Blood for Blood

- The Uncertain Journey -

A NOVEL

By

Mark M. McMillin

Hephaestus Publishing

Praise for *The Butcher's Daughter*

"... [A] pleasurable and action-packed read ... a delicious spin to the otherwise tired clichés of male captains ... the joy of the open seas - as well as the danger churning below - pulses throughout this rip-roaring, hearty tale of the high seas." - *Kirkus Reviews*

"Readers will find themselves laughing, crying, and [rooting] passionately for the heroine, Bloody Mary ... and will not want *The Butcher's Daughter* to end..." - *San Francisco Book Review*

"... [A]n entertaining read ... full of authentic historical events ... a defiant story, a narrative of strong will and perseverance which ultimately plummets to a tragic end." - *Readers' Favorite*

"... [A] historic adventure ... a beautiful romance ... I cried ..."
- *Bargain Book Reviews (5x5 Stars)*

"A wonderful novel in the best tradition of maritime literature ... authentic and rich with details, the characters are alive and passionate, and the plot is full of thrilling action, intense drama, and stunning surprises ... exhilarating adventure ... an unforgettable journey ..." - *The Columbia Review*

Blood for Blood
- The Uncertain Journey -

Copyright © Mark McMillin 2018

Author's website: www.PrivateerLukeRyan.com

ISBN: 978-0-9838179-4-9
ISBN-10: 0-9838179-4-4

Hephaestus Publishing: www.hephaestuspublishing.com

Other Works by the Author:

The New World
(1535)

Alonso de Santa Cruz, Cartographer

Foreword

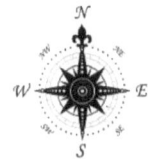

Vengeance is in my heart, death in my hand,
Blood and revenge are hammering in my head.

- William Shakespeare
(*Titus Andronicus*)

BOOK I

Lex Talionis

Chapter One

Autumn, 1588

You wish to know who I am? I shall tell you. I am a child of the gutter. I am the daughter of a whore. I am the youngest child, the bastard child, of the last of the kings of Umaill though a butcher, a commoner, raised me.

Blood for blood. I fall asleep with these words ringing in my ears each night and awake with these same words lingering on my lips at first light. I take strength from these words each and every day without fail. As I meander aimlessly about, stumbling in the dark, these words - as wicked as they may be - give my life purpose in an otherwise purposeless world. *Blood for blood* is my rallying cry. *Blood for blood* is my daily, ungodly prayer.

Revenge, raw and sweet, unbridled by any moral limits,

unrestrained by any pretense of humanity, is my North Star. Wrath is the course by which I set my compass. Except for the children, perhaps, there are no innocents. We each deserve our fate.

Some call me *el cascabela muta*, the silent rattle snake, a monstrous creature found deep in the sweltering jungles of the New World. I never cared for the comparison. The description lacks imagination and imagination is something I hardly lack. And yet I will confess the name rings true. I strike without warning. I strike without hesitation or reservation and when I strike, I feel no regret, no remorse or shame. My enemies never see me coming. They never see where I go. The wounds I inflict are fatal, always.

Despite my sex, I have a wanderer's restless spirit and the blood of warriors flows through my veins. My heart rejoices most when I am standing on a rolling deck, navigating across a boundless sea with a brisk wind at my back and fair skies above my head. This is where I can pinch a fleeting moment of peace. This is where I can quiet my troubled soul. Out on the open water I am made clean again.

But now I reek of stinking death. My clothes are stained in blood and gore. I sail across a poisoned ocean always on the prowl. I roam through hostile hinterlands relentlessly tracking my elusive, loathsome prey. Nothing can still the raging beast caged inside me and wherever I go, my grim companion Death follows me like shadow.

An eye for an eye. A tooth for a tooth. A life for a life. By God, I've put Machiavelli's principles to the test. *Lex Talionis* is the code I live by.

This is who I am. It was not always so.

The decision whether to live or die was a most difficult one for me to make. And I had little time to choose.

After slipping through a trapdoor and crawling underneath the floorboards - with scorching flames rising up all around - I left my love behind me and escaped to the world outside, gulping down cold, night air to cleanse my lungs of smoke. And as the timbers of the old mill crackled and burned, I gingerly climbed out onto the spokes of the mill's great wooden wheel, a wheel that hadn't turned in years, and worked my way down unseen to the swirling, black waters below.

My hated enemy, Dowlin's treacherous son and his brutish henchmen, stood in the woods less than a hundred paces off, watching the flames devour the mill with me inside - or so they supposed. I could hear them chuckling and exchanging ugly jokes about my grizzly end. One man lowered his trousers and started pissing on a piece of burning timber. His mates howled with laughter and stamped their feet at his crude theatrics. And then with one voice they began chanting *blood for blood, blood for blood* and cursed my name.

As I eased myself into the Carrowbeg, her freezing waters cut through me like a thousand daggers. I bit my lip, I bit down hard to stop myself from crying out though the chill at least quieted the pain in my thigh where a musket ball had gouged out a deep and bloody path.

I paddled out a ways under a canopy of bright stars. I latched on to a length of driftwood floating by and let the currents, especially strong from fresh, autumn rains that had fallen the night before, carry me swiftly downriver towards the sea. But before I drifted too far, I craned my head around for one last look at the old mill, for one final glimpse of Hunter's funeral pyre. I turned just as the mill's roof collapsed into itself in a ball of yellow and red flames, taking the mill's wooden walls, and a goodly portion of the stone wall facing the river, down with it. The old mill and my poor Hunter disappeared together in a cloud of cinder and ash.

Then I heard the sound of wood splintering, like the discordant groans of a tree when felled by the woodman's axe. I watched in fascination as the mill's great wheel, engulfed in flames, broke free from its axel and plunged into the river with a great splash. The wheel started cartwheeling towards me until it toppled over and sank. And then the night turned dark, deathly quiet, and suddenly I was all alone.

I took no solace from being alive. My heart's true joy was dead - and there would be no miraculous resurrection this time around. I fought down the urge to heave. I choked back my tears. I focused on the way ahead and kept paddling. I could wallow in my self-pity later I told myself for well I knew survival had to be my only thought.

Of course, for all my masculine bravado, I did not last long in the Carrowbeg's frigid waters. My muscles began to stiffen. My arms and legs turned heavy. I worked my way over to the riverbank before I drowned, pulled myself out of the water and crawled through muck and thorny brush on a swollen belly while I searched the ground around me for a branch or a length of wood. When I found a pole discarded by some passerby, I tucked my makeshift crutch up inside my arm and started hobbling west down a country road. I walked for miles through woods and marsh, accompanied by chirping crickets and croaking frogs.

My journey was slow and painful. My joints ached. My thigh started throbbing and began to swell. With each step I took I felt searing pain. I shivered from head to toe. Never had I felt more weary. But I dared not stop to warm or rest myself. Dowlin and his brutes would surely be on the same road as me and not far behind. Dowlin thought he had killed me and with my men scattered across Ireland and beyond, he would hurry on to Westport to seize my ships for himself. I used my belt to brace my thigh and pressed on.

And when I stumbled into town in a thick fog just before daybreak, I willed my legs a little farther to Shaw's splendid tavern as Shaw was one of mine. At that hour the tavern was closed of course so I went around to the back, broke a small window, and forced my way inside. The air inside the tavern was chiller than outside. I could see my breath. Too exhausted to start a fire, I grabbed an old horse blanket hanging on a hook against the wall, wrapped the blanket around my shoulders and curled myself into a ball on the tavern's cold, dirt floor. My last thoughts were of Hunter dying in my arms as I cried myself to sleep.

Jacob Atwood. Tall, muscular, a fine-looking Scot with a wild mane of red hair, and pound for pound by far the strongest man among my crew, broke down in tears when he saw me standing at his doorstep with a newborn baby in my arms and Efendi at my side. The hour was late to be knocking on doors, but I was in a hurry.

"Jacob, will you help us?" I asked.

The big man crossed himself, then wrapped his strong arms around me and held me close. He kissed me on the forehead.

"Oh, Mary, Mary, Mary. God's wounds, I thought you dead. Everyone thinks you are dead."

"No doubt, no doubt they do Jacob," I replied. "It is only by the grace of God, or by some fluke, that I'm still alive. Are we welcome into your house?"

"Bless me, but of course, of course you are! Mustafa, 'tis good to see you too my old friend!" The small, wiry Turk disappeared inside Atwood's huge embrace. Then he glanced down at the baby. "What child is this?"

"This little one is Aliénor Muirgheal. She is my daughter."

Atwood stared at me dumbfounded. "Eh?"

A tall, sturdy woman, more handsome than comely, brushed past Atwood as he stood gawking at me speechless. She set her lantern down, affectionately took my hand and offered me a reassuring smile.

"For the love of God, husband, after six children of your own have you no sense at all? Mary, I'm Martha, Jacob's wife. Jacob has told me much about you. Please, please, come in. Let's get you and the baby out of this unhealthy, night air. We must get something warm into you both. Jacob, stoke the fire and set out chairs for our guests. Best fetch the heavy, woolen blankets too."

Atwood dutifully nodded to his wife, then gave me another hug. "Aye, Mother, as you say. Mary, I can hardly believe my eyes. And a daughter? Come, come inside. What a story you must have!"

"I've a tale to tell Jacob, but alas it is not a happy one," I said as we followed Atwood and his wife inside. "Martha, I am pleased to finally make your acquaintance. I'm most grateful to you for taking us into your home."

"This is a good Christian home," she said sweetly. "We don't turn away weary travelers, especially when they are known to us."

Atwood, his wife and their six children lived in an unpretentious but comfortable house just outside the busy seaport of Ayr on the Clyde of Firth, a place I had never been to before. While his wife disappeared down a high-arched hallway with lantern in hand, the big Scot led us into a spacious room well-lit by a large chandelier hanging from the ceiling and from candles along the walls sitting on attractive, wrought iron sconces. I walked over to an enormous hearth built of stone to feel the warmth from a clump of dying embers.

The room, with its high ceiling planked over in dark wood and supported by heavy timbers at each corner in the Spanish style, and with walls finished in ivory wainscoting, reminded me of a church. The horseshoe arched doors were Moorish. A sturdy English oak table in the middle of the room, with eight highbacked chairs, would have made any noble proud. I smiled at some of the wood, porcelain and beaded glass objects I saw sitting on shelves or on small tables around the room. I had been with Atwood when he had purchased some of these things from the Taíno and Carib Indians. Other trinkets I saw looked Russian or Scandinavian.

Atwood's home was not a Scottish home, nor the home of a simple sailor. This was the home of an adventurer who had journeyed far and wide, of a man who had traveled between worlds.

Atwood tossed fresh logs into the hearth and set out chairs and blankets for Efendi and me. He grabbed a bottle and three glasses off the mantle and poured two fingers of whiskey into each. I did not refuse the liquor and despite his Muslim roots, neither did Efendi. I sat back in my chair and let the whiskey work its warm magic.

"I'm aware of the ambush," Atwood said in a somber voice after a quiet spell between us. "Did anyone else survive?"

"No, Jacob," I answered in a whisper. "James and thirteen good lads are dead. Only I escaped the slaughter."

I looked down at my little Aliénor as she stirred in my arms. One eye popped open. She smacked her lips and started blowing bubbles but after a deep yawn and a stretch of her arms, she fell back to sleep.

Atwood reached over to touch my forearm. "James Hunter was a good man, the best of all of us. I know you loved him. We all knew how much James loved you. He'll be sorely missed and I'm sorry for your anguish, for the grief you must bear."

"Aye, 'tis a heavy burden to be sure."

"Can you speak of these evil matters Mary? Can you tell me what happened, or are the wounds too raw yet?"

"Jacob, I will tell you, but I would first have you tell me what you know."

Atwood shifted uncomfortably in his chair. "I know very little. Like most of the lads, I set out for home after our celebration at Shaw's tavern that night. I only learned about the ambush later, after I had returned to Ayr. Men said you were dead Mary, killed by *Medusa's* crew at some abandoned mill outside of town. Merciful God, what a black day that was. The feud between us and the *Síol Faolcháin* should have ended with the death of the Twins. So much for showing savages mercy. You won over no hearts or minds when you paroled *Medusa's* crew and set them free. They say Dowlin has a son. They say he was onboard *Medusa* when you and James killed his uncles. They say it was Dowlin's son who planned the ambush and ordered your death."

Atwood paused when his wife returned holding a plate piled high with hot biscuits, fruits and cheeses. She brought warm milk for the baby.

"I have a hardy stew heating in the kitchen," she said as she set the plate down on a small table between Efendi and me. "This will tide you over until then. Mary, she is beautiful. May I hold her?"

"Aye, certainly. Thank you. She is light, but even so..."

Martha took the baby from me and sat down next to her husband. Aliénor stole a quick peek of the world around her, then closed her eyes again.

"I'm sorry," I said, "for our rude intrusion into your home. I know the hour is late, but Mustafa and I thought it best to come at night."

Atwood nodded. "You were right to do so. Like any seaport, scoundrels with nothing better to do than gossip and meddle in the affairs of others, or worse, infect Ayr. Some men would gladly sell their own mothers for a purse filled with coin. The whores are no better."

"We live in no mansion," Martha interjected with a natural sweetness in her tone, "but we have room enough to spare for the three of you. You are most welcome to lodge with us."

"No, no, thank you," I said. "Your offer is most kind, but quite unnecessary. We've taken rooms at the *Saracen* down the road. We'll not burden you further."

"'Tis no burden, Mary," Atwood said. "Do you need money?"

"Jacob..."

Atwood grunted. "Stow away your pride Mary. If you need money, a loan if you like, you need only ask."

"Thank you, Jacob."

"You've come directly from Westport I take it?"

"Aye, we've come from Westport and I'll share my story with you, with no gladness in my heart. But tell me about the others first? What news?"

"Alas, I have no news. Uncertain of who was friend or foe, I've laid low here in Ayr these many months. No doubt our lads have done the same. You were the mortar that held us together Mary and without you, well..."

"What of *Phantom*, *Medusa's Head* or *El Rojo Diablo*?"

"I know nothing about the whereabouts of *Medusa* or *Diablo* but, as luck would have it, *Phantom* is here in port."

I bolted upright in my chair. "You have *Phantom*?"

Atwood waved his hands. "No, no, I don't have her. A rich, wool merchant owns her now. How he came by her, I know not. He sold her guns off and turned our poor girl into a stinkin' freighter. She makes short runs haulin' cargo between Ayr and ports in England, Wales and Ireland. She's a mere shadow of her former glory. 'Tis sad to see."

Phantom, my magnificent warhorse, was a French-built nao and as fast and as nimble as any ship on the water. I had acquired her when I was barely more than a girl with money a man named Eoghan Dubhdara O'Malley, the last of the kings of Umaill, had left me after he died.

Medusa's Head had belonged to Dowlin's father - a clan chieftain and a smuggler. Jealous of my success, and offended by my arrogance, the elder Dowlin had decided one day to take me down a peg or two and took the life of a young girl who was very dear to me, an orphan I had rescued from the streets. Gretchen was her name. Dowlin's father was a wretched pig who needed killing and I've had no regrets about the day I cut off his head and took his powerful man o' war for myself. But after butchering a clan chieftain, I was forced to flee Ireland.

Like Christopher Columbus before me, I crossed the broad Atlantic with my men to look for new opportunities in the West Indies. We made a fresh start for ourselves smuggling goods between the New World and the old one until Dowlin's uncles, the half-witted Twins, a monstrosity of nature, hunted me down with the help of Spanish treachery. The Twins caught us napping, killed many of my men and seized my ships and treasure. They took me prisoner, put me on a ship bound for London and handed me over to the English to collect the bounty I had on my head on trumped-up charges of piracy.

I thought all was lost. I thought my life was forfeit until one day the Queen of England came to visit me in the Tower out of curiosity. She took a fancy to me, then pardoned me in exchange for my loyalty which I gladly gave. After my release, I sailed back to Ireland, took my *Phantom* back from the Twins and then purchased *El Rojo Diablo*, a fine battlecruiser with sails like burning charcoal. I handed *Phantom* over to Hunter and gave command of *Diablo* to Atwood. Both men were savvy captains, gifted seafarers and veterans of cruel, hard war. With two fine ships and an English letter of marque from the queen in my pocket, we sailed back to the West Indies to resume our life as smugglers.

I cringed at the thought of my poor *Phantom*, the noblest of ships, hauling cargo. I would have her back and my head began spinning with ideas to see it so. But any plan I devised would require men and money.

"Good grief, she's a freighter you say!"

"I'm afraid so, Mary."

"We'll just see about that," I said in a haughty tone. "What do you do to earn your keep now, Jacob? Have you found work with another ship?"

"No, leastwise I have no position as ship's master. I oversee a small fleet of herring busses for a local gentleman who treats me fair enough. It is not exciting work, neither are the wages, but the job puts food on our table. I still have a tidy sum stashed away from our adventures in the Americas, but I keep that Godsend for the day trouble might find us."

Martha took the baby over to a rocking crib in the corner of the room, tucked her in and then disappeared down the hallway again. When she returned a few minutes later, she brought two bowls of hot stew on a pewter tray, set the tray on the table between Efendi and me and returned to her chair next to her husband, taking his hand into her lap as she plopped down.

I took a spoonful of the hardy broth, full of onions, carrots, potatoes and bits of rabbit, and asked Martha about her children. She proudly described each child to me in elaborate detail as I ate. The Atwoods had three boys and three daughters. The oldest in the brood was eleven and the youngest had just turned three.

I hadn't realized how famished I was as I gobbled down my stew, or how tired. My eyelids turned heavy as I filled my belly.

Atwood caught me fading. "I'll walk you and Mustafa back to the inn," he said. "You can tell us your story tomorrow, when you are better rested."

I smiled at Atwood and his wife. I shook my head and stood to stretch my legs. I looked in on little Aliénor and found her curled into a tiny ball, chewing on her thumb. She had an angelic face and seemed happy with life. She was a wonderful baby and caring for her had been no trouble at all.

"I'm fine," I said truthfully, having caught a fresh wind and returned to my chair. "I came to talk. I know it is close to midnight, but you need to hear what I have to say and time is not our friend. Poor Mustafa has suffered through my story once already. I suspect in the days ahead, if you are both with me, you'll hear my story again."

I took a deep breath when Atwood nodded, along with a sip or two of whiskey. Six months had passed since that evil night at the old mill. For Martha's benefit, I started from the beginning. I started with the war. Atwood and his wife listened thoughtfully to me ramble on and on, soaking in my every word.

Rich and powerful Catholic Spain and Protestant England had been nipping at each other for as long as I could remember, but the war truly started back in 1585 when Queen Elizabeth brazenly sent her armies into the United Provinces to help the Protestant Dutch in their fight for independence from Spain. King Phillip II answered Elizabeth in the summer of '88 by sending *El Grande y Felicisima Armada*, the largest fleet in the history of the world, north to invade England.

Elizabeth needed every ship and every able seaman to defend her realm. She sent out a call-to-arms across the four corners of her kingdom, including one to me. Though my crew and I were Irish, and mostly Catholic, I owed the queen my life and accepted her plea for help. My ships sailed with a fine squadron of English privateers under Sir Francis Drake who, as every English schoolchild knows, crushed the Spanish Armada at Gravelines.

Drake did not purse the Spanish as they limped back home with a broken fleet. But I did. Sailing for the English had cost me plenty and so I followed the Spanish into an angry North Sea and then into the wild Atlantic hoping to pickoff a prize or two.

I lost *Diablo* off Loop Head when she sprung her bowsprit in one gale or another and while Atwood took her into Limerick for repairs, I kept *Phantom* at sea, trolling the waters between Aill Na Brun and Inishtooskert, still hoping to snag a prize before the Spanish sailed beyond my reach. My persistence was rewarded when we caught a straggler on our last day out. She was a poor ship, a Spanish galleass with a half-starved crew. I let her go - but I kept the six chests of gold

Hunter had found hidden away inside the captain's cabin - and then we sailed on to Westport, our homeport, where we waited for Atwood and *Diablo*. That was when we happened upon *Medusa's Head*, the magnificent flagship of the *Síol Faolcháin*, sailing poorly off Clare Island with a shattered mast and with her rigging in shambles. Plainly, the *Síol Faolcháin* had sailed with the Spanish as privateers and that made *Medusa* fair game.

My men and I stormed aboard the crippled ship and fought her crew hand-to-hand. And when I killed one Twin, and Hunter killed the other, the crew tossed their weapons aside and we took *Medusa* as a prize.

In one day, we had taken six chests of Spanish gold, seized a superb man o' war and cut-off the head of the *Síol Faolcháin*, ending the years of bloody slaughter between us. That was the very best of days. But oh, like the desert dunes, how fortunes shift and change.

I spared *Medusa's* crew. In a magnanimous gesture, I sent them home after each man gave his binding oath that he'd never take up arms against me again. Little did I know that Dowlin's son, and nephew to the monstrous Twins, stood amongst them.

When *Diablo* glided into Westport with a new bowsprit the following day, I released my men. I gave them thirty days' liberty, give or take, and took my officers to Shaw's splendid tavern - renamed *Fúmsa an Díoltas* in my honor, the place where the clan had first tried to kill me - to eat and drink and celebrate. After midnight men started drifting back to the ships or headed out on the road to see friends and family. Hunter stayed with me to finish-off the ale.

And then a man burst through the tavern's door looking for me. I did not know his name, but I knew he was one of Martin's men. John Martin, though he liked to pass himself off as a gentleman adventurer, was in truth a provocateur and one of her majesty's spies. More importantly to me, he was my champion at Court. Martin's man told me that Martin had been shot by desperate, shipwrecked Spaniards out by the old mill. The man begged me to follow him to the mill to help him save his master.

Hunter and I assembled what few men we could, thirteen in all, and raced out into the darkness down a narrow, country road with lanterns and torches in hand. When we reached the mill, the forest all around us erupted in smoke and flame. Martin's man had lured us into a trap.

One-by-one my men were cut down. One musket ball grazed my thigh and Hunter had to help me hobble towards the mill. Only Hunter and I reached the mill alive. We barricaded ourselves inside a room upstairs and waited for our attackers to rush in and kill us. That was when Hunter toppled over, that was when my poor Hunter died in my arms with a bullet in his back.

And then a man with a hauntingly familiar face called out my name from the woods. He introduced himself to me as Dowlin's son, the son of the wretched clan chieftain I had beheaded long ago. As his men set the old mill on fire, I could hear them chanting *blood for blood, blood for blood* over and over again.

Wounded, alone and filled with grief, I sat on the floor rocking Hunter's lifeless body back and forth as tendrils of thick, grey smoke poured into the room through gaps in the door. The smoke stung my eyes and lungs and I started choking. I found it harder and harder to breathe. But I was content with my sad end for soon I would be reunited with my beloved. Then I felt the baby kick and suddenly I was torn between life and death. I gently laid Hunter aside, touched my belly and found my reason to live.

As a young girl the mill had been my secret hiding place whenever I needed a bit of solitude. I knew every nook and cranny of that old mill. Underneath the floorboards there was a crawlspace once used by the mylnweard to access the mill's great wheel. Before the flames and smoke devoured me, I kissed my beautiful Hunter farewell and made my way to the river.

"Now you know my story," I told Atwood, brushing back a tear.

Atwood stared at me incredulously with a furrowed brow. "So, you crawled under the floor to the river and escaped?"

"I did."

Atwood stood to refill my glass. "How extraordinary. I fear I wouldn't have been that quick-witted. Ha! I wouldn't have fit into that damn crawlspace. And you were with child when we sailed out of Devonport to face the Spanish Armada?"

"Aye, I was with child then."

I could see the confusion in Atwood's eyes. I could see he wanted to ask me how it was, after all the years Hunter and I had been lovers, that we had managed to conceive a child. Mercifully, Atwood bit his tongue and did not press me.

Martha understood. She gave me a knowing nod and I nodded back, sealing a secret pact between two co-conspirators. The truth was obvious of course. I had taken another into my bed.

"I cannot imagine," Martha said, "sailing into war with a child in my belly. How remarkable. Jacob has told me how extraordinary you are. Men would never follow you otherwise. I'm so pleased to know you a little better." Then she paused to turn to her husband and poked him in the ribs. "My man here failed to tell me about your beauty though. I've not laid eyes upon a more striking woman."

I managed a small giggle, my first in many months. "Put your mind at ease, madam. Before God, I can attest Jacob is a faithful and loving husband. The islands of the New World are filled with temptation all around, but I've never seen your man stray, not once. I think it is you though dear lady who is the extraordinary woman in this room. I cannot imagine raising six children on my own and managing a household with my husband gone for long stretches of time at sea, not knowing when - or if - he'll return. You must be a strong and courageous woman."

"It is true we women do not have easy lives," Martha readily agreed. "To survive the hardships and heartbreak of this life, women must have backbones of steel. What surname will you give your daughter?"

"Ryan is my mother's family name. As James and I never married, Aliénor will be a Ryan."

"Aliénor Muirgheal Ryan," Atwood said thoughtfully, absently scratching the stubble on his chin. "Good, strong name."

"Aliénor is French. The name means *light*. Muirgheal in the old Gaelic tongue means *bright as the sea*."

"Beautiful," Martha said.

"How," Atwood asked, "did Mustafa find you?"

"After I escaped from the old mill, I made my way to Shaw's place," I answered, then paused to smile at Efendi. "He took me in, dressed my wounds and when it was my time, Mustafa was there to help me with the birth. Shaw was too squeamish and we dared not risk bringing in a midwife who might betray us to the clan."

Atwood turned to Efendi and grunted. "What the devil possessed you to look for Mary? By all accounts Mary was dead."

Efendi, a man who rarely cracked a smile, smiled broadly. "I was still in Westport when I heard the talk about the ambush. I hurried to the old mill and found the bodies of our men dumped into a ravine back in the woods. But I did not find Mary or James among them. I sifted through the rubble. The timbers still smoldered. The stones were still warm to the touch. I found only one body in the wreckage, the body of a man. I knew if Mary was alive, she would look for Shaw."

The big Scot tried to hide his tears. "Forgive me, Mary. Forgive me for not returning to Westport to do the same."

I rose from my chair and kissed Atwood on the cheek. "You had no reason to doubt the stories about my death. You were right to stay in Ayr to protect your family. There is nothing to forgive, there is nothing you could have done."

"Perhaps. Mustafa, truly you helped with the birth?"

Efendi nodded. "I did, I did indeed my friend. There was no one else as Mary has said. It was not the first time I have rendered such services."

"You're a braver man than me, Mustafa. My Martha has always known it best to keep me far away when she labored with child."

"To bring new life into the world is a solemn event," Efendi offered. "Should Allah bless you with another child, you must bear witness to this miracle Jacob."

Martha glanced at her husband askew and with an unfriendly smile. "Should I find a seventh child growing in my belly Jacob Atwood, you had best run into the hills for your life."

Atwood answered his wife with a sly grin. "Mary, what's your plan? I know something must be brewing inside that head of yours."

Atwood knew me well. This is my one, true gift. I excel most others at concocting schemes and plans.

"Mustafa and I have heard rumors about a band of brigands, a mix of Irishmen, Africans and a few Indians from the New World, hiding out in caves along the shores north of Dublin. These rumors intrigue me. There is also talk the English are assembling many ships, landing craft and men, along with vast quantities of supplies, up and down the south coast of England. Such a force is far too grand for one of Drake's raiding parties. Perhaps there is an opportunity for us there."

Atwood slapped his knee and howled. "Moors and Caribs frolicking about Ireland causing mischief you say? My, my, my."

"Shush!" Martha scolded. "You'll wake the baby and the children."

"Ah, bless me. Sorry, Mother. Mary, I've heard the same chatter about a large English force of one sort or another being assembled. Had the winds favored the Spanish Armada at Calais, England would be a Spanish province now, the queen would be without her head and we'd all be attending mass and learning to speak Spanish. Elizabeth craves blood they say. An expedition to Spain would not surprise me."

I nodded. "Nor I. The queen is a proud woman. Above all else she desires to keep her kingdom strong and secure and she'll want revenge too no doubt. I hear the best of Phillip's fleet returned safely back to Spain. The great war galleons survived both the carnage at Gravelines and the Atlantic's punishing gales. Drake's victory over the Armada was an astonishing feat. He deserves the glory. Even so, his victory perhaps is not the decisive blow many Englishmen like to boast about. Woe to England if she gives the beast time to heal."

"Quite so, Mary, quite so. Drake gave Medina Sidonia a good thrashing at Gravelines, but then the fool failed to deliver the *coup de grâce* and let the Spanish slip away. Lord only knows why he didn't try to finish-off the galleons. It'll take the Spanish months to ready their ships for action and they'll need time to raise and train new conscripts for the army and the navy. The English should hit the Spanish and hit them hard before it's too late."

I stifled a yawn and smiled. "Tell me Jacob, are you content with your fisherman's life?"

Chapter Two

I had no ships. I had no crew. Except for the clothes on my back, my two brothers at my side and an infant child in my arms, I had nothing. What little money I carried I had borrowed from Shaw. But I have started out with less.

We caught a packet ship for Westport first. I needed a safe, wholesome home for my little Aliénor. A baby in my arms would never do as I prepared myself for the violent road ahead.

I knew just the family. A priest from my childhood and a man I trusted named Friar Thomas had a brother he was very fond of in Westport named John Fitzgerald. Fitzgerald was a cooper by trade with a good business and a fine reputation. He had a kindly wife named Katerina and three lovely children, one strapping son and two fetching daughters. After I reached a fair arrangement with Fitzgeralds to look after my little one, Atwood, Efendi and I caught a packet ship to Dublin and from Dublin we traveled north on foot for some twenty miles or so to a small fishing village named Rush in the parish of Lusk within the Barony of Balrothery. We trudged through heavy snow and blustery winds and did not stop as I was in a hurry.

Rush is well-known for the tremendous quantities of ling her sons haul-in year after year. For generations Rushmen have launched their tiny fishing trawlers out into the rough and tumbly sea, dragging their drift nets across the water in fair weather and foul. Harvesting the sea's bounty is a hard and dangerous life, forging hard and dangerous men. But not all Rushmen like to fish. To the north, chiseled from solid rock by centuries of rain and surf, are many coves and caves. For men who aren't afraid of breaking a law or two, the waters there are ideal for smugglers.

We spent our days and nights sampling different taverns in and around the fishing village, mingling with the local patrons and spreading the word that we were looking for men of quality willing to sail to the New World. We spoke openly of our interest in hiring men who had been to Santo Domingo, Guadeloupe, Havana and the Port of Spain. But we were outsiders and folks greeted us with suspicion or shunned us altogether. Even so, our persistence paid off by week's end. Our peculiar questions attracted the desired attention.

As we left a crowded pub one night, a fine establishment with all the necessaries named the *Empty Pocket*, a dozen men, stout men with torches and armed with clubs, pitchforks and long sticks, surrounded us in a back alley. Atwood moved his hand to the hilt of the sword hanging from his hip while Efendi took a step to one side, the stance he favored before launching the deadly throwing knives he had hidden inside his sleeve. And I unbuttoned my coat to grab the brace of pistols I kept tucked against the small of my back.

"What is this?" I asked defiantly.

A short, stocky fellow with a crooked nose, a nose that had been broken more than once, stepped forward. "A friend of mine wants to meet you," he said evenly. "He's waiting for you down by the water's edge at the old pier. You'll come peaceful now or else..."

I raised an eyebrow at the man. "Or else what?" I asked and laughed. A dozen fishermen armed with sticks were hardly enough to intimidate me, especially when I had Atwood and Efendi at my side.

"Or you can turn around and leave Rush tonight madam and never return. You have our leave to crawl back to whatever dung-hole you sprung from."

I offered the man a disarming smile. "There's no need for any discord between us friend. We've come to your fine village without malice. We want no trouble. We'll gladly accompany you to the old pier to meet this friend of yours."

The Rushmen escorted us down to the water and then to a pier with a small storehouse at the end of it. A brazier of burning coal stood next to the storehouse. The man with the crooked nose offered us hoods and demanded we surrender our weapons.

Atwood shook his head.

"The choice is still the same," the Rushman said. "Do as I say or leave Rush tonight. Them be your two choices. There be a third choice too, but that one doesn't end well for you."

"Save your empty bluster for weaker men," Atwood scoffed and squared his shoulders back, ready for a brawl. "I'll not hand over my sword or put that filthy bag over my head. And I promise you this: you and your band of buffoons will sorely regret any attempt to force me."

Well I knew my feisty Scot was not bluffing. I've seen him fight six men at once and crack a man's skull open with his bare hands. And if Atwood drew his sword, Efendi, who thought of killing as a form of high art, would whip out his knives. A dozen good Rushmen would be dead or lying on the ground bleeding their lives away with my precious plan bleeding out with them.

I took a step forward and handed my pistols over to the lead man. "I'll go inside. Jacob, Mustafa, return to the pub and wait for me there. All will be well." I took in the faces of the twelve Rushmen surrounding us, men who were only a heartbeat away from death. "Ugh, men and your endless need to flaunt your pillicocks. We're all bound by a common cause. You boys just don't know it yet." I pointed to the leader. "You, what's your name?"

"O'Grady."

"Well Master O'Grady, it's late and I'm cold. Let's get on with it then. Lead the way."

"We'll wait for you here, Mary." Atwood said and folded his arms defiantly.

I looked over at O'Grady. "Is this satisfactory to you?"

With a nod from O'Grady, I let him slip the hood over my head and bind my hands. Then he placed my hands on his shoulder and guided me down the pier and into the storehouse where the air was thick with the pungent smell of fish mixed with the scent of freshly cut wood. I could feel clumps of sawdust and bits of wood underneath my boots.

"This is the woman," O'Grady said.

I could hear a man stepping towards me as his boots made a squishing sound against the wood shavings on the floor. My muscles tensed and suddenly felt ill. Perhaps I had made a terrible, terrible mistake. The image of Dowlin's son coming at me with a dagger in his hand sent a shiver down my spine.

The man cleared his throat. "You and your companions are strangers to this parish," he said with an edge in his tone. "You like to ask a lot of questions."

I smiled. I breathed a sigh of relief. I knew the voice.

"Questions can kill a man, or a woman, in these parts," the man continued. "I'll be asking the questions now. I want your name and the names of your friends. I know you're Irish. The big man outside is a Scot and the other fellow I suspect is from lands far to the east, Russian perhaps? You'll tell me your purpose here and if you lie to me, I'll know and things will turn messy then. Do we understand one another?"

"Michael…" I said and held my arms out. I could almost see his draw drop as I uttered his Christian name.

"What the devil? Joseph, I would see this woman's face. Remove her hood."

MacGyver stared at me wide-eyed. "Great God, Mary!" he said and reached out to embrace me.

I held him close and kissed him on both cheeks. "Michael! You are the reason why I've come to Rush! Jacob and Mustafa are outside."

"Oh, Mary, Mary, Mary!" he said as he undid my bindings. "We all thought you dead! Joseph, all is well. I know this woman. Bring the other two."

O'Grady hesitated, he removed his hat and bowed his head. "Beg pardon miss, you be Lady Mary, Capt'n Bloody Mary?"

"Aye, I'm known by both those names, as well as a few less charitable ones."

"Joseph!" MacGyver exclaimed, annoyed. "There'll be plenty of time later to chitchat with our good Lady Mary. For now, 'tis best we keep this matter to ourselves. Capt'n Mary is dead and shall remain dead until Lady Mary says otherwise. Now we have work to do."

"Aye, sir, sorry sir," O'Grady replied and started moving towards the door. "I'm sorry miss for my cross words earlier."

"All is well between us Master O'Grady," I replied.

"I know," MacGyver said as he handed my pistols back to me, "how you crave anonymity Mary. My lads are good men, but some secrets don't keep. Word will spread across the counties that you're alive soon enough."

"Not to worry, Michael. It's high time I stepped out from the shadows."

"Mary, this isn't County Mayo. Kayne Dowlin can reach you here with no difficulty at all once he learns you still breathe. The *Síol Faolcháin* has eyes and ears in every village and every seaport up and down the east coast of Ireland. Once these hounds pick up our scent, they'll not rest until they find us, until they settle every old grudge and tie up every loose end."

I brushed MacGyver's cheek with the back of my hand. "Ah, Kayne, Kayne Dowlin, you say? I did not know the bastard's given name. I'll not soon forget it. Aye, there are grudges to settle and loose ends to tie."

"What's this? Atwood bellowed as he ducked through the doorway. "God help us," he said as he lifted MacGyver off his feet and squeezed him in a bear hug, "the queen has emptied the half-wits from bowels of her jails!"

"Put me down you big lout!" MacGyver demanded.

Then Efendi stepped into the storehouse. He and MacGyver clasped each other firmly by the shoulders.

"What a day this is!" MacGyver said with a wide grin. "I never thought I'd see the likes of you two scoundrels again."

"Gentlemen, I'm chilled to the bone," I said as I tucked my pistols inside my belt and buttoned up my coat. "Let's return to the village where we can warm ourselves. I for one need a drink."

MacGyver sent his men home and we followed him back to the *Empty Pocket*. The earlier crowd had thinned out and we had our pick of tables. I claimed a table in a quiet corner and ordered a pitcher of ale from the barkeep, a huge, beefy giant who eyed me appreciatively up and down with a grin. I took no offense.

I told my story first, sorry that poor Atwood and Efendi had to suffer through it all again. I made no mention of the baby, not yet.

"James, dead," MacGyver said softly after I had finished. He brushed back a tear. "Hard to accept. He was like a brother."

I too wiped away a tear. "Aye, Michael, we all loved Hunter."

"How did you know to look for me here, Mary?"

"We heard rumors about a band of brigands, Irishmen, Blackamoors and Indians, roaming about in these parts. The rumors piqued my curiosity."

MacGyver smiled. "Kinkae, Henry and all their men are close-by. Some of our Irish lads are with us too and we have a few new men who have joined us. You met some of the new lads earlier."

"Henry and Kinkae are both alive! Wonderful!"

"Tomorrow I'll take you to them."

"What brought you to Rush, Michael? I always thought Dublin was your home. Tell us your story."

"My roots are here in Rush. I tell folks I'm from Dublin because everyone knows Dublin. I was on my way here when I heard about the shootings at the old mill. I doubled back to Westport in haste. But folks said no one survived the ambush. I knew better than to linger in town for long with the *Síol Faolcháin* on the loose."

Atwood grabbed the pitcher. "How did you find Kinkae and Henry?" he asked as he refilled each tankard.

"I hurried to *Phantom*, hoping to save her from Dowlin's filthy clutches and found our boys still on board. But we didn't have time to free *Phantom* from the dry dock and *Medusa* was of no use to us with a broken rudder so we rowed out to *Diablo*, gathered what men we could, and sailed here."

Atwood slapped the table. "Zeus's balls! You have *Diablo*?"

MacGyver's lips curled into a sly smile, a smile not unlike the smile Hunter would make when he had pulled off some mischievous, schoolboy prank. "Aye, I've got *Diablo*. She's anchored nearby in a quiet spot of water."

"Can she put to sea?" I asked excitedly.

"She could use some sprucing up, but aye, she's sound enough. We've kept ourselves busy smuggling here and there. Christ Almighty though - there be little profit in it anymore. The clans are squeezing out the independents. We can barely survive on the meager scraps they leave us. It's not like the old days, Mary. Times are lean. Men are losing hope."

I reached across the table and patted MacGyver reassuringly on the shoulder. *Diablo* was mine. I had purchased her with my own money and I had armed her with cannon. But if MacGyver claimed *Diablo* for himself, I would not object. I owed MacGyver. I owed all my men and owed them plenty. They had suffered and bled for me. Some had sacrificed everything for me, even after I had failed them. Their unwavering loyalty was a great mystery to me. I did not think myself worthy. I am a woman playing in an unforgiving, dangerous world ruled by men, a world where women are at a severe disadvantage. Despite my many failings, my men had always stood by me.

"Michael, are you with us? There'll be no hard feelings if not. If you choose to go your separate way, *Diablo* is yours with my blessing."

MacGyver looked at me with a hurt expression. "You say the most bizarre things at times Mary. Of course, I'm with you. Kinkae and Henry would shackle a cannon ball around my ankles and pitch me over the side otherwise. *Diablo* is your ship and Jacob is her captain."

I pulled MacGyver's hand to the middle of the table, placed Efendi's hand over his and then Atwood's and rested my hand on top. "Now that James is gone, *Phantom* goes to Jacob and command of *Diablo* is yours Michael. Mustafa, my fine, brave Turk, you'll continue to do what you do best. You are my sword, my shield and my will."

"You have *Phantom?*" MacGyver asked.

"No, not at present. But Jacob has seen her and she is not far away. We'll need to displace her present owner and his men. Nothing we haven't done before."

At dawn the next morning Atwood, MacGyver, Efendi and I put

Rush behind us and headed out on foot into bracing gusts blowing down from the arctic with snow flurries whirling all around. We took the north road for several easy miles until we reached a small cove protected by two fingers of land where MacGyver had *Diablo* tucked safely away.

MacGyver had understated *Diablo*'s condition. The tide was out and she sat on the sand, a sad, sad sight to see. Her hull was marred by splotches of bare wood. Paint was peeling off her rails, masts and spars. I saw rust on metal fittings and her bottom badly needed graving. Her charcoal-grey sails had been patched-over with strips of white canvas and much of her rigging was frayed. From top to bottom *Diablo* was in desperate need of an overhaul. And yet to the discerning eye, *Diablo* was a fine warhorse. Her French shipwrights had built her sound and true. She had sailed with me to the New World and into battle and had years of life in her still.

The reunion with Kinkae, Henry and all my men, about eighty strong, was bittersweet. There were hugs and tears all around and even a kiss or two. I sent a few men back into town with coin to buy fresh victuals, whiskey and ale for a proper feast and when they returned before nightfall pulling three two-wheeled carts loaded down with crates, barrels and burlap sacks, we started the cooking fires along the shore to celebrate. We ate until we could eat no more and gorged ourselves on drink. We laughed and cried as we sang the songs of our people and traded our stories. At evening's end I gathered everyone around and revealed my plan to take *Phantom* back. My words were greeted with a rousing cheer and it warmed my heart to see my lads trust in hope again.

MacGyver insisted I take *Diablo*'s great cabin when I decided to turn in. I was exhausted with a head full of whiskey and did not argue. I collapsed on the bunk and shut my eyes with a warship underneath my feet and a loyal crew at my side. But where I should have felt joy as a companion, I found only melancholy. I ached for Hunter's love. I longed to see his smile, to feel his touch and sleep eluded me.

In the morning, as was my custom before setting out on any new journey, I held a council of war with all my officers. Atwood, MacGyver, Efendi, Kinkae and Henry joined me in the ship's great cabin. They squeezed into their seats around the cabin's small table as I poured each man a glass of wine, except for Henry who preferred ale when we had no *mobbie*, a vile drink the Carib make from fermented potatoes or cassava, and I handed him a tankard of Dublin's best.

I took in the faces around me and smiled. For years we had bled together, prospered together and had survived many adversities together in two different worlds. These men were my brothers.

I laid out the particulars of my plan and - mindful of the Ten Rules - I put the matter to a vote. The Ten Rules required a unanimous decision on any proposal to put ship and crew in peril.

My plan was simple. My plans are always simple. I intended to sail north and take *Phantom* out on the open water as soon as she departed Ayr, though exactly how we would take her I did not yet know. Something would come to me. My officers all voted in favor of my plan without debate or conditions of any kind.

After breakfast we broke camp, weighed anchor and floated out to sea with the tide under half sail. Six months, a lifetime, had passed since I held a ship's wheel in my hands, since I had reveled in the exhilaration of command. I took the wheel from MacGyver once we cleared the shallows and pointed our French-built frigate towards Scotland. I gave the order to shake out more canvas. I watched the topmen scramble up the shrouds and move out smartly along the spars to untie the reef points while men on deck worked the lines and braces. *Diablo* picked up speed as she spread her wings. Though *Diablo* was not as fast as *Phantom*, she was a good sailor.

We made a quick and easy passage from Rush to Ayr under fair skies and a gentle wind. *Diablo* handled well in the light breezes.

From stem to stern she was a black ship. But when I had purchased her in Plymouth, her rails and bulwarks, her gun ports, capstan, bitticle, the fore, main and mizzen mast lowers, along with most of the wood trim around her decks, had been painted in bright red. With her garish red trimmings, and the subtle streaks of crimson running through her sallow-grey sails, resembling burning charcoal in certain light, my men had christened her *El Rio Diablo*. The dreadful name stuck even after I made the crew paint her all in black for the sake of anonymity.

In her prime, *Diablo* made an imposing sight. But now she was a poor ship crewed by men who looked like wayward fools or vagabonds. Nothing gold couldn't fix. I thanked my lucky stars for MacGyver's pluck and quick-wits in taking *Diablo* before Dowlin could sink his claws into her.

After we sailed beyond Lock Ryan and entered the Clyde of Firth, Scotland embraced us with sleet, rain and a bracing wind. MacGyver had the men take-in sail when we neared the harbor and as we passed a line of fishing trawlers heading out to sea, Atwood recognized one of his own and waved. And then, through the awful weather, I caught a glimpse of *Phantom* and I felt my heart flutter.

"There!" I cried out excitedly to no one in particular and pointed.

Ayr's harbor is too small, and the River Ayr is too shallow, to accommodate large ships. *Phantom* was the only ocean class vessel in port. She was tied against a wharf along North Harbour Street and though Atwood had warned me about her forlorn condition, I was once again unprepared for the abuse and neglect she had suffered. I saw no life in her. At first, I thought she was covered in ice but as we drew nearer, I realized some fool had applied a thin coat of whitewash over her black hull and masts. My poor, noble ship looked like some hideous apparition dressed in a gown of opaque white with streaks of black bleeding through. And yet, the crude veneer couldn't hide her quality or her graceful lines.

I would have preferred anchoring *Diablo* out in the harbor, away from prying eyes, but the harbor was crowded with fishing trawlers and small freighters riding out the dismal weather and so I stepped aside to give MacGyver the wheel as he was the best of any of us at the helm. He gently nudged *Diablo* in behind the *Phantom*, then had the crew toss out the mooring lines to secure us to the wharf.

After I paid the harbor master for the privilege of docking alongside his pier, I went to the bow to stand with Atwood and MacGyver to watch the dockmen moving bales of wool and assorted provisions onboard the *Phantom*. Plainly her master intended to sail soon, which meant we had to move quickly. I sent Atwood and MacGyver into town for a quick bit of in-and-out reconnaissance. When they returned, they greeted me with broad smiles as I met them at the rail.

"What amuses you, my good captains?" I called down from the quarter deck.

"If a bit of piracy doesn't offend you Mary," MacGyver offered as the two men stepped aboard and casually made their way towards me, "I predict a happy day ahead on the morrow."

"Her name is now the *Golden Fleece* and she sails for Liverpool in the morning," Atwood added. "I know her master, Jonathan Mackenzie. He's a good man, a capable seaman. We heard the owner will be onboard. They say he's a baron. I know him not."

"That is good, very good," I said, feeling feisty for the first time in many months. "I look forward to introducing myself to this baron, to this wool merchant who has insulted us."

Atwood and MacGyver exchanged knowing nods and smiled.

At the break of dawn on the following morning, we pushed our ship away from North Harbour Street in a swirling mist and headed out to sea. Atwood knew the mid-channel buoys well and took the wheel. I stood by his side, quietly watching the topmen brave rigging and footropes coated in ice to set our sails and was grateful I was not with them. Once we reached the Firth of Clyde, the sun burned through the fog and we started cruising lazily around in circles in a light wind, waiting for the *Fleece* to pass us by.

This was the easy part of my plan. Now we needed to lure the *Fleece* over to us, close enough to board her without spooking her crew. We didn't have the speed to run her down and our great guns, eighteen in all, were of no use as we couldn't risk sinking her, or injuring her crew, men we had no quarrel with. We needed a ruse and so, to the horror of my men, I had MacGyver disable our rudder.

Hunter had taught MacGyver how to play with explosives. MacGyver had blown off rudders before. The crew and I gathered around to watch MacGyver carefully pack black powder into three small, wooden boxes. He packed the powder in tight and then used cord soaked in lamp oil to connect all three. We hauled in our canvas, coasted to a stop and helped MacGyver over the side. After he nailed the boxes to the rudder and lit the fuse, we reeled him back in, hurried down to the main deck and ducked behind anything we could find.

With a flash and a bang, the rudder split in two. We hoisted a white flag over the main mast next and then my men fashioned crates to place over our guns while I anxiously paced back and forth on the quarter deck, guzzling down cups of hot milk mixed with coco and a little sugar.

An hour passed, then two and I began to fret. If *Fleece's* owner had delayed his voyage, we'd lose our chance. As more time passed, I racked my brain for another plan. Weeks or even months might slip by before we had another crack at taking *Phantom* back. Happily, the ship's lookout saved me.

"Sail ho!" he cried down from the masthead and pointed to the *Fleece*.

When her crew spied our ship bobbing up and down on the gentle swells with a distress flag flying off our main topgallant, her master turned his ship towards us to have a closer look. To complete our deception, Atwood sent all but a dozen men below.

I stood near the bow and kept to the shadows. I smeared soot across my face, tucked my hair up inside my felt, capitano hat and wrapped my bosom tight. I could still pass for a ship's boy if one didn't look too closely.

"Bless me, is that Jacob Atwood I see?" the master of the *Fleece* called out, followed by a hardy laugh as he skillfully eased his ship next to *Diablo*. The man was a portly fellow with a round, fleshy face and a long, white beard that he wore braided. The tip of his whiskers touched the top of his belt's brass buckle.

"Aye, Mackenzie you old rogue," Atwood answered. "Get on with it now, have your fun. A cur like you wouldn't know how to keep this little matter quiet between us would you?"

Mackenzie gave Atwood a sly smile while absently caressing his beard. "Ha, ha! I suppose not. Then again, perhaps a drink or two to seal my lips when next we meet in Ayr might persuade me otherwise. I'm hardly against a bribe. You're the master of this sorry garbage scow?"

"Aye."

"Well, far be it from me to take advantage of a fellow mariner in trouble out on the hostile sea. Honestly though, you lost a rudder in these calm waters? How does one do that Jacob? This frigate is clearly too much ship for you to handle. You best return to port and stick to those little toy fishing boats I see you playing with when the weather's not too disagreeable. This old girl needs a man to ride her."

"You're a cruel one Jonathan. Now be a good fellow and toss us a line. I have no carpenter on board. We need a hand."

As the crews tied the two ships together, Atwood helped *Fleece's* stout master step over the rail and I allowed myself a tiny smile. With the ships tied off and Mackenzie onboard, I knew my plan would work.

The two men shook hands. They exchanged friendly smiles. And then a thin fellow with pasty skin and a sour look, a well-dressed gentleman who reeked of money, followed Mackenzie over.

Mackenzie placed his hands on his hips and looked around. "When did you sign with this vessel? I've never seen her before."

"Just a week ago. We sailed her up from Dublin."

"Your deck I see is cluttered with cargo. What are you hauling?"

"We sail in ballast."

Makenzie ran his fingers along the top of a crate hiding one of the guns and stared inquisitively at Atwood. "Really? One might mistake this ship for a smuggler, Jacob."

"No, no. I don't have the stomach for law-breaking. Have a look around if you wish. I won't stop you. My instructions were to transport several gentlemen of substance and their baggage from

Dublin to Ayr and then sail on to Liverpool to pick up manufactured goods for our return voyage home. We delivered our passengers yesterday and this morning we were on our way to Liverpool when that miserable bitch bad luck split our rudder in two."

"Ah, as it happens, Liverpool is our destination as well."

"Oh? Bravo! My day is improving then."

Mackenzie winked at Atwood. "Not the way I see things. It appears you'll be late sailing into Liverpool and your new position as master of this pig boat will be short-lived. Jacob, this gentleman is Baron Reginald O'Toole, my patron and the owner of the *Fleece*."

"I know of you Master Atwood," O'Toole said. "You manage a small fleet of herring buses for Gordon."

"Aye, that is true," Atwood replied. "You've got yourself a grand ship there Baron. I'd love to put her through her paces."

"Indeed. She's a real prize. Well, we have a schedule to keep my good fellow. I regret we cannot tow you back to Ayr, but if you need victuals or spare lumber to repair your rudder, we can oblige you there."

Atwood grunted. "What if a storm should hit us?"

O'Toole glanced up at a cloudless sky, then gave Atwood a puzzled look. "Some other vessel will happen upon you later today or tomorrow I'm sure. You and your men are in no danger."

I had heard enough and stepped out of the shadows. "Pray tell us good sir," I called out as I moved towards the baron. "I am most curious. How did you acquire this fine ship of yours? She looks familiar."

O'Toole turned his attention towards me with a displeased look in his eye. When he saw only a lowly seaman, he dismissed me with a flick of his hand as if he was brushing away a pesky fly, then looked back at Atwood.

"Master Atwood, do you require any food or spare wood? If not, we'll leave you to it and be on our way."

But I persisted. "I would have my question answered."

O'Toole spun around on his heels. "Clearly," he said with a scowl on his face, "you don't know your place mister. If you value your hide, you'll shut your hole and return to your duties."

"But I like your ship," I replied in a haughty tone. "I think I'll take her for myself."

"Why you ignorant bumpkin. Are you touched in the head? I should have you flogged for your insolence. One could even interpret your words as piracy. Master Atwood, you best muzzle this dog before I fetch my cane and beat some manners into it."

Atwood shook with laughter and slapped the rail.

"I hardly see the humor in any of this," O'Toole said, unamused. "Indeed, I find this whole sordid affair distasteful. Mackenzie, these men don't need our help. The sea can take the lot of them for all I care. Let's be off."

But before O'Toole could climb over the rail, I seized him by the arm.

He spun around, he stared at me in disbelief. "How dare you! Remove your filthy hand before I cut it off!"

I tightened my grip around his arm and smiled. I removed my hat with my free hand and shook out my hair, then untied the scarf around my neck to wipe the soot off my face.

"You're a woman!" he said. "What ill-conceived jest is this? Who the devil are you?"

"Some call me Lady Mary, others know me as Bloody Mary or Capt'n Bloody Mary."

"Impossible!"

"Ah, so you've heard the name."

"Capt'n Mary was an Irish pirate, a rogue of the worst sort, and she is dead. You're a crude imposter. This awful joke will cost you dearly you filthy trollop."

When the cocksure fool raised his hand to strike me, Atwood grabbed him by the wrist. "Stay your hand coward, lest you wish to forfeit your life," he said and then blew on a whalebone whistle he had carved years ago. He blew on his whistle three times and the rest of our crew rushed up on deck armed with muskets, swords and knives. The *Fleece's* crew, few in number and unarmed, could do no more than watch.

"Why," I asked the baron, "does everyone think me dead? No matter. You said you have a schedule to keep my lord. As it happens, so do I. Your ship is in fact the *Phantom* and the *Phantom* belongs to me. I'm her rightful owner and you have my gratitude for returning her to me intact."

"Your claim is absurd on its face," O'Toole replied indignantly. "The *Golden Fleece* is mine under the law. I purchased her some months ago in Westport and have the papers to prove my good title. If you proceed with this folly, you'll be guilty of felony piracy and you - and any man here who stands with you - will be hunted down and hanged. Oh yes, you'll dance the Marshal's Dance at the end of a rope on Execution Dock and I'll gladly pay to see it."

I placed my hands on my hips and laughed. "Are you quite finished Baron? I'm taking your cargo too."

"The devil you say. That wool is worth a fortune!"

"No doubt, no doubt it is and the value of that wool will compensate me for the great guns you stole and sold. Captain Atwood, secure *Phantom* if you please and we'll need to lower away a boat for the baron and his men. Baron, you should use this time to reflect on your transgressions."

Atwood released O'Toole. "Aye, Mary, straight away! Alrighty lads, you heard the lady. Let's ready a boat for the good baron and his plum crew."

O'Toole looked at me with loathing. "You'll stand on the gibbet for this vile crime! I swear it!"

I stood toe-to-toe with the baron. "Far better men than you have tried to take my life and yet I still breathe. Now you best shut your mouth your lordship before I gag you and I pitch you over the side. That water looks mighty cold and the shore seems a trifle far, even for a strapping fellow like yourself, assuming you even know how to swim. You can live or die this day, I'm indifferent. The time for you to choose is now."

When the baron had nothing more to say, my lads hustled him down into a longboat, along with fat Mackenzie and his lame crew, and we pushed them off with only one set of oars three miles from shore near Ballantrae. As his men dipped their blades into the water, my men blew kisses and waved. It would be days before the good baron reached the law and by then we would be far, far away.

I left a skeleton crew aboard *Diablo* and took the rest of my men over to the *Phantom* with me. Atwood grabbed *Phantom*'s wheel, the honor was his as captain, and we dropped her sails and set our course for Westport with our crippled *Diablo* in tow. Spirits soared.

I disappeared below to warm myself in the galley - or so I told Atwood - but I don't think he heard me, or he chose to ignore me. The big Scot kept his hands locked firmly on the wheel with a smile on his face and his gaze fixed on the far horizon. Had I fallen overboard I don't think he would have noticed. So much for Captain Bloody Mary, the bitch men dread.

"I know that look Mary," Atwood said when I stepped back on deck an hour later. "I know that unmistakable gleam in your eye. Something has caught your fancy." Then he noticed my trousers. "God's good grace, why are your trousers soaked through and through? Have you, ahem, have you taken ill, Mary?"

I grabbed the wheel from him. "My trousers are wet from bilge water."

"The ship is taking on water? Do we need to send men to the pumps?"

"No, the ship is sound," I replied sternly, as if I was annoyed.

"Oh? I'm a bit confused. Perhaps you should go below and rest a bit?"

"No. Assemble the officers in the great cabin for me Jacob and all shall be made clear. And don't touch anything on the table, not even a peek."

My officers rose from their chairs around the table when I stepped into the cabin. I was touched by their respect as always. I ignored the blanket draped over the boxes sitting on the table and took a moment, as was my way, to look at each man.

Atwood, my affable, feisty Scot with a wild mane of red hair, was now captain of the *Phantom*. Atwood had been Hunter's equal in war and at sea and had earned his place as the first among equals now that Hunter was gone. Command of *Diablo* went to MacGyver, a serious, red-bearded Irishman who had ably commanded the *Mia Bella Donna*, my smallest ship, before Drake commandeered her and turned her into one of his fireships at Gravelines. MacGyver, who liked to tinker, had replaced *Phantom's* clumsy whipstaff years before with a clever mechanical contraption using sheaves, pulleys, rope and gears to connect the rudder to a wheel up on the poop deck, greatly improving *Phantom's* agility. Henry, a lean Carib warrior from Guadeloupe with a sword crossed over a battle axe tattooed across his chest, and with teeth filed down to fangs, was the nephew of Chief Paka Wokili, the King of Guadeloupe. Henry was the heir apparent to the throne as the king had no sons. Fearsome in battle and capable seafarers, the Carib are the Vikings of the Caribbean. Some say they are cannibals too. Kinkae, my African Blackamoor with rippling muscles and as black as pitch, had been sold into slavery in Trinidad when I found him. Tattooed around and around both of his massive arms were whips to remind him of his days in chains. I had purchased Kinkae's freedom, and the freedom of nineteen of his people, for a bag of pearls in the Port of Spain from a Spaniard named Rodriguez Miguel de Cortés y Ovando, an entrepreneur and my partner in the New World. Henry and Kinkae were brave, fiercely loyal and well-liked by the crew. And then there was my Turk, a short, wiry fellow from Istanbul who had been with me the longest, Mustafa Agah Efendi. Efendi had washed up on shore one day, the sole survivor of a band of Turkish pirates whose ship had foundered on the rocks off Louisburg. I had rescued Efendi from an angry Irish mob bent on stoning him after he had naively wandered into Westport, half frozen and starving. A better soldier than sailor, Efendi was our captain of the guns and the ship's chief petty officer with dominion over all the ratings. In all my travels, I've never crossed paths with a more dangerous man than Efendi. He can move through the world unseen and his mastery of knives and the martial arts is unmatched. Efendi had made himself my protector and never strayed too far.

These men had served with me for years and I loved them all. They were my brothers and I was their sister.

As was our custom, I played hostess and moved around the table, pouring each man a glass of wine. No one asked me about the boxes underneath the blanket.

"Gentlemen, we are back in business," I said. "Please, sit. These past few days have been most exciting. To see us reunited fills my heart with great joy. But first, a salute to the men we lost at Westport."

I raised my glass. "To fallen brothers, we shall sorely miss your good fellowship. Until we meet again in the next, new world..."

"Until we meet again," my officers repeated with one voice and tipped their glasses back.

"After we fulfilled our obligations to the English in the war," I continued, "and with the Twins dead, I thought we had put the bloodshed behind us. I, I, was terribly mistaken and we've all paid a heavy price. Though it is true that each of us are bound by the Ten Rules, I cannot, in good conscience, force any man to sail with me further. I release each of you, and the men, from your oaths and obligations. You are free to choose your own path. For any who wish to pursue other interests, I'll give them *Diablo*. For those who stay, I intend to rebuild our smuggling trade in the Caribbean. We still have good contacts in Ireland and in the West Indies and we have the *Letter of Marque and Reprisal* signed and sealed by her majesty should we wish to do a little plundering on the side. Well, what say you?"

Atwood answered me with a great yawn. Efendi tossed me an evil eye while MacGyver poured himself more wine. Henry and Kinkae simply stared at me as if I had insulted them.

But I held my ground. "Lads, do not be careless with your lives. The world is far more dangerous now. We must put this matter to vote."

"No, we do not Mary," Atwood answered gruffly. "We are adventurers and men of fortune. You cannot set aside our obedience to the Ten Rules simply because you've been touched by melancholy."

"I've not been touched by melancholy!"

"Good, I'm pleased to hear it. Now we all have a great deal of work to do. We need to whip our ships - and the men - into fighting trim. Are you finished?"

Kinkae reached over and took my hand. "We are with you, Mary."

Henry smiled and nodded. MacGyver did the same. Efendi said nothing, but I already knew his mind.

"So be it," I said softly. "Thank you. Still, there is one small matter we must discuss."

I was not above a little drama. I took my time. I stared at the blanket as I drummed my fingers on the table, savoring my guilty pleasure from the suspense I had caused. Then I yanked the blanket off.

Atwood's jaw dropped. "Nooo... Is this what I think it is?"

I pushed one of the chests over on its side and smiled. A fortune in Spanish gold doubloons spilled across the table.

MacGyver picked up one of the coins and held it to the sunlight. "This is the gold you seized from the Spanish galleass off Loop Head?"

"James," Efendi murmured.

"Aye," I replied. "We can thank James for this bounty. We took six chests of gold off the galleass that day. I found only three. James hid two chests underneath this very table in a secret compartment. Those are gone. He hid another chest behind a false panel next to the bunk. That chest is also missing. O'Toole or Mackenzie, or perhaps Dowlin's men, must have found them. But James, being a clever fellow, hid these three chests amongst the ballast stones. It took me time to find them underneath a foot of bilge water. And there is more. I found a handful of banknotes I had hidden inside the candelabra swinging above our heads. I had nearly forgotten about them."

I removed a roll of paper notes from my vest pocket and laid them over the gold. "These notes, issued by the House of Mendès, are the banknotes we took from our friend Cortés as compensation for his lack of good judgment."

Atwood ran his fingers over the gold coins. "Now I see why you were so damned determined to take *Phantom* back in a hurry. You should change your trousers Mary before you catch your death of cold."

I laughed. "And leave you five brigands alone with all this loot? Ha, I think not!"

Once we dropped anchor in Westport's fine harbor, I hurried on to the Fitzgerald home to see my little Aliénor. I found her in good health. I took pleasure in holding her, feeding her, pinching her chubby cheeks and listening to her giggle. She was a lively, happy child and it was plain to see that the Fitzgeralds had lavished their affections on her. She had my eyes and mouth. She had my raven hair. Her strong, square chin and aquiline nose were gifts from her father. I've not seen many babies in my travels, but she seemed a pretty child to me.

I could only risk spending a day or two with Aliénor as I had much to do. I sold off O'Toole's wool first and then spent the money and most of our treasure. I paid the men their shares and paid-off all my debts and then I walked down to the shipyards to hire the best shipwrights I could find to overhaul our ships. I never skimped on repairs. And I found new cannon for *Phantom*, a mix of long-barreled six-pounders and nine-pounders, French army field pieces mounted on large two-wheeled wagons. My men removed the barrels and built proper gun carriages for them before moving the guns onboard. At the end of my spending spree, I had just enough in banknotes to purchase supplies and cargo for one new adventure.

With the repairs to the ships nearly completed, I took my officers to Shaw's splendid tavern where we ate and drank like kings. The mood around the table was light, until I revealed the next part of my plan.

"My mind is firm," I said in a testy tone, surprised by the resistance around the table.

Atwood was in a pugnacious mood and repeated his objection. "Mary, again I say: the risk you propose is too great. I beseech you to reconsider."

But I would not bend. "Who can say if the queen will even agree to see me? But I must try. I, and I alone, must make the trip to London."

"What if," MacGyver asked, "Martin had a hand in the ambush at the old mill? Even worse, what if the ambush was on the queen's orders?"

"Impossible!" I replied. "Such a thing is inconceivable to me. We fought honorably alongside our English cousins in their war against the Spanish. We've given no offense to the queen, or to anyone at her Court. No Englishman has just cause to hold a grudge against us."

"An Englishman needs no just cause to hold a grudge," MacGyver replied.

"We shall all go to London with you," Atwood insisted.

"No. I need you lads here. You must see to the ships. I don't trust the men at the yards and I'll not be swindled. And we need to recruit and train new men. I want the men ready before we put to sea. Be vigilant too for any trouble from the clan."

Atwood rubbed his eyes, then reached for the pitcher of ale. "Very well, Mary. I don't like it, but there is no reasoning with you when you're like this."

"Thank you. I must know where we stand with the English before we set off on any new adventure. If I'm wrong, if I am no longer in the queen's favor, I'll not risk any of your lives for my mistake. I cannot. If I fail to return, the ships are yours as equal partners. I've already set monies aside for my daughter's care and disport. The matter is closed."

MacGyver looked at me wide-eyed. "Daughter?"

I rolled my eyes. "Auck, I forgot. There's more to my story Michael, but first I need more ale..."

Chapter Three

I know nothing about the formalities of court, of court intrigue or etiquette. I am a lowly commoner, a smuggler and a thief - though the queen had once called me *sister* when I was a guest in the Tower and later saw fit to elevate me to the lofty status of a *lady*. I had never stepped foot inside a royal court before, let alone into the privy chambers of a queen.

I arrived in London a simple passenger aboard a simple packet ship in a cold drizzle and hurried to Richmond Palace first where I learned the queen and her royal entourage had left London a week before for Nonsuch Palace in Surrey. Nonsuch, as any Englishman will proudly tell you, is a palace that has no equal in the world. I was glad to learn the queen had left London as I dislike cities. Years had passed since my last visit to England's grand city, but little had changed. London is a sad, unclean blight on the land. It is a place of foul, unhealthy odors, of mold and mildew, greasy stone, roughhewn wood and peeling stucco. Vile filth litters her streets. Rats, plump and unafraid, scurry through the slop floating down her gutters. Hucksters by the boatload roam her alleyways and beggars, wretched souls suffering from ghastly infirmities of one sort or another, reach out for a bit of charity from every passerby. The buildings and the streets, the grass and the trees, even the people of London, are forever stained in soot and grime. A dreary, disheartening place is London.

I took the first available coach I could find for Surrey, happy to leave London behind. Once we were out of the city, we passed fields of bluebells and cowslips in bloom and primroses just beginning to sprout and when we arrived in Surrey the clouds magically parted, the sun appeared and the day turned deliciously warm. I stepped off the coach at Mitcham and saw birds flittering back and forth between the trees, chirping out their love songs, and folks out and about soaking in the promise of spring, a promise with power to lift any heart. These were good omens I told myself as I paused in the middle of the village square to get my bearings. I found Mitcham peaceful, quaint and clean.

I stopped at a vendor's booth to purchase a loaf of bread and a circle of cheese from a rosy-cheeked woman with a large bosom and an easy smile. When I asked her for directions to Nonsuch, she pointed south and I promptly set out on foot, eating my breakfast along the way.

The palace was not hard to find. Nonsuch stands alone in the midst of acres and acres of soft rolling hills dotted with clusters of trees, scrub brush and wild flowers. The palace is a timber-framed, four story building in the Tudor style with ramparts all around. Immense turrets with large, onion-shaped cupolas sheathed in tiles of rich blue and deep greens stand at the corners of each wall. Rising above each copula are weathervanes with royal pennants fluttering in the wind. In the center of the palace, within an inner courtyard, is a stone castle keep with battlements and a majestic clock tower many stories high.

The outer walls are adorned with gilded panels of white slate, engraved with carvings by the Master of Modena, Nicolas Bellin. Even the timber framing is embellished with miniature carvings trimmed in gold leaf. Bellin tells the history of the world through his art, with a good bit of folklore mixed in. I saw carvings of Persian, Greek and Roman gods along with the mighty deeds of ancient heroes like Moses parting the Red Sea with his staff, David slaying Goliath with his sling and Achilles dragging Hector's corpse around the walls of Troy in his golden chariot. The grandest panel of all though was of Hercules standing triumphantly over his Twelve Labors.

They say King Henry VIII built Nonsuch as a lasting testament to the power and grandeur of his Tudor dynasty. In this he had not failed. Nonsuch is a glorious achievement, a glimpse of paradise on earth and proof, or so the royals would have we commoners believe, of the divine right of kings to rule the world.

I approached the royal grounds from the south, walking through sumptuous gardens with enchanting stone fountains, and then circled around the palace to the north wall and then to main gatehouse where four palace guards dressed from head to toe in black, black mandilions and doublets, leather jerkins, paneled trunk hoses, nether stockings and black feathered hats, lowered their gleaming halberds at me. A burly fellow with a nasty scar running across his left eye and down his cheek stepped forward.

"State your name and purpose!" the fellow demanded.

I noted the sergeant's insignia pinned to the man's lapel and nodded. "I am Lady Mary," I replied respectfully. "I'm here on urgent business with the queen."

The sergeant narrowed his eyes at me. His men chuckled.

"Sergeant," I said, "I do not expect you to take me directly to our good queen. I only ask that you summon one of her majesty's courtiers for me."

The sergeant twisted his face into a scowl as he took a menacing step towards me. "Are you feeble-minded or is this some trifling jest?"

"I'm quite well thank you kindly and I've hardly travelled all this way from Westport to play games with the queen's trusty guards."

"My, my, lads, we've got ourselves a lively one," the sergeant said, then jerked his head to one side. "Be on your way wench before I stuff my boot up your arse."

I could hardly blame the sergeant. Beyond my gang of Irish thieves, a Spaniard or two, a few Frenchmen and one Carib tribe in Guadeloupe, I enjoyed no notoriety in the world. I dress for comfort and the climate, not appearances, and wore heavy, coarse trousers with a weathered, black leather vest over a man's shirt. My boots and the fringe along the bottom of my sea cape were splattered with filth and mud. My hat was cheap and well-worn. From head to toe I looked like a *païsant femme* on her way to muck-out the royal horse stalls.

I took a step forward, I came nose-to-nose with the sergeant. "Wench is it? Huh. The queen herself bestowed the title of lady upon me, though I'm better known as Captain Mary. I'm one of her majesty's privateers."

"You must be mad," the sergeant scoffed. "A privateer, a captain, with titties? Ha! Begone with you I say. You've been given fair warning."

An ugly sot with crooked black teeth and a pockmarked face snatched my hat off my head to better see my face. He lewdly looked me up and down and licked his lips.

"Oh, pretty. I've seen this Irish strumpet before Sergeant. She likes to work the docks. She's always up for a naughty romp below decks, or so they say. Pay her well and this shipboard bitch will gladly play pirate with the whole crew!"

The sergeant and the other guards stamped their feet and howled with laughter.

When the ugly fellow puckered his lips and tried to kiss me, I took a step back.

"C'mon now love," he said. "You remember me. A few weeks back we fucked so hard we woke up half of Surrey! Give us another taste."

The sergeant yanked his man back. "Patience, Harry, patience," he said, then reached into his pocket and produced a silver coin. "My, my, Lady Mary, aren't you the rare beauty. Wait for us at the tavern in Belmont, there's only one. We'll be off duty soon. If we find your company pleasing later, this coin can be yours my lovely dove."

I looked at the sergeant with a haughty smile, leaned over and spit, aiming for the sergeant's boot but missed by a smidgeon. "Careful, Sergeant, lest you return home to your wife missing your testicles. I'm certain a man of your stature has a wife - pity that. Now, I demand to see your captain and you'd be wise to heed my demand."

The sergeant, not to my surprise, promptly arrested me. His men grabbed me roughly by the arms and dragged me into the gatehouse. They took my sword and my pistols. They clapped irons around my wrists and tossed me into a cell.

But I had come prepared. It did not take the captain of the guard long to visit me. He was a fine-looking man with unblemished olive skin, green eyes, glossy black hair and a neatly trimmed goatee. No doubt my absurd claims, and word of my beauty, had piqued his curiosity.

He unlocked the cell's door, stepped inside and waited for me to speak. But I held my tongue. Words are cheap. Instead, I reached into my cape and handed him a cloak clasp.

He whistled softly. "Real gold?" he asked as he considered the coiled sea serpent in his hand, a serpent poised to strike wrought from solid gold. The queen's own jeweler had crafted the clasp for me. The gold glittered in the torch light, the serpent's ruby eyes sparkled.

"Aye. This was a gift to me from the queen, to thank me for my services."

"What services might that be?"

"Privateer."

"You, a woman, an Irishwoman, sailed with English privateers?"

"As captain of my own ship, I did. An incredible claim I agree and yet my words are true."

The captain had more sense than the dunderheads serving under him. He had his men bring two chairs into the cell, along with a clay jug and two tin cups. After we exchanged pleasantries, the captain listened thoughtfully as I told him about my adventures in the New World, revealing just enough of my story to whet his appetite.

"You hold in your hand the mark of the *Síol Faolcháin*," I said at the end of my tale. "The clan's battle flag is a red, coiled sea serpent emblazoned on a field of green. This is the mark the one-eyed Twin burned deep into my flesh with a branding iron on the Island of Guadeloupe."

The captain arched an eyebrow in disbelief. He had never heard of the Twins, or of a female privateer.

I could see he needed more proof. I've never been shy. I undid the lace to my shirt, stood and exposed my breasts. He stared at the scar over my left breast, the scar of the coiled serpent against my heart. Then he stood and tenderly pulled my shirt back up over my shoulders.

"Mary, Captain Mary, I must confess you tell a deliciously good tale. If I take you to the queen, and she knows you not, I'll be forced to drag you in chains to the Tower in the morning. If you wish to leave Surrey now, I'll set you free and this will be the end of the matter. The choice is yours."

"I thank you for your kindness and for your chivalry, Captain. I've travelled far and at some expense to see our queen."

The captain nodded. He poured me another cup of wine before he left, then took my clasp and my story to the queen's gentleman usher who in turn would hand them off to one of the queen's ladies-in-waiting. Within the hour the captain returned with a lantern in one hand and a wet rag in the other. He removed my shackles, took a knee and used the rag to wipe the mud off my boots and cape and then he led me down a narrow brick tunnel, what I supposed to be a secret passageway running underneath the palace. He unlocked several doors along the way until we reached what appeared to be a dead-end. He removed a block of wood from the wall and used a key attached to a chain around his neck to unlock a hidden door. I followed him through two more doors and into a fabulous bedchamber fit for a queen. Never had I beheld such opulence before.

The room was filled with fresh-cut flowers in a dozen of vases. The air smelled of roses, lavender and pine. The chairs, desk, couch, tables and stands, with matching silk and leather accents, had all been polished to a high gloss. But the grandest piece of furniture in the room by far was a canopied bed of enormous size with four stout warriors, Spartan hoplites I think carved from mahogany, who served as bedposts. The warriors each carried a spear in one hand and used the other to support an onion domed canopy up on his shoulder. Silk swags, in various shades of greens, blues and earth tones, formed a tent around the bed. On the mantle over the fireplace sat an ornate clock of solid gold, a miniature replica of Nonsuch Palace, and above the clock was a large portrait of King Henry. I quickly looked away when the king's icy gaze sent shiver down my spine and turned my attention to the exquisite tapestries along the walls.

Neither the captain nor I dared sit. We stood in awkward silence together, avoiding idle chit-chat, and took in our surroundings while we waited. From some remote corner of the palace I could hear the sweet voices of children singing the spring carol *tempus adest floridum*, the time is near for flowering, a favorite melody of mine.

One tapestry, only half-finished, caught my eye. I took a closer look and smiled. The intricate weave was an accurate depiction of the great English victory over the Spanish Armada off the French coast. I marveled at the artist's skill.

I turned to the captain and pointed to the tapestry. "I was there," I said. "This is the Battle of Gravelines."

The captain nodded politely and moved to my side. He folded his arms behind his back and took a closer look.

"You don't believe me?" I asked when the captain said nothing, uncertain of whether I was amused or disappointed by his distrust.

He turned to me with a cunning smile. "I believe what the queen believes, madam."

And then we heard giggling and the light footsteps of women coming down a hallway towards us. When the queen and her three ladies-in-waiting entered the room, the captain and I dropped to our knees and lowered our heads.

"We thank you, Captain Gerrard, for your good judgment," the queen said.

"Your Highness," Gerrard replied.

"Your men, the men who took Lady Mary into custody, do you vouch for their loyalty?"

"Why I do indeed. They're good men and loyal to your Majesty."

"Good, we are glad to hear it. Their punishment need not be too harsh then."

"Majesty? Punishment?"

"A little mouse has told me that your men insulted Lady Mary. They were rude and vulgar. We think our royal guard should treat our subjects with civility, not disdain. Their actions reflect upon you Captain and your actions reflect upon me. Surely you agree Gerrard?"

"Most certainly I do your Majesty."

"Excellent. I leave the matter in your capable hands then Captain. You may leave the lady with me and see to your duties sir."

Gerrard rose to his feet and slowly walked backwards, keeping his head down until he disappeared through the secret door. I used the moment to steal a quick glance of the queen. I had never seen such opulent finery.

Her highness had always dressed in simpler attire when she came to visit me in the Tower. Now she wore more queenly garb. She was dressed in an Italian reticella lace ruff in cream over a dark blue French farthingale with elaborate Polish ornamentation. Her silk gown was embroidered in a rainbow of colors and sumptuously adorned in diamonds, rubies, sapphires and more. In place of a crown, she wore a towering, white wig dripping with pearls. I wondered if any them were from the bag of Margarita pearls I had once presented to her majesty.

She caught me staring and winked. I clumsily looked away and took in her ladies, all young beauties. One was lovelier than the next, but none was lovelier or more poised or nobler in her bearing than the queen. No, I am not smitten by royalty. Her majesty could have entered the room wearing sackcloth and my opinion would have been the same. The queen's very essence radiated power and grace.

Her ladies were tall, majestic creatures dressed in matching silk gowns in different colors. One wore light blue, one wore soft yellow and one was dressed in pale, emerald green. They used bumrolls to pad out their hips and corsets boned-in to flatten their bosoms. They wore floral garlands in their hair and had tied flowered sashes around their waists.

My world is, and has always been, living aboard a warship out on a hostile sea with rough and bawdy men where there's not much need for fashion. Even so, I knew enough to know that the ladies were wearing gowns cut in the modern French style.

In contrast to the queen, the ladies wore only modest jewelry. God forbid one of the queen's royal attendants tried to outshine the queen. The lady in blue wore a pearl neckless, the lady in yellow had a gold chain with a modest crucifix on her wrist and the lady in emerald green, the most sensuous of the three, wore a simple black choker embroidered with gold lace in a diamond pattern.

I could feel their eyes on me, taking in my coarse men's clothing. My shirt caught their attention. I prefer wearing my shirts open at the neck, partially unlaced, and I am hardly shy about using my cleavage to good advantage. The ladies made little effort to mask their contempt.

Not the queen. She looked upon me with affection.

After the captain locked the door behind him, the queen grabbed me by the shoulders and raised me to my feet. To the horror of her ladies, she embraced me and kissed me on both cheeks. I had to suppress the urge to stick my tongue out at her haughty, pampered noblewomen, at silly girls who had little notion of the world beyond palaces, manor houses, dances and picnics in the country.

"Oh Mary, Mary, Mary, how wonderful it is to see you!" the queen exclaimed. "We half-expected to find an imposter waiting for us in our chambers! Our heart was crushed when we heard the wretched news of your demise."

"I am sorry if I've caused your Majesty any anguish."

"The years slip by so quickly. How long has it been since we last embraced Mary?"

"Nearly fifteen or so, my Lady."

"Fifteen years you say? Impossible! You've hardly changed. Let us have a better look at you. My, my, still the stunning beauty - and not a blemish on you. A few freckles here and there I see and a line or two perhaps, but you still have the complexion and the figure of a young maiden! Sailing with cutthroats across the oceans plainly agrees with you - or is it war that gives you your youth?"

"Irish luck perhaps, your Majesty. And I've learned a trick or two from the Indian women in the New World. They apply an unguent made from a concoction of oils from plants, flowers and nuts to their skin to protect themselves from the elements."

The queen turned to look at her ladies. "Do you hear that my darlings? The fountain of youth is not a fountain at all - it is a magical ointment! Perhaps we should visit our lands to the west to improve our complexions." The queen put a hand to her mouth to stifle a giggle. "Better yet, I shall give each of you a ship from my royal navy. We'll sail the oceans together seeking high adventure and good fortune like our brave Captain Mary. We'll put those Spanish rascals and French buccaneers to the test! I shall be admiral of course and you ladies will be my daring captains! Mary, I shall make you vice admiral. How would that please you?"

I bowed my head. "Your Majesty is having fun I think, but I have no doubt that if you pursued this fancy you would quickly become mistress over all the great oceans. Your fame and prestige would encircle the globe like the wind."

"Ha! Flattering your queen Mary is good politics. You might do well at Court. Oh, we have missed you! When Captain Gerrard informed us that a woman claiming to be Captain Mary had tried to enter the palace gates, we were suspicious and tempted to toss this imposter into prison. But then the gold serpent was placed into our hands and joy filled our heart!"

"Your Majesty's kindness overwhelms me."

After the queen formally introduced her ladies to me, I have long ago forgotten their names, she invited us all to sit. Her majesty instructed a servant standing outside her room to bring us tea and sugar cakes and had me entertain her ladies with tales of the New World, with stories of wild Indians, conquistadors, exotic islands and buried treasure. I happily obliged the queen.

But as I recounted my adventures, I saw only boredom in the faces of the queen's ladies. They fidgeted in their chairs, rolled their eyes and yawned. Not one of the queen's ladies tried to hide her disinterest.

After we finished tea, the queen dismissed her ladies and I found myself alone with the queen. She asked me about my part in the battle with the Spanish Armada and she wanted to hear my story of the treachery and heartbreak that followed me to Westport. Except for Aliénor, and the Spanish gold we had taken off the Spanish galleass, I told the queen nearly everything. I trusted the queen, but I had no reason to trust those around her and thought it best to keep my little Aliénor a secret. As for the gold, the gold was mine. I felt no obligation to share any portion of it with the queen. I knew the English navy, notorious for ignoring its debts, would never compensate me for the *Bella* Drake had taken from me.

I doubt Queen Elizabeth had heard the story of the Spanish Armada from the perspective I offered. She listened patiently as I told her of my pursuit of the Spanish up into the treacherous North Sea, around the tip of Scotland and then down the west coast of Ireland. I told her about *Medusa*, the ambush at the old mill, of Hunter's death and my escape, describing each event in heart-wrenching detail. I even confessed my transgressions against the Scottish baron O'Toole when I took my *Phantom* back by force.

"I am unfamiliar with this minor nobleman you speak of," she said. "Unless he can produce legitimate papers to support his claim of ownership, which I am confident he cannot do, I'll have my High Lord Constable quash any warrant he might bring against you. And should he put forth any false evidence, I shall know it and he'll be the sorrier for it."

"I'm in your debt my Lady."

"As I am indebted to you, Mary. You are worthy of knighthood but alas your sex will not permit it. My father's father, King Henry VII, disallowed women from becoming ladies in the Most Noble Order of the Garter during his reign. Though I am England's sovereign ruler, I cannot undo my grandfather's decree. But you have something far more valuable than some silly title coveted by the vainglorious, you have a queen's profound gratitude for your loyalty and bravery."

"You honor me, Majesty."

The queen reached across the small table between us and placed a hand on my shoulder. "Mary, by all accounts Captain Hunter was a good man, a man of noble character, prudence and valor. War is an ugly business. Victors and vanquished alike always pay a heavy price for making war. I was saddened to learn of your loss."

"Thank you, Majesty. I did not come to England to burden you with such intimate matters though. In truth, I've come to seek your counsel."

"Oh? Well then it is good counsel I shall try to give. How may the Queen of England be of service to you, my good captain?"

"Have you any news of John Martin your Majesty? I do not know if he is dead or alive. I do not know if he is friend or foe. I think he was betrayed at the old mill as I was but it is also possible that he was one of the conspirators in the plot to kill me."

"I have not seen nor heard from Martin for many months. He disappeared when you disappeared and I do not know his fate. I doubt very much he betrayed you though. He has lands, title and family in England. He has far too much to lose. Martin has always been a devoted Englishman, a patriot, and loyal to our person."

"Then I fear Martin may be dead."

"Discrete enquiries have been made to discover who betrayed us. Time will reveal the truth. And when we learn the truth, those involved in this treachery shall feel our terrible wrath."

"I welcome that day your Majesty. After the ambush, I did not know what to think. I did not know who to trust. This is why I have traveled to Surrey. I wish to know if I am still in your good graces."

The queen rose from her chair and held my hands. "Mary, do you actually suppose your queen would renege on our agreement, turn on you or abandon you? You've held up your end of the bargain and then some. Your queen will do no less. Since I released you from the Tower, you've been a most loyal subject. You've proven your quality at sea and defended our interests in the New World. And your part in repelling the Spanish Armada has not gone unnoticed. Though he will never admit it publicly, even Sir Francis Drake admires your skill and courage."

"I still possess the letter of marque signed by your Majesty."

"That commission is as valid today Mary as the day I impressed my seal into the parchment. England and Spain are still at war. True, we gave the Spanish a good thrashing at Gravelines, but we have unfinished business. The Pope's puppet, that scoundrel Phillip, still craves to have my head mounted on a spike on London Bridge for all the world to gawk at. He may yet succeed. We live in uncertain, violent times."

"There's talk your Majesty about a large English fleet being assembled. Many suppose this expedition will sail against the Spanish to administer your just vengeance, swift and sure."

The queen returned to her chair and considered me for a moment before answering. "Indeed? How men love to gossip as they while away the hours in their bawdy taverns, drinking and whoring about and playing games of chance when they should be at home comforting their wives and children. It is no secret England is marshalling her armies and assembling her ships. If you seek Drake out, you may tell him you do so with my blessing. England will need her finest for the struggle to come. What say you to that Mary?"

"I'm intrigued, Majesty."

"Splendid. After the battle at Gravelines, I was informed about your pursuit of the Armada into dangerous waters when all my admirals thought it best to return home."

"We were sailing for home ourselves," I replied vaguely and made no mention of my desire to take a prize.

The queen smiled. "I see. There are safer routes to Westport I'm told. You're a fighter Mary. You've shown great courage and tenacity in the face of England's enemy. I'm less sanguine about the will of some of my admirals. Oh, it is true we won a great victory over the Spanish, but I fear Spain's power is only a little diminished. The heart of the Armada still beats."

"To be fair, Majesty, my men and I took an awful risk following the Spanish into the North Sea. I would not fault your admirals too much. Many a commander would see prudence in returning to port after a battle of the likes of Gravelines to care for the wounded and to replenish their stores of shot and powder."

"Perhaps. My commanders have claimed as much. Or perhaps they simply missed their wives and sweethearts and a warm, comfortable bed. We want lions not kittens to lead my navies and my armies! Once a lion sinks its fangs into its prey, it does not let go. Spain has men and ships aplenty to topple us yet. If only my admirals had pursued the Armada with your audacity. But here we are. Now

England will sacrifice more lives and spend more precious treasury on a risky campaign. I take no pleasure in sending fathers and sons into war."

"How soon, Majesty?"

"Only Drake knows the answer to your question. I pray he launches his ships soon. Assembling large numbers of ships, men and arms, and procuring sufficient supplies, is no easy task, but we are losing precious time. And then there are the politics."

"Politics, Majesty?"

"There are always politics Mary. Politics and the cunning games men like to play to increase their wealth and power, to advance their own ambitions."

""The curse of avarice and cupidity," your Majesty."

"Ah, you know your Chaucer."

"Long voyages at sea allows me ample time to read."

When the queen stood again, I stood with her as I understood it was time to leave. She took my hands into her own once more.

"Mary, if you are game, go to Plymouth and speak with Drake. Be mindful of the dangers. There's been an outbreak of the sweating sickness in Devon recently. Good men have already lost their lives. With Martin's disappearance, your eyes and ears would be most welcome. Oh, I have my spies as you might imagine. But a woman's perspective can be useful. Our navy might benefit from a good dose of your swagger as well."

"As you wish, your Majesty, I shall leave immediately for Plymouth. In all candor, I don't know if Drake will embrace me or arrest me though."

The queen chuckled, then moved over to her writing desk. She took a seat, dipped a quill pen into the ink jar and began scratching words across a sheet of paper. Her penmanship was well-ordered and precise. Once she was satisfied with what she had written, she sprinkled sand over the wet ink and blew across the paper, then held a stick of green wax over a candle, dribbled the melted wax next to her signature and pressed her signet ring into the hot goo.

"This is a letter of safe conduct," the queen said and then began to read the letter to me. "Be it known: the bearer of this letter is to be accorded unconditional safe-passage. Let no insult or harm befall the bearer, or to any person in her company. If there is a debt owed, or some dispute at issue, no matter how grave, you are commanded to accompany the bearer of this letter safely back to England and we shall see the matter justly settled. Elizabeth R."

"Thank you, Majesty," I said and bowed my head in gratitude.

"Men, leastwise English nobles, will know this seal Mary."

The queen handed me the letter, then kissed me on the cheek. "I pray your wounded heart heals in time Mary. It would seem God has chosen heavy burdens for you to bear in this life. Who can know the why of such things? I pray He keeps thee safe and well as you embark upon your uncertain journey. Go now with my love."

I left Nonsuch Palace behind me, sent a letter to Westport to let my officers know that all was well and hurried on to Plymouth next. On a whim, I hired a horse instead of taking a coach and was glad I did. Not long into my journey the rains started. Relentless, heavy showers drenched England for days, turning the road from Surrey to Plymouth into a morass of sticky slime. I passed coaches mired in mud or sitting on the side of the road with broken wheels or splintered axels. I pressed on as best I could for if I dallied, I risked missing Drake. After two hundred miles of hard riding, I reached the busy seaport of Plymouth cold, wet, filthy and exhausted.

Nearly nine months had passed since I had last seen Drake. My first voyage with the admiral had been back in 1587 when Drake had set out with thirty warships, give or take, to raid the Spanish coast. The admiral's mission was to strike Cádiz, to disrupt Spain's preparations for war. Drake had assigned my ships to a wonderful squadron of privateers. Most were Englishmen, all of them were first-rate.

I did not care for England's great hero at first. Drake struck me as humorless, pompous and vain. Modest in stature, plain of face and cursed with a thin, high voice, he hardly embodied the qualities of a ship's captain let alone what I imagined an admiral to be. He liked to surround himself with young English noblemen, men of questionable abilities barely old enough to shave, and sought their counsel on everything, no matter how trivial, before making any decision. I thought him weak.

But I must confess my judgment of the man was clouded by my jealousy. Without a pair of stones between my legs I could never achieve his fame or glory. My opinion of Drake was also tainted by what I knew about his part in the massacre of the rebellious Clan MacDonnell at Rathlin Island. After capturing the MacDonnell stronghold, the English massacred every living soul, except for Sorely Boy MacDonnell himself. They say Drake forced the Scottish chieftain to watch as his soldiers slaughtered all of MacDonnell's men. And when the English found the women and children hiding in nearby caves, Drake's men forced them out and off the cliffs to the sea below. Hundreds perished.

And it was plain Drake did not like me. He and his gaggle of young cavaliers did not trust me or my Irish, Catholic crews, men they thought of as thugs and most likely traitors to the Crown. Drake had kept us at a goodly distance during the expedition to Cádiz. At Nonsuch the queen had assured me though that, contrary to my suspicions, Drake in fact held a good opinion of me after my men and I did our part in the colossal struggle with the Spanish Armada in the summer of '88.

A biting wind ripping across the harbor cut into my bones as I walked my horse down the narrow streets of the old Barbican Quarter where Drake was using the home of a wealthy merchant as his headquarters. Captain Gerrard had given me a good description of the merchant's residence and I had no trouble finding the stately, red brick and white stone building. I tethered my horse to a wrought iron fence and climbed a slate stairway up to an impressive portico supported by six Grecian columns. I struck the head of a bronze lion bearing its teeth with a ring knocker several times before an elderly gentleman opened the door. The manservant offered me a kindly smile and waved me inside out of the cold after I introduced myself. I kept my coat on and walked around in circles trying to keep my teeth from clattering after he left me in a large, oval foyer, a drafty place with only one small bench, and disappeared down a hallway.

I was grateful Drake did not keep me waiting long. He greeted me with a genuine smile, bowed and kissed my hand.

"Captain Mary! How good to see you again. You are blue in the face with cold. I trust you are in good health otherwise?"

"I'm well enough your grace. And you?"

"Tolerable, most tolerable."

I was surprised by Drake's appearance. He had aged. His eyes had sunken back into their sockets and had lost their brightness. His ruddy complexion had turned pale and his tar-black goatee was now grey with streaks of yellow.

"I am glad, Sir Francis."

"I received word from Surrey only yesterday that I should expect you. I did not think to see you so soon. I hear the roads are nearly impassable in places. How is it you arrived in Plymouth only a day after the queen's good messenger? Did you sprout wings and fly?"

"Alas, I left my wings behind in Ireland. I traveled by horse. Hunger and misery inspired me to ride hard."

"Ha! Two powerful incentives to speed any traveler along his way. Let us retire to the library. I use the room as my office. This house belongs to an old friend of mine who is off in Italy somewhere. The library is blessed with a sturdy fireplace where we can chat in comfort whilst you warm your bones."

"You are most kind your grace. I'm grateful to you for your hospitality. A commander of your stature must have many important matters to attend to."

Drake slipped his arm inside mine as if we were dear friends and led me down the hallway. "Nonsense. You and I are old fighting companions, warriors bound by blood. After Admiral Medina Sidonia quit Gravelines and took the Armada north, I understand you pursued his ships around Scotland and Ireland and all the way back to Spain. A courageous move by God! I'd like to hear your story.

Any profit in it for you? Did you take any prizes?"

I forced a giggle. "What you've heard is a bit of an exaggeration Sir Francis. We pursued the fleet only as far as Limerick, no farther, and for our efforts we managed to snag only one, poor galleass carrying pots and pans intended for Parma's army. Not much of a story there for the bards to sing about."

Drake burst out laughing. "Pots and pans you say? The spoils of war fit for a tinker! Well, if you have an appetite for another go at our hated foe, perhaps we can find more enticing opportunities to prosper from."

"That is why I've come to Plymouth, your grace. And I am here with the queen's good blessing. It is no secret you are assembling ships and men for a large expedition, though for what purpose I do not know."

"Do you still have those fine battlecruisers, Mary?"

"Aye, indeed I do."

"Excellent! Let's sit by the fire shall we and get some hot soup into you. The cook made a batch of fresh biscuits earlier with jellied fruit. After you've eaten, we can discuss how best we can help each other. I believe our interests are aligned. Ha! Pots and pans indeed Mary!"

After a pleasant morning chatting by the fire with England's great admiral, I caught a packet ship for Westport, the stronghold of the O'Malley clan and for years my safe haven. Drake had not shared much with me in Plymouth. I knew at least that he intended to launch his expedition within several weeks, which left me with precious little time to prepare.

Once I reached Westport, I gathered my officers and men, won their consent to sail with the English and we set off for England in a hurry. We made good time and found the fleet still anchored in Plymouth. Though Drake had disclosed nothing about his plans to me, he could not hide the sheer vastness of the undertaking. A forest of masts and spars had sprouted across Firestone Bay and along the River Tamar. On the docks we saw teams of men, animals and carts moving supplies of every sort and the storehouses looked filled to bursting. Plymouth was bustling with more sailors, soldiers, craftsman and laborers than I could count.

We had arrived late to the merrymaking and were forced to park our ships far out in the middle of the bay with a long row to shore. I gave my men their liberty and took Atwood, MacGyver and Efendi into town with me where we found Plymouth's taverns and gambling dens abuzz with idle gossip and wild rumors.

Some thought Drake was planning to circumnavigate the globe again, as he had done in 1580 with the *Golden Hind*, eclipsing the greatness of Fernão de Magalhães, Spain's famous navigator who had died during his voyage around the world sixty years eariler. Queen Elizabeth had knighted Drake for his astonishing feat, and for the fabulous wealth he had returned with. I prayed these rumors were not true for the passage had taken Drake three, long years to complete. I dreaded the prospect of spending so many monotonous years at sea.

Others thought Drake would sail west and invade the Americas. Many Englishmen wanted to colonize the territories to the north of Florida before Spain gobbled up all the land, lands rich in timber, game and fertile soil they say. I was as much at home in the West Indies as I was in Ireland, more so, and an expedition to the Americas would have suited me just fine. But I did not think Drake would sail around the world or to the Americas, for either course of action would have left England without her wooden wall and vulnerable to invasion.

The English victory over the Spanish Armada in the summer of '88 changed nothing. True, Spain had lost half her ships and 15,000 dead, but Spain is rich in gold and men and her great dreadnoughts had survived the awful debacle. Of the Armada's twenty-two Castilian and Portuguese galleons, all but two returned home. The war was far from over.

I am no Caesar, but even I understood England's precarious military predicament. As long as Spain ruled the oceans, she ruled half the world and all the wealth in it. A river of gold, silver and pearls, and other commodities of great value, was flowing into Spain from the New World uninterrupted and as Spain's wealth and power multiplied, England's own diminished.

Queen Elizabeth understood this stark truth. One strong gust of Spanish wind would topple her from her thrown. The struggle between Spain and England was to the death and as long as Elizabeth lived, there could be no peace.

Regnans in Exelsis, the papal bull issued by Pope Pius V in 1570 excommunicating Queen Elizabeth from the Church for her Protestant heresies, had set the two kingdoms against each other. Pope Pius declared Elizabeth's crown forfeit and handed all of her lands, wealth and titles over to Spain. But the two kingdoms did little more than snarl at each. Then in 1587, after Queen Elizabeth had her cousin Mary, the Catholic Queen of Scots, beheaded for treason, Pope Sixtus V resurrected Pius's papal bull. The Vicar of Christ urged all good Catholics across England, Scotland, Wales and Ireland to rise up against Elizabeth and encouraged Spain to help them. In truth, Sixtus had signed Elizabeth's death warrant. The Pope's holy edict was the inspiration that drove the Spanish Armada towards the shores of England in '88.

A week after my arrival to Plymouth, Drake and Sir John Norreys, known as Black John by his men because of his tar-black hair and dark complexion, summoned the fleet's senior officers to a council of war. I was invited too and stood on the main deck of the *Revenge*, Drake's forty-six-gun flagship, pressed shoulder-to-shoulder with the others. We all looked up at Drake and Norreys as they looked down upon us from the quarter deck like two demigods. The night air was chilly. The ship was quiet. The crew had been sent ashore.

I studied Drake and Norreys with fascination. There was nothing particularly impressive about Drake in the flesh. He was a diminutive fellow with an unremarkable face and spoke with an unfortunate, tinny voice as I have said - and yet he towered over all of us. With fearless guile, this English Odysseus had plundered Spanish lands and seized Spanish ships for decades against great odds while foiling every attempt to capture him. Drake was a legend. Norreys, no less a titan among men, had proven his mastery of war across the battlefields of Europe time and time again. And Norreys was blessed with height, broad shoulders and a booming voice. In speech, demeanor and stature, Norreys was every inch a warrior prince.

The queen, in her wisdom, had bestowed joint command over the expedition, or the Counter Armada as some were calling it, to Drake and Norreys. England's greatest admiral would command the ships and England's finest general would lead the army.

Drake cleared his throat, he leaned over the rail. "I see the hand of God standing before me. Surely it is through His divine will that we are gathered here this night. Surely, He favors our just cause. Now, before I say more, I would hear each of you reaffirm your unwavering loyalty before God. Repeat after me: I do solemnly swear that I will be faithful and bear true allegiance to our Sovereign Lady Queen Elizabeth, to her heirs and successors, and that I will as in duty bound honestly and faithfully defend Her Majesty, her heirs and successors and her dignity, against all enemies and will observe and obey all orders of the generals and officers set over me, so help me God."

We all repeated the oath as one.

Drake nodded. "Good. Welcome my fellow crusaders! Spain is our destination. Spain is where we'll seize new glory for queen and country!"

All around me the officers on deck erupted into thunderous cheers and applause. They shook hands. They slapped each other on the back - as if the victory had already been won.

Drake raised his hands for silence, then removed a scroll from his jacket. He began rattling off the names of every ship in the fleet and assigned each ship to one of five squadrons. To my annoyance, Drake didn't keep the privateers together as one unit as he had during the raid on Cádiz in '87 and again in '88 when we fought the Spanish Armada. He parceled the privateers out piecemeal. My ships were assigned to the second squadron, Norreys's squadron, which would carry the English army. After Drake finished doling out our assignments, he stepped aside for Norreys.

Norreys spoke with a voice brimming with power. "Her Majesty and Her Majesty's Privy Council have entrusted this expedition with three objectives. First, we are to finish-off the galleons. According to our spies in Spain, the galleons are sitting in port damaged and undermanned. None are fit for action. Once we've destroyed Spain's precious dreadnoughts, we're to sail on to Lisbon where we'll help our honored guest, Dom António, the Prior of Crato, find his crown."

Norreys waved the exiled king out of the shadows over to his side. I knew nothing about the man except for what the queen had told me. The Spanish had taken away António's crown after easily routing his army at the Battle of Alcântara in 1580. António's reign had lasted barely twenty days. Despite his dubious credentials, António had won the Privy Council's favor after he promised the Council that the Portuguese would rise up against their Spanish oppressors if England restored him to throne. A bold claim perhaps, and yet Portugal has never been Spain's willing bride.

"Gentlemen," Norreys continued after António joined him. "I give you the King of Portugal." The officers applauded politely as António, an exceedingly plump fellow, took a bow. "After we've taken Lisbon with the help of our new Portuguese allies, our third objective is the Azores. Our cause is righteous, and if God is with us, who can be against us? Who is with me?"

All around me, men cheered wildly again. No doubt the cocky English were itching to take the war to Spain, but it was the Azores that inspired. The strategic archipelago sits astride the sea lanes between the Iberian Peninsula and the Americas and if England held the Azores, she could launch endless sorties against the Spanish treasure fleets. The opportunity for great wealth was not lost on any man.

The English plan was audacious and I was excited by it. England had never attempted such an enormous military campaign across the ocean before. We all felt the hand of destiny that night. Men would talk and write tales about our exploits for generations to come - and an English victory would create many new interesting prospects in the Americas for a rogue with warships and men-at-arms under her command like me.

But well I know that plans are fragile things. Even a good plan can go awry for an infinite number of reasons and any plan not properly nurtured will wither and die on the vine.

Though Drake and Norreys had assembled a huge force - the expedition would sail with one hundred and fifty ships in all, along with dozens of supply barges and troop transports and twenty-three thousand men - numbers can deceive. Drake in fact had only twenty battlecruisers: six race-built galleons, the navy's smallest, and fourteen heavily-armed privateers. Sixty lightly-armed merchantmen of dubious quality, fitted out by London investors, and another sixty Dutch flyboats, fine ships from the United Provinces crewed by able sailors but reluctant allies from what I had seen in port, and twenty unarmed pinnaces, good only for hauling supplies, made up the rest of the fleet.

And while Norreys had fourteen full regiments under his command - fifteen thousand men - only two thousand of these men were professional soldiers. The rest were gentlemen adventurers, hirelings and mercenaries of unknown quality with questionable loyalties. I have fought with and against their kind before and never thought much of them.

In truth, Drake and Norris were sailing into war against a colossus with a measly twenty warships and two thousand professional soldiers, augmented by three thousand hard-bitten, battle-scarred privateers. The problem I learned later was money. Drake had asked the Privy Council for one hundred warships, twenty thousand professional soldiers and £80,000 to fund his expedition. But after three years of war, England was broke.

The queen funded the expedition in part with £20,000 of her own money, provided the six Royal Navy galleons and the two thousand professional soldiers. To make up the difference, the Privy Council formed a joint-stock company to lure private investors. The scheme worked. Thousands bought stock in the expedition or volunteered their services. Drake, the most celebrated man in England, and the most reviled man in Spain with a bounty of twenty thousand gold ducats on his head, had always returned home from every voyage with ships full of Spanish treasure. *El Draque* was a man worth betting on.

Chapter Four

n the morning the thirteenth day of April in the year of our Lord 1589, the boom of heavy cannon startled me from my slumber. I heard three shots fired in rapid succession, the signal for the fleet to weigh anchor. I quickly dressed and hurried topside. My men were already turning the capstan to raise the anchor when I stepped out on the quarter deck.

Atwood greeted me with a wide grin. "Mornin' Mary. Fine day."

I took in the sky and nodded. The first shafts of sunlight were peeking over the rooftops of the city. The air was crisp and clean.

"A fine day, Jacob," I said. "For many a lad though, this may be the last English sunrise they'll ever see."

Then I saw Efendi moving across the main deck towards us with Henry and Kinkae in tow. When embarking upon any new voyage, it was our custom to take breakfast together.

"Gentlemen, how are we today?" I asked.

"All is well," Efendi answered. "Hancock has been hoarding eggs for over a week. He is scrambling the eggs, adding bits of shallots and mushrooms, and has made fresh biscuits. Desert is a slice of marzipan."

"God bless our cook," Atwood said, patting his belly.

Kinkae pointed over the stern rail. "Look Mary, Drake is underway."

We all turned to watch *Revenge* sail past us under half sail. And then one-by-one the galleons *Dreadnought*, *Swiftsure*, *Nonpareil*, *Foresight* and *Aid* pulled away from the wharfs to follow her. The expedition at last was on the move.

All of Plymouth turned out to see the grand spectacle. All along the waterfront we saw music, dancing, entertainment and street peddlers selling food and drink. The mood was festive and hopes were high.

Once the *Aid* lazily slipped past Artillery Tower at Devil's Point, we privateers moved out slowly into the channel with the rest of the fleet falling in behind us. At the edge of one pier stood a section of scaffolding three-stories high erected by carpenters the day before and as *Revenge* led us past St. Nicholas Island, hundreds of sparklers ignited all at once across the face of the scaffolding spelling out the name *GLORIANA* in huge, white-hot letters. This wonderful display was soon followed by colorful fireworks bursting over our heads. The fanfare was grand. Plymouth was sending her favorite hero on to victory in style.

But I had an uneasy feeling in the pit of my stomach. I always begin every journey with the very best men I could find and with fully-provisioned ships in prime condition. I never skimped on skills, or on supplies, or on maintenance for the ships. As I looked over the stern rail at the merchantmen clumsily moving into line, I did not like what I saw. And then our cook appeared with a hot breakfast and fresh coffee and my mood instantly improved.

Once the fleet cleared Plymouth Sound, the galleons fanned out into a single line abreast and then reduced speed to let the rest of us catch up. My ships slipped in behind our squadron leader, Norreys's magnificent flagship *Nonpareil*, a French word meaning 'without equal.' At five hundred tons and a length of eighty-five feet at the keel, *Nonpareil* was considered a second-rate galleon. She was armed with sixteen heavy guns and fourteen light guns and had a ship's complement of two hundred and fifty souls.

With the squadrons assembled, we set off towards Spain with a friendly wind under fair skies in five parallel lines, leaving England behind well before the first spring harvest. The timing of our departure was important for the queen had confided in me at Nonsuch that a man named John Dee, a mathematician who dabbled in occult philosophy and astrology, had prophesied an English victory if England attacked the Armada before the first spring harvest. But the seer's foretelling also came with a warning: *flame devours wood, iron breaks against stone.* Neither the queen nor I knew what to make of Dee's warning.

It was an effort to keep our racehorse from outpacing *Nonpareil*. We had to take in sail. I had asked Norreys for permission before leaving port to reconnoiter ahead and around the flanks of our squadron, but the general had dismissed my proposal with a flick of his hand. Like Drake, Norreys didn't like or trust the Irish and so we kept to our station within the squadron, plodding along in boredom.

On our third day out, misfortune struck the fleet. A powerful spring gale blowing in from the west swept over us with ferocious winds and pelting rains. The winds shredded sail and snapped lines. Heavy seas knocked the fleet around all through the night. Spectacular lightning bolts and booming thunder kept many a merchant sailor cowering below deck.

My men and I had sailed through worse, far worse, and took the storm in stride. We reefed our main sails and let the storm jib fly. Big wind, small sail is the rule we mariners live by. We kept *Phantom* and *Diablo* on a slow but steady course while all around us less experienced crews struggled to keep their ships from foundering. When the skies cleared in the morning, thirty English merchantmen - a fifth of the fleet - showed their backsides to us as they sailed for home. Drake and Norreys were powerless to stop them.

We sailed across an empty sea for three more days before Spain, appeared in a shimmering haze off our port bow. Drake led us straight at the white walls of A Coruña, brought us in close, and then led us north. I wondered what the Spanish thought as they watched the English flaunt their power so near to shore. We sailed past the blue waters of the Ría de Coruña and then past the Ría de Betanzos. Both bays were teeming with fishing trawlers and a few modest freighters, but we saw no sign of the Armada. The fleet dropped anchor at the mouth of the Ría de Ferrol.

"What does it mean?" Kinkae asked as he stepped up to the quarter deck with two tins of hot coffee and handed one to me.

"It means," Atwood said, "that the bear has crawled back deeper into its cave. The Spanish surely knew we were coming and have moved their galleons. Now tell me Kinkae, why does Mary have coffee and the captain of this ship does not?"

Kinkae grinned and pointed to the bow. "I know the captain of this ship. He's a Scot, a big, powerful man with strong legs. If he's forgotten where the galley is, it is that way."

"Look!" I said and pointed over the rail to a small sloop with a single sail. I had seen her leave Coruña earlier, about three miles away, and thought nothing of it but now she was sailing straight for *Revenge*.

Atwood grunted. "I don't see a white flag. Apparently, it's not King Phillip coming over to surrender Spain. Must be Englishmen. Perhaps they can find the Armada for Drake."

Not long after the sloop pulled up alongside Drake's flagship, I was summoned over to *Revenge* with the rest of Drake's senior officers. The ship's great cabin was already packed with men when I arrived. The admiral was sitting behind his desk, surrounded by his young cavaliers.

Drake rose from his chair. "Lady Mary, welcome aboard. Mary, gentlemen, you may have noticed a small sloop with three men pull-up alongside *Revenge* earlier. These Englishmen were put ashore some time ago to keep an eye on the Armada. The Spanish have moved the galleons east, across the Bay of Biscay, to Santander and San Sebastián for repair and refitting. Only five warships are nearby, one galleon, two man-o-wars and a pair of galleasses. The galleon is a real prize though. She's the *San Martín*, High Admiral Medina Sidonia's flagship."

I knew better than to open my mouth but did so anyway. "So, we'll sail east your grace?" I asked brazenly.

"No, Mary. We attack the enemy where we find him. The enemy is here."

Drake turned on his heels to address the cabin. "We have

another matter to discuss. To my utter dismay, I've learned we have shortages of victuals and fresh water. God's bones, we're less than a fortnight into the campaign and already we need to replenish our supplies! I sent out explicit instructions to every ship's master prior to quitting Plymouth that they must procure sufficient foodstuffs and fresh water for a long cruise. It would seem we've brought some fools along with us. Each of you are seasoned officers and I trust all of you heeded my orders. I trust your ships are well-stocked. Circumstances compel me to ask each of you to provide my quartermaster with an inventory of your stores. We'll need to redistribute the surplus to those in need."

I thought it curious Drake failed to mention the thirty ships that had abandoned us, ships that no doubt carried supplies for the fleet. There was grumbling around the room, but no one dared challenge the queen's favorite, the hero of the Nombre de Diós, of Cádiz and Gravelines and a dozen other battles in-between - except for me.

"Admiral, my ships carry no surplus," I said. "Those loggerheads you speak of should return to England at once to resupply or raid a Spanish town or two along the coast and take whatever they need."

"Lady Mary, I'll not risk this expedition's primary objective by delaying our attack whilst we send out foraging parties for food and water. My orders stand."

I held my ground. My men and I were private citizens. Drake did not own me.

"Your grace, I mean no disrespect," I began with a feisty tone. "But we must make haste and depart these waters immediately for Santander and San Sebastián to destroy what is left of Phillip's fleet. Surely the garrison at Coruña has sent riders out by now to warn Madrid of our arrival. You'll want to move swiftly before the garrisons at Santander and San Sebastián bolster their harbor defenses with reinforcements. We have lost surprise, but time may yet favor us if we move out smartly."

I could see the rage building in Drake's eyes. I could see all the goodwill I had found in Plymouth melting away. He set his jaw. His cheeks turned crimson. The officers standing next to me stepped aside, as if to avoid being hit by flying shrapnel.

"I answer to the Queen of England madam, not to the likes of you. I'll not debate strategy with a woman, especially an Irishwoman. We attack Coruña and you'll comply with my orders or so help me God, I'll charge you with insubordination and confiscate your ships."

Had the queen been with us, I was confident she would have countermanded Drake's orders. She would have told him to ignore Coruña and sail for Santander and San Sebastián without delay. But the queen had asked me to be her eyes and ears, no more, and so I bit my tongue and looked away.

Satisfied that he had shut me up, Drake looked at the faces around the cabin. "Gentlemen, once we take Coruña there'll be plunder aplenty to go around. You'll each be handsomely rewarded for your efforts. I expect my quartermaster will have your inventory lists in his hands before midnight and that is the end of the matter."

Ah there it was, the ugly truth for all to see. Drake wanted plunder.

I know little about warfare on land. My home has been the open sea. But after years of sailing between two worlds, I know something about the Spanish. They like to protect their precious harbors with lofty battlements built from enormous blocks of stone and concrete reinforced with iron. They favor thick walls and large calibre harbor guns and are especially fond of demi-culverines, huge monsters capable of hurtling a thirty-pound ball with enough punch to sink a ship a mile off.

I returned to *Phantom* in a foul mood and summoned my officers to me for my own council of war.

"What happened next?" Atwood asked.

"Oh, the other captains hemmed and hawed of course," I replied, "but they offered no objections. I can hardly blame them after Drake's harsh rebuke of me. Drake promised plunder to compensate them for the supplies they must surrender."

"What will we do, Mary?" MacGyver asked.

Atwood stood and drained his glass of wine. "Drake's spies must have reported seeing something of value in Coruña. Why else would he attack a fortress? As for our stores of victuals and water, the fleet's quartermaster can't possibly validate the inventory of every ship. Mary, I suggest we offer some token amount, the least of what we have. Drake saves face and we'll still have enough food and water to spare. We could sail all the way to the Americas with what we have stowed below."

I surprised us all when, begrudgingly, I nodded my consent.

As the stars began to fade and the sun began to rise, I scanned a pale blue sky as I stood on wet sand. The air was still and warm with hardly any breeze. The surf splashing over my boots was little more than a ripple. Except for the commotion farther down the beach where the English were assembling, the morning was pleasant, serene and quiet.

I did not fully appreciate what it meant to be attached to Norreys's squadron until my men and I, one hundred strong, climbed into our boats before dawn and followed the first wave of the English army, two regiments strong, ashore. We were privateers and raiders, not infantry soldiers trained to fight on land and I was not at all pleased with my new orders.

We landed without opposition on a deserted stretch of beach directly in front of Coruña. The Spanish army did not show itself, fearing no doubt they'd be too exposed to the English navy's heavy guns.

Coruña is actually two towns. High Coruña sits atop a plateau overlooking the ocean. It is an impressive fortress with thick stone walls, intermittent watch towers and batteries of heavy cannon. Below the castle, sprawled around the foot of the plateau, is Low Coruña, a village crowded with houses, shops, inns, churches and a few stockyards sprinkled in-between. Low Coruña has no high walls or artillery.

A handful of villagers emerged from Low Coruña out of curiosity. But when Norreys's men shouldered their muskets, pikes, crossbows and halberds and started marching in a column towards their town, the villagers quickly melted away.

My orders from Norreys were simple. My men and I were to form a skirmish line to the north to protect the army's left flank. A company of German mercenaries was to do the same on the army's right flank to the south. Two thousand Englishmen, Norreys's best, his professionals, marched forward to the sound of fife and drum with battle flags and royal pennants flying high above a sea of glittering steel helmets. The English, dressed in dark-grey baggy trousers with light grey stockings, and wearing pale-blue shirts underneath their steel breastplates, made a handsome sight. Norreys, dressed all in black, helmet, breastplate, shirt and trousers all black, trotted out confidently in front of his men on a black stallion, the only horse in the expedition, with two enormous feathers, one white and one red, bouncing up and down on his helmet as he rode.

As Norreys led his men forward, my men and I moved parallel to the column with about two hundred yards of open field between us. With Efendi at my side, I led my men in single file up the dunes to a narrow, rocky ridge where we had an excellent view of the world around us. We could see Norreys's entire column below us and the Germans beyond to the south. On our left, to the north, we could see *Revenge* leading the galleons and ten English privateers into the Ría de Coruña to search out and destroy any Spanish warships.

We were standing in the midst of a great battle, watching history in the making, and I can't deny the elation I felt. Even so, I was grateful Norreys had decided to use my men as auxiliaries in support and not in the front lines. I had no desire to risk the lives of my men in pitched battle. My men and I were fighters, good fighters, adept at hit and run tactics on the water - but we weren't too proud to hide behind cover or to turn and run if we didn't like the odds.

Some five hundred yards or so from the edge of town, Norreys halted the column, reformed his men into a solid phalanx, two hundred men abreast, ten ranks deep, and waited. For what I did not know.

Long minutes passed. And then we heard the boom of heavy

cannon in the bay. Drake had found something to his liking.

Then Norreys drew his sword and rode up and down the front ranks, whipping his men into a blood frenzy with words about duty, honor, God and country. A trumpeter blew the signal to advance and the phalanx lumbered forward over flat ground in good order.

There was not much to the fighting that first day. When the English came within a few hundred yards of the town, a Spanish force of nearly equal strength, a mix of regulars and militia, emerged from Low Coruña like a horde of wild barbarians.

The Spanish were led by a conquistador of high rank judging by his resplendent golden armor. The regulars, dressed in buff, baggy trousers with red sashes and red stockings and wearing brown leather doublets over their yellow, red-striped shirts, were easy to spot. Half were armed with muskets and half carried swords and pikes. Their polished steel *capacetes* glittered in the morning light. The militia wore the simple clothing of farmers, laborers and fishermen and had no helmets or armor. Many carried muskets, others had armed themselves with shovels, axes, clubs and pitchforks.

To my astonishment the Spanish didn't pause to form a battle line. The militia broke ranks and charged wildly at the English, screaming and yelling incoherently while the more disciplined regulars moved forward at a walk in tight formation. My men and I took up positions behind the rocks along the ridge and watched.

The militiamen discharged their muskets on the run and Englishmen fell. English soldiers in the rear ranks rushed forward to plug the gaps as the phalanx continued advancing. When the English and Spanish were within fifty yards of each other, the English front rank took a knee and raised their muskets while the second and third ranks moved in behind them, forming a solid wall of six hundred muskets.

Even from a distance I could hear Norreys's voice. "*FIRE!*" he bellowed.

Six hundred lead balls ripped through the center of the Spanish mob. Militiamen stumbled and fell by the bushel. The survivors staggered backwards. A handful, just a trickle at first, panicked, spun around and darted for the town and then the trickle burst into a flood. Spaniards by the score tossed away their weapons as they ran. The entire Spanish center was collapsing. But the battle was not over. On the Spanish right flank, a company of pikemen with two companies of *tercios*, elite Spanish shock troops, started moving towards our ridge.

My men and I stood and fired a volley into them. My lads were good marksmen. Spaniards fell. But to my horror the Spanish didn't stop or even slow down. Spanish sharpshooters took-up positions around the base of the ridge and fired up at us, trying to keep us pinned down, as three hundred of their mates started scrambling up the side of the ridge to kill us.

I had only seconds to decide whether to hold our ground or bolt.

"Stand fast!" I screamed, even though we were heavily outnumbered. Maybe I had just killed us all I thought, but if the Spanish overran our position they could outflank and come up behind the English. I wasn't going to run and let Norreys blame me if the attack went badly.

We hastily reloaded our muskets for one final volley before the Spanish reached the top of the ridge. We drew our swords and long daggers for the hand-to-hand fighting to come. But then we heard a Spanish trumpeter blow several sharp notes on his horn. The *tercios* spun around and retreated down the ridge. Unable to stop the rout in the center of his line, the Spanish commander knew the battle was lost and decided to recall his men. I took a deep breath and thanked my lucky stars.

I looked over at the English just as the fourth and fifth ranks stepped past the first three ranks and discharged their muskets into fleeing Spaniards. More Spaniards tumbled into the dust. Englishmen cheered. To the south I could see two Spanish companies engaged with the Germans falling back in good order.

Norreys then stood up in his stirrups and used his sword to raise his helmet above his head. Sergeants rushed about pushing and pulling men back into formation and then the English rushed forward at a half-run across a field soaked in blood and littered with bodies. Norreys waved at me and then turned and waved at the German mercenaries, urging us to join the English attack. I led my men down the ridge and across the field and we reached the English just as the front ranks started scaling over a three-foot dirt berm hastily thrown up by the Spanish the day before.

Except for a few civilian stragglers, mostly shopkeepers hoping to protect their shops and wares, we walked into a deserted town. The Spanish army and the rest of the village were fleeing up the plateau, into the safety of the castle. Having nothing with him to batter down castle walls, Norreys kept one company at his side and unleashed the rest of his men. To my disgust, all discipline evaporated as the English disintegrated into gangs to ransack the village and look for plunder.

From start to finish, the battle for Low Coruña had lasted about thirty minutes. The Spanish left behind five hundred dead, the English lost only twenty men. Norreys was off to a good start.

I took my lads to a small church where we stretched out on across the pews and ate our noonday meal of cheese and hard biscuits in peace. Each of us carried three skins of water and had plenty of rations, though some fool had left the wine behind on the ships.

Later, we wandered through the town and stumbled upon an army too drunk to fight. The English had found large stores of beer and wine hidden away in a cellar and had helped themselves to all of it. We saw soldiers staggering aimlessly about or sprawled out on the streets napping or standing in the alleyways vomiting their guts out. When one soldier after another started begging us for food, we realized that the English were drinking on empty stomachs. Drake had concealed the full gravity of the fleet's shortages. The English had been on half rations since leaving Plymouth.

After the sun settled on the water, my men and I returned to the church for supper and then I took a stroll. The evening was peaceful and not to warm. I watched English burial details strip the dead and toss their bodies into a mass grave just outside of town. Along the castle ramparts mothers, wives and sweethearts, overcome with grief, wailed and pulled their hair as they watched the English work. I'll never forget the heartbreak I saw along that wall.

Then the English returned to their campfires to eat their suppers. For an army that had won the day, I saw little joy. Men ate their food quietly and cleaned their weapons. No one seemed to know what the morning would bring. Low Coruña was in English hands but the army had no heavy mortars, no battering rams or siege towers or catapults, nothing to use against the castle and unless Drake found a way to resupply the army soon, the English would starve before the Spanish would.

In the morning I saw Drake and his entourage of young noblemen strolling through the streets on their way to Norreys's command post. I was not invited.

After Drake returned to his ships, Norreys summoned the rest of us to the village square. The general was not a happy man. Drake, Norreys informed us, had destroyed thirteen merchant ships in the bay, but the Spanish warships had slipped away, into some estuary or down one river or another, and were beyond Drake's reach. I had to bite my tongue to stop myself from snickering. We should have sailed for Santander and San Sebastián. The merchant ships meant nothing. Taking Low Coruña meant nothing.

But that was not the worst of it. A captain asked Norreys if he should start moving his company down to the beach to be ferried back to the fleet.

"That will not be necessary Captain," the general replied, shaking his head in disgust. "The breeze feels pleasant here, but out on the water strong, blustery winds from the north are keeping Drake locked-up inside the bay. The galleons can make no headway against those winds. For now, Drake's attack squadron is trapped. The rest of the fleet will stay put at Ferrol and we shall stay put here until the winds shift in Drake's favor."

I couldn't help myself and laughed. Norreys shot me a warning glance, but otherwise let my indiscretion pass.

"Gentlemen, have the men grab their shovels and pickaxes. We have some digging to do. Lady Mary, your men will take up positions on the northeast side of town to watch the army's flank and when I find our German friends, they'll do the same on the southeast. Let's get to it then."

Later that afternoon, Norreys sent a lieutenant to the church to guide my men and me to our new positions on the northeast edge of town. We spent the rest of the day cleaning our muskets and rebuilding an old stone wall that had been neglected for many years. Drake and Norreys had agreed to launch a full assault against the castle while Drake's ships sat idle in the bay. Though Coruña was an important port for the Spanish navy, the city had no strategic value and trying to take the city's stronghold without siege equipment would cost many lives. But the queen's commanders were in a pickle. They needed to give the queen a victory.

I was lucky Drake had not dragged my ships into the bay with him. Atwood moved *Phantom* and *Diablo* to the small island of O Boi Grande and every day before sunrise, while the English dug their trenches around the castle and sent out their patrols to probe Spanish defenses, Efendi and I took a squad of men down to the Costa da Morte, the Coast of Death, where we'd meet Atwood on a small spit of land just south of Farum Brigantium, better known as the Torre de Hércules, the oldest lighthouse in the world they say built by the Romans some two thousand years ago. Atwood brought us victuals, wine, beer and water. My men and I ate well as the English grew thinner by the day. I pitied our English allies of course, but there was nothing I could do for them.

"How does the day find you, my good Captain?" I called out to Atwood one morning as his crew shipped oars and let their longboat slide up onto the beach.

"All is well, my Lady," Atwood replied cheerfully as he stepped off the boat with a wide grin. "Have you taken Coruña yet? The men are growing bored on O Boi Grande watching goats graze and fornicate all day."

I laughed. "Nay, Norreys has yet to ask me to."

"We should pack-up and sail home before the Spanish fleet appears on the horizon one morning, before the Spanish bull returns and gores the English lion."

"And what would you have me tell the queen, our royal protector?"

Atwood sighed. "Aye, Mary. Still, I pray we're far away from here if this campaign turns into a disaster. The destruction of the Armada serves our purposes, but Coruña is not our fight."

"Fair enough. Any sign the winds might shift soon?"

"None. Spring's a fickle bitch. Norreys has been digging up dirt for days now. Any word when he'll attack?"

"No."

"I'm sure more than one Englishman on the line has wondered whether he is digging his own grave. Better the English than us."

"Norreys is a shrewd tactician they say. He's up to something."

Atwood kissed me on the cheek and handed me a half bottle of whiskey before he stepped back into the longboat. "When the attack comes Mustafa," he called out as my men pushed the longboat out into the water, "don't let Mary do anything rash. Nothing good ever comes from beating your head against a stone wall."

I suddenly recalled Dee's warning to the queen: *flame devours wood, iron breaks against stone.* Dee's words sent a chill down my spine.

My men and I were not the only ones being resupplied. Every few days a pair of Spanish galleasses would slip past Drake's ships at night and bring supplies up to the castle. One evening I caught a glimpse of one of the galleasses and recognized her. She was Captain Antonio Marcus's ship, the very one I had taken off Limerick with six chests of gold. I was glad to see Marcus and his men had survived the journey home.

The days passed by slowly as the English dug their trenches. A week went by and then another and then the English brought two culverins and two demi-culverins onshore from *Revenge* and started lobbing shot and fuse bombs at the castle. My men and I spent the days lounging in the shade, playing cards and dice.

"English iron can't punch a hole through Spanish stone with those thirty-pound shots?" Atwood asked as he jumped off the longboat with our daily supplies.

"The English are making a few ugly pockmarks, no more," I

answered as Atwood handed me a crate. The big Scot had no qualms about treating me like one of the men.

"Well, Drake best do something soon before he has no fleet."

"Oh?"

"A few ships have quietly abandoned the expedition. No surprise there. But last night a whole squadron of Dutch flyboats left Ferrol for La Rochelle, taking three thousand men with them."

"How do you know this Jacob?"

"Because before he sailed the Dutch commander dined with me aboard *Phantom*. He was a most unhappy fellow. No one, he told me, had agreed to sail all this way to lay siege to a Spanish castle, particularly one of no worth."

I nodded. "What a fine mess this is. Drake still can't get his ships out of the bay and Norreys hasn't been able to starve the Spanish out of High Coruña. We've lost precious time. Surely Drake will quit this nonsense and hurry on to Santander and San Sebastián once the winds change."

"I pray you are right Mary. You should know we lost two good men during the night."

"The sweating sickness?"

"I know not. Others have taken ill, but all have recovered. Henry had a rough time puking his guts out but seems to be on the mend today."

My heart skipped a beat when I heard Henry's life might be in jeopardy. "Should I go to him?"

"No need."

"The ships are well-stocked with soap - use it."

"Mary, I don't think - "

I already knew what Atwood would say and cut him off. "Jacob, I want the men to scrub the ships down and wash themselves and their clothes with soap and water. The task will give them something to do if nothing else. Might even do some good."

Atwood sighed and nodded. None of my men believed in the curative powers of soap.

"Very well, Mary. I'll see to it. I'll return tomorrow with a cake of soap for you and the lads. What's good for the goose..."

I rested my hand on Atwood's shoulder and smiled. "Is good for the gander."

"Perhaps I should stay with you, Mary? Michael can handle the ships just fine."

"Of course, he can. Even so, I want you with the ships."

"Where's Mustafa today?"

"The English were up and about early this morning. Something is afoot. I left him with the lads."

"You only need give the signal Mary and we'll come fetch you and the lads away from this putrid shithole."

"Agreed."

As my squad and I walked through the town in the dark carrying our supplies, we saw the English regiments up and mustered for action. Whole companies were moving into the trenches. We hurried back to our camp.

"Where are the others Mustafa?" I asked Efendi when we reached our camp and found him alone.

"The English are preparing to attack. Norreys sent a messenger around and ordered us to move forward."

"Into the trenches?"

"No. We are to provide covering fire."

"Merciful God, thank you," I said, relieved. I was grateful Norreys hadn't ordered my men into the trenches. He saved me the trouble of disobeying his order.

"I found good ground close by for us, Mary. The men are already in position."

Efendi led us down a dozen narrow streets until we reached the east side of town where my men had taken cover inside houses, behind trees, a stone well and behind three carts they had flipped over. The castle towered over us several hundred yards away. To the north, though gaps in the buildings, I could see Drake's ships anchored in the bay. The sky was overcast. The air was sultry with not even a wisp of wind. Drake's ships weren't sailing anywhere.

"This is a good position for us, Mustafa. But I can't see the

English line."

Efendi winked at me, then pointed to a nearby four-story building with windows all around. "You can see the English from up there."

I followed Efendi up four levels of stairs of an empty hostel. We sat quietly together, staring out a window facing the castle with a fine view of the English trenches. An hour past and nothing happened. We heard no digging. We heard no officers barking out orders or talking. Everything around us was still and peaceful. I began wondering if Norreys had decided to call off the attack. When the sun broke through the clouds, I went downstairs to pull my men into the shade. I handed out strips of dried goat meat and skins of wine. I ate my meal sitting underneath a tree with several of my men, then closed my eyes and started nodding off when a horrific BOOOOOOOOOOM! jolted me awake.

The blast snapped my head back hard against the tree. A searing pain shot through my head and I nearly fainted. Then a cloud of dust rolled over me. I started choking. Pebbles and sand fell on top of me as I struggled to my feet.

At first, I thought a shot from a Spanish mortar had landed on us. My men were covered in dust and coughing, but no one seemed injured. I hurried back to the hostel where I had left Efendi. He pointed to a huge, gaping hole in the castle wall when he saw me, a hole large enough for five men abreast to walk through.

"English pioneers," I whispered. "A tunnel."

Efendi nodded. "The English must have packed several shiploads of powder into that tunnel."

English soldiers stood and cheered. A trumpet sounded and three companies of musketeers closest to the breach climbed out of their trenches and started racing up the plateau. I could almost see the horror in the faces of the Spaniards standing along the ramparts. A sea of starving Englishmen was coming for them and neither side was much for mercy.

Spanish musketeers and crossbowmen frantically fired down into the English multitude storming up the hill. Norreys's men were easy targets in the open and many fell, but no one stopped. The surge kept sweeping up the hill towards the breach. I called down to my men and gave the order to fire. Efendi and I placed our muskets on the windowsill and fired too, but we were too far away to do much good.

I watched in awe as the first wave of Englishmen climbed over the rubble at the base of the wall with no care for their lives. They disappeared through the breach and into the castle and more followed. We heard the trumpet's blare again and three more English companies rose out of their trenches and charged up the hill. Englishmen weaved their way around broken stones and broken bodies. They dodged a hail of bullets and bolts. The Spanish didn't have enough men on the wall to stop them and many started fleeing.

And then I saw the most amazing sight. A woman, a bold and fearless woman, climbed to the top of the battlements near the breach and began waving a spear above her head and shouting out a challenge. When the fleeing Spanish soldiers saw her, they found their courage, turned around and rallied to her side. But even this woman's bravery couldn't stop the English torrent. Up and down the English line we heard men shouting *Victory! Victory! Victory!* as more and more men poured through the breach.

Norreys ordered a full attack. The entire English army started up the hill. I imagined Norreys's men placing captured Spanish battle flags at his feet by day's end and dubbing him the *Lion of Coruña*. And then, in the blink of the eye, the world turned upside down.

A miracle so terrible and bizarre in nature, that it could only have been by the hand of God, unfolded before our eyes. Standing next to the breach was a massive stone tower, the tallest watchtower of the castle. Every man froze in horror as the ground around the tower rumbled and seemed to shift and give way. Then wheelbarrows of dirt and rock started cascading down the plateau. The tower began to wobble. One stone broke loose from the tower, followed by another and then another and then the whole edifice toppled over. Tons of stone, timber and debris tumbled into the breach in a great cloud of dust. When the dust settled, the breach was sealed.

An eerie quiet settled over the battlefield as Englishmen and

Spaniards alike stared at the pile of rubble in disbelief. The English, caked in dust and sweat and blood and with nothing left to attack, slowly turned away and shuffled back to their trenches. The garrison held their fire. They raised no victory cheer. All along the ramparts Spaniards shouldered their arms and stood at attention to honor English bravery.

The misfortune cost the English dearly. Four captains and nearly three hundred Englishmen perished in the attack that day. Many were crushed in the breach and those trapped inside the castle were never heard from again.

The following morning the winds at last, miraculously, shifted in favor of the English and Drake was able to move his squadron out of the Ría de A Coruña. Norreys ordered the army to break camp and by midafternoon long lines of exhausted, disillusioned Englishmen were wearily moving down to the beaches to board the transport barges.

Later that evening Drake sent boats out to all commanders with new instructions. I was disgusted when I read them. Instead of sailing east across the Bay of Biscay to destroy the Spanish Armada, Drake was taking the fleet to Lisbon. I passed Drake's instructions around the table for all my officers to read. No one had much to say, not even Atwood. With all his caustic wit and love of sarcasm, Atwood didn't utter a word.

The next morning, we were moving under full sail, heading south for Portugal. When we reached Cabo da Roca, a rocky headland of austere beauty at the westernmost tip of the European Continent, Drake ordered the fleet to drop anchor and summoned his senior officers to join him on shore.

I decided to bring Atwood and MacGyver with me. We beached our longboat next to a long line of other boats and joined the men gathering on a stretch of beach nestled in-between two jagged promontories. Above us, at the top of Cape Roca, stood a modest fort. I suppose Drake had a mind to flaunt the might of England before the Portuguese who would, in turn, report what they saw to Lisbon.

Despite the fiasco at A Coruña, Drake appeared to be in good spirits and in good health. Norreys had Drake and the officers standing with him roaring with laughter at one joke or another.

The laughter couldn't hide the thin and weary faces I saw. I discretely removed a piece *ch'arki* from my mouth and let it fall to the sand. *Ch'arki*, the Inca word for dried meat in their Quechuan language, had become a favorite snack among my men. We carried barrels of *ch'arki* aboard our ships. Our Carib Indian friends in Guadeloupe had taught us how to prepare, season and store the meat.

Drake acknowledged me with a polite nod. Norreys must have given the admiral a favorable account of my actions at Coruña. After the last boat glided into shore carrying four more officers, Drake held up his hands for silence.

"Gentlemen, my Lady Mary, ahem, it is God's will that has brought us here. No man can command the wind. We lost time bottled-up at Coruña. We lost some ships too. Good riddance to those English moneymen who have no stomach for a little rough weather I say. Good riddance to those effeminate Dutchmen who bolted at the first sound of cannon. The loss is of little consequence for England has the best of what she needs standing on this beach."

"Hear-hear, hear-hear!" men shouted with one voice as they punched the air with their fists.

Atwood leaned close to my ear. "What does effeminate mean?" he asked in a whisper.

"Womanish," I whispered back and smiled. I hadn't heard the newfangled word myself before my visit with the queen.

Atwood nodded his approval. "Good, strong word for the Dutch."

Drake held up his hands again. "I know each of you shares my disappointment with the happenings at Coruña. Whilst we beat the Spanish on the field, we were robbed of a greater victory by evil luck. But think not upon the past. Our luck will change in Portugal.

General Norreys and I are of a like mind. We march on Lisbon next. My lord Dom António, your day has arrived and with God's good grace, we shall see you restored to your rightful place as the legitimate King of an independent Portugal!"

Men clapped their hands and hooted their approval. The Prior of Crato, the head of the Order of the Knights of St. John of Jerusalem, took a step forward and bowed. From head to toe, he was clad in his magnificent black armor trimmed in gilded gold leaf, armor strong enough to stop any bullet they say. I must admit he looked the part.

"Do you, my grace," I asked Drake in a respectful tone after the silly applause had faded, "have good intelligence on the Armada? Are Spanish warships anchored nearby? Should we expect action at sea?"

Heads turned towards me.

"I shouldn't think so, Mary. The same foul winds that plagued us at Coruña would have prevented the Armada from leaving either Santander or San Sebastián. I would have preferred to sail for those ports after we quit Coruña, but we must replenish our provisions first. We need victuals and we need gunpowder before we can take on the Armada. We used large quantities of powder to breach Coruña's walls. After we take Lisbon and have restored his Highness Dom António to the throne, we'll be able to resupply our ships. Then we can make a run at Santander and San Sebastián. Then we can avenge our queen."

I dreaded the prospect of fighting alongside the army again in pitched battle or wasting precious time in another siege. "Admiral, I urge you to at least release the privateers. We can sail south along the Spanish coast and stir up trouble. We can land at Huelva, Cádiz and Málaga and take whatever supplies we need with little risk."

All eyes stayed fixed on me as Drake considered my words. I saw a mix of admiration, disdain and lust in the faces staring at me.

"An interesting notion, Mary," Drake said. "If we were in the Caribbean with a choice of remote islands to rally at, I might agree to split my forces. But in the home waters of our great enemy, with provisions running low and our men on half rations, prudence dictates we keep our forces whole and apply all of our strength against our prime objective. Lisbon is the prize."

But I was not ready to yield. I took a step forward and I bit my lip, bracing myself for the dressing-down that was sure to follow. I was not disappointed.

"But my grace," I asked, "if we couldn't take poor Coruña, how can we possibly hope to take Lisbon, a far grander city and better fortified I hear?"

Drake grit his teeth, then looked at me with raw contempt. "My dear Captain Mary, and for the benefit of all here, Phillip has placed his nephew, the Cardinal-Archduke Albert of Austria, in command of the city. The Archduke is not a military man. Worse, he only has a few Spanish companies of infantry to support him, men of inferior quality. The rest are Portuguese, men who will rally to Dom António's banner once the people know their rightful king has returned. We merely need to squeeze Lisbon a little - she'll crack like a walnut in our hands."

Dom António stepped into the middle of the crowd and began walking around in a circle. The unfortunate king had neglected to oil his armor and with each step he took the joints squeaked. He cleared his throat and stretched out his arms as if he wanted to embrace us all.

"My lords and graces, honored gentlemen and dear lady, the Admiral is precisely correct. My people despise the Spanish. They yearn to be free from the yoke of Spanish tyranny. The Spanish will flee like cockroaches once my people rise in revolt. And trust me when I say: my loyal subjects will revolt when they see this glorious fleet. The time for celebration, gaiety and feasting is near. An easy victory awaits us if we move swiftly and decisively. Dread will fill every Spanish heart when the fleet drops anchor off Lisbon. Hope will embolden every Portuguese soul into action."

I dared not say more.

Drake bowed his head to the deposed king, then took a map of Lisbon from a young adjutant standing close-by and spread the parchment over the top of a boulder. The council gathered around as

Drake and Norreys led a discussion about possible plans and was quick to reach a consensus. The army would land at Peniche and march on Lisbon from the north while the navy moved into the Tagus to attack the city from the south.

Drake nodded his satisfaction. "Excellent. It is settled then. We'll come about and land General Norreys and six regiments, augmented by our valiant privateers, at Peniche. I shall then take the fleet south and land my lord General Devereux and the marines at Cascais, accompanied by his grace, Dom António. After your Highness has secured the rebellion, I'll move the fleet off Lisbon and we'll have the city's neck in a noose. With a bit of luck, the Portuguese garrison at São Jorge Castle will join us and the Spanish will take flight. If the Spanish try to hold the city, we'll bombard Lisbon day and night by land and sea. By God, we'll hit the Spanish hard. Let's pray for a quick and easy victory. Questions?"

When there were no questions, Drake adjourned the meeting and men started for their boats. I lingered for a bit to take a closer look at Drake's map and while I considered the English plan, I caught Devereux starting at me out of the corner of my eye. Robert Devereux, the Second Earl of Essex and Master of the Horse, was a dark, ruggedly handsome fellow known to be one of the queen's favorites. Though few could match Devereux's overweening arrogance, he was a man of considerable charm and was well-liked by one and all. The rumor, one of many in the fleet, was that the queen, fearing for the earl's safety, had forbid Devereux from sailing with the expedition.

"Will you accompany your men ashore again Mary?" he asked with an appealing grin.

"Is there any other way to lead my lord?"

Devereux placed his hands on his hips and laughed. "Bless me woman, you are a match for the best of us!"

"I see my men have our boat in the water and are waving me over. I'll see you in Lisbon, God willing."

"I know Lisbon well. Perhaps after we take the castle, you'll permit me to show you Lisbon?"

Back in Plymouth, Devereux had tried to lure me into his bed on more than one occasion. I was not above toying with him. I battered my eyes flirtatiously at the earl and smiled sweetly.

"A most tempting offer my lord. But I think you mean to say *if* we take the castle."

We swung our ships around for Peniche, an easy sail away, and landed on the beach that very night at two of the clock despite the buffeting winds and a ferocious surf. Haste cost the English dearly. Two flatboats, carrying fifty men apiece, capsized in the heavy seas, taking one hundred Englishmen down to the bottom in their heavy armor.

I brought one hundred of my crew ashore with me again, this time with Atwood and Efendi after both men vehemently refused to stay behind, and left MacGyver in command of the ships. I would have preferred taking more men with me as we were plunging deeper into enemy territory, but we'd be marching inland and out of reach from our ships and supplies. We stuffed our pockets and our oiled leather pouches and backpacks full of *ch'arki*, sea biscuits and dried raisins, figs, apples and pears. We took as much food and water as we could carry.

At first light we quickly moved off the beach and walked into the small village of Peniche without a fight. When Peniche's modest garrison saw six thousand Englishmen standing outside their fort's flimsy, wooden walls, the Spanish commander opened the gates and surrendered without a fight. The English spent the morning buying as much dried fish and bread from the Portuguese as the villagers were willing to sell them and then Norreys formed his regiments into a single column, six men abreast, and we headed-out down a winding, dusty road towards Lisbon. The day turned hot and the road was long. We moved up and down hills, through thick brush and forest. We had no cavalry to scout ahead and no cannon to deploy if attacked.

An hour into our march, men began wilting under a blistering Portuguese sun. With heavy steel breastplates and helmets, one company even wore greaves, the English suffered worse than my men and me.

We had marched no more than five miles when the Spanish first hit us. My men and I were with the rear guard, at the tail end of the column, and couldn't see the action ahead. But we could hear the sounds and see the smoke of battle. Word quickly travelled down the line: Spanish light cavalry was striking the column here and there where the ground favored them. Spanish lancers and *ginetes*, light horsemen armed with swords, javelins and heart-shaped Moorish shields, emerged from woods or from behind hills and ambushed the English without warning. They'd smash right through the column, killing or wounding any in their path, and then melt back into the countryside before the English could form a skirmish line.

By mid-afternoon the column had been attacked three times, putting every man on edge, but Norreys kept us moving. When we found ourselves plodding through dense woods, the air turned stifling. Each breathe I took burned my lungs. The day was like a furnace. My shirt was drenched in sweat and the straps around my backpack had rubbed my shoulders raw. Some of the older men collapsed along the side of the road. But Norreys kept us moving.

When I had to piss, I stepped away from the column to find a bush to squat behind. As I did what I needed to do, I heard men whispering and walking on dried leaves and when I glanced up, I saw a line of Spanish musketeers advancing towards me. I pulled my breeches up and ran. The Spanish raised their muskets and fired past me at the English and I heard men cry out.

When I reached the road, I saw mayhem everywhere. Spanish infantry was emerging from the woods on both sides of the road and to the south Spanish cavalry had cut the rearguard off from the rest of the column. I could see my men scrambling to form a square but couldn't reach them so I fell in with a platoon of Englishmen as a sea of Spaniards came at us from every direction.

Spaniards madly attacked our lines. Like a fool, I had left my musket behind in the woods so I grabbed my pistols, hit both of my targets and then I drew my sword. A young Spaniard with a fresh face and a rapier in his hand, an officer I think, stepped in front of me and we started trading blows. The fellow was short and slight of build but he was an excellent swordsman. With Englishmen pressed against me working their long daggers and halberds, I could gain no advantage on my opponent and as the Spanish threw themselves at us, I could feel our line slowly caving in. I could feel myself losing my duel with the Spaniard.

Suddenly Spaniards broke through gaps in our line and it was every man for himself. The fighting all around me turned savage. Men fought hand-to-hand with desperation. I saw men rolling around in the dirt, clawing at each other with bare hands, biting, gouging and using rocks to smash in heads.

The Spanish swordsman in front of me suddenly went down with a stray bullet to his thigh. He clutched his leg and looked at me with pleading eyes. I nodded and let his men drag him off.

I suddenly found myself in the open and alone and then I caught the attention of two lancers on large, brown steeds. The riders circled around me. They wedged me in-between them, toying with me as I struggled to keep my footing. The thought of being trampled to death struck me as an ugly way to die.

I grabbed the lance of the trooper on my left and held on with everything I had. The Spaniard just smiled at me, amused, as his companion on my right tried to skewer me with his lance. I thrashed my sword wildly above my head to parry each thrust. Their horses neighed and pressed against me with a wild look in their eyes as I struggled to keep my life.

Then the horse on my left rose up on its hind legs and I lost my grip on the trooper's lance. I saw my killer grit his teeth and raise his lance above his head to deliver the final blow. So, this was the end I thought. I hastened to tell God that I was sorry for all my failings, then closed my eyes and braced myself for death.

Instead of pain, I heard a terrifying voice, howling like some wild beast. Atwood. I opened my eyes just as the big Scot ripped the trooper off his saddle and threw him to the ground. Atwood smashed the heel of his boot into the Spaniard's face so hard the man's helmet popped off. I turned to his companion and knew not even Atwood could save me. The tip of the Spaniard's lance was an inch away from my heart.

All around us the fighting was subsiding. English reinforcements were advancing up the road for us and Spanish infantry was falling back into the woods. The trooper saluted, dug his heels into his horse's flanks and trotted off to find his unit.

I fell on one knee to catch my breath. I fought down the urge to heave.

"Whew, Mary, that was close," Atwood said as he moved to my side, pausing for a moment to wipe the beads of sweat off his brow with his sleeve. "I thought for certain you were dead."

As Atwood helped me to my feet, I took in the bodies of the dead and wounded all around us and squeezed Atwood's arm. "As did I, Jacob, as did I. Thank you, Jacob. You saved my life. God only knows why I brought us here. This was a mistake."

Then Efendi joined us, holding his right arm with blood spreading across the sleeve of his shirt. I gently pulled his hand away to have a look.

"The wound is deep, Mustafa. The blade nicked the bone but not the artery."

Atwood grunted. "So, you've finally met your match my friend? There's a Spaniard out there quicker than you?"

Efendi managed a smile. "No. An Englishman standing near me was careless with his dagger, thrashing it all about. He did this."

"Well," I said, "we best stitch you up Mustafa and disinfect the wound. You'll live. Did we lose any men?"

"I saw McGowan fall, shot through the lung, and we have wounded."

"Aww. He was so young."

"He had a good death."

"That won't matter to his widow or to his two young boys," I said. "He often spoke of his wife and children with pride."

An English captain then grabbed the Spanish trooper who had nearly killed me by the arm and raised him to his feet. The Spaniard stiffened when he saw the captain draw his sword.

"Stop!" I shouted.

But the captain ignored me and plunged his sword into the Spaniard's belly. The Spaniard looked over at me, confused, sank to his knees and died.

"Why?" I asked the captain.

"Those are my orders, my lady. No prisoners."

"But we released the prisoners at Peniche."

The captain gave me a smug smile. "Did we now?"

"I was there when the Spanish garrison give their paroles. They pledged not to raise arms against us in exchange for safe passage out of Portugal. Those were Norreys's terms and the Spanish commander accepted."

The captain shrugged his shoulders. "Madam..." the captain began to say, then paused to remove a dirty rag from his pocket to wipe the blood off his sword. "I can assure you that those poor Dagos will never see Spain again."

I could feel the fury rising inside me, but I bit my tongue. The Spanish, I knew, were no better.

The captain bent over the dead trooper, pulled something off the man's uniform and tossed the object to me. "Beware my lady of these Spanish horsemen who wear the scarlet capes. They're a special breed. They're fanatics who believe they are the soldiers of Christ doing God's holy work."

I reached down to pick up a crucifix with crossed swords lying at my feet. "Templars?"

"No, not Templars. These men serve the *Tribunal del Santo Oficio de la Inquisición*. They call themselves *Los Jinetes de la Muerte*. Death Riders."

"Ah."

"You hold in your hand one of the seals of the Inquisition. If we lose this war, these men will show us Protestants and our families no mercy. These Catholics serve a cruel and wicked God."

I silently nodded to the captain. I pitched the crucifix into the woods.

"I'm sorry for the men you lost my lady," the captain said sadly and started walking off, then turned to look at me again. "I lost more and will lose even more before this campaign is over."

We tended to the wounded. We took those who couldn't walk over to the supply wagons, crude two-wheeled carts we had commandeered in Peniche, and helped them up. While the English buried their dead in shallow graves next to the road, I cleaned and stitched Efendi's wound. My men wrapped McGowan's body, a man who had sailed with me for years, and the bodies of two new men I barely knew, in their bedrolls to take with us. I wanted to give them a proper burial after we made camp for night. Once we returned to Ireland, I would see to the needs of their families as was our custom.

When the column took up the march again, word came down the line from Norreys that he wanted three more miles out of us before we stopped for the night. Those three miles were some of the hardest of my life.

The distance between Peniche and Lisbon is a two day walk for any man with strong legs who moves along with purpose. It took us six. The Spanish harassed us the whole way, striking the column three or four times a day and using the terrain to maximum advantage. Causalities mounted, moral plummeted. And the Spanish were clever. They burned every village between Peniche and Lisbon to the ground. They put the torch to every crop and fouled every well with dung, animal parts or other kinds of filth. They striped the land of anything useful. Men grew weaker by the mile as we staggered through a wasteland with little water or food.

The English professionals and my men accepted our hardships with stoic perseverance. Among the mercenaries though there was a good bit of grumbling. Many were unaccustomed to hardship and spoke openly about returning home. There were even a few desertions. No one had joined the expedition to fight Spanish regulars in the backwoods of Portugal.

When we at last stumbled into Lisbon late in the evening a week after landing at Peniche, we were a ragged, filthy lot walking on empty stomachs and parched throats. The Portuguese locked their doors and closed their shutters to us as we marched by.

Norreys released half the army to gather water and look for food while the rest made camp just outside the high walls of São Jorge Castle. Norreys issued strict orders that no harm, under penalty of death, was to befall any Portuguese. No home or shop was to be disturbed, no plunder taken. No church was to be desecrated. The English needed Portuguese good will for the battle yet to come.

From the camp we could see the castle's garrison patrolling the ramparts. We could see the gun crews standing by their batteries. But we saw no English ships in the Tagus River. We saw no sign of Devereux or his marines. I watched Norreys explode in a fit of rage when his scouts returned with their reports. We were on our own.

That night for supper I had my first taste of cat, roasted on the spit. I forced the tough, stringy meat down only after Atwood threatened me. Later I tended to our sick and wounded. Despite my best efforts Efendi's wound had become infected and he was burning up with fever. The thought of losing Efendi depressed me greatly. I stayed by his side through the night, applying cool compresses to his forehead and sponging his body down with clean water.

At daybreak, I took Atwood, Efendi and a dozen men with me to join Norreys and a company of his men. Norreys was on his way to Cascais, some fifteen miles away, to find Drake. While I had no wish to see Drake, I needed to reach my ships. I needed medicine for Efendi and wholesome victuals for my men. None of us had much taste for cat, dog or rodent.

Norreys led us through the city down to the Tagus where we turned west on a road running parallel to the river. Lisbon is a rich and pretty metropolis. The city's streets are clean and the shops and homes are attractive and well-maintained. Most of the buildings are white stucco with red tiled roofs. The Portuguese love arches and columns and balconies decorated with flowers. Even the waterfront, where we walked through a spacious, open plaza next to the main docks, is clean and inviting.

On the road to Cascais we passed through one sleepy fishing village after another. Spirits soared as we walked down the narrow streets of Algés, Paco de Arcos and São João do Estoril. The Portuguese were friendly and happily sold us fresh bread, baked fish and steamed vegetables, at least what they could spare. In Estoril though Efendi's legs buckled and my men had to carry him on a makeshift litter the rest of the way. We lost a little time when we kept well clear of Torre de Belém, a fortress built on the water to guard the mouth of the Tagus River.

We reached Cascais a little past noon and saw the English fleet riding anchor off shore. Sentries led us to Drake's command tent, which had been placed next to the stone ruins of what had once been a castle keep long ago. I saw Devereux sitting on a small barrel by a fire near the tent, leisurely smoking a cigar. After Norreys disappeared inside the tent, I sent Atwood and the others on to find our ships and then plopped down next to Devereux. I kept Efendi with me.

Devereux handed me a tin of coffee. "Who's this brave fellow resting on the litter?" he asked.

"His name is Mustafa Agah Efendi. He was wounded in one of the skirmishes with the Spanish whilst we were on the march. How does the day find you, my dear Devereux?"

"I'm most well thank you and in fine spirits Mary. You on the other hand are splattered in dried blood and dirt from head to toe. You look like you crawled out of the bowels of hell."

"Ah, the words every woman longs to hear."

Devereux smiled, then reached over and placed his hand on Efendi's forehead. "Your man has a fever."

I was touched by his concern for a man he did not know. "Aye, the wound is infected. I've sent my lads off to find our ships."

"You have medicines, a ship's doctor?"

"We have both."

"How fortunate for you. You came better prepared than we English did. I take it you saw a fair amount of action on the road to Lisbon?"

"Aye, each day the Spanish hit us hard with a mix of cavalry and infantry. Thanks be to God their numbers were small, thank God they had no artillery."

"Well, 'tis good to see you came through the fight unscathed. Let me make amends for my thoughtless remark earlier. Even splattered in blood and begrimed in the filth of the road your beauty is intoxicating. You are a lovely vision in this sad place."

"Ah my grace, now you flatter me too much. There's no beauty in stink or filth."

"And yet, I speak the truth. Do you not think me handsome and virile?"

"You are a bold rascal my dear Earl! Aye, you are a fine-looking gentleman and I have no doubt all the girls at Court swoon whenever they see you coming. About your virility sir, ahem, I wouldn't know."

"A bold approach can sometimes bring rich rewards."

I smiled. "A bold approach can kill a man too."

Devereux chuckled good-naturedly. "One has no chance of winning the game without throwing the dice. Why will you not share my bed? Great God, you're not a virgin like our beloved queen?"

"My, you are a frisky fellow, persistent too. I'll give you that. I've heard some say your heart belongs to the queen. She's a jealous sovereign and I should like to keep my head. That is reason enough I think to keep matters between us simple."

Devereux sighed. "How true, how true. You have wits to match your exquisite beauty my lady. Well, since you've denied us any carnal pleasures, the topic of the day seems to be war. Did Norreys suffer many causalities?"

With the flirtatious banter over, I relaxed and took a sip of coffee. "I lost four men, twice as many wounded. Norreys doesn't share his casualty lists with me but, between the Spanish, disease and desertions, he lost scores of men from what I saw, perhaps as many as a hundred altogether. Tell me, why is Drake sitting on his rump here in Cascais? We expected him to be outside of Lisbon's gates waiting for us. Truth be told, we had hoped to find you and your marines inside São Jorge's walls with victory banners flying overhead."

"That would have pleased old Black John, I'm sure. We

unleashed António on Portugal but have yet to see the promised uprising. São Jorge Castle is a powerful fortress with three rings of thick stone walls and many batteries heavy cannon and you must have walked past Belém Tower. The tower is well-defended and in a fine spot to protect Lisbon's flank. No, the fleet would lose any duel against those two fortresses. Without Portuguese support, Drake cannot hope to take Lisbon."

"Aye, I saw São Jorge up close and we skirted around Belém. The Spanish will not leave Lisbon willingly."

"I fear your words at Cape Roca were true. If the army couldn't crack Coruña, how can we possibly take Lisbon? Drake is too proud to admit it, but he knows. The expedition's fortunes will rise or fall with Dom António."

"Do you think António can deliver?"

Devereux shrugged his shoulders. "Who can say? The admiral seems to have doubts. Drake sent a ship back to London a few days ago with letters to both the queen and the Privy Council. He has asked for more supplies and the siege equipment we'll need to smash in Lisbon's walls if the Portuguese fail to rebel."

"What news from António?"

"Nothing, not a peep."

"Norreys's men are slowly starving. What is the fleet's situation?"

"We've found enough stores of grain and flour to feed the expedition for a week or two. Foraging parties have been sent out but have returned with nothing. The Spanish have devastated the countryside."

"Aye. We saw these same tactics, your grace. The Spanish cleansed every village we passed through."

"My dear Mary, please call me Robert. There is no need for formalities between us. Down that path there is a tent for officers with a tub. A hot bath and some fresh clothes would do much to rejuvenate your spirits. On my honor, I'll protect your privacy and keep an eye on your man here."

A hot bath. Not since the jungles of Panama during our search for Aztec gold, when Hunter had shaved my head bald to relieve my misery, had I yearned so much for a hot bath.

"A most tempting offer, Robert. I'm much obliged. But my men will return soon and I must see to Mustafa first. Perhaps later I shall take you up on your offer."

"I applaud you, Mary. Your loyalty to your men is well-known. Speaking of loyalty to one's men, did the Spanish take any of your lads prisoner?"

"No, why do you ask?"

"The Portuguese have told us that the dungeons at Torre de Belém hold a number of English prisoners. I suspect some are privateers. The tower is a stronghold of the Inquisition."

"Dear God, the Inquistion."

"Dear God, indeed."

"Surely Drake won't leave them there?"

Devereux looked absently down at the fire. "That would be an unthinkable trajady Mary. But without seige engines..."

Chapter Five

s I was exchanging information with Devereux, Atwood liberated a sturdy fishing trawler to look for our ships and after he found them in the midst of the English fleet, he sent the trawler back with our ship's physician, a down-on-his-luck newcomer from Munich we had saved in Plymouth from his creditors named Joachin Stachel, and medicines. Despite his weakness for the gambling tables, Stachel had shown himself to be a kind and consientious soul and a competent physician and I was glad to have him.

With Devereux's help, we carried Efendi to the English hospital tent where Stachel went to work. He opened the stiches first to draw pus from the wound using hot compresses boiled in water and a poultice of one sort or another with a godawful stink. After Stachel thoroughly cleaned the wound, he applied a paste made from coconut oil, honey and garlic to speed the healing he said and then carefully re-stitched the wound, boiling the thread and needle in water first. I didn't know if our German friend knew what he was doing but the English surgeon must have approved of Stachel's methods as he watched the German work because he later invited Stachel to look in on the English wounded with him.

I sat with Efendi through the night. I kept cold compresses on his forehead and gave him plenty of *cinchona*, a white powder that comes from the bark of the *cinchona* tree, the fever tree as the Indians call it, found mostly in Peru. The powder can be mixed with wine or water and is good for relieving mild pain and reducing fevers. *Cinchona* is a wonderful medicine and we kept ample quanties of it onboard our ships. We also had Paracelsus's Laudanum, good for easing severe pain, but it is very hard to come by and we never had much of it. Stachel offered Efendi a spoonful, but Efendi refused as laudanum is a strong drug that can play tricks on the mind. In the morning my prayers were answered when Efendi's fever broke.

With Efendi on the mend, and while Drake and Norreys were debating what to do, I used the time to take *Phantom* upriver to bring food and medicines to my men. I took both Atwood and MacGyver with me. We reached Lisbon before sunset, found a deserted wharf just west of the city to dock our ship and after we hid the supplies for our men in some woods, we strolled into the English camp. We stayed only long enough to collect our sick and wounded and returned to our ship before sunrise with the English none the wiser.

I let the currents carry us slowly downriver as the sun rose over our stern. I was in no hurry. I waved to Kinkae and Henry to join Atwood, MacGyver and me up on the quarter deck for breakfast. The ship's cook served us hot porridge, bacon and fresh biscuits straight from the kychen's brick oven. As we leisurely ate our meals, with Belém Tower off our starboard bow, a deliciously wicked came to me. At high tide Belém is an island and stands alone against the riverbank. The castle is not large as castle's go, but its white walls are thick and well-protected by a good number of harbor guns with excellent fields of fire.

"Do you know what is in Belém?" I asked no one in particular as I kept I kept my gaze fixed on the fortress. Belém is more than a formidable stronghold, Belém is a work of art, as beutiful as any cathedral. The Portuguese had lavished money on the Tower's ornate, Gothic archtecture.

Atwood shot me a warning glance. "A lot of trouble Mary," he said. Atwood's abilty to read my thoughts was often uncanny.

MacGyver was the conciliatory soul among us. "I'd like to know Mary. What is in Belém?"

"I'm delighted you asked Michael," I said and poured him more coffee. "It might interest you gentelmen to know that the Inquistion uses the Tower to hold and interrogate prisoners."

"Interrogate?" Kinkae asked.

"One of those new words I learned in London. It means to question someone."

Atwood sighed. "Every castle has a dungeon to keep prisoners. What of it?"

I smiled sweetly at Atwood. "Nothing. I just find this information interesting."

"Ah, ha," Atwood replied and rolled his eyes. "So we'll have no more talk about what might be inside Belém?"

I glanced up at the sky, the sun was not too hot yet. I took a moment to relish the pleasant ocean breeze caressing my skin.

"What a glorious morning this is," I said as I sipped my coffee.

As soon as we dropped anchor off Cascais, I went ashore to look in on Efendi. I found him outside practicing with his knives. His color had returned and I thanked God again for his good health.

I placed my hand on his forehead. "Good, good. The fever is gone. How do you feel?"

"I'll feel better when these stitches are out and my aim is true."

"If you work that arm too hard, you may pull those stitches. Rest, let your body heal. I insist."

After Efendi put away his knives, I sought out the young Earl of Essex next and found Devereux close to where I had left him. He had his back against a block of stone close to Drake's tent with a book in his hand, dozing in the shade.

"Robert, what news?" I asked, gently nudging him on the shoulder. I offered him a friendly smile when he opened his eyes.

"Ah, Mary there you are! You are looking refreshed and clean. You found time to bathe after all."

"I did. I took your good advice and I'm the better for it."

"Come, sit with me. I'll have one of the sentries fetch us a skin of wine. Where did you disappear to yesterday if I may ask?"

"I made a quick run up to Lisbon," I replied evenly. "I needed to fetch my wounded and left a few meager supplies behind."

I have a reputation for honesty, but some lies are useful, even necessary at times. My ships were still well-stocked with victuals of every sort, including pigs, goats and chickens. We had fresh meat, eggs, butter and milk, delicasies the English might kill for.

"I see. Well, the news is the same as it was the day before. We are all waiting on *Senhor* António to deliver the promised rebellion, or for our gracious and pious queen to send us something to break down São Jorge's sturdy walls."

"It would seem we'll be fighting this war sitting on our bums, waiting on others to do what must be done as we relax in the shade."

"Ha-ha! You do like blunt speach Mary. I don't think Drake appreciates your caustic wit. No, I am certain he does not. He can be a bit too grim for my taste. I rather enjoy your liveliness, your biting tongue. Norreys is leaving Cascais today to rejoin his army. Will you accompany him, or will you stay here with your ships?"

"I doubt the fleet will see much action. I'll follow Norreys back to Lisbon I suppose."

"Pity, I find your company most invigorating."

"You're an incorrigible scoundrel, Robert. Perhaps we can find something more stimulating for you to do other than reading books."

I was not above using my feminine charms on men. I was not beyond using flirtation to good advantage. Devereux was easy prey and took the bait.

"When in the presence of exquisite beauty, I can think of several stimulating things to do."

"There now, you've made me blush. I have ten years on you or so - we need to find some younger trinket for you to play with, one who can keep pace with your virility."

"Beauty is beauty Mary."

"I suppose, but there are many fetching, young creatures no doubt here in Cascais who, I'm quite certain, would do anything to please an English lord, especially when he is the Master of the Horse. But whilst I have your attention, your martial skills are what interest me now, not the other, leastwise not today and not when you hold the queen's interest."

Devereux smiled and tossed his hands up in defeat. "I am undone, madam. You tantalize to draw your prey in and then you push away. Tactics better suited for war than love. Well, tell me.

What is rattling around in that pretty head of yours?"

"I've been thinking about what you said the other day, what you told me about English prisoners being held at Belém."

"Oh? How so?"

"Let us see how it goes with the siege of Lisbon. If Lisbon falls, Belém will certainly fall with it and we'll not need to discuss my plan. But if Drake and Norreys fail to take Lisbon, we must make an effort, a stout effort, to deliver our brothers-in-arms from the Inquistion. I cannot in good conscience leave such good men behind to be torured and murdered, especially when we are only a stone's throw away. We must at least try to rescue those poor souls before we sail off."

"Attack Belém? Such an attempt would be very risky without the fleet, nay impossible, and Drake will never permit it."

"I don't intend to attack Belém and I don't require Drake's permission."

Devereux raised an eyebrow.

"I only ask you to give the matter some thought Robert."

"I have."

"Wait until you've heard my plan. Perhaps then you'll agree to give the matter some more thought."

I left Devereux with his book and returned to Lisbon with Norreys. We slogged along muddy roads in heavy rains the entire way. Efendi had refused to stay behind with the ships and walked with me. Atwood had wanted to come along too, and had been rather ornery in his persistence. But if Drake took my ships into action, I needed Atwood in command.

The days in Lisbon slipped by slowly with little action. Norreys contented himself with bombarding Lisbon's great castle using two meager batteries of long-barreled sakers Devereux and a company of his marines had hauled up from Cascais. Short on shot and low on powder, the English contented themselves with firing-off a few symbolic volleys here and there. It hardly mattered. The twelve-pounders did no damage against São Jorge's thick walls. The Spanish garrison took pleasure in taunting the English gunners as they watched along the battlements.

Meanwhile, back in Cascais, the brilliant hero of Nombre de Diós, of Veracruz, Cádiz, the Azores and Gravelines, and of a dozen other daring raids against the Spanish, a man of action, luck and daring, kept the fleet anchored in the mouth of the Tagus River and did nothing. Norreys asked Drake to move the fleet upriver to join him in an all-out assault against Lisbon by land and sea, but Drake declined. The admiral's paralysis was a mystery to us all. Old age, melancholy, or some infirmity perhaps was to blame. No one knew for certain what troubled Drake. Perhaps the queen's rebuke had stung his pride. Word spread through the English camp that the queen was most displeased with Drake. She wanted the Armada destroyed more than Lisbon taken and refused Drake's request for siege equipment or supplies.

And as for the Portuguese, no one rallied to António's banner. Portuguese nobles would not risk their necks unless Drake took Lisbon first and Drake would not risk the fleet unless the Portuguese declared their allegiance to England and rebelled against Spain. The days passed by with inaction, supplies dwindled and the English were forced back on half rations.

Bored with siege duty, I took twenty of my men with Norreys's consent to reconnoiter the countryside. We went as far north as Santarém, forded the Tagus there where the river is narrow and shallow and can be walked across at low tide, and then traveled south to Aledia Galega, a small village directly across the river from Lisbon. The Portuguese greeted us warmly in every village we passed through and gladly sold us whatever they could spare. On our way back to Lisbon, we passed a Spanish patrol of about forty men or so just outside of Santarém. The Spanish were heading north as we headed south. They ignored us and we ignored them.

A week after leaving Lisbon, we returned to the English lines with a cart filled with food and wine. A sentry took me to a sergeant major who led me to some nobleman's house where Norreys and his officers were gathered. I left the cart with the sergeant major as a gift and sent my own men back to camp.

Norreys and his officers were sitting around a table with a map of Lisbon spread across it when I arrived. The great warrior welcomed me with a weary nod and dark half-moon circles under his eyes. He had an irksome cough.

"Captain Mary, welcome back," Norreys said. "What news?"

"From Lisbon to Aledia Galega and back General, we covered over one hundred miles of ground. We came across one Spanish patrol at Santarém heading north but saw nothing else of interest."

"Please take a seat. I've been handed a note about the victuals. Most appreciated."

"We returned with barely enough to feed a company of men for a week I fear. The Portuguese don't have much to share."

"English foraging parties have fared no better and none have travelled as far behind enemy lines. My compliments to you and your men. Mary, gentlemen, I know the hour is late and the evening is dreadfully hot, but our situation is becoming more precarious by the day. Our scouts have reported spotting fresh reinforcements joining the main Spanish army encamped around the hills of the Serra de Motejunto. Whole regiments are flocking to Motejunto. The Spanish are assembling an impressive force of infantry, cavalry and artillery and they are well-supplied. My quartermaster informs me that we have enough grain to feed the army for another four weeks, five at most. We are losing men to disease and desertion and morale is low. Our pioneers have probed the fortress's defenses but have found no weakness. I've ordered a halt to the bombardment to conserve what is left of our gunpowder. We can expect no help from the Portuguese. Our predicament here is less than satisfactory."

As Norreys's voice trailed off, Devereux cleared his throat to speak. "General, our present circumstance is most unfortunate, especially since our Portuguese spies have reported that the Spanish garrison cannot hold São Jorge's triple walls without the Portuguese auxiliary units. What a pity the Portuguese people do not rise up against their Spanish masters. On a cheerier note, we've hardly lost the campaign. Once we resupply and regroup, we can still sail north to destroy the Armada."

"I admire your enthusiasm to continue the good fight Robert.

Every man here is a loyal and righteous Englishman, bound by duty and love of God, queen and country. I've served with none better. I include our feisty Captain Mary in my praise. Earlier today though I received a dispatch from Drake with distressing news. A powerful squadron of Spanish war galleys - over twenty strong - has been sighted off the Estoril Coast. Drake believes Admiral Alonso de Bazán is in command. Bazán is a capable seaman, a good fighter."

"This news is indeed troubling, General," Devereux replied solemnly.

Norreys stood and leaned over the map on the table. "This new development complicates our tactical position to put it politely. Bazán has just shut the door to the Armada on us, I think. Drake will not risk trying to bludgeon his way through such a large Spanish force. Our mission is doomed if we do not take Lisbon in the next week or two. I'm prepared to order a general retreat to Peniche before the Spanish army grows much stronger. God forbid the Spanish pin us against the walls of Lisbon whilst Bazán traps the fleet inside the river."

"Why return to Peniche, General?" Devereux asked.

"We left two hundred men in Peniche to guard our rear, along with the flatboats. We'll need to get them."

No one had much to say after Norreys explained the army's dire predicament. Norreys asked for a vote and to a man, his officers agreed to continue the siege for one more week to give António a little more time to deliver his rebellion.

I pulled Devereux aside after Norreys dismissed us all. "Robert, do you recall what I said to you in Cascais?"

Devereux nodded. He was only twenty-two years old and had been full of vigor in Plymouth. Now he looked and moved like a man twice his age. I reached into a leather satchel and produced a half bottle of wine, a bag filled with strips of bacon and a large block of cheese with only a touch of mold around the edges.

"Take these."

His eyes lit up. "Where did you find these wonderful delicacies?"

"From a few of my Portuguese friends," I answered with some

truth.

"Mary, you must look after yourself."

"Do I look ill-nourished to you?"

"No, in truth you appear to be in wonderful health. I'm amazed by your stamina and constant good cheer." He paused for a moment as if he were trying to catch some fleeting thought alluding him. "Ha, I think war agrees with you!"

I forced the bottle and food into his hand. "I can't spare much, but I won't miss these things."

"Thank you for this kindness Mary. I'll share this bounty with my men, the men who need it most."

"The gift is yours to do with as you like."

An easy, boyish grin came to Devereux, the kind a man makes when there is a bit of mischief afoot. I could see why the earl had won the queen's heart.

"Ah, I see it now, this is a bribe! Mary, you could roll out cartloads of fresh meats and vegetables and the best wines in all of Portugal and still I wouldn't be able to pry away any English ships from the fleet to help you attack Belém. Even if I could, Belém's batteries would make short work of us."

I shook my head. "My gift is not a bribe and I don't need any English ships. But I do wish to make a point. You are right, we can't force our way into Belém. If nothing else, Drake has at least cut Belém off from the world. The garrison must be as desperate as the English for food, perhaps more so, which gives us one good card to play."

"And you intend to do what? Oh, silly me. You're an Irish smuggler with goods to sell. God's wounds, you're not a papist trying to give aid to the enemy?"

"No need to burn me at the stake my good Master of the Horse. I'm neither a papist nor a Protestant. I'm a free spirit and I pray God is comfortable with that. But you are right. I'm an Irish smuggler, a blockade runner with an Irish, Catholic crew and I have supplies to sell to any who would pay me a fair price."

"For prisoners?"

"For prisoners."

"Two trips? You slip over to Belém to introduce yourself one night, cut a deal and then return the next with your cargo?"

"Quite so."

"And then?"

"And then? And then we'll insist the garrison allow a small party inside the castle to work the hoists - to avoid any damage to my ship as we lift pallets up the seawall - and we'll insist on counting the gold the Spanish pay us before we start offloading our cargo."

"A clever pretense Mary to get your men inside. Even so, you won't have enough men to overwhelm the night watch."

"True. That is why we'll hide men and arms inside some of the crates. Once we take the south rampart, we'll toss ropes down to the ship and bring more men up. The seawall is not too high."

"'Tis a daring plan, inspired truly, but it is too risky. I fear even if you succeed in bringing your whole crew into the castle, you still won't have enough men to bludgeon your way into the tower and down into the dungeons. The garrison will be hundreds strong."

"Aye. Lucky for me I have a master of explosives aboard my ship. A dozen barrels of gunpowder ought to even-up the odds. I could use you and some of your marines. My men and I will keep the garrison occupied whilst your men free the prisoners from their cells."

"Huh. I've underestimated you. But why risk your life and the lives of your men in this Mary? What are these English prisoners to you?"

"I once knew a man, an Englishman, who was very, very dear to me. He barely escaped imprisonment from a place like Belém. I do this in honor of him. If he were here, standing with us now, he wouldn't leave fellow Englishmen behind, not when half the might of England sits just a few miles away."

"Yes, I've heard of this man. Hunter was his name?"

"Aye, Hunter was his name."

"Very well, I will help you."

"Marvelous."

"If this all goes very wrong, there'll be the devil to pay. You and I will be sharing a cell in London if the Spanish don't kill us first. Ah, one cell, one bed. Perhaps my fortunes are improving!"

"You're impossible!" I said with mock anger and stormed off with a smile.

We Irish have no love of the English. The English subrogation of the Irish and the confiscation of their lands in favor of the New English under the brutal laws of Plantation is an abomination of the worst kind, an unforgivable sin against God, or if not God, against nature. Since the days of King Henry VIII, the English have displaced and killed thousands of Irish men, women and children, or sent them off to the New World as slaves. If my men had not signed with me, many of them would be back in Ireland killing Englishmen.

But war can forge bonds between men stronger than blood. A man you wouldn't share a drink with at home can become your brother in war. In Portugal we were brothers-in-arms with the English facing a common enemy, men linked together by loyalty, hardship and death. And despite the Catholic faith they share, the Irish have no love for the Spanish.

In accordance with our Ten Rules, I put the matter to a vote before the whole crew. Every man stood with me.

The first part of my plan succeeded without flaw. We brought *Phantom* in carefully under a moonless night in light breezes with a large, white flag flapping off the mizzen gaff. We eased our ship up close to the fortress's seawall and hailed the Spanish garrison to introduce ourselves. A captian of the guard studied us with curiosity. He had his men lower a rope ladder down from the ramparts and allowed two men - the ship's master and another - into the bastion. I sent Atwood and MacGyver. A full platoon of Spanish muskateers kept their muskets trained on the rest of us.

When Atwood and MacGyver worked their way down the ladder an hour later, Atwood patted me on the shoulder as he stepped back onboard. "As you suspected, Mary, the Spanish are in desperate need of victuals. Only a few small boats have managed to slip past Drake's picket ships with supplies for the garrison. The commander is Captain-General Guilherme de Martinez, who also happens to be the *Alcalde* of Algés. Martinez is a congenial enough fellow and his English is quite good. He believed our story - and he has gold to pay."

"Good, very good. Did you see any English prisoners?"

"No, but our host spoke openly about them. He had no reason not to and we shared information about the English with him, nothing useful. He did seem surprised to learn that the Spanish still held Lisbon. I think we gave him hope. He questioned us of course about how we were able to slip past the English fleet."

"And you're certain he believed your story?"

"Aye, Mary," MacGyver interjected. "He was plainly annoyed that no Spanish ship has tried to run the blockade to resupply his men, but he believed us. He saw no threat from one Irish smuggler sitting underneath his heavy guns."

"When does he want us to return?"

Atwood stretched his arms and yawned. "Tomorrow night, Mary. Plenty of time to prepare."

"What is your impression of the captain-general? Does he seem trustworthy? Is he a fighter?"

"Martinez appears to be a reasonable fellow to Michael and me. I doubt he tries to double-cross us as we might be useful to him again. If we can pull-off the second part of your plan, it won't matter. As for whether he is a fighter or not, I'd say he's no fool but I suspect he's more politician than soldier."

"This is most welcome news. I am encouraged."

I was more than encouraged. I was ecstatic. I had felt out of sorts, even lost, since leaving Plymouth. Now I had found purpose again.

It was the darkest of nights. The river's surface was flat. Visibility was poor. A warm, sticky mist mixed with pin drops of drizzle seemed to hover over the water. Luck was with us. But then luck has always been at my side whenever I set a plan into motion, leastwise in the beginning.

We approached the castle with only our main tops'ls set and let the gentle currents of the Tagus carry us along with four covered longboats in tow. Atwood and Efendi stood with me as MacGyver worked the wheel with his delicate touch, easing *Phantom* over to the castle.

"Each man understands what he must do?" I asked, trying to hide the anxiety in my voice.

Atwood nodded. "Aye, Mary. The crew knows what to do. Each man understands the role he must play."

"A lot can go wrong, I know. But, if we finesse this just so, and if chance is kind to us this night, we can pull this off without bloodshed and both sides win."

Atwood took my hands in his. "Rest assured Mary, the lads are ready. We'll triumph. The plan is sound. In any case, we can't turn back now."

"No, we can't. *Allons*, we go..."

I don't like complexity. The more moving pieces in play, the more that can go wrong. My plans have always been simple. This plan had too many moving pieces and left me queasy and nauseous. We needed surprise. We needed coordinated actions between several teams of men scattered about the castle and most of all, we needed a heavy dose of luck. Win or lose, in my heart, I knew Hunter would have approved.

MacGyver gently nudged *Phantom* against the wooden pilings set against the seawall. The Spanish had lit dozens of torches along the wall and inside the double Moorish bartizan turrets standing at each corner. My men tied us off underneath the castle's guns poking over the lower bastion terrace while Spanish soldiers scrutinized us from the upper ramparts with muskets and crossbows at the ready.

The Spanish dropped a rope ladder down for us and extended a pair of sturdy hoists with cargo nets over the seawall. Atwood led ten men up the ladder, including me. I had tucked my hair inside my hat, bound my bosom tight and smeared soot across my face, transforming myself into a lowly ship's boy once again.

Captain-General Martinez greeted us in plain clothes with a wide grin as we climbed over the castle wall. He was a bow-legged man with heavy jowls and receding hair. He used a thin goatee to good advantage to give his face some character.

His men, I counted fifty on duty in all, were in full battle dress with polished breastplates, helmets and greaves. These men were an elite guard of one sort or another, not the common garrison troops I'd seen before. I felt sweat dripping down my armpits and my throat went dry. I glanced uneasily at Atwood. I had given him the power to call off the raid if he didn't like what he saw.

"Welcome, my friends," Martinez said and reached over to shake Atwood's hand. "All is in order Captain Atwood? No problems?"

"No problems, my lord. The English are slovenly folk. I have dogs back in Scotland that keep better watch. Our ship is heavy in the water with cargo and we carry more in the boats in tow."

"*Muy bien.* Excellent. If you deliver the quantity and quality of what you promised last evening, I have the gold to pay."

Atwood bowed, "*Mucho gracias, Señor.*"

Atwood turned to me. "You there boy, and the rest of you lazy, filthy heathens, shake a leg and haul that first pallet up! I want to show the good Captain-General a sample of what we've brought. And take heed: by Christ Almighty, I'll peel the flesh off the bone of any son of a bitch who damages my ship or cargo. You best believe I will."

The Spanish soldiers stepped aside to let us work. I helped work one of the hoists and within minutes we had the first pallet up and over the battlements. I took a crowbar and pried the lid off each barrel for the captain-general's inspection.

Atwood scooped up a handful of grain from the closest barrel. "Grain, coffee, tea, rice, flour, cured meat and tobacco to start with."

I watched Martinez's men stare at their commander wide-eyed in the flickering torchlight as he plunged his arm deep into each barrel to satisfy himself that every barrel was full. And then I realized that underneath their pretty uniforms the Spaniards were more skin and bone than muscle. These men were starving, worse than the English.

Martinez scooped a handful of coffee up to his nose to savor the rich aroma of the beans. "¡Ah, *delicioso*! Nooo - what do I see here. *¿Ch'arki*, you brought *ch'arki* with you?"

Atwood beamed at the Spaniard. "*Si, ch'arki*. You've been to the West Indies *Señor* Martinez?"

Martinez popped a chunk of dried beef into his mouth. "*Si*. I have been to the New World. Come my dear Captain, let us retire to my quarters as your men off-load the rest of the cargo. We can relax, chat and dry ourselves near the fire. I am certain you have a good story or two to tell."

"Most kind sir, most kind. I think your suggestion is excellent."

"I am sorry to say I have no wine or ale to offer. We finished-off the last of our spirits weeks ago."

"Ah, not to worry there. I've brought gifts with me to celebrate our new friendship. I have cigars from Havana and a decent Portuguese wine."

Martinez rubbed his hands together. "¡Oh, *maravilloso*!"

Before the captain-general led Atwood across the courtyard to his quarters in the Tower, a four-story structure on the north side of the bastion, he scooped up a heaping handful of *ch'arki* with both hands and passed the pieces out to his men along the seawall. The Spaniards greedily devoured the treats.

It pleased me to see the captain-general cared for his men. His humanity might play into our favor very soon. I anxiously watched for the signal. If Atwood rubbed his nose, the raid was on. If he coughed, we hauled the rest of the cargo up, returned to the ship and left. To my surprise, Atwood rubbed his nose before strolling off with Martinez.

My men and I resumed the tedious work of lifting cargo up into the castle. We brought up the smaller, lighter cargo first and then I waved more men up the rope ladder to help us haul in the larger, heavier loads using both hoists in tandem. We took our time and worked with care.

We stacked some of the cargo neatly against the seawall and

some we lowered down into the courtyard. Every crate and every barrel, each box and cask, was marked. An hour into our labors, Efendi, playing the part of Atwood's first officer, led the captain of the guard away with a bottle of whisky, fresh bread and a round of cheese while I magically produced a dozen bottles of wine and a basket of bread and handed them out to the night watch. No man refused my gifts.

As the Spanish ate and drank and fell into a mellow mood, my men and I continued lifting crates, barrels and boxes into the castle. I allowed myself a smile as more than one Spaniard sat down and closed his eyes. After we hauled the last pallet up, we swung the hoists around over the courtyard, leaving the last pallet suspended in midair. Then we went around and pried the larger crates stacked in the shadows against the seawall open, crates stuffed with muskets - the new snaphaunces, a huge improvement over the old matchlocks and snaplocks - pistols, swords, rope and men. After we tied the ropes around the merlons and dropped the ropes over the wall, I leaned over the battlements and waved the rest of my crew up.

I could feel my adrenaline pumping hard as I watched my men scramble up the seawall. One-by-one they slipped through the stone embrasures and quietly dropped down into the castle. Then Devereux's company of marines, hiding underneath the tarps on the boats we had in tow, moved out smartly and followed. It was a glorious thing to watch.

"Lads," I whispered. "Quickly now, we need to disarm our friends. Remember, tonight we spill no blood. It is to our advantage to keep matters civil."

My men one-by-one rounded up the night watch without much fuss. Devereux led his company down a stone staircase to the terrace directly below and spiked the harbor guns, seventeen deadly brutes in all, that would have made any escape impossible if left intact.

And then, without warning, silly woman that I am, I felt a tear stain my cheek when I imagined Hunter standing by my side. I could see his face and hear his voice. I could feel his arms wrapped around me. I bit my lip, shook the vision off and forced myself to focus.

We couldn't disarm every Spaniard of course. Once we had secured about half their number, the rest realized what we were doing and fled back to the Tower, crying out for help. Scores of half-dressed Spaniards and Portuguese started pouring out of their barracks onto the courtyard with swords and muskets in hand.

I saw Martinez stagger into the courtyard, struggling to keep his balance with Atwood walking a step behind him. A dozen soldiers moved to Martinez's side as others scrambled down the cloisters along the east and west walls. My men and I held the upper seawall. Devereux and his marines held the terrace below.

Martinez stopped in the middle of the courtyard and drew his sword. "What is this madness?" he demanded as he looked up at the ramparts where my men and I stood. Then Devereux and his marines stepped out of the shadows and formed a skirmish line. Martinez took in the English uniforms and considered the numbers against him.

I removed my hat, shook my hair out and looked down on Martinez. He stared at me, confused.

I couldn't help myself and laughed. "*Mi querido Capitán-General*. I am *Capitana Maria*, known by some as Captain Bloody Mary."

"*Capitana*, eh? I know you not. But I know this: I'll blow your ship to hell and kill you and all your men if you do not lay down your arms and surrender to me now! I have more men than you and I have cannon. I hold the advantage."

"I beg to differ, *Capitán-General*. I think it best for all concerned if you order your men to stand down."

"Ha! You are outnumbered by two-to-one or better or can you not count?"

"Oh yes, *Capitán-General* Martinez, I can count. Can you? And I know when I hold the far better tactical advantage."

"What foolish game is this you play? If I give the order, you and all your men shall die!" Martinez raised his hand and snapped his fingers to give his words more power. "Poof!"

Atwood then pushed his pistol against the captain-general's ribs. "I've enjoyed your good company so far, *Señor* Martinez. But if you give that order, you'll be the first to die this night."

"Enough!" I called out in a calm tone. "Let me answer your question about numbers more thoroughly. Your men may outnumber mine, but on my signal, more ships will come. I hold the seawall and your cannon. I also have taken thirty of your men prisoner. Of more concern to you should be those barrels suspended above your head. Those barrels are packed with gunpowder and rigged to blow. I light the fuse I hold in my hand, drop the pallet and boom! What a mess all that powder will make. I think that evens-up the odds considerably between us, don't you? But calm yourself my friend. We didn't come here to fight. We aren't here to take your precious castle."

Martinez carefully considered the barrels above his head. "No, this is a trick. I know about the attack at A Coruña. You English must have used most of your powder stores in the tunnel - why else would Drake not move his fleet up the Tagus and fire on Lisbon? For two months your fleet has sat idly off Cascais. Even if *El Draque* had gunpowder, he'd never waste it on Belém when Lisbon is the prize."

"Sound reasoning, *Señor*, sound reasoning. But we are not English. What Captain Atwood told you last night is true. We are Irish smugglers. The powder in those barrels hanging above your head belong to me." I turned to Efendi. "Mustafa, bring the highest-ranking prisoner to me. *Señor* Martínez, I'll prove to you that my words are true."

Efendi found a sergeant major among our prisoners and pushed the man my way. My men pulled the pallet in a little closer and I removed the lid off one barrel for the sergeant major. He put a handful of powder to his nose, stared at me wide-eyed and looked down at his commander with sweat oozing from his pores. He removed his helmet and bowed his head.

"*Capitán-General Martínez*," the sergeant major said in a shaky voice, "*lo que dice la señora es cierto. Los barriles se llenan de pólvora.*"

"This is madness!" Martinez shrieked. "Madness! You'll kill us all."

"No one need die this night."

"I will not surrender Belém."

"As I said, I do not want your castle. Keep your arms and keep your castle. We can avoid any ugliness. We can both win tonight. I have a proposal for you."

"What? What is this proposal you speak of?"

"I wish to conclude the deal you made with Captain Atwood last night. I want the payment promised in exchange for the cargo we have delivered."

"What buffoonery is this? Why do you do this for a deal already struck? You think I will double-cross you?"

"That thought did cross my mind, but no. This little demonstration has another purpose. We must make a slight amendment to our contract. You are holding prisoners in your dungeons. I want them."

All around the courtyard and along the battlements men stood still, waiting for Martinez to answer. His next words would decide the life or death of many.

Martinez shook his head. "All this trouble for a few prisoners?"

"How much longer can you and your men hold this place without supplies, Captain-General? That should be your only concern this night. The English seige of Lisbon could drag on for months. Your men appear gaunt and weak and they are are cetainly slow. Your men are starving. Soon they'll fall prey to disease and die."

The Spaniard hesitated at first, debating what to do. "You will leave the supplies?" he asked.

"For the gold and all the prisoners, yes."

"The powder too?"

"No, not the powder."

"Then we have no agreement."

Martinez's final demand surprised me. Spanish pride.

"I'll compromise with you. I'll leave you six barrels of powder, half of what I have."

All eyes turned to Martinez as he considered my offer. He considered the forces arrayed against him, took in the sad condition of his men and weighed his options one last time.

"Very well," he said, "I agree to your terms."

I felt my heart skip a beat and breathed a sigh of relief. "Excellent. And just so there is no misunderstanding between us, we've spiked all your guns along the seawall and we'll keep our Spanish prisoners until we're safely away."

Martinez nodded. "I will summon the jailer and have him release our English prisoners."

"No, not just the English prisoners, *señor*. I shall have every prisoner in your possession."

"*Si, si.* Very well. And just so there is no misunderstanding between us, today you have made yourself known to the *Tribunal del Santo Oficio de la Inquisición*." Martínez turned and pointed to the Tower where two priests were standing at a vestibule watching us from an open window. "I fear by your actions tonight my lady, you have cut your own throat."

"Ha!" I scoffed in a loud voice for all to hear. I never took threats well. "Let those twisted demons come for me if they dare. I have no qualms about slicing up priests." I drew my sword and pointed the blade at the priests. "Do you hear me you pathetic, dickless, turds? I'll be waiting for you and by God, I'll show you hell. *¿Me oyes, pequeñas mierdas? Te estaré esperando y por Dios, te mostraré el infierno.*"

Martinez crossed himself as if to ward off some evil spirit, then ordered his men to shoulder their muskets and stand at ease. Then Atwood disappeared into the Tower, dragging Martinez with him and a platoon of Devereux's marines to find the jailer.

As I tried to stop my heart from racing, a pair of strong hands grabbed me from behind and lifted me off my feet. Devereux twirled me around and around and laughed.

"Your reputation is well-deserved Mary! The plan, your poise and bravado, what a show. What a night to remember!"

"We're not free yet," I said. "I pray you feel as charitable towards me tomorrow should Drake have us standing side-by-side in front of a firing squad."

When Atwood returned to the courtyard with forty ragged, filthy souls and three chests of Spanish gold, we quickly scrambled over the seawall to our ship, taking our thirty Spanish prisoners and six barrels of gunpowder with us. The Spanish garrison rushed to the battlements to watch us leave, but I don't think any man wished us ill. I saw no anger in any of their faces. I saw only hungry, lonely men far away from home.

We cast-off the mooring lines, pushed our ship away from the seawall and once we were clear, we put our Spanish prisoners into the longboats we had in tow and set them free. Atwood then gathered the crew around and led them in a rousing cheer. Devereux and his marines happily joined in.

"*Hooray! Hooray! Hooray!*" men shouted in one, thunderous voice.

"By God's infinite grace," Atwood bellowed for all to hear and raised his hands up to the heavens. "You did it Mary!"

I shook my head. "But for the courage of each man here, I could have done nothing." I glanced over at the men we had rescued, men who looked like death. "You men there, you owe your liberty and your lives to my crew. We're Irish and yet we risked our lives for you. You remember that should you ever find yourselves in Ireland. And you owe the Lord Devereux and his marines your gratitude as well. They too risked their lives for you."

From stem to stern the ship again erupted with shouts of "*Hooray! Hooray! Hooray!*"

One of the prisoners, dressed in filthy, tattered rags, stepped forward. His left eye was swollen shut and his nose had been broken. His lips were cracked and caked in blood. Someone had worked him over. Then I saw the hair matted against the side of his head with dried blood and winced. The Spanish had cut off the poor fellow's left ear.

The man knelt before me and kissed my hand. "As I've told the queen from time-to-time my dear lady, what a remarkable woman you are. It is good, so very good to see you again. I never thought I would. I heard you were killed at the old mill. Oh Mary, Mary, Mary..."

The man started shaking and wouldn't release my hand. I raised his chin to see his face.

"John Martin," I mumbled to myself in disbelief. I pulled Martin to his feet and embraced him. We wept together in each other's arms, oblivious to the world around us.

For all things there is a price, a price that must be paid.

Drake looked none too pleased as I stood before him in his gloomy command tent back in Cascais. The lackeys at his side glared at me like a pack of ravenous jackals. But a lioness has no fear of the jackal. Devereux stood off to the side with a defeated look in his eyes. He'd survive Drake's wrath - and so would I.

Drake took a step towards me. "Did you think you could slip in and out of Belém without me knowing?"

"I hid nothing, your grace. I sailed into Belém in plain view."

"By whose authority did you engage the Spanish?"

"By my own - I'm a freeborn woman. My crew are freeborn men. My ships belong to me and to me alone to do with as I please."

Drake started circling around me with his hands locked behind his back. "My authority Mary, my authority on this expedition is absolute!"

"I dare say your grace, not even the queen's authority is absolute. I never agreed to join your navy. I am a privateer and carry her majesty's commission to engage her enemies where and when I find them. For a few crates and barrels of sundry provisions - provisions that were mine to give - we obtained the release of forty desperate, broken men, most of them English, men who would have languished in awful pain and eventually died in the dungeons of Belém had we not freed them."

"Hogwash! By your actions you've given aid and comfort to the enemy! You've supplied the Spanish with food and powder. You risked the lives of my marines in a reckless, ill-conceived ploy for fame and fortune. I've always suspected your loyalties to England were insincere. You are a schemer and an interloper. Gold is your only god."

"I did no more than save the lives of forty men."

"By risking the lives of hundreds! I've often thought you should be taken down a peg or two - and now you've handed me your head. I'm sorely tempted to charge you with treason. It is one thing to entertain the queen with puffed-up stories over tea and cakes. It is quite another to be one of her majesty's noble knights and a trusted counselor. Let me enlighten you, let me show you the difference. Guards, arrest this woman for insubordination. I'll have her ships and provisions seized as well as the Spanish gold! Devereux, you'll do the honors and see that my orders are carried out properly."

"Sir Francis!" Devereux blurted out and took a step between the guards and me.

"You'll hold your tongue sir," Drake barked. "Do not interfere!"

I waved Devereux off. "All is well, Sir Robert. I can fend for myself. My dear Admiral Drake, you cannot arrest me. Neither can you seize my ships or my provisions or the gold. You don't have the, what did you call it? You don't have the authority. Rescind your order now, I insist."

Devereux grabbed my arm. "Mary, please, don't make matters worse for yourself."

Fury filled Drake's eyes. He pointed his finger at Devereux while continuing to look at me.

"Not another word from you, Robert," he said sternly. "And you, woman - what insolence! If you were a man, I'd strike you down. Clearly you don't grasp the grave predicament you are in. I've always heard you are a clever woman. Perhaps not so much?"

I forced a smile. "I only wish to spare your grace from further indignities."

"Indignities? What gibberish is this? I have no patience for childish riddles madam. Guards, we are finished here. Take her. I'll see you at week's end for your court-martial, Captain Mary."

I slapped the first guard to lay his hand on me across the face. The man must have known me by reputation as he withdrew his hand and took a step back. I reached into my vest pocket.

"You'd be well-advised to read this Admiral," I said defiantly and handed Drake the letter the queen had given to me at Nonsuch. "You no doubt will recognize her majesty's royal seal."

After Drake read the letter, he carefully folded the paper and handed the letter back to me with a subdued look. "Begone madam, leave my sight," he said wearily and turned his back on me.

Devereux followed me outside. "Mary, I'm sorry I could not do more. I argued strenuously on your behalf, but Sir Francis would hear none of it. I've never seen him so angry. And when he decided to arrest you, I had no chance to forewarn you."

"Thank you, Robert. Does he intend to court-martial you?"

Devereux laughed nervously. "No, no. He gave me a good dressing-down let me tell you, but what else can he do to one of her majesty's favorites and a nobleman with rank to boot? What is in that letter?"

"This is a letter of safe conduct, given to me by the queen."

"Ha! I've never seen anyone get the better of Drake. The queen is a shrewd woman."

"She is shrewder than we know."

"I don't think Drake likes you very much. It might be best to avoid him until the dust settles. You're both stubborn in your pride. In this you are alike."

"I'll never understand Drake's animosity towards me. I've never been his enemy. I've never offended or slighted him in any way. Perhaps he dislikes me because I'm Irish, but I've heard Drake has Irish friends. Perhaps he dislikes me because I'm a woman playing in his world."

"Perhaps he is simply jealous."

"Jealous? Of me? Nonsense, Robert. His accomplishments far exceed my own."

"As you say. So, what will you do now Mary?"

"Plainly, I'm no longer welcome here. And you?"

"You are not the only one with a letter from our queen. I received a letter from her majesty yesterday, commanding me to return to England at once."

"Good. There are no riches or glory for you here. What will

become of the expedition?"

"Black John will return to Peniche with the army and then sail home to England. He'll take the sick and wounded with him. Drake intends to sail for the Azores next. Without the army, he can't possibly take the Azores for England now. He hopes to find the Spanish treasure fleet."

"So, you are off to England with Norreys?"

"No, I will sail with Drake."

"What? And risk the queen's wrath?"

"Oh, Elizabeth will rant and rave for a bit but she'll forgive me with time."

After I bid the Earl of Essex farewell, I sent MacGyver with *Diablo* upriver to retrieve our men encamped in Lisbon. Then I went to visit Martin and found him in the English hospital tent, resting on a cot.

"You are as thin as a reed my friend," I said and pulled a stool over to sit next to him. "And yet I see improvement."

He offered me a weak smile as he struggled to sit up. "I doubt I'll fatten-up any in this wretched place. The rations are rather meager here and the service is dreadful. I take it Drake is running low on supplies?"

"Aye, supplies are a knotty problem on any long campaign. Did you eat better at the Tower? Should I return your pathetic carcass over to the Spanish?"

Martin cracked a smile and shook his head.

"Good. That is why I brought you this basket filled with assorted treats and a few necessities. I also have a salve to help your wounds heal faster. The clear ointment in this jar is strong medicine to ward off infection and will numb your pain. There isn't much, so use it sparingly."

"I find myself in your debt once again my lady."

"The slate is clean between us."

"What a spectacle you put on at Belém! But why, Mary? Why risk everything for a handful of English prisoners?"

"Truly, I do not know myself. I suppose I did it for James. I know he would never have left good men behind."

"The men who kidnapped me in Ireland told me about the ambush at Westport. They said they killed you and James at the old mill."

"Aye, James is dead."

"I'm sorry to hear about James. As you know, he saved me from the headman's axe on a whim upon a time. He was a good man."

"The very best."

"Considering your disdain for a safe, if humdrum life, and your careless disregard for your own welfare, fortune favors you, Mary."

"Aye, I was born under a lucky star. Those closest to me though seem to pay an awful price for my charmed life."

"Rubbish. I'll not listen to such foolish talk."

Uncertain of what to say, I looked away and wiped a tear off my cheek.

"Mary, do you know who the culprits are?"

"Aye. The *Síol Faolcháin*."

"I thought as much. I fear one of my own men betrayed us too."

"Aye, I know. And I know how to deal with betrayal."

"Yes, I know you do. Coping with sorrow is a heavier burden I think. But you are stronger than you know."

The tent had a stove and I stood to brew a pot of hot tea for Martin. I added a pinch of laudanum to his cup to ease his pain. His Spanish interrogators had not been gentle with him. The army's physician had to splint one arm and wrapped Martin's shoulder tightly in heavy gauze to help with a fractured collarbone. Other than to clean the wound, there was nothing to be done for his severed ear. After he drank his tea and rested for a bit, we exchanged our unhappy stories.

There was not much to Martin's story. Martin's man, the same fellow who had lured me away from Shaw's tavern, claiming that Martin was grievously wounded at the old mill, had sold his soul to the *Síol Faolcháin*. The clan snatched Martin, put him on one of their ships bound for Lisbon and delivered him to the Spanish for the price he had on his head. The Spanish had a long list of Englishmen they wanted dead and were willing to pay gold to any who delivered.

I had first met Martin in '73. He had been with Drake when Drake, commanding a fleet of English privateers and French buccaneers, intercepted Spain's fabulous Silver Train in the jungles near Nombre de Diós. This particular train was very large, nearly two hundred mules carrying tons of gold and silver. But a Spanish army quickly closed in on Drake and his men and so they carried what they could back to the ships and then buried the rest along the Panamanian coast. Martin and dozens of others, including the French commander, Captain Guillaume Le Testu, were captured. The Spanish beheaded all the prisoners except Martin, the only Englishman, hoping they could persuade Martin to tell them where Drake had buried the treasure. Martin had landed on my ship in Havana bound in chains just as we were preparing to sail for Santo Domingo. Hunter had persuaded me to set Martin free.

"So Spanish inquisitors tortured you at Belém to learn where Drake buried the silver and gold from the Silver Train?"

"No, the Spanish recovered the treasure from the great Silver Train raid years ago. I am an English spy and a pirate. I was just good sport."

"The army's physician believes you'll mend?"

"He does."

"Good. We both have unfinished business."

"Indeed we do. The gossip around the camp is that Drake is quitting Lisbon, that António is finished. Drake is readying the fleet to sail. That much I know. What will you do Mary?"

I took Martin's hand. "Aye, the Earl of Essex has told me as much. I've had a bellyful of Englishmen for awhile. I'll return to Ireland and after that - truly I do not know."

Martin squeezed my hand reassuringly and smiled. "Devereux came to visit me earlier. Our families are well-acquinted and the relationship between us is cordial. I do believe the earl is smitten with you."

"I think our good earl is smitten by any woman with a fair face and a shapely figure. He'll need to find more willing game to quench his lust."

"Only Devereux, Drake, and you know about my work for the queen."

"You can count on my discretion, John."

"Thank you."

"You're welcome to sail with me if you like. I'll gladly return you to England."

"A gracious offer, Mary. But my duty is here. As you say there is unfinished work to be done and my work starts here in Portugal."

"Ah, the mysterious Master John Martin is on the move again, full of secrets and keeping to the shadows to do the queen's bidding. Are you certain you'll be strong enough to do whatever it is that must be done? You'd recover from your wounds more quickly back home."

"I'll manage."

"The queen will want to see you."

"Yes, I suspect her majesty will want to see me. But I'm of little use to the queen if I cannot answer the questions she is bound to ask me. Our English house needs a good cleaning."

"I think I understand. Then fair thee well my friend. No doubt our paths shall cross again."

"No doubt they will my lady and soon I pray. And I swear by all the saints in heaven, we'll set matters right."

"Those are the words I long to hear John. Those are the words that bring my heart great joy."

After leaving Martin, my past again caught up to me. The Iberian sun was roasting everything in its path. I kept to the shade as I walked towards the waterfront, slipping in-between buildings and trees as best I could. Then I spotted a man resting underneath a fine, leafy carob tree with a bottle in his hand and a large floppy hat with a distinctive yellow plume lowered over his eyes. I knew the outlandish hat. I knew the man.

"Captain Guillaume Le Testu!" I called out.

The handsome Frenchman pushed his hat up off his forehead and grinned. "*Incroyable*, Mary!"

He jumped to his feet and we embraced one another in the middle of the road.

"You're looking fit, Guillaume."

"And you are a match for lovely Aphrodite, Mary."

"Do you charm all the girls this way, likening them to your warship?" I asked with a giggle. *Aphrodite* was the name of Guillaume's very fine Caribbean raider.

Guillaume looked at me perplexed. His English was good, but he didn't always understand my humor.

"I compare you to the goddess of beauty and love," he said in a wounded tone.

"Frenchmen, always flirting. Your lofty praise is too much for me *mon ami*. And yet, if we mortals do take after the gods, I'd much prefer to be like Athena."

He made a graceful bow and kissed my hand. "Athena the warrior princess it is then. Even better. She too was a beauty they say."

Like his famous father, Testu had chosen the life of a French buccaneer. We had first stumbled upon each other in the Caribbean off the Spanish Main near Columbia when he had tried to steal my ships from me. He had mistaken my ships for Spanish treasure ships ripe for the plucking and had attacked my two ships with his three. But I got the better of him that day. Our paths crossed a second time when I found *Aphrodite* bobbing up and down with her main mast in the water. I boarded Testu's corsair and took him prisoner, but the Frenchman won me over with his easygoing manner, gallantry and quick wits and we made peace between us. I agreed to tow his broken ship into the Port of Spain and then I set him free.

Testu was as handsome and as charming as my Hunter, or nearly so. His love of life and carefree spirit, his amusing nature and French flamboyance affected everyone around him. He was the most loveable of rogues.

"What brings you to Cascais?" I asked.

"I am with the fleet."

"What fleet?"

"The sixty freighters from France and the Hansetic League."

"I know nothing of this fleet. France and the League have sent ships and men to support England against Spain?"

"No, no. Our destination is Lisbon. We sailed to Portugal unaware Drake was here. Imagine our surprise when we made our turn into the Tagus and found an English invasion force sitting off Cascais! The English seized our ships. Outrageous conduct, a clear act of piracy as France and the German principalities along the Baltic Sea are neutral kingdoms! Surely you've heard some news of this?"

"No, I've been occupied with other matters. If France and the German kingdoms haven't allied themselves with Spain, why did Drake seize your freighters?"

"For plunder, why else? We carry naval stores including powder, copper and various other materials of value purchased by the Portuguese."

"Why did the English release you?"

"When Drake saw my name on a list of ships' masters, he sent for me. Drake and my father were allies as you know and dear friends. Drake released me and gave me money to make my way back to France. He is a generous man."

"Aye, your father and Drake took the great Silver Train together. A brilliant feat-of-arms men still talk about with reverence. For his dalliance with the devil though, your father paid with his head. Drake would indeed feel an obligation to the son of his ally and friend."

"And you, Mary, what fate has brought you here? Where is James and Jacob and that mysterious Turk of yours?"

I glanced away. Despite all his manly bravado, Testu sensed my sorrow. He took my hands and let me sob against his shoulder.

"Shh, shh, shh. Come, Mary, let us find a quiet place where we can sit and talk."

Nearly a year had passed since our paths had last crossed in the summer of '88 in Devonport where Drake and Lord Howard Effingham had been preparing England for war. I can't recall ever being more bored as we sat in port for weeks, waiting for the Spanish to appear. My head still rebels at the thought of the monotonous card games, the tedious hours of endless, heavy drinking and the dismal weather that kept us cooped-up indoors.

Testu had sailed from the Caribbean and was on his way to France when he put in at Devonport to repair one thing or the other on his ship. He stumbled into me by pure chance at a tavern near the waterfront. Following a long bout of drinking, Hunter and I returned to our room at a nearby hostel. The English navy back then occupied the whole of Plymouth and rooms were impossible to find so we brought Testu with us and both men fell into my bed. For years I thought I was barren until that one indiscretion. I can only suppose Hunter, knowing his seed was unfruitful, wanted a child with me and to that end he made Testu his unwitting accomplice.

Some might see our night of passion as an immoral act of debauchery. Shame on them I say. *Judge not lest ye be judged.* I saw our licentious revelry as a night of unselfish love, an enchanted night that produced a beautiful child.

Testu and I walked a little ways until we found a dusty, old tavern that served only warm, bitter ale and watered-down Madeira. As I told my story, I eased my sorrows with drink. Testu had heard nothing about the ambush at the mill or of Hunter's death. He patiently listened to me prattle on and on in-between my sobbing spells.

After I finished my sad story, I drained my glass, debating what to do. Testu was Aliénor's father but, for no particular reason I knew of, I decided not to burden him with this news, leastwise not yet.

Testu reached across the table and gently took my hand. "All will be well. You loved James. You lament his death and now you feel empty and alone. This pain will pass. Time is what you need. When you are ready, you will find your way. You must learn to find joy in life again. This is how we honor those we love who have passed on."

What woman in her loneliness doesn't seize the chance for a roll between the sheets with a virile, handsome man? Testu's tenderness touched me. When I leaned across the table to give Testu a peck on the cheek, our lips brushed, our mouths parted and we kissed. I had not felt a lover's touch in a very long time. I yearned to be held. I longed to feel a man's skin against mine, to feel his soft caresses. With desire building and racing hearts, we bolted from the tavern and took a room at the nearest inn with a bed that we could find.

Testu was sweet and gentle with me. But I was in the mood for more. Raw, unbridled lust is what I craved. I ripped off his clothes. I pushed him on the bed. I taught the frisky Frenchman a thing or two. I taught him how to please a woman unencumbered by inhibition and in return I took my time pleasing him, in satisfying his every carnal desire.

After we had spent ourselves, we fell back on the bedsheets exhausted and drenched in sweat and I rested my head against Testu's bare chest. I found comfort in his strength. His body was lean, smooth and wrapped in thick muscle. I savored the peaceful stillness in my soul as he stroked my hair and held me. For a fleeting moment, I allowed myself to feel soft and vulnerable.

I invited Testu to accompany me to Ireland as we lingered in each other's arms. Though I had said nothing about Aliénor to him, I decided it would be wrong not to introduce father and daughter. But he declined my invitation. He needed to return to France he said. He had lost the *Aphrodite* in a storm off Calais a few months back and had commissioned a shipyard in Boulogne, home to some of the finest shipwrights in the world, to build him another. He had sailed to Lisbon only to pass the time. He asked me to join him in a new venture to the West Indies after his new ship was ready and I agreed to consider his proposal.

When I felt Testu's lust rising in the palm of my hand again, we indulged one another in a second bout of raucous lovemaking. Testu held nothing back this time and in return I did nothing to stifle my screams as wave after wave of exquisite pleasure swept across my body. After Testu fell asleep, I quickly dressed and left the room to fetch my men.

"You look well-rested, Mary." Atwood said as I took a seat at the table. Atwood, MacGyver and Efendi were passing the time playing cards at a tavern on the water. "I'm glad to see it. We still need to fatten you up some."

"After you boys are through, let's round up the men."

"Where away?" MacGyver asked.

"Westport. Our work here is finished."

Atwood nodded. "Good. And then?"

"Damned if I know gentlemen, damned if I know. I was hoping one of you smart lads might have a suggestion."

Atwood cleared his throat. "Mary, you know you have our loyalty and you have the loyalty of the veterans who have sailed with us for years."

I interrupted Atwood with a wave of my hand. "I'll have plain speech between us, Jacob. Say what you need to say."

"Very well. There is talk amongst the lads, not much, but talk even so. Some worry your grief has clouded your good judgment. Some think you weren't bluffing at Belém. They fear you would have ignited the powder and killed us all had Martinez not agreed to your terms."

"I see," I said calmly, though in truth I was seething inside. I didn't like being questioned by my crew. "And what say you boys?"

"No one is better at playing a hoodman's blind than you, Mary."

I grabbed Atwood's tankard and took a swig of ale. "I've been known to bamboozle a fool or two. Tell the lads all is well. They're alive aren't they? Now finish your drinks."

We combed the taverns, gambling dens and whorehouses around Cascias to collect our men. A handful had disappeared, lost to love or to some new adventure or perhaps to illness or even to foul play. I know not the reasons why and didn't care. We stayed in Cascias for one more day for any stragglers and then put Portugal behind us with the first outgoing tide.

The voyage to Ireland was leisurely and without mishap. We sailed under fair skies with a bracing wind and made good time. After we dropped anchor in Clew Bay, I gave my lads sixty days' liberty, a generous stretch of time in port to visit friends and family as I needed time to concoct a new plan and for the first time in my life, I was returning to Ireland with my own family to see. The prospect made me both happy and anxious.

Our adventure with the English had been folly. I had lost men in battle for a cause not our own and lost a dozen more to disease or desertion. The gold we took at Belém barely covered my expenses. The voyage had been a disaster. My losses though were insignificant compared to England's own. Not long after we reached Westport, we heard the news that Norreys had returned to Plymouth with only half his men. Spanish infantry, cavalry and artillery, and squadrons of the Inquisition's Death Riders, had attacked Norreys's army relentlessly throughout his retreat to Peniche. Thousands perished on the road. Many of Plymouth's sons were among the dead and missing. Dark despair gripped the seaport hard we heard.

When Drake returned to England with equally tragic losses, shock swept across the kingdom like a tidalwave. Drake had found no treasure of any consequence in the Azores, but Admiral Bazán had found him. When Bazán's fast and well-armed war galleys appeared on the horizon, Drake was forced to flee. The Spanish hounded the English day and night all the way back to Plymouth.

The expedition's losses were staggering, incomprehensible, worse that the losses suffered by the Spanish Armada a year before. Drake had lost fifteen thousand dead and forty ships, all for a paltry one hundred and fifty Spanish cannon and £30,000 worth of plunder taken at Porto Santo in Madeira.

The military fiasco diminished England's power and left the queen's own survival in doubt. Her two finest commanders had been beaten. Drake and Norreys had flagrantly disobeyed the queen's wishes to destroy Spain's galleons to look for plunder. They say Elizabeth was furious. But, to my astonishment, neither man was disciplined for their insubordination.

I loved the queen. But England's woes were not my woes - except for one. Spain was now the undisputed mistress of the oceans. My men and I would need to find a way to survive in a far more dangerous world.

Chapter Six

lace one burden on a scale and one burden of like kind on the other and you start with equal portions. Add two burdens to the left scale and one to the other. Add three burdens to the left scale and two to the other. Inexplicably, with no warning, three burdens suddenly disappear from the left scale and reappear on the right scale. It matters not which way the scales tip my friend. We are all dust in the end, swept away by fate and time. The game is rigged. None of us can win. The best we can do is to choose how we lose. With cowardice or grace, with defiance or perhaps with nothing more than indifference. I've won, I've lost. I've won and lost again. If nothing else, they will say when I am gone: *she lifted herself up, she fought with all she had.*

Truly, I do not know if God will embrace me or cast me out when it is my time. Or perhaps in the end when we close our eyes we simply sleep forever. Such were my rambling thoughts as I rocked little Aliénor back and forth in my arms, wondering what joys and sorrows life would bring her.

From the window on the second floor of the Fitzgerald home, I could see the first of my men trickling back into town. I placed Aliénor in her basket and grabbed my sword and pistols. It was time to take to our ships, time to return to the open sea - though I was still uncertain of our journey and that annoyed me greatly.

Rest easy I told myself. Ride whatever wave God sends you. Not a very satisfactory plan, I know. But no matter what we do, I whispered into Aliénor's ear, the sun will rise and the night will fall and the stars and the moon will circle around the heavens forever and should we awake on the following morn', we pray it is to God's sweet song. Then I kissed my darling daughter's eyes and bid her a sorrowful farewell.

"Well?" I asked my officers as we sat around a table at our favorite tavern eating supper. Shaw had served us a splendid banquet of succulent duck, roasted pig and a hearty vegetable stew in a rich, brown gravy while a talented musician entertained us with his lute. "What say you all? Or have you let strong spirits and the tender affections of the fairer sex pickle your brains these past few months?"

We needed a plan to find new fortune. I had more clarity of what our options might be in the old days. I looked around the table for help.

Returning to the West Indies was the logical choice for us. But then there was the *Síol Faolcháin* to consider. Their power reached far and wide, as far as the Caribbean and perhaps even extended beyond. If the clan didn't yet know I was alive, they would soon enough. Though Dowlin and his murderous thugs never strayed far from my thoughts, I didn't have the money or the muscle to take on the *Síol Faolcháin*.

The Orient was tempting. The Portuguese were expanding the boundaries of their empire, sending their ships south around the Cape of Good Hope and then east to find faster trade routes between Europe and Asia and new territories to colonize. Portuguese traders willing to gamble were fetching huge profits from the Spice and Maluku Islands and from the Moluccas where nutmeg, mace and cloves grow in abundance. We heard stories of spice merchants reaping obscene profits - as much as four hundred percent. But such journeys across vast stretches of open water are fraught with untold perils and not for the faint hearted. I'd rather take my chances with an angry Irish clan and told my officers so.

Then there was the lucrative slave trade between Africa and the Caribbean. New investors in greater and greater numbers across Europe were putting their money into slavery each day. Both Queen

Elizabeth I and King Henry III of France had turned a blind eye to the wickedness of men enslaving men in favor of higher tax revenues, but I would have none of it.

The notion of plying the waters between the kingdoms of the Old World, scratching out a living as honest merchants, was repugnant to us all. And no one had any desire to sail with the English again.

Atwood picked Testu's letter up off the table and took a second look. "So, our friend Guillaume is in Boulogne purchasing a new ship and he is inviting us to join him in a private expedition to the West Indies. How did he know we'd still be sitting in Westport I wonder?"

"Testu and I happened upon each other by chance in Cascias," I replied as one of Shaw's boys, his youngest son, moved around the table, topping-off our tankards with ale. "He was with the French-Hansetic fleet, until Drake seized the fleet for England. I agreed to consider his proposal."

Testu's letter was all business, no playfulness, and there was no harm in passing the letter around the table.

"It would be good, Mary," Kinkae said, "for the Africans to return to the Caribbean for a time. Many have family in the islands. We've been away a long time."

I reached across the table for Kinkae's hand. "That is a strong consideration, my friend. No matter what plan we decide upon, I'll see to it that any man with family in the New World, or in Africa, can return home if that is his wish and I'll cover the cost of their travel. We are hardly penniless."

Kinkae squeezed my hand. "Thank you, Mary."

I turned to Henry. "I'm certain you and your lads would be happy to return to the Caribbean as well Henry. And I think I know the mind of Jacob and Michael." Then I looked over at Efendi. "What say you, my noble Turk? Any opinion Mustafa?"

Efendi shrugged his shoulders. "It matters not to me. Wherever we travel and whatever we do, there is bound to be a good amount of amusement with you at the helm. Certainly, none of us will complain of boredom. I'm game for any adventure Mary, east, west, north or south."

I smiled. "All these years, Mustafa, and you've never once asked me for anything for yourself. Truly, you have no preference?"

"My lady, where you lead, I follow. It has always been so between us and life is good."

"Zeus's balls, Mustafa," Atwood cried out and slapped the table hard in mock disgust. "Your words drip with honey and reek of horseshit! What seaman with any pride kisses his captain's arse in plain view for all to see like this? Truly disgraceful. I thought you Turks had more pride."

Efendi seemed to ignore Atwood and said nothing. But then he removed a stone from his pocket, reached into his sleeve for one of his knives and quietly began sharpening the blade against the stone.

Shaw's boy, standing next to me with his pitcher, put his fist to his mouth and cleared his throat to get my attention.

I glanced up at the boy. He was a stocky, good-looking lad with curly black hair and an easy smile.

"Robert?"

"Beg pardon, ma'am. Are you hiring more men?"

"We are always looking for good men. Why do you ask?"

"I'd very much like to sail with you. I want to see new worlds."

"You're just a boy!" Atwood scoffed.

"I'm nearly a man, sir!"

"A man you say?" Atwood asked. "A boy I say. Out of curiosity, what skills have you, Master Robert?"

"Well sir, I know everything about this tavern. I'm good at fishing and hunting game."

"Those are hardly shipboard skills worth bragging about, lad. Or are you looking to sign aboard as a ship's cook?"

"No, no, sir. I want to be a sailor, a soldier. The life of a gentleman adventurer would suit me fine."

Around the table my officers chuckled. But not me.

"I was," I interjected, "younger than you working a tavern like this, a tavern not far from here, when I decided to see the world. It is not all grand adventure young Robert. A mariner's life is hard and fraught with dangers. The days and nights are long and filled with boredom. You'd be far away from your Papa and your brothers for long stretches of time. Even the bravest, most skilled sailors die at sea."

"Rob!" Shaw's father cried out from behind the bar, unsure of what was being said. "You have work to do. Don't be pestering Lady Mary."

The boy ignored his father. "My mind is firm, Lady Mary," he persisted. "If not with your ship, I'll find another."

I offered the boy a reassuring smile. "I'll say this for you, you're an eager young lad. And well I know you come from hardy stock. Did you know, before you were born, your brothers saved my life once in this very tavern?"

The boy rolled his eyes. "I've heard the story, ma'am, too many times to count."

I glanced over at Shaw and winked. "Well, you best take heed of your father's instructions and see to your chores. You discuss this matter with him and, if you can win his blessing, then you and I can chat about your future. Run along now. My officers and I have matters of importance to consider."

Realizing he had a fighting chance, the boy broke into a wide grin before rushing off.

MacGyver was the first to sense my shift in moods, to see the sadness in my eyes.

"Are you all right, Mary?" he asked.

"Aye, why Michael?"

"We all remember Billy, that's all."

William Ferrell, Billy, the sweet boy from Castlebar, was younger than Shaw's son Robert when he joined our crew some years ago. With unthinkable brutality the clan had forced young Billy to betray me. His treachery had cost me dearly and had cost him his life. With one quick pull of a knife, the clan rewarded the boy by opening his jugular in front of me.

After some discussion, and more ale, we all agreed to sail on to Boulogne to rendezvous with Testu. The Frenchman had good contacts with the Hansetic League and with Dutch brokers, men who could procure all sorts of finished and manufactured goods, the kind that fetch the best prices in the New World - provided one didn't pay the *quinto*, the thirty percent tax imposed by the powerful *Casa de Contratación de Sevilla* on imports originating outside of Spain. Testu and I had already agreed we'd both contribute half of the capital needed to fund our joint venture and split the profits equally.

We left Westport a few days later with a lively, autumn wind rounding out our sails. I had my two battlecruisers, completely refitted and in top condition, and three hundred men - along with one handsome boy with an easy smile. Our ships were armed with thirty-eight great guns, a mix of long-barreled falconets and sakers mounted on rolling carriages and carronades, sixty swivels and enough muskets, pistols, swords, pikes, crossbows, grenades and knifes to equip a small army.

I took *Phantom's* wheel with *Diablo* trailing close behind us, savoring the exhilaration of setting out on a new adventure. The sky was brilliant blue, without blemish, and the sea did not fight me. I reveled in the cool breezes flowing through my hair and the warmth of sun on my face.

We made an easy passage from Westport to France. I took my officers into Boulogne, found a large inn named *le Porc-épic*, the Porcupine, and led them down a narrow staircase into a spacious cellar that had been transformed into a refined establishment favored by gentlemen of substance. I spotted Testu at a table off to the side sitting with his first officer, a Blackamoor named Maurice, quietly sharing a pitcher of ale. I've encountered many a strong seaman over the years, but Testu's first officer had been chiseled out of stone. Maurice was a *Cimarrón*, the Spanish word for wild or untamed. The Cimarron were once slaves who had rebelled against their Spanish masters and then fled into hills of Panama to carve out their own kingdom. When Drake and Testu's father raided the Spanish Main together, they formed a strong alliance with the Cimarron and it was the Cimarron who had led the two men to the Silver Train near Nombre de Diós in '73.

"*Une bonne journée à vous mon bon monsieur,*" I called out to Testu.

Testu bolted from his chair when he heard my voice, embraced me warmly and kissed me on both cheeks. "And a good day to you, *ma dame*. Please, please, sit and join us."

"*Je vous remercie.* That, I fear is the extent of my French."

"Pity. You breathe life into the words. I would be delighted to teach you my native language."

I looked over at Maurice and nodded. "Maurice, you are looking very fit. The years have been kind to you."

Maurice grinned. "It has been too long, my lady," he said and bowed his head respectfully. "Guillaume has told me of your brush with death, and your loss. Your sorrow is my sorrow."

"Thank you, Maurice. Gentlemen, I brought my officers with me so we can all become better acquainted." I turned to my lads standing in the shadows next to staircase and waved them over. "I believe you've met them all before when we towed your ship into the Port of Spain some years ago. You remember Jacob Atwood, captain of the *Phantom*, and Michael MacGyver, now captain of *El Rojo Diablo*. And these three fine looking scoundrels are lieutenants Mustafa Efendi, Kinkae and Henry."

Testu reached out to shake each man's hand. "I remember you all. Welcome to Boulogne my friends. Come, sit, sit."

"Do you," I asked as we took our seats, "still have that ship's cook of yours? I don't recall his name." Testu had an Italian in the Caribbean with him, a runt of a man and a sot with the bottle but a magician with food.

"Ha! I do. I can't seem to lose Antonio. I've tried to maroon him on one island or another time and time again."

"Aye, Antonio, I remember now. I'm jealous."

"I would be most happy Mary," Testu offered, with a subtle playfulness in his tone, "as your friend and ally, to share resources between us."

"Sharing resources you say? An excellent suggestion! I'm looking forward to seeing this new ship of yours."

"She's a three-masted man o' war mounting sixteen six-pounders and two long barrel stern chasers. She's square rigged for speed and weighs close to five hundred tons. She's very fine."

"Impressive. Did you keep the name *Aphrodite?*"

"No, she is the *Cerberus.*"

"*Cerberus?*"

"*Oui, Cerberus.* You know, the Hounds of Hades, the three-headed dog that guards the gates of the underworld, or so the Greeks believed."

"Ah, you're an educated man, well-versed in ancient Greek godlore?"

"I know only what I hear in the taverns, brothels and gambling dens around town as I whittle away the hours in port. Such is my education."

"I like the name *Aphrodite* better."

Testu made a fist and punched the palm of his other hand. "The goddess of love must amuse herself with other interests as we embrace our brother War!"

"I see. But if you dare compare me to these dreaded bitches of yours, I'll slice you open from your privates to your navel." My officers looked at me, confused. "A small joke between Guillaume and me," I explained.

"Fair enough, my lady. But if my fate is to be eviscerated at the hands of Ireland's very own Aphrodite, I will die a happy man!"

Atwood laid his large hand on Testu's shoulder. "I can think of better ways to die than at the end of Mary's sword. But tell me friend, you have two ships I hear?"

"Indeed. We also have *Vengeance,* a superb corsair. She has a few years on her, but she is sound and she is fast and her draft is shallow. Maurice is her captain."

"*Vengeance,* eh?" I asked. "I pray her name was not inspired over the little spat between us when our ships traded a locker's worth of iron."

Testu smiled. "Maurice and I have forgotten that awful day off the coast of Columbia."

I laughed. "Well, I haven't. Who could forget such a glorious day where a mindless, silly woman got the best of a man in battle!"

"You had the bigger ships and bigger guns back then," Testu said defensively. "And the winds unexpectedly shifted in your favor. Gloat all you like Mary, it was an unfair match."

I raised an eyebrow. "An unfair match you say? If memory serves, you had three ships to my two sir and you choose the time, the place and the line of attack."

"Ah, how true, how true my dear lady. I humbly concede these points to you. If only I had *Cerberus* back then."

Atwood howled. "No ship, no matter how fine, can conceal her master's pitiful lack of skill!"

Testu laughed good-naturedly. "You Scots are a cruel, heathen race."

I raised my glass. "To Captain Testu of *Cerberus* and Captain Maurice of *Vengeance*, we salute you. Have you taken *Cerberus* out for her sea trials yet Guillaume?"

"We have Mary. You will be consumed with envy when you see her flying across the waves!"

"That sounds like a challenge."

"I am always up for a friendly wager..."

"We shall see," I said. "We shall just have to see about that *mon ami*."

Though I had been cocky with my words, and it was true I had out-sailed Testu off the coast of Columbia, I reminded myself that only exceptional men survive the New World as brigands for very long. Testu had survived and prospered far from home in hostile waters for years.

With the pleasantries over, and after the hard drinking was behind us, we agreed to return to our ships straightaway and assemble our tiny flotilla in Boulogne's modest harbor. I had been looking forward to one night of wanton pleasure in Testu's bed, but I could think of no good excuse to delay our journey and had to put my unchaste thoughts aside.

My men and I lined-up along the rails to watch Testu ease his new battlecruiser into the harbor. His crew dropped the tops'ls as he edged his ship towards us. The man and his ship were impossible to miss. Testu, wearing his distinctive, ridiculously large floppy hat with the long, yellow plume cocked to one side of his head, worked the wheel of a ship painted in gaudy blues and bright reds.

As the flamboyant Frenchman waved and circled around us, his crew raised a string of outlandishly long pennants of every color of the rainbow from the forestay at the bow to the top of the fore mast, across the main and mizzen masts, and down the backstay to the stern rail. And then his men hoisted three flags, enormous in size, up each mast, adding more theatrics to an already absurd spectacle. *Cerberus* was like a miniature Nonsuch Palace floating on the water. When Testu came around again on a second pass, I caught my first glimpse of the three-headed figurehead mounted to the prow. The hideous creature was standing up on its hind legs, bearing its fangs and snarling at the world. I did not care for it. *Cerberus's* stern though was a work of art. Opulent, gilded carvings in the new Baroque style decorated Testu's cabin windows with colorful coats-of-arms set in-between. The cabin even had a modest balcony.

The pomp and circumstance were too much for me. Had I not known Testu, I might have mistaken him for bumbling royalty on his pleasure yacht or a clown, a dashing, fine-looking clown, but a clown just the same. Despite her colorful veneer, *Cerberus* looked formidable. Her design was similar to *Phantom's* and though she was not as sleek or as heavy, she looked like a racer capable of taking on all challengers. But many a handsome vessel are little more than flimsy, false pretenders. She would prove her quality or not in the crucible of rough weather and then again in battle.

With far less fanfare, Maurice then joined us out in the middle of the harbor with his fine ship. *Vengeance* was a two-hundred-and-fifty-ton battlecruiser armed with twelve great guns. She looked like she could hold her own. She too was painted in bright blues with red trim to match her sister. Adrestia, the Greek goddess of just retribution, all in white, graced her prow.

By comparison, my ships were bland. I had learned a hard lesson in humility many years before. I had learned the value of obscurity.

Our ships were unadorned and painted black. Everything above the waterline, planking, masts and spars, was tar black. We blotted out any colorful art work, we removed the figureheads and obliterated every decorative carving. We vandalized anything that made our ships standout. My men and I craved opacity. We practiced stealth.

And then a squat, two-masted freighter fell in behind the *Vengeance*. She was a portly, swaybacked, ugly little thing, a sixty-footer at most.

I cupped my hands over my mouth and leaned over the rail. "What is this third ship following us, Guillaume?" I called out.

"I named her *le Petit Cochon*. Fitting, yes? I won her a week ago playing dice against a rich nobleman. An earl from Nantes, or so he said. He rolled aces and I am the richer for it!"

I shuddered at the thought of sailing aboard such an ungainly freighter in rough seas. The *Pig* did have some bite though. Protruding through her gunports were the stubby noses of six three-pounders and I saw four swivels mounted to her forecastle.

"I might," I called out, "have gambled for a different prize, perhaps a galleon or a caravel. That old bucket is going to slow us down considerably."

"A small price to pay to bring more wine with us!" Testu said and laughed.

I waved Testu off, turned to Atwood and nodded. Atwood barked out orders to the lieutenants and the lieutenants turned to their divisions. MacGyver did the same aboard *Diablo*. Men moved out smartly. Six men turned the capstan to raise the anchor into the cathead while others manned the braces as the topmen moved out over the spars along the footropes to let out the sails. My men were a match for any disciplined crew on any ship. I soaked in the beehive of activity swirling all around me, pleased with what I saw.

The winds in the Channel were frisky and the seas were up. Six-foot swells and better smashed over *Phantom*'s bow. Atwood had the topmen let out more sail to increase our speed, but no more than prudence would allow, while Testu's crew spread out enough canvas to take the lead. I wasn't surprised.

We headed north in a single line for Amsterdam, hugging the Côte d'Opale, the Opal Coast, where we had cargo for the New World waiting for us. We drove through cold drizzle and patches of fog the entire way.

Amsterdam is an enormous seaport, teeming with ships and boats and trawlers and barges of every kind. It is the greatest seaport in all the world men say. I marveled at the number of vessels in her bustling harbor and the many church steeples and spires rising above the city.

We tarried in Amsterdam only long enough to claim our cargo and pay the brokers their due. We crammed as much as we could into the holds until the ships were filled to bursting and then we stuffed every nook and cranny with the smaller containers and boxes. Once our ships were fully loaded, we cast off the mooring lines and dropped our sails and made our way down Channel. Testu and I agreed to put in at Cherbourg to buy fresh victuals before setting out across the broad Atlantic. We entered Cherbourg's fine harbor the next day without flags or pennants of any kind. Testu gave his men three days' liberty and so did I.

I took advantage of the time. What I could not have in Boulogne was available to me in Cherbourg. I've never been shy or felt guilty about satisfying my desires. After a fine supper with our officers on our last night in Cherbourg, I discretely ran my tongue across my lips while Testu was watching and then excused myself to retire to my room.

"I have always heard you Irish are like cold fish in bed," Testu said after I rolled off him exhausted, but fulfilled.

"And I've always heard you Frenchmen are far better at seducing women than pleasing them."

Testu winked at me and laughed. "Ha! Lies spread by jealous Englishmen who would rather make love to their hand than to a woman. But tell me fair lady, what is your own opinion on the subject now, now that your heart is racing, your face is flushed and you are wet between the thighs?"

"How can I possibly judge a whole meal by sampling only one

morsel *monsieur*? So far I have no complaints."

Testu started nibbling on my ear, then slowly worked his way down my neck and to my breasts. He took his time trying to please me.

"I'll have you begging me for more," he said as he ran his tongue across my nipples.

I could feel his cock beginning to swell against my leg. "You, sir, are a resilient fellow. I'm impressed! But you best return to your own quarters now. The morning watch will be around to wake us soon. It would not do for the men to find you in my bed."

"But how can I prove my resiliency to you, eh?"

I kissed Testu on the nose and then kicked him off the bed. "I suspect you'll have more opportunities to prove yourself in the coming months - the journey is quite long I hear."

Testu laughed again and jumped to his feet. He stood before me naked without a trace of inhibition. His dark, smooth skin glistened in the candlelight. I couldn't look away from his muscled, well-proportioned arms and chest. His legs were long and strong. One glance at his fine physique would set any girl's heart aflutter. He leaned over me, cupped my left breast in his hand and pressed his body against mine. He slipped a finger inside me and forced his tongue into my mouth. I couldn't help myself and yielded to my desires. My body started grinding against his. I guided his stiff cock between my legs and started moaning when he drove himself deeper inside me. But for the crow of a cock just outside the window, he would have won me over.

"GO!" I said and pushed him off me. "'Tis later than I thought."

Testu left my room with a wounded look. I washed and dressed and hurried down to the waterfront and when I saw Testu had reached the city gates before me, he looked none too happy. A dozen of his crew had lost their nerve and had vanished during the night, though how they managed leaving the city without the night watchmen noticing was unclear. The city is surrounded by a high wall and has three gates with three drawbridges. All three gates were still locked. The drawbridges were still raised. We lost a full day while

Testu and Maurice scoured the seaport recruiting new men.

We departed Cherbourg with mid-autumn closing in, with ornery, biting winds blowing down from the north carrying a strong taste of winter. The Kings of Oak and Holly were on the march. We sailed in close formation, plunging in and out of frenzied whitecaps and fighting contrary winds. We made slow headway the first few weeks sailing south-by-southwest, slipping in and out of minor squalls. But we crossed no hostile sails and we lost no men.

Five hundred miles west of the Azores the weather turned fair and the winds shifted in our favor. We laid on more canvas and picked up good speed - nothing we could brag about later but satisfying just the same. The days turned warmer as we sailed south. The sunrises filled the mind with glorious color and the sunsets dazzled the senses with wonderment.

Forty days out from Cherbourg spirits soared when *Phantom's* lookout spotted the first hazy smudge of land on the horizon. I ordered one salvo fired to alert the others and then went below to the galley to fetch two tins of hot coffee and a loaf of warm bread.

When I returned to the helm, the sun was just rising over our stern, painting bands of fiery reds and mellow turquois across a canvas of deep blue. Scavenger birds, the first we'd seen in over a month, circled around our ship looking for scraps of food and off our starboard bow, I could see the faint silhouettes of ships taking form, sailing in different directions between the islands of Barbuda, Antigua and Guadeloupe.

"How are we this fine day, Jacob?" I asked and handed Atwood a tin of coffee.

"All is well, Mary. Ah, hot coffee and fresh bread, thank you."

"I fear the last of the jellied fruit has disappeared, but here is a dab of butter and I've asked our cook to set aside an egg for you, provided the chickens do their part. I see our good Captain Testu is up and about, strutting around the main deck like a peacock. Let's have some fun, shall we? Let's see what his ship can do."

We were fifty miles or so northeast of Guadeloupe by my reckoning with a gentle breeze on our starboard beam and a mellow current under our keel. Not ideal conditions for a racehorse like *Phantom*, but good enough. Our modest flotilla was sailing in a line with *Cerberus* in the lead, followed by *Vengeance*, *Pig*, *Diablo* and then *Phantom*.

Atwood grinned. "Aye, Mary! Be good to put that haughty Frenchman in his place. Henry, call your division on deck and get your boys aloft. Have 'em shake a leg. Drop all sail, extend the stuns'l booms and set the stuns'ls too. Our girl can handle it. I want *Phantom* soaring across the waves before I finish my coffee!"

Henry beamed with excitement. He loved a good race as much as any man, and he was nearly home. He called his division into action and led them up the shrouds himself.

Carib warriors make wonderful topmen. Carib are short, slight of build and agile and have no fear of heights. Henry's men deftly followed him up into the rigging and spread out along the footropes, working with one mind in nearly perfect harmony as they shook out the royals, topgallants and coarse sails, each one unravelling with a loud flap, on the fore, main and mizzen masts. Kinkae's Blackamoors grabbed the braces to trim the yards, then went forward to set the sprit sail and aft to adjust the lateen-rigged sails on the mizzen and bonaventure. *Phantom* lurched forward with impressive speed.

We sailed by *Diablo* on our starboard and then passed the lumbering *Pig* on our port and after we overtook the *Vengeance*, it did not take us long to nudge ahead of *Cerberus*. When Testu understood my intentions, he doffed his floppy hat with the long yellow plume to accept my challenge and used *cajolerie* to whip his crew into action.

To my utter annoyance, thirty minutes into our race *Cerberus* was close to overtaking us. Neither MacGyver nor Maurice had any chance of catching us and the poor *Pig* was barely a speck on the water a mile off our stern. Except in flat seas with little wind, no ship had ever equaled *Phantom*'s speed before. I could see Testu standing on the bowsprit urging his men on, trying to squeeze every knot of speed out of his racer.

He had skill, but so did I. I looked for Atwood and found him standing at the wheel.

"She's handling well, Mary," he called over to me when he saw the perplexed expression on my face. "Henry and Kinkae and the lads have been superb. Our girl is giving us her very best. She's holding nothing back. She'll out sail any ship with a good wind. But in these fluky, light breezes as we approach the leeward side of the islands, *Cerberus* has the advantage. I'm sorry Mary, I fear Testu has the faster ship this day."

Atwood was as good at driving ships as any man and I loved him with all my heart. But those were not the words I longed to hear. At times I thought him too cautious. I bit my nails, something I rarely did, debating what to do. A gracious loser I've never been.

"Humph!" was the only reply I could muster as I joined Atwood at the wheel. I paced back and forth on the poop deck, racking my poor brain for a new plan.

Then Efendi hurried to my side with a grin on his face. "You are pouting Mary. Pouting does not become you. If humbling French vanity is this important to you, let's run out the guns and fire a warning shot across *Cerberus's* bow. Testu will back-off then..."

Atwood howled with laughter and stamped his feet. "A grand suggestion Mustafa! I'd pay gold to see Testu's face as we sent a ball flying over his head!"

I stopped my silly pacing when an inspiration struck me.

"I know that look, Mary," Atwood said, wiping a tear away from his cheek from laughing.

"Mustafa, ready the men," I ordered. "On my signal, I want to make a hard turn to starboard."

Atwood stopped chuckling and shot me a warning glance. "God's wounds, Mary. *Cerberus* is too close to cut across her bow. She may not be able to turn in time and ram us if we try. Even if she turns with us to avoid a collision, we'll still be sailing on parallel courses. We'll still lose this race."

Efendi nodded. "Mary..."

I stepped in-between both men, I wrapped my arms around their shoulders. "Gentlemen, have a wee, tiny, smidgen bit of faith. If the wind *Phantom* longs for will not come to us, we must go to the wind."

We had already slipped past Antigua and I could see Montserrat off our starboard rail. If I strained my eyes, I could even make out the northeast tip of Guadeloupe ten miles to the south. Our present course would take us past the leeward side of Guadeloupe and then up around the south-east coast until we reached the grandest of all the Carib villages nestled in-between two mountains.

The breezes from the south then freshened and we suddenly found ourselves bucking against stronger headwinds. Both *Phantom* and *Cerberus* lost speed. We had to make our turn soon or not at all.

I took the wheel from Atwood. "I'll only have myself to blame if this goes badly. Look lively brothers!"

I glanced over at *Cerberus* as Atwood and Efendi barked out orders. I considered our tack and the trim of our sails. I considered the wind and currents.

"Wait for it. A moment more. Now! Hard over to starboard!"

Men let some lines go slack and pulled in others as I spun the wheel around. When *Phantom* heeled sharply over on her side, water spilled over her starboard rail, soaking me through-and-through.

Cerberus was sailing straight at us. I could hear her crew shouting and cursing. I could see them dashing about, frantically trying to turn their ship to port to avoid smacking into us. But once *Phantom* righted herself, we picked up speed and cut across *Cerberus*'s bow with plenty of water between us - or so I told myself.

"Mary!" Testu shouted angrily as he threw his arms up in the air. "Have you lost your mind?"

When I didn't answer, he shrugged his shoulders. "You are sailing in the wrong direction," he scoffed. "The race is mine and I'll expect a proper reward from you, a trophy, when I reach Guadeloupe before you."

Cerberus resumed her course south as we headed west. Testu had the shorter distance. I had the better wind.

Atwood moved to my side with a bottle and two tin cups in his hand. He poured one thimble-full of whiskey for me and another for himself.

"Jesus, Mary. That was close."

"Nonsense," I said in an uneasy tone and knocked the whiskey back. "Well, then again, perhaps we shouldn't try that again."

Atwood poured me a second and took a swig from the bottle. "Wise, very wise."

As I savored the warmth of the liquor spreading across my chest, I suddenly realized that I hadn't thought about Hunter once all day. I felt an odd sense of both guilt and relief. I handed Atwood the wheel and made my way to the bow to relieve myself at the privy, or so I said. In truth I didn't want Atwood to see me shaking.

Phantom found her stride and picked up good speed as we sailed along the northern coast of Guadeloupe. But after we rounded the northwest corner of the island and made our turn south, *Phantom* truly found her wings. We sliced through the waves at breakneck speed. I didn't know if we could win the race, but I was pleased with myself for trying, for gambling boldly. I'm a lioness in a jungle of men and I thought it good to remind my crew of it from time-to-time.

We reached the tip of the southwest peninsula of Guadeloupe in fading light and when we made our final turn to the north, we saw smoke rising from the Carib cooking fires. I had my men raise our battle flag, the flag with a red sea serpent poised to strike emblazoned on a field of yellow-gold, the mark the one-eyed Twin had burned deep into my flesh on those very same shores years ago, a mark the Carib knew well. I absently slipped my hand inside my shirt to touch the scar.

My crew lined-up along the rails, anxious to see if *Cerberus* had beat us into the bay. But we saw no sign of Testu.

Atwood started laughing. "There she is," he said and pointed. "There's *Cerberus* to the east! She's flopping all around like a mackerel out of water, trying to tack against strong headwinds."

Atwood had a keen eye. I could barely make out *Cerberus's* sails. She was fighting a stiff, westerly breeze, the same breeze spilling into our sails and speeding us along. *Cerberus* had no chance of catching us.

"Jacob," I said softly. "I want the main course sail brought down."

Atwood stared at me confused with his jaw agape. "Beg pardon, Mary? What do you mean "brought down?" If we hold this line the race is ours. We've won!"

But Efendi knew my mind. "Let the Frenchman have his pride, Jacob. Let him think he's won. We will need some minor mishap to keep him from becoming suspicious."

"Precisely," I said. "A cracked brace, a fitting that has rusted through and given way or a snapped line might do. Whatever you think best Jacob. Such misfortunes are not uncommon when a captain pushes his ship too hard."

Atwood chuckled. "I'll see to it, Mary, and no one will be the wiser. Mustafa, keep the men clear after I climb into the rigging..."

Another hour passed before I reached the shore. Testu was waiting for me on the beach with a broad smile. But he was gracious too and waded into the surf to offer me a helping hand.

"Mary, what a wild day you gave us!" he said as I took his hand to jump down off the boat. "I will gladly give you a rematch. Your turn to the west caught me by surprise. Dangerous, but clever. It is a shame *Phantom's* main spar gave way. The race would have been much closer."

"Congratulations, Guillaume," I replied with a sincere smile. "*Cerberus* is very fast and she has a gifted master, one of the best I've seen. Fine, fine sailing. You didn't win by much though so your prize will be rather small..."

"Just to survive the experience with you is a good day."

"Beg pardon?"

Testu winked at me. "I've heard the stories, the stories of a female pirate captain in these waters who will cut your throat for nothing more than an offensive glance."

"Ha! How men love to spin their tall tales. Rest easy my friend. I've given no thought to taking your head today. Hmmm, it is odd the Carib have not come out to greet us."

For the first time in our travels to Guadeloupe, Chief Paka Wokili was nowhere to be seen. I looked for Henry among my men as *Phantom's* second longboat drifted in.

"Ah, Henry there you are," I called out. "The chief is not here. Should we wait for him on the beach or walk on to the village? I see the Carib moving about. Nothing appears out-of-sorts."

"Come, come," Henry said and gestured for me to follow him as he started for the village.

Carib women greeted us with open arms and smiles as we walked into the village. The children flocked to me and pulled on my jacket. They liked the gifts I always brought. I had been good to the Carib over the years and they had been good to me. We had bled together as allies against the Spanish and I was, after all, the chief's adopted daughter. I was royalty.

We saw only a few young men in the village and soon learned from the women that Chief Paka Wokili had sent most of the warriors off to one of the islands to deal with a rival tribe. The Carib war party had left a week ago in their great war canoes but were expected to return home soon.

Henry led us to the chief's hut where two priests were sitting outside keeping vigil. The priests allowed us both inside. We found the chief lying on his bed, too frail to rise, with a young woman at his side, braiding his long, white hair. The chief managed a thin smile when he saw Henry. The woman nodded and left.

Henry knelt next to the bed. He kissed the chief's hand and I did the same.

The old chief was more bone than flesh. His eyes were thin slits and had lost their keen brightness.

"*Kemar*," the chief whispered and raised a crooked finger to point to a spear leaning against the wall.

Henry grabbed the spear and placed it in the chief's hands. The chief said a few words, then closed his eyes and drifted off to sleep.

"What was that all about Henry," I asked after we stepped outside.

"Paka Wokili has given me his spear."

"Oh, I take it this is a great honor?"

"Yes, Mary."

"The word *kemar* means spear?"

Henry smiled. "No. Kemar is my Carib name."

"Oh, and all these years I've only known you as Henry. Shame on me. I pray you are not offended. The men gave you the name Henry as a token of their respect."

"I am proud of my English name."

"Good. I'll address you by your proper name if you prefer."

"On the ship, I'm Henry. To my people, I am Kemar Wokili. Like you, Mary, I have my feet planted in two worlds."

"So you do. I fear the chief may not live much longer Henry."

"He knows. By giving me his spear, he has made me *ubutu*."

"*Ubutu?*"

"He has made me chief."

I smiled and bowed before my Carib lieutenant. "Your Highness."

"No, no, Mary. Please, please. You cannot stoop before me. You are my captain!"

"A chief outranks a captain, leastwise whilst I stand on your island. What will you do now Henry?"

"I know not, Mary."

I placed my hand on Henry's shoulder. "I know how much you love the sea Henry. Even so, you must think on this matter with care. This is a great honor. Only you can decide what is best for you and your people. Whatever decision you make, I am your friend."

"And you are my sister. Chief Paka Wokili has made it so."

I curtseyed before my lieutenant, before the island kingdom's heir apparent.

When Henry and I returned to the boats, we saw the lanterns of three ships dancing on the water to the east. *Vengeance*, *Diablo* and the squat, little *Pig* were slowly coasting into the bay. Along the shore men were busy pitching tents, starting the cooking fires and slaughtering our livestock for a proper feast.

After a wholesome meal of roasted meats, and fresh fruits and vegetables provided by our Carib friends, I gathered all our men around, Testu's men as well as mine, and laid down the law. The Carib had been my friends and allies for years and I would let no man jeopardize the sacred bond of trust between the Carib and me.

The Carib didn't much care for wealth. There wasn't much gold or silver or pearls in the islands for men to pilfer. I worried more about the women. Many Carib women are quite lovely and it was not unusual to see them walking about bare-chested or even completely naked. The Carib think nothing of public nudity. Our men were surrounded by temptation and I warned them all: any act of violence against the Carib would be punished severely and I reminded them of the great pox too. I had seen men go mad and die from the ravages of syphilis. The Indian curse is an ugly, painful way to leave this world.

Every man nodded that he understood. Even so, I knew we could not linger on the island long. Men being men cannot shackle the lust burning between their loins.

Several more days passed before Chief Paka Wokili's eyes closed on him forever. I like to think the old chief was content to let go of life once he knew his people would have a strong and noble king to lead them. And when Paka Wokili's warriors returned home a day later, none contested Henry's right to rule. No doubt the sight of four heavily-armed battlecruisers anchored in their bay cooled the ambitions of any rival.

I stood at Henry's side as holy men prepared Paka Wokili's body for burial. By Carib law, the priests carefully examined the body first, looking for any sign of sorcery or foul play. Satisfied the chief had died of old age, they sponged his body clean and then painted the body from head to toe in red. Red is the color of the gods Henry told me. Next the priests allowed the chief's six wives into his hut. The women combed the chief's long, white hair and applied scented oils to his skin.

Then men dug a round pit four feet across and six feet deep at the spot where Paka Wokili's spirit had left him. They lowered a stool into the pit and then sat the chief upon the stool. For ten days the village mourned. Women cut their hair and wept. Relatives brought food and water for the chief's journey into the afterworld while the priests tended to a fire around the open grave to keep the chief warm at night.

On the tenth day, as an enormous fiery ball melted into a black sea, men filled the grave with dirt and the mood of the Carib turned festive. A great banquet was held. The Carib took turns dancing over the grave while a bard sang the songs of their ancestors with music from drums made from hollowed-out logs, claves and dried calabashes filled with pebbles. And when the feasting came to an end, the Carib burned the chief's hut and all of his possessions in a spectacular bonfire.

Henry was crowned chief the following day. His coronation took place in the great council lodge of the elders where women and foreigners were forbidden. An hour later Henry emerged from the lodge washed and plumed. He wore a feathered headdress of many colors and a matching robe across his shoulders with a simple loincloth around his waist and wooden sandals on his feet. In one hand he carried the spear Paka Wokili had given him, symbolizing his great duty to defend his people, and in the other he held a fish, symbolizing his great duty to feed them. All bowed and cheered before the new King of Guadeloupe, of Dominica and of all the lesser, far-flung islands in-between.

"The king is dead," I mumbled to Atwood. "Long live the king."

"He'll always be simply Henry to me," Atwood whispered back.

The chief led everyone down to the shore where the Carib had prepared another great feast in his honor. We ate roasted pig and drink our fill of ale and wine while the women danced seductively around the campfires, swaying their hips and swirling their breasts to the undulating beat of the music. Carib and European men alike leered at the women like a pack of ravenous wolves.

In the morning we prepared our ships to sail. Henry's old division, nineteen Carib seamen in all, chose to remain with me and I gave them permission to elect one of their own to lead them. They chose a tall, stick of a fellow known as Fish, a nickname the crew had given him because of the sharks he had tattooed around his neck.

As the men broke camp and started drifting back to the ships with fresh victuals and water, I went to see the new king. I took Efendi and Kinkae with me.

Over the years, with Paka Wokili's blessing, I had created a web of spies in the West Indies. Kinkae recruited African slaves for me, slaves who worked in the homes of prominent men and who knew how to read and write. I paid these Blackamoors well to be my eyes and ears. My Blackamoor spies passed their messages on to Carib warriors recruited by Henry. The Carib moved from island to island with amazing speed and efficiency in their great war canoes. As I never tarried long in one place, finding me before the information turned stale had always been a challenge and it was not unusual for my spies to send three or four copies of the same message to me out to different islands. Sometimes my spies would simply mail me a letter. The Spanish run a very efficient post service across the Caribbean using packet ships and post riders. Even pirates are fond of mail and leave the packet ships alone. Efendi too had a crucial role to play in all of this. Among his many talents my Turk was a master at devising secret codes and using invisible inks.

I was particularly proud of my secret fraternity. Men and women risked their lives to help me and without them, I would have been sailing blind in the Caribbean - a good way to meet an early end. The new king happily agreed to help me restore my web of spies.

I took all my officers over to *Cerberus* next to sketch out a plan with Testu and Maurice before we sailed where I received a cool reception. Testu was in a testy mood and short with me. I took no offense for I had eluded Testu during our time in Guadeloupe. I had spurned all of his advances.

Bittersweet. Returning to Guadeloupe had been bittersweet for me. When Hunter was alive the island had been a special haven for us. We'd disappear together when we could, looking for some lovely spot to rest and play. Our favorite hideaway was on the top one particular mountain where the breezes are always brisk and you can see the Caribbean's shimmering waters stretching across the horizon in all directions for miles. Underneath this mountain is a stream that flows through caverns until the water spills into a ring of boulders on the side of the mountain, forming a natural pool, before cascading down to the sea below. Hunter and I enjoyed striping off our clothes and relaxing in the pool's cool waters until our desires got the better of us. Then we'd hurry to the mountaintop, lay a blanket across the grass and indulge ourselves in every erotic pleasure. And after we had spent ourselves, we'd share some bread, some cheese and wine and then fall asleep underneath the stars, wrapped in each other's arms. No, I could not share Guadeloupe with Testu.

The Frenchman thrust a glass of wine into my hand as I took a seat at the table in his great cabin. "Mary, we've been mired in this place for too long."

I nodded. "It couldn't be helped, Guillaume. The death of a king is no small matter."

"The chieftain of a small, inconsequential island little bigger than a rock is not a king."

"Chieftain or king, our interests are well-served by keeping a strong alliance with the Carib."

"When the Spanish grow bored with other matters," Testu said gruffly, "they'll turn their attention to the Lesser Antilles and crush the Carib as they did the Taíno, the *Borinquen*."

"Perhaps. Who can know the future? I only know today. Today the Carib are our friends and a powerful ally. Someday you may be glad that this is so. But like you, I am eager to sail."

"Good. Do you still intend to meet this Spanish entrepreneur of yours? What is the fellow's name?"

"Cortés."

"Ah, *oui*, Cortés. And this *caballero* has influence with the Spanish authorities you say and can arrange good prices for our cargo?"

"Quite so, Guillaume."

Testu sat back in his chair and took a sip of wine. "*Très bien, mon amie.*"

A peace offering. I nodded.

"Mary, once we conclude our business with Cortés, we must

plan our attacks on the Spanish. There are ships and towns to plunder."

When our paths had crossed in Portugal, when we had discussed the possibility of a joint venture, I knew this issue would become a quarrelsome one between us. Testu was more buccaneer than smuggler - and his hatred for the Spanish ran deep, down to the very marrow of his bones.

"Guillaume, *mon ami*, you saw with your own eyes what happened to the English in Portugal. Drake and Norreys squandered English might in their vain attempt to take Coruña and Lisbon. The cream of the Spanish Armada is intact. Spain's power at sea is nearly absolute. England won't have the muscle to challenge Spain again for many years I suspect. The game has changed Guillaume."

"But we agreed in Cascais. We agreed to raid Spanish ships and towns together."

"I agreed to do so only when we were presented with a good opportunity. Until that day, we can make fat profits from our cargo with far less risk. Not even King Phillip has enough ships to chase down every smuggler. But for pirates - he'll spare the ships and men to hunt those rascals down and he'll show no mercy."

"I can't believe my ears! *Le Capitaine Marie, maîtresse du Phantom mortel, que tout le monde sait sans peur, a peur des Espagnols!* You fear Spanish steel and iron?"

"Fear? No. I respect the Spanish, Guillaume. And I like to play the odds, weigh the risks, before I step into a brawl. I tell you this: with the English navy no longer a threat to Spain, Spain will flood the Americas with more soldiers and more warships to protect her possessions here. We are facing a far deadlier adversary now than before. We must be prudent and tread carefully."

"We shouldn't," Atwood interjected softly, trying to break the deadlock between Testu and me, "move with too much haste or press our luck too hard."

Maurice surprised me when he nodded to Atwood and turned to Testu. "Captain, my blood is hot for action. I long to plunge my sword deep into a Spanish heart. But I see wisdom in Mary's words, wisdom worthy of reflection."

"Very well," Testu said with a long sigh.

I rose from my chair. "Gentlemen, we are about to make a substantial sum of money and the profits we reap selling Old World goods in Europe will be even better. Perhaps when you feel the heft of the coins in your pockets you'll have an appetite for more."

With nothing left to be said, I took Atwood, Efendi, Kinkae and Fish with me back to *Phantom* to make ready while MacGyver rowed himself back over to *Diablo*. Once the crew secured the longboat, we raised the anchor, dropped our sails and followed Testu out into deep water to look for my old friend.

Chapter Seven

ortés kept two residences in the Caribbean. He had a lovely home in Santo Domingo on the Island of Hispaniola and owned a modest plantation, a *hacienda*, not far from Havana on the large island of Cuba, or *Cubao* in the Taíno tongue, meaning the place of abundant, fertile land. Cortés grew his own sugarcane and tobacco and raised his own cattle at his *hacienda*. He had his own mill, or *ingenio*, to process his sugarcane and he cured his own tobacco. Europeans gladly paid handsomely for both. Each year around August, Cortés slaughtered his cattle and sold the meat to the great Spanish treasure fleet before the fleet sailed across the ocean carrying unimaginable quantities of gold, silver and pearls back to Spain.

I decided to put in at Havana first. If Cortés wasn't in Havana, he'd be in Santo Domingo or in the Puerto de España, the Port of Spain, where he and I had brokered many a profitable deal.

Our voyage to Cuba was pleasant and routine. We sailed under fair skies with a hint of fall in the wind and I relished the drier air. A pod of dolphins entertained us for a time playing hide-and-seek in-between our ships and we passed many vessels from many kingdoms traveling in all directions. The West Indies had changed since my first voyage to the New World years ago. I had been little more than a girl back then and the Caribbean had seemed a vast and lonely place. Now the New World, at least what I knew of the Americas, was smaller and far busier.

We reached Havana two weeks after leaving Guadalupe under a warm sun and azure blue skies. Havana's fine harbor, known as the Puerto de Carenas, was covered in a forest planted thick with masts and spars and bustling with ships sailing in and out of every sort and size. Most were freighters but we also saw impressive warships flying the Cruz de Borgoña, a diagonal, barbed red cross embossed on a field of white, the ensign of the dreaded Spanish Royal Navy.

The citizens of Amsterdam are quick to boast that their city is the most important seaport in Europe but in the New World, Havana is the queen of ports. She offers the finest anchorage in the Americas and in shipbuilding, Havana surpasses even Amsterdam. The Island of Cuba is blessed with cedar, eucalyptus and mahogany, highly prized woods used in making the finest quality ships. Shipwrights around the world flock to Havana's massive shipyards to ply their trade. The work is plentiful and the Spanish pay in gold.

I signaled our tiny fleet to heave to and took a longboat over to *Cerberus* with Atwood and Efendi at my side. Entering Havana with all of our ships at once would only set the tongues of the local flibbertigibbets a-wagging. One ship would do and Testu agreed.

I stood at the helm next to Testu sipping wine as we sailed *Cerberus* into the channel under half sail. We took in Havana's largest shipyards nestled in-between the small fortress of San Salvador de la Punta and the monastery of San Francisco de Asis on the west side of the harbor. Even from a distance we could see the yards were glutted with work. Teams of men, no bigger than specks, were crawling over keels and ribs and sheathing the skeletons in planking using saws, mallets, planes, chisels and sheer brawn.

"Do you know the meaning of the name Castillo de los Tres Reyes Magos del Morro?" Testu asked.

I did but I shook my head, pretending not to know. Cortés had taught me much about the history of the New World. But men's egos are fragile things and sometimes need a little pampering.

"Castillo de los Tres Reyes Magos del Morro is the fortress on our port," Testu said and pointed, clearly pleased with himself that he knew something that I did not, or so he supposed. "The castle is named for the three Magi who followed the Star of Bethlehem across the desert to witness the birth of our Lord and Savior."

I kept my eyes fixed on the castle, watching the stonemasons at work. They were tearing down a tangled mesh of scaffolding standing against the north wall. The Spanish had nearly finished transforming the old, flimsy harbor palisade, originally built from only earth and fascines, into a mighty fortress of stone, mortar, iron and concrete.

"Jacques de Sores," I whispered.

Testu looked at me with surprise. "Pardon?"

"Jacques de Sores was the French pirate who burned Havana to the ground in 1555. *L'Ange Exterminateur*. One might say he built the Three Kings."

"*Oui*, de Sores, the Exterminating Angel. You know your history."

"A little. I wonder if Jesus, a man of love and peace they say, would approve naming a monument of war after the three wise men."

Testu removed his hat and ran his fingers through his long, black hair. "Ah, you are a philosopher Mary. I have no clue what Jesus would say if he were here. I pray I live to see the day when this abomination is toppled into the sea. But I am looking forward to our visit into town. I do enjoy Havana."

"This is not your first visit to Havana?"

"Not at all. I've been known to sample Havana's pleasures from time-to-time."

"I'm surprised Havana survived you," I replied, keeping my gaze fixed on the Three Kings. "I've visited Havana on occasion myself to look after my interests here. I once saw the Spanish treasure fleet preparing to sail."

Testu smiled. "A tempting target. But for the half dozen galleons sailing escort, I'd take the risk. Speak of the devil! Look Mary, look over there around the bend. My, my, what a beast!"

I whistled softly. In the middle of the bay sat the largest galleon I'd ever seen. She was a three decker, a behemoth, armed with dozens of monstrous guns. A single blow from just one of her cannon would send any of our ships to the bottom.

Testu had his crew drop anchor in the harbor near Havana's third fortress, the Castillo de la Real Fuerza, the Castle of the Royal Force, an impressive five-point star fortress constructed from huge limestone blocks re-enforced with iron beams. A broad moat surrounded the castle, making any frontal assault by infantry nearly impossible.

I dragged Testu, Atwood and Efendi ashore with me and we walked through the streets of Havana looking for Cortés. The town, soon to be elevated to the lofty status of a city by King Phillip if the rumors we had heard were true, was larger and far more impressive than the Havana I remembered. Havana had always been a charming, clean village. But the Havana I knew had been a simple place, an outpost in the wilderness with dirt roads and flimsy buildings made of wood and thatch. Now we strolled down a brick pathway next to a cobblestone street with concrete curbs and gutters. The buildings we passed by were handsome structures of stone and brick with pillars, arched cloisters and tiled roofs. We saw spacious parks with shade trees, flowering plants and ornate fountains. The proud and industrious Cubanos had rebuilt Havana into a place of great beauty that reminded me of Lisbon, but with more color. Cubanos love to paint their homes and shops, and even some of the grander buildings, in bold blues and vivid yellows with soft green, red or varnished wood accents. Havana is the Caribbean's most radiant jewel.

I knew the taverns Cortés liked to frequent and we stopped at each one. But when we did not find the Spaniard, we decided to look for him at his *hacienda*, ten miles or so to the west of Havana.

We walked down a long, dusty road in sweltering heat, passing hundreds of slaves toiling in the sugarcane fields along the way. The men moved across the land in a line using machetes to cut down the sugarcane while their women followed, singing unfamiliar chanties as they stopped to gather the stalks into bundles. They tied cord around the stalks and then carried the bundles on their backs or on their heads to nearby wagons parked along the road. The sugarcane fields stretched across the horizon like the ocean with islands of forest or rocky hills scattered about here and there.

We reached Cortés's property by mid-afternoon caked in dust and soaked in sweat. Cortés's home stood in the middle of an open field enclosed by a simple, split rail fence. The house was a plain, one-story building with beige stucco walls, a red tiled roof and arched wooden shutters and doors. A hundred yards to the south were small shacks used for curing meats and tobacco and beyond the shacks stood a dozen long, clapboard buildings set out in a neat row, used to house Cortés's slaves. There was also a barn with horses, cows, pigs and chickens roaming about and farther down the road I could see men and oxen in the distance working Cortés's mill.

An older man, as black as night with snow-white hair and a deeply wrinkled brow, stepped onto the porch as we approached. He waved us towards the house and smiled.

"Lady Mary, how good to see you again," he said in English as he knew my awful skills with Spanish. "Come, come. You and your friends must come inside, out of this horrid heat."

I embraced the old man. "Jesús, you are well?"

"I am Lady Mary, I am."

Jesús was a *Negros Ladinos* and Cortés's trusted steward. He was tall and lean and despite his age he had a muscular build from working in the fields alongside the *Negros Bozales* many years ago.

"Good, good. I'm glad. Is your master here?"

"No, no. *Señor* Cortés left yesterday for Trinidad."

"Puerto de España?"

"*Sí, sí.* From there he will sail on to Santo Domingo. I am sorry you have traveled all this way for nothing. Please, come inside. You must be parched and hungry Lady Mary. Let us find something cool for you to drink and I will see that you and your men are properly fed."

Always a gracious host, Jesús led us into the kitchen, the coolest room in the house, and served us a fine meal of smoked ham, fried plantains and *ouicou*, a favorite drink of the Carib made from fermented cassava. After we filled our bellies and quenched our thirst, Jesús sent a boy out to the barn to fetch Cortés's carriage and a driver to take us back to Havana. We thanked Jesús for his hospitality and returned to Havana in comfort, rolling past the army of slaves still toiling in the fields under a broiling, Caribbean sun.

Displeased our voyage to Cuba had been for naught, Testu was in a foul mood during the ride. I let him brood. I had accomplished what I had set out to do. Jesús was very valuable to me. He was one of mine. Efendi had slipped a pouch fat with gold coins into his pocket when Testu wasn't looking. Jesús would discretly spread the word across the island for me: Captain Mary had returned and had gold to spend.

We reached Havana just as the lamplighters were making their rounds. We combed through the inns and taverns once more, searching out other Spanish merchants who I had done business with from time-to-time. I introduced Testu to a man or two worth knowing, though none had Cortés's resources or influence. Cortés was the savviest of them all. He had the best political friends. On my very first voyage to the New World, he had introduced me to Gregorio González de Cuenca, the *Capitanía General* of Santo Domingo, and after Cuenca returned to Spain, Cortés secured the friendship of Juan de Tejeda, the *Capitanía General de Cuba* and the *Presidente de la Real Audiencia*, the highest court in the Americas, making him a very good man to know.

We returned to *Cerberus* before dawn, collected our ships and sailed for Trinidad next. Testu insisted. I let the Frenchman have his way as Testu had a price on his head after all and Trinidad was the one port in the West Indies where he and his men could relax and enjoy life's pleasures with little fear of the Spanish.

We cut across the Caribbean sailing south towards Venezuela until the north-west tip of Trinidad appeared off our port bow. Then we turned east and south again, hugging the tidal mudflats and mangroves common to the island until we saw the silk cotton trees and mud-plastered huts, called *ajoupas*, favored by the town folk of the Port of Spain. We coasted into the port's busy waters one-by-one so as not to arouse attention, slipped past the harbor's ridiculous fort - a sad, little shack with three measly field cannon, one crooked flagpole and a low, dirt parapet any child could scale - and found a quiet spot of water to drop anchor.

The Port of Spain is nothing like lovely Havana. Hunter had once described the port to me as a filthy pit of lechery, treachery and villainy. The port is indeed a cesspool infested with vermin and unscrupulous sorts who have no qualms about eating their own, or snuffing out a life over the smallest slight. But under an unwritten truce between the Spanish and the pirate chieftains, malefactors of the worst kind, the port is a safe haven for all. The Spanish tolerate a certain amount of lawlessness in Trinidad in exchange for a certain measure of peace in other parts of the Caribbean. Any infractions of the truce are dealt with harshly by the pirates themselves. Their terrible justice can be seen nearly each day in the bodies, men and women who did not die well, washing-up on shore.

The Port of Spain is where the slavers bring their human cargo from Africa to the New World. The Africans are led down the gangplanks in shackles to the piers where obedient *Negros Bozales* are waiting with brushes and buckets of soapy water. After the *Bozales* strip the Africans naked and scrub them down, the slavers herd the Africans like animals down the port's narrow streets to the auction blocks using whips and clubs.

I stepped off the longboat onto the main wharf with Atwood at my side and prepared myself for the ugliness ahead. The waterfront reeked of urine, sweat and excrement and the overpowering, pungent smell of rotting fish saturated the warm, humid air. Atwood and I had to push our way past throngs of seamen, laborers, tricksters, whores and unclean beggars to reach the marketplace in the center of town.

We found the marketplace crowded with people moving back and forth between hundreds of colorful tents and makeshift tables where merchants from around the world come to peddle their wares and services of every sort and kind. On the eastside of the square stand the auction blocks and holding pens, made of wood and wire mesh. The pens were filled to bursting with naked Africans. Business looked brisk. My thoughts strayed to Kinkae and my Blackamoors whom I had purchased from Cortés for a bag of pearls.

The Africans were not alone in their misery. Atwood tapped my shoulder and pointed to a long line of half-starved Irish men, women and children, whole families, dressed in filthy clothing waiting to be sold. These hapless souls were the victims of Plantation. I was powerless to help them and looked away.

We ignored the merchants and the evils all around us and made our way to our favorite tavern on the square. Part inn, part whorehouse, gambling emporium and opium den, the tavern offered all the essentials to men who had the coin. We found an empty table, ordered a pitcher of ale and waited for Testu and Maurice.

"Ah, there you are," I cried out and waved when our friends strolled through the tavern doors several drinks later.

Testu plopped down next to me and helped himself to my beer. "It is good to be home," he said, casting a glassy-eyed stare in my direction. My beer was not his first drink of the day. He smacked his lips and smiled.

I snatched my tankard back and made a toast. "To home," I said.

Testu grabbed the pitcher off the table and took a long draught. "To home," he said. "Any sign of this man Cortés of yours?"

"No," I replied. "I take it you and Maurice had an errand to run?"

"Errand? Ha! Yes, yes, we did indeed have an errand or two! We made, made, a quick visit to the *Pearl*."

I knew the *Pearl*. I had only been there once or twice before. It was a large shithole of a place on the waterfront, but a favorite of many mariners whereas our tavern, which oddly had no name, catered to men of substance, to merchants and entrepreneurs with money.

"Did you find anything to your liking there?" I asked.

"We did! We found old friends and passed the time rem, reminiscing."

"And might these old friends of yours be interested in any of our cargo?"

Testu tried to stifle a giggle. "I suspect not."

"Ah, fellow buccaneers then. That is why you insisted in coming to the Port of Spain, Guillaume. You wish to renew old alliances with rogues and cutthroats? I thought as much. Or perhaps some of these friends of yours are blessed with pretty faces and generous bosoms?

No matter, I'm here strictly for Cortés."

"Mary, you seem annoyed."

"Not at all *monsieur*. I hear thunder and rain. Let's stay, drink and be merry. But before we consider our next move, I trust you'll agree that we must sell our cargo first and to fetch the best prices, we need Cortés."

After supper, and too much drink, I took a room above the tavern. I paid thrice the regular rate so I wouldn't need to share the room with strangers. Heavy rains had been pelting the island for hours and for once I was glad not to be out on the open water.

A little after midnight, Testu found his way into my room. I should have shown him my displeasure and the door. I needed to be in Santo Domingo to catch Cortés before the Spaniard slipped off to another island or worse, returned to his home in Barcelona. But I welcomed Testu into my bed. I longed to feel his hands, his mouth and tongue on me. My flesh burned with desire and Testu had bathed, shaved and had put on fresh clothing for me, which made me want him even more. I stood and unlaced my shirt. I undid the buttons to my trousers. But when Testu kissed me on the cheek and started nibbling on my ear, as if I were some delicate virgin, I pushed him away.

"You must have me confused with one of your coy, little pets you keep hidden away in Boulogne, Guillaume," I said. "I'm a woman on fire, not some silly girl looking for her first kiss. I don't want gentle. I want rough and hard - ravish me. Take me like you've never had a woman before. Tonight, we are two wild horses."

Testu did not hesitate or disappoint. He stripped off his clothes, savagely tore my shirt off and ripped my trousers apart. He pushed me on the bed, pinned my arms against the headboard and mounted me. He kissed my mouth, my neck and my nipples and slipped his cock inside me. I arched my back to let him plunge deeper into me and when I pressed my breasts against his chest and raked my nails across his back, the Frenchman thrust himself even harder into me. He lost himself to reckless, raw lust without restraint and so did I. Testu knew how to make me moan. He knew how to make my body shudder with breakers of delirious pleasure and when I was satisfied, I gladly took my time to return the favor.

I found no sleep afterwards. My mind would not rest. I listened to the rain beating against the windowpane. I listened to Testu snoring. I stared at the flickering flame of a single candle sitting on the nightstand and let my mind drift. Something deep within me was amiss. I felt an emptiness, a void Testu could not fill. Perhaps no man could. The blame was mine I knew. I was and am deeply flawed. Testu was a witty, handsome and virile man. Women everywhere desired him. But Hunter was in my heart and I ached for him.

After wasting a week drinking and playing cards in Trinidad, Testu finally agreed to roundup our crews and sail for the Island of Hispaniola next. I thought about sending letters to Cortés before departing, but I was uncertain whether Cortés would wait for me or bolt if he knew I was on my way to his home. We set out under grey skies and a contrary wind.

After three weeks of hard sailing through unrelenting squalls, we shortened sail as we approached the Ozama River under the watchful eyes of the garrison at Fortaleza Ozama, an impressive citadel of thick stone walls, sturdy ramparts and tall watchtowers protected by batteries of heavy cannon. We had left *Cerberus*, *Vengeance*, *Diablo* and the *Pig* out-of-sight in a small, secluded cove several miles west of the city, a spot I had used before, and dropped anchor in the river. I took Testu ashore with me.

Santo Domingo, known as the Puerta de entrada al Caribe, the Gateway to the Caribbean, is the first city of the New World. This is where settlors by the tens of thousands from Europe and beyond enter the New World each year before catching packet ships for other destinations around the Caribbean. Santo Domingo is a grand city laid out in neat squares with paved streets, parks and buildings made of brick, mortar and stone. The construction of New World's first cathedral, the Basilica Santa Maria la Menor, where they say the great Christopher Columbus lay buried, was completed in Santo Domingo in 1540. Built with coral limestones, the cathedral is a charming blend of Gothic and Romanesque architecture. Columbus's son,

Diego Columbus, built the New World's first palace in Santo Domingo, a stately residence with many columns and arches named the Alcázar de Colón built from blocks of coralline.

I saw no evidence of the *ternado* spawned from the awful *huracán* of '73 as Testu and I wandered through the city. The beastly *huracán* had caught my men and I unawares out on the open water and we narrowly escaped with our lives. Santo Domingo was less fortunate. When we coasted into the port to make repairs, we saw the frightening power of a *ternado*. Vicious, twisting winds had ripped through the city, leveling wooden homes with their thatched roofs, uprooting trees and killing anyone in its path. Hundreds perished. After the *ternado* devoured large chucks of the city, the monster turned west, carving out a wide trail of destruction through the jungle.

We were greeted at the door of Cortés's home by a plump, Blackamoor woman with fine grey hair, kind eyes and a handsome face. Esmeralda welcomed me with a large smile and a warm embrace.

"¡*Capitána Maria, Dios es bueno*! You are alive. You've come home!"

Esmeralda was a Castilian *Negro Ladino*, as refined and as cultured a lady as any European noblewoman and like *Jesús*, she was one of mine. She had been the first to join my ring of spies.

"It warms my heart to see you again, Esmeralda. You are well?"

"Yes, yes. *La vida es buena mi Señora María*."

"Life is good. Esmeralda, this is Captain Guillaume Le Testu. He is a friend."

"You be French, sir?"

Testu nodded. "Yes, though the Caribbean has been my home for many years."

"*El Amo, Señor* Cortés, will be most pleased to see you, Lady Mary. I am sure."

I laughed and squeezed Esmeralda's arm. "Oh, my sweet Esmeralda, we both know that isn't true."

Esmeralda covered her mouth to hide her smile.

"Is he here?" I asked.

"No. He left this morning to go into the city. Rest assured, he will return for supper."

"With your permission, I should like to wait for him here," I said and pressed a bag of gold coins into Esmeralda's hand while Testu wasn't looking. The bag quickly disappeared into the folds of her skirt. Esmeralda was a special soul and dear to me. Over the years she had used the money I had given her to help her kind, never for herself. I had offered to secret her away from Santo Domingo and set her free once, but she declined. Her work in Santo Domingo was too important she had told me.

"Please, you and *Capitán* Testu will stay for supper. I will let the cook know we have guests. *Señor* Cortés has his daughter Elizabeth with him. She is a lovely young lady. I think you will enjoy her company."

"Oh, how splendid!" I said and followed Esmeralda inside.

Cortés's home was spacious and well-built. The roof was tiled, the walls were sandy brick. The inside walls were finished in *marmorino*, a popular Venetian plaster among the rich. The floors were made from expensive, polished stone. Cortés's home also had luxuries like glass windows, a water closet imported from Córdoba and elegant, bronze chandeliers. The kitchen stood apart from the main house in a red brick building with double stone chimneys. On the grounds behind the house were shacks for curing meats and tobacco and larger buildings resembling *barracas*, used by the Spanish army to quarter soldiers, to house his slaves.

Testu and I decided to wait for Cortés outside on the back veranda as the day was overcast and pleasantly cool. We played cards to pass the time while Esmeralda plied us with good wine and tasty treats to tide us over until supper.

I was considering the cards in my hand when I heard a familiar voice call out my name behind me. I turned in my chair to find Cortés standing in the doorway. The lean, handsome man I once knew had turned into a portly fellow with receding hair and stooped shoulders. Cortés looked at me with cold, dull eyes.

I stood to embrace him and kissed him on the cheek. He reeked of tobacco.

"Rodriguez, you look surprised to see me," I said and took his hand, the hand missing a little finger, and led him to a chair next to mine. I did not know if Cortés had heard about the ambush at the old mill. Perhaps he thought me dead.

"Yes, well, ahem, it has been several years."

"Indeed it has Rodriguez, indeed it has. Allow me to introduce Captain Guillaume Le Testu to you."

Cortés bowed his head. "An honor, *Señor*. The name Testu is familiar to me."

"No doubt it is," Testu replied. He stood and nodded but he did not bow or extend his hand. Testu's dislike of Spaniards ran deep. "My father was an explorer, a brilliant navigator and a gifted cartographer. He was well-known throughout the West Indies."

"Ah, that Testu. The commander of the warship *Harve* as I recall."

"*Oui.*"

"He and the Englishman Drake sailed to Nombre de Diós and took *el Tren de Plata* together in the great raid of '73."

"*Oui*, Drake and my father took the Silver Train."

"He died in Panama."

"Murdered, he was murdered in Panama. The Spanish took his head."

"Well," I said brightly and smiled. "Let us talk of more pleasant matters, shall we? I hope you don't mind Rodriguez, but Guillaume and I have invited ourselves to supper. Esmeralda is out at the kitchen and has the cooks preparing a wonder feast for us! Good thing too as I'm famished!"

Cortés did not return my smile.

We took our seats and then I heard a voice, a young woman's voice inside the house.

"*Padre, veo que tenemos invitados. ¿Es que no me presentara?*"

Cortés turned. "*¡Elizabeth! Por favor, vuelva a su habitación. Estos son socios de negocios, nada más.*"

A young woman, barely more than a girl, a striking beauty with large, sensous eyes, full lips and flawless olive skin stepped out onto the veranda. She wore her raven hair long, pulled over one shoulder. Instead of the traditional black farthingale favored by the Spanish wealthy, she had on a pale yellow gown with rose colored embroidery, cut to excentuate her trim figure. The style was bold and flattering.

She looked me up and down, unsure of what to make of me, and smiled. There was nothing shy about her. I instantly liked her.

I clasped my hands together. "Ah, you must be Elizabeth!"

"*Sí.*"

I turned to Cortés. "Business partners indeed Rodriguez! Elizabeth, do you speak English?"

"My English is good, *Señora*," the girl replied and curtsied.

"Wonderful. My Spanish is shamefully lacking. Please stay and grace us with your presence. Your father has told me many things about you and your sister Isabela."

"Thank you, my lady."

"Come here child," I said and stood to embrace her. "Let me have a better look at you. Your father and I are more than business associates, we are old and dear friends. I am Mary."

"I am honored."

"What an exquiste creature you are. You must have an endless parade of suitors knocking at your father's door. Is Isabela in Santo Domingo with you?"

"No, my lady. Isabela is married and lives in Barcelona with her husband and two children. After the fever took my mother, my father brought me here to the Americas."

I held her hands in mine and kissed her on both cheeks. "I am sorry about your mother, but I am delighted to make your acquintance. Tell me now, how do you find the New World?"

"It is beautiful and exciting. I am most happy to be here. I hope to see more of the land and the people one day."

"I share your opinion. I'm certain we shall become fast friends."

Testu removed his hat and bowed. "*Por favor, querida señora, sentarse con nosotros. Soy el Capitán Guillaume Le Testu, su muy humilde servidor.*"

Elizabeth simply nodded at Testu's flamboyance.

I caught the gleam in the Frenchman's eye. Men, always on the prowl for new conquests.

"Pay that miscreant no heed," I said. "He's French. You need know nothing more about this horrid rascal than that. Come, sit next to me."

Cortés winced, but wisely held his tongue. I could not tell if what I saw in his eyes was loathing or horror. I hardly cared.

Esmeralda served us one of my favorite meals. She brought us plates heaped high with slices of delicious smoked pork, roasted slowly on the spit and crisp around the edges, baked plantains, Spanish rice and *boniatos*. And for desert we had sweet chocolate, or *chocolātl* in the Aztec tongue, served warm over slices of banana, prickly pear and chunks of pineapple. We ate and drank to excess while we exchanged harmless chit-chat. After we finished our meals, Esmeralda instructed two household servants, young girls, to clear the table while she went around the veranda to light the lanterns, then she served us after-dinner cordials from a fancy, silver tray.

"Rodriguez," I said, "you've been unusually quiet this evening. What troubles you?"

"Why nothing, Mary. My day in the city was long. I had to review a thick stack of accounting records, a most tedious, unpleasant task."

"Has the year been profitable for you?"

"I have seen better years. I've experienced only one or two that were worse. The war between Spain and England should be to my advantage but, alas, the war has cost me business."

"Well, perhaps your luck is about to change. Our ships are nearby and loaded down to the scuppers with European cargo of high quality. I'm here to increase your wealth."

"You said ships?"

"Aye, ships. Five in all to be precise."

Cortés smiled despite himself. "Elizabeth, it is time for you to retire. Lady Mary and I have import matters to discuss."

"¡Pero el padre!"

"*Ningún argumento, buena hija la noche.*"

Elizabeth reluctantly rose from the table and nodded obediently to her father. "Lady Mary, Captain Le Testu, I bid you both a good night. I very much enjoyed this evening. With all sincerety, I pray we meet again."

"I promise we shall Elizabeth," I said. "You are a delightful young lady. *Tu padre debe estar muy orgulloso.*"

"*Muchas gracias, mi Señora.*"

Testu placed his hand over his heart. "*Mademoiselle*, you have bewitched me, you have stolen my heart," he said smoothly, then knelt before her and kissed her hand.

Most young women would have giggled or blushed from the handsome Frenchman's exaggerated attentions. Instead, Elizabeth responded with maturity and poise. She offered Testu a confident smile, nodded politely and walked off without a word.

"Circumstances have changed, Mary," Cortés said gruffly as he watched his daughter disappear into the house. "I trust you have heard of Spain's great victory over the English navy? Drake has finally been beaten. I dare say Spain has shamed Drake and chastened England. I have seen the official dispatches from Madrid. The English suffered horrendous losses. Half the English fleet was destroyed. Thousands of Englishmen perished."

I was quick to show the Spaniard my displeasure. "Save your Spanish haughtiness for some upstart less worldly-wise than me, Rodriguez. Spare me you condescending tone. I was with the English fleet when Drake and Norreys invaded Spain and Portugal. I would hardly say the Spanish defeated the English. The English beat themselves."

"A distinction without significance. Spain's power is unequaled. England is finished. She is no longer a threat to Spain. The French are weak. The German and Italian kingdoms are divided and fight amongst themselves. Warships, soldiers and arms are pouring into New Spain. The treasure ships sail in convoy now. They are well-protected by the great war galleons. The oceans belong to Spain."

"England, finished you say?" I scoffed. "I hardly think so or

Phillip would have landed his armies in London by now. No matter, I do not wish to quarrel with you, or to be lectured by you. I have no care for treasure ships or galleons. I've not returned to the Caribbean to make war on the Spanish. I'm here to trade."

Cortés offered me a cocky smile. "The king is determined to put an end to all smuggling, privateering and piracy. You will not find the West Indies very hospitable to your kind these days. Spain's power and glory are ascending. Spain has made the Caribbean her *mare nostrum*. You should return to Ireland, Mary, while you still have your head."

I was sorely tempted to reach across the table and grab Cortés by the throat. He thought he held the upper hand. He did not.

I smiled sweetly at him. "I'm grateful to you, sir, for you concern about my welfare. I'll consider all you have said but, for now, I have cargo to sell and you will help me sell it."

Cortés lit a cigar with a certain smugness in his demeanor. He offered one to Testu and Testu accepted. "You should bring your cargo through the *Casa de Contratación* and pay the *quinto* like the other merchants wishing to import goods into the Americas," he said, pausing to blow a ring of smoke through the air. "To do otherwise is far too risky these days."

I stood to stretch my legs. Cortés flinched when I walked behind him.

"Have you forgotten your pledge to me?" I asked, as I circled around the table a second time. I could see the beads of sweat forming across his brow.

Cortés shifted uncomfortably in his chair. "No, Mary. No, I have not forgotten. But the world has changed as I have said."

"Medina Sidonia returned to Spain a broken man with a broken fleet in '88. Drake returned to England after his disastrous voyage more or less the same way. You say Spain has won? No, my friend. Power ebbs and flows like the tide. Today Spain is first among kingdoms, I grant you this. But she is surrounded by jealous rivals, resilient challengers who perhaps are not as weak as you suppose. Tomorrow England or France, or perhaps the Ottoman Empire, will eclipse Spain's glory. But I'm indifferent to such matters. My allegiance is to myself and to my men. My only interest is surviving and prospering where I can."

I stopped behind Cortés. I rested my hands on his shoulders. I could feel his muscles tense. I leaned close to his ear.

"I spared your life once, Rodriguez, despite your poor judgement in your choice of friends. Surely you remember? Old Havana, the warehouse? A severed finger? Do not make me regret my mercy."

Testu stared at me, confused. He knew nothing about the history between Cortés and me, or of Cortés's treachery.

Cortés chuckled nervously. "Of course, of course I will help you with the *Casa*, Mary, if that is your wish. I do not overstate the risks though. Hispaniola will soon have a new *capitán-general*. A man named Lope de Vega Portocarrero is on his way to Santo Domingo from Spain. I hear he is immune to corruption. He accepts no favors or gratuities. Men say he will enforce the king's will with an iron fist."

"We've had to dodge and weave around incorruptible officials before. He'll be a nuisance, nothing more. The New World is a very large place Rodriguez. Tell me though, I am curious. You've not asked me about Hunter."

Cortés betrayed himself when he glanced down at his shoes and failed to answer.

"Ah, so you know."

"I have, I have heard talk Mary. Some say James was killed in Ireland by your enemies. That is all I know."

"By enemies you mean the clan."

"*Sí.* Yes, the clan."

"And Don Villanueva? Where is he?"

"I have not seen him. I have not heard from him. Villanueva left the islands years ago and has not returned."

"You mean he fled like a dog once he learned I had survived the Twins."

Cortés craned his neck around to look up at me, no doubt fearing I held a knife in my hand. "Yes, Mary, he fled for his life."

Testu cleared his throat. "This," he said as he blew his own ring of smoke into the air, "is a most excellent cigar."

We left Cortés at his home, unbloodied, and returned to *Phantom* with a plan to sell our cargo. Testu wisely asked me no questions about the past Cortés and I shared.

Two days later Cortés delivered - as I knew he would. He quietly gathered several investors at his home and held a private auction on my behalf. We sold off our pots and pans and tools, our bolts of silk and fine linens. We sold off our finely crafted furniture, our French dresses and German muskets and our finished metalwork of every sort and size. We sold it all and fetched excellent prices though we had no cause to celebrate, not yet. The risk remained with Testu and me until we placed the goods into the buyers' hands. I agreed to offload half of our cargo on the shores of Hispaniola and then sail on to Cuba to deliver the rest, though the additional run to Cuba would cut into our profits with more bribes to pay. No matter. The tax-free profits Testu and I would reap would make the stingiest merchant smile.

The following day Testu and I returned to *Phantom* and then sailed a little ways west to rejoin our small squadron. When I saw Cortés with his three buyers ride up to the beach on their horses, I went ashore to greet them just as night began to fall.

Cortés and the buyers had brought pack animals, two-wheeled carts and dozens of men with them. The laborers planted torches in the sand and then brought rafts hidden away in the jungle down to the water. They started rigging the rafts with the rope I had brought ashore, tied at the other end to our ships, while my men moved our cargo up on deck. The air was sticky and humid with not even a whiff of breeze. I hadn't lifted a finger as I watched but was still soaked in sweat.

After my men pulled the rafts back the ships and loaded them down with cargo, they waved lanterns back and forth to signal the men on shore. Cortés's men carefully reeled the rafts back in with rope, tackle and brawn. They went about their work efficiently, quietly, bringing three or four rafts in at a time. After they removed the crates, barrels and boxes and stacked them neatly along the beach, my men pulled the empty rafts back across the water to load more cargo. The work was cumbersome and slow but safer than trying to sneak tons of material through port with prying eyes all around.

After the buyers inspected the cargo and were satisfied with the quality and quantity of their purchases, their men loaded the containers onto mules or into carts for the journey back to the warehouses hidden deep in the jungle where they'd break the bulk cargo down later for resale. Some goods would be sold in the city and some would be transported on the small coasters favored by the local smugglers to other islands.

I stood next to Cortés watching him meticulously record each item accepted and the price to be paid into his ledger. Standing next to us was an agent of the *Casa* to validate his take. The agent had already prepared false tax stamps for the merchants. After the last of the cargo was brought on shore and accepted, Cortés tallied up the final numbers and even with his cut and the bribes, our profits were obscene.

The buyers, I never knew their names, paid me with chests of gold and silver. One gentleman paid in part with a roll of banknotes issued by the House of Mendès and that was fine by me.

As the caravan disappeared into the palm trees with the first shafts of golden light streaking across the sky, I turned to Cortés and the buyers. "Well gentlemen," I said as I shook each man's hand, "it has been a pleasure. I trust each of you is satisfied with your purchases and I look forward to future business with you. I bid you each a good day."

"The pleasure is mine," one of the Spaniards replied and kissed my hand. "You delivered exactly what you promised. Rodriguez, I look forward to participating in more auctions where Lady Mary is the seller. Farewell dear lady."

The other two merchants nodded in agreement and then all three men walked over to their horses. Cortés turned to join them.

"My dear Rodriguez," I said and grabbed his arm. "Where are you going?"

Cortés looked at me with a pained expression on his face. "I beg your pardon?"

"We have cargo to deliver in Old Havana."

"All the necessary arrangements have been made, Mary. You do not need me in Cuba."

"Oh, but I do you silly goose. I'll feel much more secure with you standing by my side."

"But, Mary, I..."

"Hush now, Rodriguez," I said and took his hand, the hand missing a little finger. "I understand your reluctance. I understand your reluctance full well. We both have painful memories of Old Havana seared deep into our souls. I no less than you. Indeed, my memories are far worse. The longboat is waiting for us. I've already written letters to Esmeralda and to Elizabeth to let them know you'll be away for several weeks, but I assured them both that you'll be in good hands. The buyers can deliver the letters to your house as they return your horse. Shall we? I do insist..."

Old Havana. Some thirty-five miles south of new Havana as the crow flies is Old Havana. Old Havana is where the first settlors to Cuba came to build their golden city. But nature had cheated Old Havana. She did not have Havana's Puerto de Carenas, the splendid bay on the north side of the island. After discovering the New World's vast riches, the Spanish needed a defensible, deep-water port from which to launch their great treasure fleets back to Spain and abruptly abandoned Old Havana for Havana.

Old Havana is where the Twins, flying the colors of the Spanish Royal Navy, had ambushed my men and took my ships while I was recuperating in Guadeloupe from one malady or the other. Old Havana is where the Twins had murdered Thomas Gilley, a man dear to me like a father, along with Benjamin Green, Albertus Fox and

Hadley Ferguson - all because of my wicked, unbridled arrogance. Old Havana is where I exacted my revenge on Cortés for his part in the ugly deed. Hunter, Atwood and Efendi had very much wanted to snuff out Cortés's life. But I did not think Cortés evil and so I let him live. I took his little finger instead.

I would have preferred not to return to Old Havana. My wounds were deep and still raw despite the years that had passed. But the sleepy, little fishing village had a good anchorage and serviceable piers and was ideal for smuggling goods in and out of Cuba.

We made a quick and easy passage from Santo Domingo to Old Havana. I rarely saw Cortés. He stayed below and kept to his hammock for most of the journey fearing, I suppose, that Atwood or Efendi might do him harm. He may have been right to think so. The big Scot especially made no attempt to hide his contempt for the Spaniard.

We entered Old Havana's peaceful waters in light winds, floating by several dozen fishing boats of modest size. While *Cerberus* and the rest furled sail and snuggled up to the piers, I kept *Phantom* out in deeper water to stand watch and went ashore with Cortés and twenty men in a longboat.

As the crews secured the ships to the pilings with mooring lines and fashioned gangplanks to offload our cargo, a wave of scruffy, barefooted boys in shabby clothing, looking to make a coin or two, rushed towards the waterfront to offer their services. I stood off a ways under the shade of a small shack with Cortés at my side, taking in all the commotion around us. When two carriages arrived from Havana with agents for the buyers, Cortés took out his ledger and went to work.

The mule train hired by the buyers was late so we moved our contraband into the storehouses along the wharf, or what was left of them. The Spanish had abandoned the buildings long ago, leaving them to rot. I had interrogated Cortés in one of them.

The exchange went smoothly as before and after the agents accepted the last pallet, they paid us in in chests of gold and silver and pearls. With our business concluded, the local magistrate stopped by to introduce himself and to collect his end, an exorbitant sum of money I thought but, all-in-all, I was pleased with our final take.

I had my men pass out silver coins to the village boys and then pulled Cortés aside. "Rodriguez, your fair share is in that small chest over there against the door. You did well and I'm paying you in full. The same arrangement as we had before. The gentlemen from Havana have agreed to take you with them. You'll travel in comfort back to your *hacienda*."

Cortés looked at me surprised. He assumed I suppose that I would cheat him out of his commission. I took him by the arm and led him to the chest. I knelt down and opened the lid for him, to show him the gold bars stacked inside.

"Eh, *mucho gracias* Mary."

"You're welcome Rodriguez. This is how partners respect each other and keep trust between them. These first shipments are a good start, but I intend to do more. The Twins are dead - but the clan is alive and well. I suspect there will be more killings in the days ahead. You must stay clear of all of it."

I looked for Efendi, found him teaching the village boys a wrestling move and I waved him over. "Mustafa, please, come join us."

Cortés could see the malice in Efendi's eyes as he approached and took a step backwards. I rested my hand on his shoulder to calm him.

"Rodriguez, I've learned a very hard lesson and will not be the victim of betrayal a second time," I said harshly. "Swear to me again that I have your unwavering loyalty. Make me believe your words are true."

I could see Cortés's lips begin to quiver. I could see the tears pooling in his eyes.

"Yes, yes, Mary. Yes, you have my loyalty. I swear on my life before God that you can trust me. I too have learned from my mistakes."

I nodded. "Good, good. I believe you. Mustafa, show Rodriguez that I will hold him to his oath."

I had barely finished my sentence when Efendi, quicker than the eye can see, whipped out one of his throwing knives tucked inside his sleeve and flung it past Cortés's nose. The blade buried itself with a dull thwack deep into the center of a door to a toolshed a good thirty paces away.

"I want no harm to come to you, Rodriguez. But there will be consequences for any who betray me, even if I'm not alive to savor the retribution that I swear will follow. And if Mustafa falls with me, I have others on retainer - nameless, faceless souls, men and women, who'll set matters right. Some are Carib, some are Negro slaves. You won't know who your killer is until they step up behind you and slit your throat. Even from the grave, my reach will be long. Do you understand?"

Cortés nodded vigorously.

"Good. Fare thee well then Rodriguez. I expect you to look for goods and materials we can take back to Europe with us. As always, I want the things that will fetch the best profits. Hardwoods, tobacco, sugar, spices and the like."

Cortés bowed his head and kissed my hand before he turned away. He tucked his chest of gold underneath his arm and hurried to the carriage where the men from Havana were waiting.

Before we departed Cuba, I invited Testu and Maurice and all my officers to join me in my great cabin. The men sat quietly around the table waiting for me to speak, listening to the ripples of water slapping against the rudder and to the pintles grinding in their gudgeons. Up on deck, we could hear *Phantom's* crew preparing the ship to sail. I raised my arm and pointed to twelve, large chests filled with treasure stacked against the cabin's fore bulkhead.

"Thank you for coming," I said as I went around the table to pour each man a glass of wine as was my custom. "We did exceedingly well, even with the higher costs of doing business. Guillaume, six of those chests belong to you, you can pick which six."

Testu smiled. "What is the take?"

I turned to Atwood. He had a gift with numbers. "Jacob?"

"Values of gold, silver and pearls fluctuate of course, but I think our profit is roughly about twelve thousand pounds sterling, give or take."

"Gross or net?" Testu asked.

"Net of course. Mary has already seen to the expenses."

Testu whistled. "My, my. This is most excellent. Mary, you predicted this would be a good day and *voilà!*"

"I'm glad you are pleased," I replied. "I've sent Cortés home with instructions to procure new cargo for the voyage home. We've always made even heftier profits selling New World goods to the Old World."

Testu stood and walked over to the cabin's open windows to watch two seabirds squawking at each other, fighting over the table slops the cook had just pitched over the side. The rest of us waited for him to speak.

Testu turned and smiled. "A good day. But I have men who long for the hunt. They are accustomed to more Mary."

"More than a share of six thousand pounds sterling?"

"*Oui.*"

"It is hard for a man to want more from life when he is dead."

"Everything has risk. My men are wolves, not sheep."

I grit my teeth. "I see no sheep sitting around this table Guillaume."

"Ouch! The lioness's claws are sharp."

"Why look for trouble when there is a fortune to be had in smuggling?"

Testu pointed to fore bulkhead. "Imagine taking a galleon carrying a hundred chests like those."

"Imagine *Cerberus* resting at the bottom of the sea with all hands, or with a Spanish noose around your neck."

Testu tried to disarm me with one of his boyish grins. "I prefer to imagine Spanish prisoners standing before me in chains with a hundred chests of gold resting at my feet."

"Your mind is firm on this matter, Guillaume? You intend to raid Spanish ships and towns?"

"Yes."

Atwood cleared his throat. "Our lads will follow you whatever you decide Mary. That I can promise."

I nodded. "Jacob, your words warm my heart."

The sun was hot, the breezes warm. I stood on the quarter deck at the fore rail drenched in sweat, pacing back and forth, weighing matters in my head as *Phantom* and *Diablo* bobbed up and down tethered together. I stopped to consider the men assembled on the deck below me.

"Lads," I said, "I'm prepared to return to Ireland and issue every man his proper share from the profits we've made. I'll wager your share will be a goodly amount more than any of you could earn in a year by other means. When you signed on with me, you signed aboard this ship knowing that we'd be smuggling goods into the West Indies. Now Captain Testu proposes we turn away from smuggling and ready our ships for action. He is setting out to prowl the Caribbean and take whatever plunder he can find. Risky business that is. In my hand I hold a commission from the Queen of England. This document gives us the legal authority to raid Spanish towns and ships. England and Spain are still at war. But make no mistake: the Spanish punish privateers, buccaneers and pirates the same. We'll all dance the hangman's jig on the gallows if we're caught."

A stillness settled over both ships as I paused to let each man absorb my words. "Well now," I continued. "Are we buccaneers or are we smugglers? One is more lucrative but more dangerous than the other. Not a decision to be made on a whim. The choice is yours to make. Talk amongst yourselves. I would know your thoughts before we sail."

"What," a faceless voice in the ranks cried out, "if we can't all agree my lady?"

"I'm prepared to accept the vote of the majority. If the vote is to sail with Captain Testu, then we sail with Testu and I'll release any man who is opposed."

Chapter Eight

There was a time, not so long ago, when I eagerly embraced the thought of war. No more. Perhaps I had seen too much blood. Or perhaps having a daughter had changed me. I know not the reasons why but when my men overwhelmingly chose to sail with Testu, to scour the Spanish Main for plunder, I felt sadness in my heart.

A handful of men decided to part ways. I paid them their shares, with a little extra for the passage home, and put them ashore in Old Havana. I tried to send Robert with them, but the boy refused to go. The sea had seeped into his soul and like most young men, war seemed like a glorious adventure. I had grown fond of young Robert. I looked past his insubordination and reluctantly agreed to let him stay with one condition: I handed him over to the Turk and only if he survived Efendi's training, would I take him into battle with me.

I pitied the boy when he accepted my terms with a cocky smile. The days and weeks and months ahead for the young lad would be long and grueling, filled with pain, sweat, blood and tears followed by more pain. My magnificent Hunter, a great champion among great warriors, was the only man I knew able to finish Efendi's training. I shared all of this with Robert of course. The boy didn't flinch.

I had the skiff lowered away. I thought it only proper to give Testu the news he longed to hear in person. He was standing amidships against the rail, smiling down at me as the skiff bumped up against *Cerberus*. Testu dropped a line down to me to secure the boat and tossed a rope ladder over the side.

"Welcome, Mary," Testu said as he took my hand to help me up on deck. "Jacob, Michael, welcome. Ah, your eyes betray you Mary.

You've decided to sail with me!"

"Aye, Guillaume," I answered without any enthusiasm. "I put the matter to a vote to my men. We've rowed over to discuss your plan."

Testu rubbed his hands together with glee. "*Splendide!* I'll have my lads raise the red ensign for the hunt!"

"Do as you please. You'll see no crimson banners flying from my ships. We sail as privateers under the commission given to me by my queen."

"But of course you are privateers! Let us share some wine, relax and enjoy this magnificent evening. It is nearly time for supper. I'll ask Maurice to join us."

Antonio, the ship's cook, served us strips of roasted chicken marinated in a tomato paste and spices wrapped inside a light pastry. Once we devoured those treats, he brought out bowls of corn mixed with haricot beans, rice and peppers smothered in a rich wine sauce, a dish the French call a *cassoulet* he told me proudly. Antonio's skills at cookery had not diminished and I gladly accepted a second helping.

"What are your thoughts?" Jacob asked Testu as Antonio cleared the table.

"We sail wherever the wind takes us," Testu answered. "We sail until we run across a ship or village worth plundering."

I tried to suppress a burp. I was not accustomed to rich food.

"That's your plan, Guillaume?" I asked. "Surely there is more?"

Maurice laughed. "Testu only knows one plan."

Testu caught me rolling my eyes. "Very well," he said. "Panama."

"Panama, why Panama?" I asked. "There'll be no treasure in Nombre de Diós. The treasure fleet would have sailed months ago."

"True," Testu replied. "But the Cimarron are there and Maurice has many friends among them. The Spanish can do nothing in the Istmo de Panama or Nueva España without the Cimarron knowing. *Vous avez vos amis Carib et j'ai mes alliés Cimarron, oui ?*"

I took a sip of wine and nodded. "Yes, you have your Cimarron allies. I have my Carib friends. Very well then, Panama it is."

I could see Atwood studying me out of the corner of my eye as he pulled on the oars. We had already returned MacGyver to *Diablo* and were rowing back to *Phantom*. It was late, I was tired and my stomach was on fire.

"Out with it, Jacob. What is on your mind?"

"Nothing, Mary. All is well."

"Jacob..."

"Oh, very well, but only because you insist Mary. I was wondering who Testu is to you. There is often tension in the air between you, undercurrents of sorts beyond my reckoning. I find it odd. There, I spoke my mind. Michael has observed no less."

"Michael has observed no less you say? Ha! My two captains, swapping gossip between them like two old spinsters. Did you imagine I'd be cross by your question?"

"I asked no question."

"No, I suppose you didn't. Forgive my tone Jacob. You are right. I find Guillaume to be, at times, frustrating."

"Frustrating?"

"Aye."

"Mary, ahem, might, ah, might you and Guillaume be, well, friends?"

I couldn't help myself. I caught the giggles like some silly school girl. I blamed the spicy food.

"Guillaume and I, friends? The saints protect me. He's a skilled mariner to be sure and has a fine warship. He's brave and honorable and we share a common enemy. That makes us natural allies, not necessarily friends."

"That explains it then."

"I've explained nothing. You are being gracious Jacob. You are a true friend and you are very dear to me. I'm touched by your concern and grateful for your delicacy. I'll tell Michael the same when I see him next. We women are curious creatures. I cannot explain what I do not understand myself. It would seem Testu's fate and mine are intertwined - for the moment at least. That is what I know."

Atwood said no more. I tied the skiff off when we reached the *Phantom* and followed Atwood up the rope ladder.

"Great God Almighty!" I heard Atwood thunder as he stepped on deck.

I hurried to reach his side. "What is it, Jacob?" I asked.

"Look," Atwood said and pointed up to the quarter deck.

With only a loincloth wrapped around his waist, Robert was swaying back and forth precariously on one leg with a heavy wooden yoke resting across his shoulders. Hanging at each end of the yoke was a bucket filled with sand. I could see the sweat dripping from his skin in the lantern light.

Atwood bolted up the steps to the quarter deck. "Are you drunk or have you lost your wits boy?" he asked gruffly.

I grabbed Atwood's arm and pulled him back. "Pray you tell us and tell us quickly Master Shaw what you are doing."

Efendi startled me when I heard his voice behind me.

"The boy is training," he said matter-of-factly.

"Training?" Atwood barked. "Training for what?"

Efendi cracked one of his rare, thin smiles. "You told me to prepare him, Mary. I began his lessons at once. The boy has surprised me. Rob has a very sharp eye and extraordinary reflexes. I was curious to see what other basic skills he might have."

Atwood snickered. "Let me guess Mustafa. You're training the boy how to put out a fire with a broken leg?"

"I am testing him."

"For?" I asked.

"Balance, endurance, strength and focus."

I nodded. "I see. How long has he been standing there like that?"

"Oh, nearly ten minutes."

"Ten minutes!" Atwood bellowed. "Impossible. Wait. You were down below. How do you know he didn't cheat?"

Efendi pointed up to the ship's crow's nest. "Gilligan has the watch. I gave him strict instructions to keep a close eye on my young apprentice and to report any, ahem, any irregularities."

"Apprentice?" Atwood asked.

"Yes. I've rarely seen such skills in one so young. And he is most eager to learn. I intend to train him beyond the martial arts if he continues to show promise. I'm concerned how clever the lad is though."

"Oh, how so?" I asked. Robert had always shown good, strong common sense in my presence.

"Had he asked Mary, I would have let him set those buckets aside five minutes ago and would have praised him for his fine effort. But there he stands, enduring pain he need not endure."

I couldn't help myself and smiled. "Hmmm. From what I've observed since leaving Ireland, I think the lad is clever. Plainly he's headstrong."

"Yes, yes, I agree Mary." Efendi said. "Very much like the owner of this ship, who years ago also happened to be one of my most promising students."

Efendi never spoke much about his past. I knew he had been a soldier in the Sultan's army upon a time before he awoke one day shackled to an oar aboard a Turkish pirate galley. And I knew he had studied Vadi, Fechtens and Monte starting at a very early age. He began training me when I was barely more than a girl. We spent long, hard hours practicing koshti, ringen, fencing and working with knives, garrotes, hira-shurikens, muskets and a host of other weapons.

A sudden crack of wood startled all three of us and we turned to look at Robert. The yoke had slipped off the boy's shoulders and struck the deck and he was falling too. I watched helplessly as he smacked his head against the bitticle. I envisioned spending the rest of the evening setting a broken bone or stitching up a nasty gash but luckily a bump on the noggin, and perhaps some wounded pride, was the worst of it.

Nombre de Diós is roughly three hundred leagues due south of Old Havana. We enjoyed fair skies and calm seas during our journey, but we could not sail any faster than our slowest vessel and made poor time. Better had the *Pig* sprung a leak and sank. It took us nine days to reach the Isthmus of Panama.

When Nombre de Diós appeared on our starboard, I walked to the bow, not to use the privy, but for a bit of space. Either way the crew had long ago learned to give me privacy. Standing at the bowsprit, I could just barely make out the fishermen along the shore working on their nets. I could see the old fort sitting atop the hill overlooking the bay. One of the happiest days of my life had been in Panama.

Name of God is where Hunter, Efendi and I, and one hundred of our men, had emerged from the jungles exhausted but triumphant. Through cleverness, and a good bit of luck, we had recovered a fortune in buried, Aztec gold. I wondered if the captain of the small Spanish garrison, who had let us return to our ships unaware of the treasure we had hidden away in our supplies, was still alive. Without Hunter's map, without Efendi's skills at deciphering invisible codes and one seaman's knowledge of the Gospels, a sailmaker named Pike, we never would have found that gold. I like to think my own perseverance added a little to our success. The memory made me smile.

And then I turned weepy as Hunter filled my thoughts again. After I brushed away a tear, I admonished myself for my melancholy and returned to the quarter deck, no worse or better.

We followed *Cerberus* past the village to a small, secluded bay to the east, a bay surrounded by uninhabited jungle known as Guna Yala. When Testu had his crew drop anchor, we did the same and I followed Testu and Maurice ashore with Efendi and Robert in tow, the boy begged me to take him with us, and forty of our men. I left my captains with the ships as they knew what to do if trouble found us. Even from a hundred yards off and standing in a crowd, Testu was easy to spot in his distinctive floppy hat with the long, yellow plume.

I stepped off the longboat and walked over to Testu and his cluster of men. "Guillaume, Maurice, I trust you are both well and in good spirits."

"I am most excellent," Testu replied, smiling broadly to show-off his new, pencil-thin moustache. The look suited him.

"Good. What the devil are we doing on this Godforsaken beach?"

Maurice produced a crude map. "We are here, Mary. We must cut through the jungle along this path until we reach this region, a *palenques*, where there is a village on the Pacific at the mouth of the Chepo River. The Maroons, or Cimarron if you prefer, call their village Ronconcholan."

"I've heard stories about this place. A man named Bayano led a revolt of the slaves against the Spanish I think and built Ronconcholan?"

"Yes. Bayano rose up against his Spanish masters at Nombre de Diós and inspired dozens to join him. The dozens turned into hundreds and the hundreds multiplied into thousands. Bayano was a great man blessed with *karisme* and the Cimarron made him their king. My mother and father were both slaves. They joined Bayano's rebellion and settled in Ronconcholan. I am a freeborn man."

"Ronconcholan," Testu interrupted, "is where my father and Drake first met with the Cimarron to plan the robbery of the Silver Train as the caravan made its way down from Ciudad de México."

"Off to Ronconcholan we go then," I said indifferently and shouldered my musket.

Carrying as much food, weapons and ammunition as we could carry, Maurice led us down a narrow foot path into the jungle in single file. As the crow flies, Ronconcholan is not far from Name of God. But Panama is rugged, mountainous country covered in thick foliage with steep ravines, streams and swamps. The road to Ronconcholan was difficult and hot. We climbed up and down mountains where the footing is treacherous, waded through putrid water infested with snakes, leeches and mosquitos and forded across fast flowing streams. The journey took us the better part of three days.

Scores of villagers, men and women, rushed out from behind Ronconcholan's wooden walls with open arms when they saw Maurice. There were hugs, smiles and laughter all around. Most of the Cimarron were Blackamoors, but I saw a good number of Indians too and even a handful of European men.

Then a burly fellow wearing the helmet and gold breastplate a conquistador, who I took to be the captain of the guard, rushed over and embraced Maurice. After the two men exchanged a few words, the man led us inside the walls.

I leaned close to Maurice's ear. "How can eighty heavily-armed foreigners walk through the gates so easily? Security seems lax."

Maurice winked at me. "The Cimarron have been watching us since we landed on the beach. They could have slaughtered us at any time."

"I see. I had a sense we were being shadowed during our journey but never saw a soul."

We walked past mud *ajoupas* laid out in neat rows and everywhere I looked, I saw stacks of arms. Muskets, machetes, swords, crossbows, recurve bows and spears were within easy reach of every Cimarron. In the center of the village stood three Spanish field pieces with a cart parked next to each loaded down with barrels of gunpowder and iron shot. Ronconcholan was more war camp than village.

"These are my people," Maurice said softly as dozens of curious boys and girls suddenly rushed towards us. The braver ones darted in and out to touch me.

"What have I done to be honored so by these little ones?" I asked.

Maurice smiled. "To the best of my knowledge, you are the first white woman they have seen and you carry a sword and musket. They will talk and wonder about you for days, perhaps even weave wild tales about you."

"I'm flattered."

Maurice tilted his head back and laughed. "You may feel less flattered should you hear the bawdy tales they spin about you. Cimarron boys become men at a very young age."

"Indeed!"

"Every Ronconcholan boy and girl learns how to hunt and kill with every kind of weapon before they learn to play."

"I doubt you not. The skill and bravery of the Cimarron in battle are well known, even to Europeans. And yet I wouldn't want to defend this position against a large Spanish force."

"There will be no battle here."

"Oh?"

"Our fortress is the mountains. Ronconcholan is just a village, a place to rest and eat. Nothing, no man or beast moves through the lands between México and Venezuela without the Cimarron knowing. The Spanish have tried to crush the Cimarron before. We fight them in the mountains and in the swamps and the Spanish leave behind many dead for their troubles."

"The Indians I see, Aztec?"

"Many, yes. We have some Carib with us and a few from other tribes."

"The Cimarron and the Indians are allies?"

Maurice locked his hands together. "The Cimarron and Indians in Panama are one people. We live and die as one. My father's father was a Spaniard and his mother was a Negro slave. Under Spanish law, that made my father a *mulatto*. My mother was a *mestizo*. Her father was Aztec, her mother was a Negro slave. The Spanish would call me a *pardos*, a person of mixed European, Negro and Indian blood."

"I see. A new race of men for a new world. How extraordinary. You've spent time in France. Have your travels taken you to Spain?"

"Yes."

"Then you've had a glimpse of Spain's enormous power and wealth. You must know that when the Spanish decide to take Panama, and they will someday, the Cimarron will not be able to stop them. The Spanish army will sweep across these lands like locusts, killing and destroying everything in its path."

Testu, who had been listening quietly to Maurice and I chatter, moved closer to me. "Such glum forebodings, Mary. The English and French have fought side-by-side with the Cimarron for years and will do so again."

"I wouldn't count on that my friend," I said. "The English fiasco in Spain has changed everything."

"Not everything, I think. Not long ago the Spanish began rounding-up slaves at random from Nombre de Diós, slaves who had done no wrong. They hanged one or two each day, demanding the Cimarron surrender. The Cimarron answered the Spanish in kind. They went out and captured dozens of Spanish soldiers. They crucified one prisoner each day on the road to Nombre de Diós until the hangings stopped. An eye for an eye..."

Maurice turned to face me. "These great matters between the great kingdoms across the ocean are beyond the Cimarron. Every soul you see in this village is condemned. My people understand this truth. Under the *Ordenazas para los Negros*, slave owners have the right to punish runaway slaves however they please. The longer a runaway is absent the harsher the punishment. Whippings are most common. A slave who goes missing for an hour might receive a dozen lashes. If he is gone a full day, a hundred lashes. Sometimes an ear or a nose is cut off as a warning. A slave who runs away more than once is hobbled so he can never run again. A master can put a slave to death anytime he wishes for any reason. The Spanish sentenced the Cimarron to death long ago, our executions are long overdue."

"The same fate," Testu added with a wry smile, "awaits any who help the Cimarron."

A silence fell between us as we continued walking. Through an embrasure in the wall, resembling a keyhole turned upside down, I caught my first glimpse of the Pacific Ocean. I couldn't imagine sailing across such an enormous expanse of water. We walked past the small artillery park and continued walking until we reached a magnificent lodge of striking beauty.

Made from heavy, roughhewn timbers fitted together with exacting precision, I saw no nails or pegs, the lodge looked very much out of place amidst the village's crude, mud huts. Long wood panels, as tall as a man, had been fitted over the timbers like tapestries. Each panel told a story using carvings in high relief. I saw pyramids, mountains, forests, oceans and lakes. I saw men on the hunt, men at war and women fishing and cooking. The lodge's gabled roof was made of thatch with exposed eaves and decorated rafters and soffits, incrementally stepped up on each side towards the highest gable in the center. Massive wooden spires in the shape of spirals rose high above each gable.

Maurice led Testu, Efendi and me through the lodge's large double doors, richly decorated with images of deer, jaguars and wild boar impressed into sheets of copper on one door and with dolphins, whales and manatees on the other. Our men remained outside and rested in the shade while Cimarron women happily moved amongst them with pitchers of water and baskets of fruit.

The lodge was dark inside, devoid of any decorations. The Cimarron used the building as an armory. Barrels of powder and racks of spears, halberds, swords and muskets had been stacked against the walls and off to one corner I saw Spanish helmets, breastplates and greaves thrown into a large pile.

Then two men, a Blackamoor and an Indian, stepped into the lodge with a young boy between them. The Blackamoor, a bald, short, thickset fellow with massive forearms, had a serious face with a full beard. The Indian was lean and tall with long, black hair and a sharp face. He considered me with confident, but not unkind eyes. The boy looked like a miniature copy of him. Both men were dressed in European clothing. The boy wore nothing more than a loincloth, called a *maxtlatl* I learned later.

The Blackamoor warmly embraced Maurice and Testu. "¡Mis hermanos! ¡Ha sido demasiado tiempo!"

Over the years my Spanish had improved, but I still struggled with the language, especially when spoken with a heavy provincial accent. When I gave Efendi a puzzled look, he leaned close to my ear to translate the words for me.

Maurice placed his hand on the Blackamoor's shoulder as he looked over at me. "Mary, this is Alonso, though some call him by his African name, Chidimma, which means God is Good in his native tongue. You will give no offense if you chose to call him by his Spanish name. And this tall tree of a man is Xicohtencatl. Xicohtencatl means angry bumblebee in Nahuatl. I call him *Ze-kow-tah* and you may do the same. Zekowtah is Aztec, and a great warrior among his people. And this fearsome young lad is his son, Iztli, the name means obsidian. Iztli will leave the village in the morning with the other boys his age to go on their first raiding party. When they return to Ronconcholan, they will return as men. This is the Aztec way."

"Obsidian?" I asked.

Maurice pounded on the boy's chest. "Hard as lava rock."

"Ah, impressive," I replied. "His rite of passage into manhood sounds most challenging." I thought back to my own rite of passage into womanhood, the day the clan murdered my stepfather in front of me and then violated me. "Is Alonso the king of the Cimarron?"

"No, no. Alonso and Zekowtah are generals and command the army of Ronconcholan. Each Cimarron village has two generals and a garrison of several hundred warriors. When a raiding party is sent out, one general leads the raiding party whilst the other stays behind to guard the village."

"Maurice, please tell both men it is a great honor to meet them. Tell them I come with the gift of friendship."

Testu winked at me. "Maurice has vouched for your good character already."

Alonso looked at me and said something I could not understand.

"Mary," Maurice said. "Alonso has heard the stories of a young Irishwoman who led men into the jungle north of Nombre de Diós years ago looking for buried treasure. He wishes to know if you are that woman."

I nodded. Maurice had already warned me that the Cimarron prize honesty as much as loyalty and bravery and to be caught in a lie would poison any chance of friendship between me and the Cimarron.

Then the Indian spoke and Maurice translated his words for me. "Zekowtah asks if your given name has meaning. Names are very important to the Aztec. They choose the names of their sons and daughters with great care, and only after they have consulted with a holy man."

"Hmmm. Mary, or so I've heard, comes from the Hebrew name Myriam which means rebellious one or something of the sort."

The Aztec nodded his approval after Maurice translated my words and then spoke again. "The name Mary suits you Zekowtah says. Had you been his daughter though, he would have named you

Moyolehuani, the enamored one. This is meant as a compliment."

"I'm flattered," I said and bowed my head. Then I turned to Efendi. "This is one of my most trusted officers, Mustafa Efendi. He is a Turk. Mustafa. Does your name carry some meaning in the language of your people?"

"Mustafa means the chosen one, Efendi replied. "It is meant as an epitaph for the holy prophet Muhammad, *salla llahu ʿalayhi wa-alehe wa-sallam*."

After Efendi repeated his words in Spanish, Alonso asked me a question and I understood most of what he said. "Aye, we recovered buried gold not far from Nombre de Diós," I said. "We concealed our booty in burlap sacks and rowed back to our ship with the Spanish none the wiser."

"Did you find this gold near the ocean or deep in the jungle?" Testu asked.

"Deep in the jungle, why?"

"Because," Testu said, "the Silver Train Drake and my father ambushed was especially large as you know. They seized tons of gold bars and silver ingots, too much to load onto the ships with the Spanish army closing in on them. The English only had time to move a fraction of the loot. Drake buried the rest along the coast."

"I should have known, Guillaume," I replied in a sharp tone. "You brought us here to look for the treasure Drake and your father left behind."

"*Oui*, of course. Why not? Looking for buried treasure is less risky than raiding Spanish ships and villages, no?"

"Perhaps, perhaps not. But as the rest of the story goes, the Spanish recovered what Drake buried."

"That is the Spanish claim. Certainly, Drake must believe it to be true as he has never returned to Panama to try and recover any of it. Something interesting happened recently though. A Spanish deserter offered the Cimarron information about the treasure in exchange for refuge. He claims the Spanish recovered only part of the gold and silver. Alonso sent word of this to Maurice and me and here we are."

"So, if the Cimarron know where the treasure is buried, why

haven't they taken it for themselves?"

"The Cimarron do not know where the treasure is buried. The Spaniard can only show us the place where the Spanish found a portion of the treasure. The English buried the chests in different places. Even if the Cimarron knew where to find the rest, the treasure belongs to Drake and my father. The Cimarron would never betray their allies. And besides, the Cimarron have plenty of wealth. Hidden in the riverbed of the Chepo is a king's ransom in Spanish treasure, riches taken over the years by the Cimarron in raids to the north and south. The Cimarron use their plunder to buy what they cannot find in the jungle."

"This Spaniard can lead you to the spot where the Spanish recovered several chests?"

"That's the gist of it."

"But if the Spanish couldn't find the rest, how can we?"

"Perhaps the Spanish did not look hard enough."

"That's rather thin Guillaume."

"Thin?"

"Weak."

"Ah. I think perhaps you and James began your own quest for buried treasure with less."

"A fair point. So, we'll return to the ships and sail somewhere west of Nombre de Diós?"

"No. The Spanish keep a close watch on all ships sailing in these waters. They will know about our ships anchored at Guna Yala soon enough. As there is nothing at Guna Yala, I doubt the Spanish will feel any urgency to investigate. Landing men west of Nombre de Diós is a different matter. Such a thing would attract attention. We must travel by land. The Cimarron have agreed to accompany us with a strong war party."

I could feel my heart sink. I could feel an ache forming between my shoulders. I had spent three long weeks in the jungles of Panama and had never been filthier, more exhausted or miserable. I dreaded the thought of wading through swamps and cutting a pathway through thick vines in torrid heat until my hands and feet blistered and bled.

"When did you devise this plan with your Cimarron friends? We just arrived in Ronconcholan."

Testu smiled mischievously before answering. "Maurice and I met Alonso and Zekowtah two days ago outside of camp whilst you and your men were sleeping."

We spent the next three days in Ronconcholan doing very little. My men did not complain. Unlike our Carib friends in Guadeloupe, Cimarron women place little value on monogamy or virginity. Producing warriors, lots of warriors, was the duty of every Cimarron woman. My men happily obliged all offers.

I spent the time exploring the Pacific coast a little and mingling with the villagers. Eking out a thin existence in the jungles and mountains, surrounded by a merciless enemy of overwhelming strength, had forged a tough and stoic people with a grim resolve about their fate. The Cimarron had no illusions. Without French or English support, the Spanish would invade Panama someday, destroy their villages and kill them all. The Cimarron prepared for that unhappy day by turning themselves into a race of fierce warriors. Men and women excelled at hand-to-hand combat, at staging ambushes and employing hit and run tactics and using the mountains, forests and swamps to deadly purpose. For decades the tiny Cimarron nation had kept the Spanish colossus at bay.

On the morning of our third day in Ronconcholan, Iztli and his war party returned bloodied and bruised but brimming with pride. Under Cimarron law, once the boys passed through the village gates, they passed through the gates as men.

The Cimarron held a great feast that night to honor them. We ate pig, duck and chicken roasted on the spit, steamed fish, crab, lobsters and oysters. The women moved around the campfires serving boiled vegetables and chunks of cornbread and the Cimarron had plenty of Spanish wine and ale to share. There was music, song and dancing around the bonfires and the merriment was grand.

I sat with Testu, Maurice and Efendi, quietly eating my meal when Alonso and Zekowtah joined us at our campfire.

The two men thanked me as I handed each a clay cup of wine. "Zekowtah," I said slowly as Maurice once again translated my words, "you must be proud of your son and happy for his safe return."

The Aztec pursed his lips and nodded as he gazed into the fire. "Iztli is a fine man. He will accompany us. He has the skills and the heart of a great warrior, but he has much to learn. Yes, I am proud of my son. I delight in our days together. It is not given to us to know who will see the light of a new day and who will not. Mother Earth takes who she will with no care for time."

"I think I catch your meaning."

Alonso turned to Efendi. "You are a quiet one, Mustafa. Do you have sons or daughters?"

"Once, no more," Efendi replied in a whisper.

"I am sorry if I've stirred up sad memories my friend. Mary?"

I lied. "No, and you?"

"None that I know of!"

Testu raised his cup. "To bastards and the lovely trol, trol, trollops who bore them!" he said, slurring his words as he spoke. "What would the wor, world be without their good com, company!"

"Guillaume, you sound like a man with some experience in these matters," I offered lightly, masking my annoyance as I am, after all, the bastard of a trollop.

Maurice erupted in laughter and slapped his knee. "More than once I've seen a young lass chasing Testu's bones down an alley with a baby tucked inside her arms, demanding money to help feed *his* bastard child."

Good grief I thought to myself. Little Aliénor had half-brothers or half-sisters somewhere in the world. "Well, gentlemen, I will leave you to your lewd stories. 'Tis a glorious evening. The stars are bright and clear and I feel a cool breeze coming off the ocean. I think I'll stretch my legs along the beach before I sleep. I bid you all a good night."

"I will be pleased to, to es, es, escort you mad, madam," Testu offered with a sly smile. "For your safety."

"I doubt you can even stand," I replied.

When Testu tried, he fell.

"Well," I said, shaking my head. "At least it would seem Cimarron women are safe tonight from you as I doubt any part of you can stand."

I turned and walked off in a huff to the roar of laughter behind me.

In the morning the two generals of Ronconcholan drew straws. Zekowtah won the honor of leading the Cimarron war party while Alonso would stay behind with the garrison.

We sent word back to the ships of our plan and set out before breakfast in the dark, one hundred and fifty strong. The Cimarron marched in front, followed by the French and then my men. The Spanish deserter came with us too. We travelled light, carrying only our weapons, waterskins, shovels and pickaxes. The jungle would provide everything else we'd need Zekowtah had assured me. I had my doubts. I had seen Carib warriors living off the land, munching on bugs and raw snake. I resigned myself to a meager fare of nuts and berries.

The Carib, renowned across the Caribbean for their bravery and skill with spears, axes, bows and blow guns, prefer to hit and run like the Cimarron, but they have no fear of pitched battle. They can move whole armies across vast stretches of ocean in their great war canoes at impressive speeds. The Carib are the Vikings of the New World and feared by all. Beyond bravery, I did not know what to expect from my new Cimarron friends.

We marched west in more or less a single file along the coast with the Pacific on our left and jungle on our right. When we turned into the trees, I saw Zekowtah step away from the column and he waited for Testu and Maurice to reach him. He walked with them for a time and then stepped away again to walk with Efendi and me.

He had traded in his boots, trousers and shirt for sandals, a loincloth and a royal blue cape. From head to toe his body was all taut muscle. His calves and thighs were particularly thick. His flesh had been scarred in many places.

"You are well Lady Mary?" Zekowtah asked me in English as we walked.

I raised an eyebrow. "You speak English?"

"Of course. We have been friends with the English for many years."

"Indeed. I'm well thank you. We seafaring folks are not accustomed to long marches, but we'll manage. How far must we travel, how many days' march do you think?"

"If this was an Aztec war party three, perhaps four days. Because our white friends move like the sloth, nine or ten."

"We are moving at a very good pace it seems to me. How could your warriors reach wherever it is we are going in one third of the time?"

"We run."

"All day?"

"Yes, all day and often through the night if we must."

"Impressive. This cape of yours is splendid. I take it only officers wear capes?"

"Yes. Generals wear blue *xiuhtilmatlis*, captains red and junior officers wear brown, green or yellow war capes."

"I saw one of your men wearing black."

"We honor a warrior who has shown great courage in battle, bravery beyond any of his peers, with the black cape."

"I don't recall ever seeing any of the Carib in capes."

"A Carib king wears a headdress and a robe. His officers wear feathered armbands of different colors to show rank."

"I see. I pray you forgive me if my next question seems indelicate, but I am curious, how many are the Aztec? The Spanish conquistador Cortés destroyed your kingdom, yes?"

"Sadly, this is true. Hernán Cortés, the Great Christian Devil, the Bringer of Death and Tears, destroyed everything that might someday threaten Spain. When Cortés captured the great city of Tenochititlan, he took Cuauhtémoc prisoner, the last of the Aztec kings, and killed him. The Aztec nation died with Cuauhtémoc. The Aztec who live among the Cimarron are the last of my people."

"A great and terrible tragedy. The sorrows of the world are born from the deeds of wicked men."

"Yes."

"The Cimarron and Carib are fond of their tattoos. I dare say many of my men are too. But I see no tattoos on you."

"A warrior is great because of his deeds in battle, not by the images inked into his flesh. The scars I bear from battle are my tattoos."

"I have a scar or two myself. I haven't seen your son."

"I sent Iztli and three of his brothers out last evening to make sure the path ahead is clear."

"Ah, scouts. Was your father a warrior?"

"Yes. From father to son, from mother to daughter, we pass down the history and the brilliance of our people and will do so until we are no more. According to the stories of my people, my father's father was one of the *Cuachicqueh*, one of the Shorn Ones, the greatest of all the Aztec warriors, greater than even the *Cuauhtli*, the Eagle Warriors, or the *Ocelotl*, the Jaguar Warriors, the bravest of the brave. The *Cuachicqueh* shaved their heads, leaving only a long braid over the left ear, and painted their bodies half blue and half red before battle. Until Cortés and his conquistadors landed on these shores, the *Cuachicqueh* had never retreated in battle, they had never tasted defeat."

"Perhaps your people will one day rise to become a great nation again."

"No. We are too few. Our time is at an end. When my son marries, he will marry a Cimarron or Carib woman or perhaps even a woman from the Totonac or Tlaxcalans tribes, once our hated enemies. And when his son or daughter is of age and marries, they will do the same. Blood will mingle with blood until the Aztec disappear forever."

"When my wise Turk here is unsure of what to say, he will tell me it is of no consequence, that we simple creatures cannot fathom God's great plan and we should not fret about things to come. All is as it should be."

"All is as it should be..."

"You've known Maurice for a long time?"

"As small boys we hunted and fished and played games together until one day he left with Testu to see new worlds. We are brothers. Maurice has told me you are a great warrior, a shrewd tactician and a chief respected by men. Most of our women are warriors, fine warriors, but we have never seen a warrior woman among the whites. This puzzles me. From what I know, the women of your race are soft and weak."

"Maurice," Efendi interrupted, "does not exaggerate. I and many in our crew have sailed with Mary for years. We have followed her into many battles, fought with her side-be-side. I will sail with Mary until the end."

"How extraordinary. Are there others like Mary in your world across the ocean?"

"Like Mary? No."

I rolled my eyes. "Gentlemen, all this praise will go to my head if you continue. Well, if you'll excuse me, I need a moment to water a tree."

Confused, Zekowtah turned to Efendi.

"Mary is no goddess," Efendi said. "She needs to take a piss."

"All is as it should be," Zekowtah said and howled with laughter as he started back towards the head of the column.

We ate our noonday meal on the march, I devoured the hunk of cornbread the Cimarron women had made for us before departing Ronconcholan. We continued marching and didn't stop until we reached a large clearing just as the day's light began to fade. I had no clue where we were, but I knew we had moved inland miles away from the ocean because of the stifling heat and disagreeable humidity. Zekowtah sent four teams of three men each out on patrol and passed the word around: we were in hostile, Spanish territory, no fires and no noise. I plopped myself down against a tree exhausted, filthy and famished.

Testu sat down next me holding two small bags. "Supper," he said in a hushed voice and handed me one bag.

The bag was in fact a large leaf, wrapped around a treasure trove of *ch'arki*, dried fish, nuts, berries and cornmeal.

Testu laughed. "Ah, the look on your face, Mary. It is only food, not gold."

I greedily stuffed my mouth full with a chunk of cornbread. "Mmm, better than gold," I said as I chewed. And then I noticed the Cimarron moving around the camp passing out leaves to each man. "Where did this bounty come from?"

"We are resting on a Cimarron *dépôt d'approvisionnement*. Over there is an underground vault. A Cimarron war party from a village to the north stocked these supplies here for us yesterday. You thought you'd be feasting on raw monkey meat tonight?"

"A disgusting notion! I'd rather go hungry."

"Ha! You would be surprised what one will eat to survive. I suspect we will dine well enough until we reach our destination. After that, I am less certain of the cuisine."

"I'm glad you are feeling better."

"Pardon?"

"Last night, you were slurring your words and couldn't stand. I feared you were suffering from one vile ailment or another."

"Perhaps I overindulged a bit."

"I should say so."

"Ah, I nearly forgot," Testu said, pausing to remove a waterskin strapped around his shoulder and offered the skin to me.

"I have enough water, *merci*."

"Water? I'm French dear lady. This is wine. Take just a sip."

Maurice and Efendi, having posted the night watch together, then joined us with their suppers. As the men ate and chatted, I leaned my back against the tree, wrapped my sea cape around my shoulders and closed my eyes. I instantly fell asleep.

And so it went for the next eight days before we reached the east coast, somewhere far west of Nombre de Diós. The journey, mercifully, was not as demanding as my first adventure into the wilds of Panama, but the march was hard enough and my men and I were hungry and bone-weary. Our Cimarron allies seemed oblivious to hardship, especially the Aztecs. They ate less, rested less and moved faster than any of us. Not even young Iztli appeared fatigued. I marveled at his stamina. My poor Robert, about the same age as Iztli, appeared half-dead by comparison. Even so I was proud of him. Not once did he complain or fall behind.

We set-up camp before sunset near a stream with good water that emptied into the Caribbean a short walk away. Efendi and Robert stood watch as I stripped off all my clothes on the beach and waded into the ocean with a cake of soap. I washed away the sweat and grim, scrubbed my clothes clean and then rinsed the salt water off in the stream. Despite the boy's loud protests, I made Robert and Efendi bathe too.

And then I sent them both off to do a quick reconnaissance of the area while I returned to the camp. I saw Testu, Maurice and Zekowtah sitting by a rock and joined them.

"So, where are we?" I asked. "What is this place?"

"I have no clue," Testu said. "During the raid in '73, I was aboard the *Harve*, sitting a thousand yards off Nombre de Diós. My father would not let me go ashore with him. I could see our men setting fire to the village, though I knew not why. Then Spanish soldiers suddenly emerged from the smoke and there was fighting in the streets. Men scrambled for the boats with the Spanish close behind. Barely half of our lads made it back to the ships. The rest were killed or captured and as you know, the Spanish executed their prisoners, starting with my father."

"And where were you Maurice?" I asked.

"I was here," he replied. He stood and walked over to the stream, waving me to follow him. He stepped into the stream, the water was only several yards wide and shallow, and pointed to a small pile of smooth stones at his feet.

"The great Drake himself stood at this very spot and placed these stones here. I stood about where you are standing now Mary, watching him. The English ships were anchored just over there. This place was the English rallying point."

"Drake buried the treasure here?" I asked.

"No, but we must be close. After the English and French ambushed the Silver Train, Drake and Testu decided to divide their forces when the Spanish army caught up to them. Testu took his Frenchmen to Nombre de Diós, hoping to draw the Spanish off to give Drake and his men time to reach the English ships with the treasure. Drake led us here. We had two hundred mules and many carts loaded down with gold and silver and the Spanish were closing in. We heard fighting between the Spanish and the English rear guard to the south. Drake and his men loaded as much gold into the longboats they could and sent the boats back to the ships. Then he took his raiding party farther west to find a place to hide the rest. The Cimarron stayed here with the English rear guard slow the Spanish down."

"You couldn't have been much older than Iztli back then."

"Younger."

"You remained behind with the Cimarron?"

"Yes."

"Then you don't know how far or in what direction Drake went?"

"That is true. But our Spanish friend knows. He says we need to travel another five miles or so."

"And then what?"

Maurice picked up a stick and used it to poke ten dimples in the dirt. "Do you recognize this?" he asked.

"Well, I, um. Hmmm. Wait, stars, the hunter Orion?"

"Quite so, Mary. I was squatting behind that tree over there relieving myself when I heard Drake tell the men in the longboats that he intended to bury the rest of the treasure in ten places in the shape of the great hunter spread out over an area of five hundred square yards. He wanted his men with the ships to know where to look for the treasure in the event the raiding party failed to reach the next rendezvous point."

"I understand now. The Spaniard can show us the vicinity where Spanish army recovered some of the treasure and with what you know, we have a chance of finding whatever the Spanish did not."

"Yes. It is possible the Spanish recovered all the treasure. Then we have risked our lives for naught. But our Spanish friend has no reason to lie, he has made no attempt to flee or to betray us. I believe his story to be true."

"What happened after Drake left this place? How did you and Guillaume come to sail together?"

"After Nombre de Diós, the French sailed to Guna Yala. *Harve's* men went ashore and traveled to Ronconcholan, the French rallying point, hoping to find their captain. Guillaume went with them. I returned to Ronconcholan with the Cimarron war party just as *Harve's* men reached the village. A few days later a wounded Frenchman wandered into Ronconcholan, the sole survivor of the slaughter at Nombre de Diós. He had witnessed the Spanish behead Captain Testu and the others. I too lost my father in the raid. He stepped in front of a Spanish pikeman, not far from this very spot, to save me. Two boys, overwhelmed with grief, became fast friends. When Guillaume and his father's men returned to their ship, I went with them."

Efendi and Robert then strolled into camp. With nothing to report, we all joined Testu and Zekowtah and quietly ate a cold supper of nuts, fruit and roots from different plants. Zekowtah would not allow any cooking fires. I found a spot of soft ground to stretch across after supper with a pleasant ocean breeze and quickly fell asleep. I didn't stir until I felt a hand pressed against my mouth.

"Shhh," Efendi whispered as he put a finger to his lips. He pointed towards the ocean.

I turned and saw dark forms moving along the beach. Spaniards. A company of fifty men or more were marching east towards Nombre de Diós in the middle of the night. I glanced to my right and then to my left. Every man in camp was awake with his musket at his side.

Once the Spanish disappeared, Zekowtah gave the order to break camp and within minutes we were on the march. I picked a banana off one tree and mango off another and ate my breakfast as we walked. When dawn broke, I saw one of the young Cimarron boys carrying six coconuts in his arms without a stitch of clothing.

I moved up the line to find Testu and Maurice. "Good morning, gentlemen. Why the devil is that poor lad walking naked and carrying coconuts?"

"Zekowtah," Maurice began to say, pausing while Testu plucked my mango out of my hand and took a bite, "is punishing the lad for nodding off as he stood watch. Because of his weakness, the Spanish nearly stumbled into our camp unnoticed."

"Poor fellow."

"No. Zekowtah is a great warrior and a fine leader, but he is soft with the younger warriors. In the Spanish army the boy would be beaten or worse depending on the commander."

"Pity," quipped Testu as he devoured my mango, "Zekowtah did not find you asleep while standing watch Mary. I would have enjoyed witnessing your punishment. How many coconuts can you carry in the nude my lady?"

I rolled my eyes and ignored the Frenchman. "Maurice, be a good fellow and tell me again about the dart frog. How does one extract the poison from its skin? Three minutes to lay a man low with a single drop I think you told me? I may have need for such a subtle weapon very soon, certainly before our journey ends."

Maurice glanced over at Testu and smiled. "With pleasure my lady, I will happily teach you."

By midafternoon we reached a clearing of tall grass on high ground with a respectable stream cutting through the center of a large field. I saw two crocodiles, not more than fifty paces away, sunning themselves on a sandbar in the middle of the stream. I swallowed hard and looked around in all directions before I stepped into that stream. In my haste to cross though, I tripped over a branch and landed face-first in the water. The crocodiles glanced my way but didn't move. No one dared laughed as I picked myself up.

I saw our Spanish guide pointing to several holes in the ground to Testu and Maurice, who were standing on top of a large boulder. The holes had been dug-out by men not too long ago judging by the amount of erosion. We had reached Drake's field, a field roughly five hundred yards deep and five hundred yards wide. Zekowtah sent his warriors out in all directions to secure a perimeter. I saw the boy who had fallen asleep during his watch among them, clothed, armed and determined to reclaim his honor by the look I saw in his eyes.

Testu waved Efendi and me over. "I must say, you are looking fit Mary," Testu said in his easy-going manner. "Traipsing through the jungles of the New World agrees with you."

In truth I felt exhausted, but I forced a weak smile. "A hot bath and a hot meal with a deck under my feet would suit me better."

"Perhaps I can help you with one of the three. Rains are coming. Zekowtah's lads over there are fashioning a small hut using fronds and mud to make an oven. Zekowtah has agreed to allow one cooking fire once the rains come to mask the smoke. We will eat well tonight!"

"The Spaniard is certain this is the place?"

"Our Spanish *amigo* Filipe stood on this very ground with a whole company of his friends. Filipe was on the digging detail."

The Spaniard hurried over to us when Testu called to him.

"Tell me again, for the benefit of the lady, you are certain Filipe?" Testu asked him.

"We found," the Spaniard said, stamping his feet over a depression in the dirt a few yards away, "chests of silver buried here. I dug around this very spot and found the first chest, though the hole has since filled with sand."

"How many chests did the Spanish find?" I asked.

Filipe removed his straw hat. "I do not know my lady. A large Indian war party attacked us. The Indians overran our camp and killed many men. They killed our horses, mules and oxen too. Colonel Gonzales, our commander, ordered us to withdrawal to Nombre de Diós. Without pack animals, Gonzales had us empty our backpacks and each man refilled his pack with silver. Perhaps there was enough silver to fill ten chests? After we reached Nombre de Diós, my company, what was left of it, was reassigned to Ciudad de México. I heard Gonzales returned to this field later with a larger force. I do not know if he found more silver."

"How did the Spanish know to look here?"

"Ten years ago, the navy seized an English pirate ship in these waters. One of the English prisoners was with Drake during the great Silver Train raid."

"The man talked?"

"Sí. The Englishman confessed his sins in exchange for his life. He claimed this field was only one of several places Drake used to bury what he stole."

"There are other fields we must look for?"

"Mary," Testu interrupted. "We will find what we will find."

"And if the English prisoner told the truth and Drake buried only some of the treasure here?"

Testu shrugged his shoulders. "As I said, we will find what we will find. We know Drake had his men dig ten holes in the pattern of the Great Archer, a fact the Spanish did not know, so we have a map of sorts to help us."

"And we know Filipe found one chest here, so we use this spot as our reference point."

"Yes, Mary." Maurice interjected.

"If we find anything, we'll need the ships."

Testu nodded. "Zekowtah will send a runner to Guna Yala with instructions to our men to bring the ships here, with your permission of course."

I took a moment to survey the land around us. "Gentlemen, if we were making wagers, I'd wager this hole is Orion's right foot."

"And why do you think this, Mary?" Testu asked.

I pointed to the ocean behind us. "Drake and his men were marching along the beach down there with their ships within easy reach shadowing them. Drake was in a hurry. He saw the stream and this plateau and followed the stream up to where we are standing now, where he could see the whole field and still see his ships. Drake would have considered the terrain from this very spot as we are doing now. Look at the natural contour of the high ground. This clearing is shaped diagonally, running from here to the south-west and then to the south-east and then back again to the north-east."

Testu glanced down at the ocean, then spun around to consider the plateau. "I see what you see Mary. The Spanish were digging haphazardly with no rhyme or reason. Yes, yes, this is the Archer's right foot. Maurice?"

Maurice nodded and grabbed four spears. He walked around the field and planted one spear at each corner. Then he went to the center of the field with six more spears. He planted one spear in the ground every one hundred paces to make Orion's belt and then used the last three spears to make his sword.

I turned to look at Testu. "God be praised Frenchman, there is a brain behind that pretty face of yours. Pray tell me, for I am famished. What is for supper?"

"Why you passed supper just moments ago."

"What?"

"Crocodile *mon ami!*"

"Ugh..."

Testu jumped down from the boulder and laughed. "Be of good cheer, Mary! You will like crocodile, trust me, though I do wish Antonio was with us. Crocodile meat is tough. Antonio would know how to make the meat tender. Do we send for the ships?"

"*Oui, monsieur.* What choice is there?"

All through the afternoon our men vigorously attacked the earth with their pickaxes and shovels. Even when the rains came, they didn't stop. A wave of excitement swept through the camp when Testu's men found a wooden chest at the bottom one hole, but the chest had been split in two and was empty. Spirits plummeted.

When night settled over us, we put our tools aside and rested. I sat with my back against the boulder with Efendi and young Robert at my side and tried my first taste of crocodile. I heard Testu, sitting a few yards away with Zekowtah, snickering as I struggled to swallow the meat.

"I knew you would like crocodile," Testu shouted.

"I'm grateful the meat is cooked at least," I said. "I don't suppose you have any wine left?"

"Alas, no. But when the ships arrive our fortunes will improve, unless the men have broken into the ale and wine stores and have drunk themselves into a stupor."

"I heard no musket shot. How does one kill a crocodile? Certainly an arrow is not enough to penetrate their thick hides?"

"Mahuizo, the young warrior Zekowtah punished for nodding-off whilst on watch, he brought the animal down."

"How?"

Zekowtah raised a bow off the ground. "With an arrow tipped with poison."

I suddenly felt ill. I spit out the crocodile flesh in my mouth.

Testu laughed. "Easy there Mary. You're turning green. The meat is safe to eat."

Efendi and Robert smiled when I handed them my portion.

Maurice then came over and sat down next to me with a short reed in his hand. "Mustafa had me teach him before we left the village. Would you like me to teach you?"

"Teach me what?"

Maurice tilted the reed so I could peer down inside. "Do you see the frog, Mary?"

"Aye."

"Behold," Maurice said as he removed a thin stick from his pocket. "After you stuff the frog down this hollow reed, you take a stick sharpened at the tip and force the stick down the frog's throat like this, then push until the tip pierces one of the frog's rear legs. See?"

I have a strong stomach for blood and gore. But my stomach turned on me as I watched. I felt the urge to heave.

"Come now Mary, you've seen far worse things done to a man."

I nodded and took a sip of water.

Maurice carefully removed the stick from the reed with the frog impaled on the stick. The frog, no bigger than my fingernail, was frantically squirming to and fro trying to free itself. Its skin was brilliant yellow with bright green stripes along its body. Its legs were purple with yellow spots.

"When the frog is threatened it secretes a sticky, white froth from the pores on its back. See?"

"I do."

"This is the poison. Extraordinary, yes? One of the smallest creatures in the jungle is the most dangerous, feared by even the largest predators."

Maurice pulled an arrowhead from his belt. "You take the arrowhead, or a sword or a knife, and run the edge of the blade across the frog's back like this. Never let the poison touch your skin. Never. If you have a cut, a bug bite or even an open blister or a sore, the poison will seep into your body and you will die."

I nodded solemnly. "How many arrows did the boy use to kill the crocodile?"

"One."

"Only one?"

"Yes, the poison from the dart frog is very powerful."

"Good God. Is there an antidote?"

"None. And the poison is always fatal. The victim is paralyzed first and then cannot breathe. Death comes swiftly, within three or four minutes."

"How long can the poison hold its potency?"

"I've shown Mustafa how to store the poison after it has been extracted. The poison will last for many months if stored properly, perhaps as long as a year."

Efendi took the stick from Maurice to take a closer look. "An elegant way to kill."

At first light we started digging anew. We dug all day, found nothing and when dusk fell, we wearily set our tools aside for supper. Zekowtah would not risk another fire, so we ate cold meals in the dark.

I could not eat the raw fish or the cassava or batata roots the others were feasting on and contented myself with nuts and berries. I took a stroll along the beach afterwards with Testu and Maurice to keep me company. The tide was rolling in. The surf was rough. The breeze was fresh and cool. All the brilliant stars in heaven were out and shining brightly. We stopped to gaze up at Orion as the Archer wheeled around the heavens with his bow, staring down on us, perhaps even taunting us.

I rested my hand on Testu's shoulder. "Guillaume, you must not be disappointed if we find no treasure."

Testu nodded. "Not every adventure ends with riches. I will have no regrets. Our trek across Panama has been a worthy gamble."

"I agree and I admire your spirt."

Maurice grunted. "Don't be fooled, Mary. He'll be miserable and in his cups for weeks if we return to the ships empty-handed."

"Ah, there's the truth of it!" I said. "And what say you Maurice about our chances of finding treasure?"

Maurice took in the night sky. "Tomorrow I think will be a lucky day. Orion smiles upon us."

In the morning I brought water around to the digging details. Fifty men were hard at work looking for Drake's silver and the day was turning hot. Bare-chested and sprouting new muscles each day, Robert, buried up to his neck in dirt and mud, looked up at me with a huge grin when I stopped to give him water.

"I see you like playing in the dirt Rob," I said in a playful tone as I handed him a waterskin.

"Lady Mary, could you grab that shovel and help me?" he asked, still grinning. "If a little hard work doesn't offend you, I could use an extra hand."

My hands were raw from digging but before I could say no, he tapped his pickaxe against something solid. When I looked down at his feet, I saw the top of a wooden chest. I eagerly grabbed a shovel and jumped into the hole to help Robert clear the dirt around the chest. We found the chest intact - and locked. Too heavy for us to lift the chest above our heads, I cried out and dozens of men rushed over to help us.

The entire camp gathered around as Maurice smashed the rusty lock with a rock until it broke. He opened the lid, stood back and we all stared slack-jawed at the shiny silver bars stacked neatly inside the chest.

"*Whoo-hoo!*" Testu shouted and embraced Maurice.

Men slapped each other on the back and hooted. Robert passed one of the bars around as Testu raised his arms for silence.

"Gentlemen, my lady, this is a good day. Let us not forget the many good men, my father, Maurice's father, who paid dearly in blood for this treasure. We split our booty equally with our Cimarron brothers and our Irish friends. Grab your shovels lads! The silver calls to us!"

Men resumed their work with renewed vigor. We recovered nine more chests buried in Robert's pit and in the late afternoon, after tearing up acres of field, two of Testu's men found more treasure. By day's end we had recovered close to six thousand pounds of silver in all, nearly ten percent of the thirty tons the English had taken.

A fine drizzle fell on our camp that night. A gentle mist rolled in from the sea. A scavenging party sent out by Zekowtah earlier returned with two deer, an ocelot and one wild boar and Zekowtah reluctantly allowed one cooking fire to celebrate the day. We would eat well.

Zekowtah plopped down next to me as I watched the boar roasting on the spit a few feet away.

"We have been extraordinarily fortunate so far," he said.

"Yes," I replied.

Testu and Maurice then joined us.

"We invite misfortune," Zekowtah continued, "if we stay in this place much longer. One Spanish patrol or another will stumble upon us soon."

Testu tossed a faggot on the fire. "I know in my bones there is at least one more cache of silver hidden somewhere out there."

Zekowtah kept his eyes fixed on the fire. "Considering what we have, is one more chest of silver worth a man's life my friend?"

"My men knew the risks and accepted them. I forced no man to come with me. If I put the matter to a vote, I promise you my men will vote to stay. As for your people, this silver will buy many weapons and armor for the Cimarron. This silver will make your people stronger."

"What you say Guillaume is true," Zekowtah replied thoughtfully. "But this is poor ground to defend. If the Spanish find us, how will we move six thousand pounds without mules or horses or carts? We risk losing all."

"Perhaps gentlemen there is a compromise to be made," I offered. "The ships will be here soon and when they arrive, we leave. But before we depart, we should restore the land as best we can so the Spanish won't know what we've done. If we find no more treasure in the next day or two, you can return later on your own Guillaume if you wish to look for the rest."

Zekowtah stepped over to the fire, took his knife and sliced off a thick piece of boar for me. "We are agreed then?" Zekowtah asked.

Testu nodded.

"Good," I said and savored my first taste of wild boar. "What is this silver worth?"

Testu turned to look at Maurice as he spoke. "Before we left France, gold was pegged at about two hundred and twenty-five French *francs* per pound in the trading houses. That is roughly equivalent to about one hundred *pesos* I think. I am not sure about silver. Maurice?"

"Silver was trading at about thirty-five *pesos* per pound," Maurice said. "That is why Drake took the gold and buried the silver. We have found sixty chests with one hundred pounds of silver in each. Those chests over by the trees should be worth, give or take, roughly two hundred thousand *pesos*."

"What did Drake take with him?" I asked.

"Drake left Panama with over a thirteen hundred pounds of gold worth about one hundred and thirty thousand *pesos*," Testu replied. "And he took an equal weight in silver with him, or so I've heard."

Chapter Nine

estu was stubborn in his greed. At first light he and his men began attacking the far edge of the field with their pickaxes and shovels in a steady rain. I assembled my men to help the French, though my heart was no longer in our quest for treasure. Half my lads were struggling with the runs or with fever. I made the unwell rest and administered what little *cinchona* I had left to the sickest among them. The Cimarron seemed immune from our afflictions and oblivious to our hardships. Zekowtah continued sending out his patrols.

When I needed a bit of solitude, I headed down to the beach to walk along the shore alone. Efendi could scold me later. I did not walk far before the rains letup and sun broke through the clouds. And when the mist began to lift, I saw a dark stain on the water slowly moving towards me. The stain took shape, spouted sails and divided itself into two, three, four and then into five parts. Five ships were moving from east to west sailing unusually close to shore. I hurried back to camp.

Just as a reached the knoll, one of Zekowtah's men, a lookout perched up in a tree, cried out his warning. When Zekowtah saw me, he raced towards me with Testu close behind.

"Five ships." I said.

"Ours?" Testu asked.

"They're too far off yet, but..."

I called to Maurice and Efendi and we all hurried down to the water.

The ships were too small for galleons and none were flying the white flag with the jagged red cross of the Spanish navy. One ship had dark sails and the last ship in the line was a squat, smallish thing.

Maurice quickly had the men stack green wood and brush on the beach and lit a signal fire. The ships swung towards us and within the hour their men dropped anchor in front of us a hundred yards off shore. Only *Phantom*'s crew though lowered a longboat away.

"Jacob!" I cried out and waved as Atwood worked the tiller while the oarsmen struggled against an angry surf. The boat plunged up and down precariously in the heavy swells.

"Been awhile since we were rummaging around in the jungles of Panama on a treasure hunt, Mary," Atwood said as he gracefully jumped over the side into knee-deep water. He was agile for a big man. "Have ya been havin' fun?"

I kissed both his hands and kissed his cheeks. "All is well?"

"Aye, more or less. We've lost a few men to one affliction or another."

"Who?"

"Among our own, Blackwell, Murphy and Moore," Atwood said, then reached over to shake Guillaume's hand and beamed when he saw Efendi. "Ah, Mustafa, and Maurice, good to find you both alive my friends. Any luck Guillaume?"

"Sixty chests, one hundred pounds of silver in each," Testu answered proudly.

Atwood whistled. "I had my doubts Guillaume about this little adventure. I did indeed. My compliments to you, sir, and to you Maurice."

"To be honest, I had my own doubts too," Testu said. "Maurice is the one who had faith. He is the one who insisted we return to Panama. Any trouble whilst we were away?"

Atwood took a handkerchief to wipe the sea spray off his face. "Great God, who's this tall tree of a fellow?"

"This is Zekowtah," I said. "He's a full-bloodied Aztec warrior."

"I pray he's with us."

"He's a Cimarron general and a friend."

Zekowtah nodded, Atwood returned the nod and then turned to me. "Mary, we've had eyes on us since we put in at Guna Yala. As soon as we raised anchor and set our sails, six warships swooped down on us from Nombre de Diós and gave chase. We lost them in the rains during the night but I doubt they're far behind. We shouldn't tarry here long."

Testu scanned the horizon. "I see no ships but ours. We have our men and six thousand pounds of silver to move. We should wait for the surf to calm."

Atwood shook his head. "The Spanish will not wait Guillaume. They could appear on our flank at any moment and if they do, they'll have us pinned here against the shore."

Zekowtah took a step closer to Testu. "We should make haste and leave this place Guillaume. The Cimarron can help you bury the silver in the woods, or perhaps the swamp would be better, then I'll take my men back to Ronconcholan."

"Who the devil is that?" I asked and pointed to a man running hard towards us along the water's edge.

"One of mine," Zekowtah replied.

The man, barely winded when he reached us, spoke to Zekowtah in Nahuatl.

"The Spanish are here," Zekowtah said calmly. "Their ships landed a large force on the beach beyond the bend about three miles to the east."

"How many?" I asked.

"Three hundred."

"Look there!" Maurice said and pointed.

Sails, the size of stray pieces of lint suddenly appeared in the distance. The Spanish had found us. My mind started spinning as I considered all that had been said.

And then we heard a thunderous cheer rise over the camp. The men had found more silver.

And then another one of Zekowtah's scouts, a lanky fellow as black as night and as thin as a reed, raced down the stream for us. He spoke to Zekowtah in Spanish and I understood his words. A reinforced Spanish company of musketeers, over one hundred strong, was moving up from the south through the jungle towards us and were less than two miles away.

Testu and Maurice started arguing. With our predicament turning grimmer by the minute, I drew my sword and plunged the blade into the sand.

"Silence!" I roared, startling everyone except for Atwood and Efendi. All eyes turned to me. There can only be one commander and after Coruña and Lisbon, I was in no mood to surrender or share the privilege again.

"We have no time for silly squabbles. We have no time to move the men to the ships or to bury the silver. The Spanish have blocked any retreat to the south. A battalion is coming at us from the east. If we move west, we'll be running deeper into Spanish territory and farther away from our ships and God help us if we run into another Spanish force coming down from México. We'll be caught in a vice. We have an hour at most before the Spanish reach us. We need a plan!"

"Your orders, Captain?" Atwood asked with a voice like rolling thunder. He set his jaw, he squared his shoulders, leaving no doubt who was in command.

I retrieved my sword, slipped the blade back into the scabbard and turned my gaze to Testu. "We stand and fight. We have no choice."

Testu narrowed his eyes at me. "No! Maurice was uttering the same gibberish. Zekowtah can hold-off the Spanish company to the south whilst we load the silver into the boats."

I grit my teeth, vehemently shaking my head. "There is no time, Guillaume."

Maurice stepped to my side. "We risk capsizing the boats in this surf Guillaume if we try."

Testu shook his head. "We cannot win a pitched battle against four hundred Spanish regulars!"

"We can and we will," I said and meant it. "Gentlemen, the Spanish don't know our numbers. They don't know who we are or why we are here -."

Testu cut me off. "Enough, Mary!" he roared angrily. "We are wasting time bickering. We can bring all the boats in and move the silver to the beach. We do it now. Zekowtah, we need you and your men to purchase a little time for us. Maurice, have the men begin moving the silver."

But neither man moved. I kept my poise. Arguing with a hot-headed Gaul is always futile.

"I'll not risk any of our lives for silver," I said evenly. "Jacob, go. Return to the ships. Do whatever you must to protect the ships. I need the *Pig*. Have her captain beach his ship here, right here on this very spot upon which we stand. Tell him to drive his ship into the ground hard and have him be quick about it too."

Atwood smiled and nodded. "I think I understand your plan. If all goes wrong, we rendezvous in Cartagena?"

"Aye, Cartagena, Jacob. Can you handle the Spanish flotilla?"

"Without their vaunted galleons, the Spanish navy will rue the day they tested us."

"Good. Guillaume, if you wish to return to *Cerberus* to fight this battle on the water, leave now with Jacob. I'll compensate you for the *Pig* later - if I survive the day."

Testu sighed and bowed his head. "I will remain here," he said in a softer tone. "Maurice, go with Jacob. You have command."

Maurice nodded and climbed into longboat with Atwood. Zekowtah and Efendi pushed the boat off.

"You want *Pig's* guns?" Testu asked me.

"Aye, we'll build Fort Pig on this spot. That should even up the odds."

"I will take my men," Zekowtah said, "and delay the Spanish to the south."

I nodded. "Thank you, Zekowtah. Guillaume, Mustafa is more soldier than sailor and he is exceptionally talented at soldiering, will you permit him to oversee our defenses whilst you and I wait for the *Pig*?"

"Of course."

"Good. Mustafa, go."

"I will see it done," Efendi said and hurried off with Zekowtah back to the camp.

As Zekowtah assembled his war party, Efendi moved men and arms around while Testu and I stood quietly together on the beach, watching Atwood's longboat rise and fall on the waves, struggling to make headway. I took his hand to let him know that all was well.

"The surf is strong," Testu offered meekly and said no more.

Twenty minutes later the *Pig* came straight at us under full sail. Testu and I stepped aside before her bow plowed into the beach in a cloud of sand and an awful groan. And then we saw muzzle flashes streaking across the water off in the distance, followed moments later by the crack of musket fire to the south. Our ships were trading broadsides with the Spanish navy. Zekowtah and his men had engaged the Spanish musketeers.

While Atwood kept the Spanish navy busy, we would fight on high ground from behind the stream using the pits we had dug for cover. The Cimarron would hold our right flank, which extended down to a large swamp to the south. The French would hold the center and my men and I would defend the left flank with support from the *Pig* - and I prayed to God that nothing came up behind us from the west.

"*Capitaine* Henri, welcome to Panama," I called up to *Pig's* master as he looked down upon me from his ship's bow with a puzzled expression.

Testu put his hands on his hips. "Alexander, you old drunkard, you've run my ship aground!"

A squat, portly little fellow shaped like a pear, not unlike his ship, lowered himself awkwardly down on a line.

"*Ma dame*," he said, tilting his head to one side. "Atwood told me you needed to be rescued, though I am uncertain whether he meant I am to rescue you from the Spanish or that I am to rescue you from Testu." He turned to Testu. "Guillaume, this old cow is a floating coffin and I've done us all good service by breaking her back. What is our situation here?"

Testu patted Henri reassuringly on the shoulder. "Over four hundred angry Spanish regulars are closing in on us. That is our situation my old friend."

"*Merde*. You need *Petit Cochon's* guns."

"Quite so, but don't look so glum Alexander. We found thousands of pounds of treasure!"

"I pray we live to spend it."

"Have faith. You and I have fought our way out of worse predicaments than this."

"We were younger back then and more foolish."

"Ah, but we have Lady Mary with us now. She holds the rank of general and you will obey her commands."

"How many men have you?" I asked.

"Thirty souls in all."

"Very well. You'll need to work fast. First, have your men lower your starboard guns over the side and start moving them up to the knoll over there. You won't need them. Have your men bring plenty of powder and grapeshot ashore too. Next drop your sails, topple the mizzen and have your lads cut a hole here at the bow, below the waterline. *Petit Cochon* must look like she's been shipwrecked and abandoned. On my signal, you'll engage the Spanish with your port guns. You must hold this position. If the Spanish take the *Pig*, they'll take the knoll and then all is lost."

Henri looked to Testu.

Testu nodded. "You have your orders, Alexander. We shall be entertaining our guests very, very soon I think."

"And if the Spanish board my ship and overwhelm us?"

"How many boats have you?" I asked.

"Only one. She'll hold twenty if we squeeze in close and cozy like."

"We'll support you from the high ground as best we can. I'd have that boat ready to launch off the stern. Cartagena is our rendezvous point. If the boat is full, the others will need to swim ashore and try to reach our position up on the plateau. Ugly business I know, but there it is."

From the boulder atop the knoll, I had an excellent view of the field and the ocean. From the sea to the edge of the swamp, I watched our men prepare.

Henri's crew moved out smartly with axes, rope and tackle. The Frenchman knew his business. His men felled *Pig's* mizzen mast as fast as any woodsman while others chopped a hole into her hull. The damage looked convincing. Others hoisted *Pig's* three starboard guns over the rail, laid planks across the sand and rolled the guns over the planks while my men on the knoll pulled on rope and tackle to help them. I saw Efendi and Testu moving up and down the field checking lines of fire and distributing extra ball and powder to the men taken from the *Pig*. Once we had the guns in place, I helped my men fashion a berm using sand, logs and fronds to conceal them.

And then I saw Zekowtah and his men return. Wearing only *maxtlatls*, their skin glistened with sweat, their bodies were splattered in blood. I grabbed an armful of waterskins and rushed towards them.

Zekowtah gladly accepted a skin. "Thank you," he said, took a long sip and then poured the rest over his head.

"What of the Spanish?" Testu asked after he and Efendi joined us.

"We led them into an ambush in a gully. We bloodied them but could not hold them. They are close. The men we fought are tough, seasoned veterans, professionals. This day will not be easy. Where would you have my men, Mary?"

"Guillaume and Mustafa have prepared positions for you. Your warriors will hold the right flank, from about here down to the swamp. The French will hold the center and my lads and I will defend the left with Captain Henri and the three-pounders. With the sea to the north and the swamp to the south, the Spanish cannot turn our flanks. They'll need to come straight at us."

Zekowtah surveyed the field and nodded his approval. "This is all well-done Mary."

"Aye, but if the Spanish have more men coming at us from the west..."

"I very much doubt they will, but I have scouts out to the west to warn us if I am wrong."

It was a strong defensive position to fight from and I was pleased with myself. The Spanish were marching headfirst into men dug-in on high ground supported by artillery. Without their ships, the Spanish could not turn our left flank and any attack through the swamp would be slow going through knee-deep water. The Spanish could swing south around the swamp and come around behind us from the west, but I did not think their commander would take such a risk. The maneuver would require him to split his forces against an enemy of unknown strength and take too much time - and if our ships returned before his, he would find himself surrounded, or so I imagined.

And then we heard the sounds of fife and drum floating on the breeze. The ominous melody had the desired effect as men turned to one another with uneasy glances.

"Take your positions!" Efendi cried out.

Men jumped into the holes or took cover behind logs and trees.

"God be with you," I said to no one in particular and hurried back to the knoll.

Moments later, the Spanish company on our right emerged from the trees moving in a single line abreast. I counted about eighty muskets in all. Zekowtah and his men had done good work. The Spanish halted before the stream, took a knee and waited.

On our left I could hear the music drawing nearer. I moved to the edge of the knoll where I had a clear view of the *Pig* and the beach and then I saw them. A battalion, three hundred strong, a mix of musketeers, pikemen and crossbowmen wearing steel *capacetes* and baggy, black trousers with brown leather doublets over their crimson shirts, came around the bend marching in a column.

The column halted. Officers barked out orders and soldiers scrambled. The Spaniards reformed themselves into a solid phalanx, into a show-of-force to freeze the blood.

Out on the water, I could still hear the boom of heavy guns. But the ships were too far off and obscured by smoke and haze to see who was winning.

Testu and Efendi suddenly appeared at my side. Testu gently took my hand.

"Mary, if the Spanish overrun our position, take Mustafa and head west and then north as fast as you can. The land turns mountainous not far from here. If you keep moving and are careful, the Spanish will never find you in that rugged country."

"I'll not abandon my men," I said tersely.

"Mary, I have bowed to your will this day in all things. Now you must do this for me. You must not let the Spanish take you. They will show you no mercy. Survive this day Mary, avenge us on the morrow if we fall. Mustafa has sworn to me that he will see you safe away."

"Mary...." Efendi said softly.

"Very well Guillaume," I said. "I'll not let the Spanish take me."

"Excellent," Testu replied cheerfully. "I look forward to gorging ourselves on wine with both of you tonight and pray Maurice, Jacob, Alexander and Zekowtah can join us. But if not, we shall meet again in some other far-away world."

I kissed both men on the cheek before I sent them back to their positions. And then we waited. We did not wait long.

An officer bellowed, a trumpeter blew his horn and the phalanx lumbered forward. The battalion commander, a man of limited imagination, ignored the broken *Pig*. He led his battalion across the stream and up the knoll, smack into the noses of our three-pounders hidden behind the berm. The company of musketeers on our right also advanced, leaving a gap of roughly three hundred yards of open ground between themselves and the battalion, a tempting gap worth exploiting had we more men. The Spanish advanced without skirmishers, uncertain of the terrain ahead and ignorant of our strength and deployment. I thought the Spanish commander stupid.

And then an enterprising young lieutenant took a platoon of thirty men, some carrying ladders, and peeled away from the battalion to have a closer look at the *Pig* and I realized my cockiness had been premature. The Spanish placed the ladders up against both sides of the *Pig* and started climbing. When they reached the rails, they were greeted by Henri's men who rose up from behind the bulwarks and fired.

"Roll out the guns!" I shouted. "Fire when ready!"

The gunners brushed the fronds aside and pushed the noses of our three-pounders over the berm. I covered my ears just before the gun captains brushed their linstocks against the touchholes.

BOOM! BOOM! BOOM!

Clouds of white smoke fouled the air. I heard men scream. And then I heard *Pig's* three-pounders bark, belching smoke and flame. When I raised my head above the berm, I saw heaps of mangled flesh lying in the sand in front of us, and all around the *Pig*. The wounded on the slope were already slithering their way back to the beach.

Up and down the line men on both sides discharged their muskets. One of my gunners keeled over with a soft groan and a bullet in the eye.

I steadied my nerves. I considered our situation. To the left, reinforced with a second platoon, the Spanish were storming aboard the *Pig* and fighting the French hand-to-hand. They were pushing Henri and his men back towards the stern. To the right the Spanish company had crossed the stream and were moving inside our lines. In front of me, less than fifty yards away, I saw the Spanish commander swinging a tasseled sword above his head, urging his men on. One more good push and his battalion would be on top of us. We had killed and wounded Spaniards, but not nearly enough. My gunners had fired too high. I wondered if I had just killed us all.

My gunners struggled reloading. The guns had recoiled off their wooden tracks and the carriage wheels could gain no purchase against the sandy soil. I put my shoulder against one muzzle to help the crew push the brute forward.

Then we heard the blare of a Spanish horn again. The trumpeter blew three sharp notes on his trumpet and the phalanx disintegrated into a swarm of angry bees. Men fanned out in all directions. The Spanish commander kept fifty musketeers with him, had them form two ranks and take a knee. They fired at our battery while their mates charged up the knoll. Musket balls punched the sand up all around us and I saw two more of my men fall.

"Lads!" I screamed. "Push these bitches back into place. Push for all your worth!"

We put our backs into it, frantically working the muzzles over the berm. One of my men, an industrious fellow, suddenly appeared with an armful of wood. We wedged the pieces underneath the rear wheels of the first two guns to lower the elevation while the crew on the third gun struggled to move their gun into place. The gun captains primed their guns with priming powder, checked their aim and fired.

BOOM! BOOM!

I didn't even look to see the damage. I grabbed a flexible rammer, bolted over the berm and swabbed the first gun's muzzle down as shots whizzed by all around me. I placed a powder charge into the muzzle next and rammed the charge home, then grit my teeth and pushed a canister filled with shards of metal against the charge. I knew the drill. My Hunter had had taught me well.

But when I moved over to the second gun, a pair of strong arms pulled me down. The man ripped the rammer from my hands and scrambled up the berm, cursing as he moved. Two more men followed him carrying charges and canisters. Then the third gun fired.

I glanced down to my right and saw Testu directing his men to cover my men as we reloaded the three-pounders again. I peeked over the berm and saw Spanish pikemen, not more than twenty feet away, struggling to reach us. But for the loose sand shifting under their feet, I think they would have reached the top of the knoll and sent us all to hell.

With our guns primed and loaded, I told my gunners to hold their fire until we saw a face. And when we saw that first Spaniard stick his head over the berm, all three guns fired as one. I grabbed my pistols, climbed over the berm and jumped up on top of the boulder. I fired into the Spaniards fleeing down the hill, many were tripping and falling over themselves as they ran. From the boulder I had a good view of the entire battle. I saw carnage on a ghastly scale. Our three-pounders had shredded scores of Spaniards. My gunners raised a cheer, but the battle was far from over.

Aboard the *Pig* the Spanish had Henri's men cornered against the stern. The French were fighting desperately for their lives with nowhere left to run. The Spanish commander then changed tactics. He rallied his men around him and threw everything he had at the center of the field. His battalion charged across the stream to join the company of musketeers near the swamp. Testu's men couldn't stop them and the French and Cimarron suddenly found themselves locked in grisly hand-to-hand fighting. And then I heard Efendi's voice, I turned and saw him helping the sick and wounded into the line. From left to right and in the center the battle hung in the balance. We needed every musket.

"Musketeers!" I cried out to my men. "Shift right and make ready to fire a volley into the center of the field. On my command we'll rise as one and fire. You gunners, shift your guns to the right as best you can. Stagger your shots this time. On the command *gunners stand*, you men on the first gun will rise and fire when ready. You men on the second gun will then rise, adjust your aim as needed and fire and you men on the third gun will do the same. Make each shot count or all is lost. Understood?"

My men, drenched in sweat and covered in dust and soot, answered me with grim nods.

The sun was at its zenith, scorching everything in its path. The humidity was stifling. The air had turned thick with clouds of acrid, white smoke. I steadied my breathing as I reloaded my pistols. I brushed the sweat off my brow. I stole a quick glance of the sky, then took in the sea, the sea that I had loved so much in this life, and braced myself for the end.

"Musketeers! Ready. Steady... Stand and *FIRE!*"

I cocked the hammers on my pistols back, rose with my men and came face-to-face with a Spaniard wielding an axe. The man was quick. He hurtled his axe before I could fire. By the grace of God, he missed. Then a ball struck the pistol in my right hand. The shot ricocheted into the man next to me. He clutched his stomach and crumpled to the ground, alive or dead I did not know.

"Gunners stand!" I said awkwardly, suddenly realizing I badly needed to piss. "When ready: *FIRE!*"

BOOM!

BOOM!

And then nothing. I turned, saw the third gun captain slumped over his gun's muzzle. I took the linstock from his hand, checked my aim and fired.

BOOM!

I watched in disbelief - horrified - as angry Spaniards emerged from the smoke on top of the berm. One man raised a rock above his head to bring me down, until he doubled-over with a knife in his gut. The rock slipped from his hands as he fell on top of me.

Efendi reached down to pull the dead man off me and helped me to my feet. "God is great, Mary."

I stood and drew my sword, ready to get back into the fight. But all across the field, the Spanish were on the run.

I buried my head in Efendi's shoulder and wept. "I thought the battle was lost when the Spanish came over the berm."

"Shhh, and yet we live," Efendi replied softly and let me weep.

I took Efendi by the hand and led him to the top of the boulder to survey the world around us. To the far right, the Spanish company was falling back in disorder with Zekowtah and his warriors sprinting after them, swinging their spiked war clubs and sharp battleaxes for the close-in work. The Cimarron raised a chilling war cry as they ran - and they'd show the Spanish no mercy. Then I saw a small crocodile crawl out of the swamp to retrieve a severed head. I felt a shiver run down my spine as he moved backwards into the water. In the center, the French were cautiously advancing, stepping over crumpled bodies lying across the field, and on the left Spaniards were jumping off the *Pig* to rejoin their battalion.

"And yet we live," I whispered.

"A hard day to get clear of," Efendi said with a touch of introspection in his voice.

"I did not want this Mustafa. You are unharmed?"

"*Tâlih* was with me today. I am well."

I caressed his cheek with the back of my hand. "May your luck hold fast always," I said, then turned my gaze to the ocean. "What do you think?"

"Have faith Mary. On the water, Jacob is as good as any man."

Then Robert caught my eye as he climbed out of his pit. The top of his shirt was stained with blood and I called him to me.

"You're a lucky man, Rob," I said as I inspected the wound to his forehead. "A ball grazed your temple. You'll need stitches. Find some shade and rest. I'll tend to you shortly."

"Not until you rest first, my lady."

Efendi smiled, plainly proud of his young protégé. "You fought with skill and bravery today Rob."

"You've taught him well Mustafa," I said. "Though I'm concerned by this relentless insubordination of his."

"Will it be an ugly scar?" Robert asked.

"Women love a good scar on a man," I replied and patted the boy's shoulder. "Especially a scar earned in battle. Did you shoot anyone?"

"Aye, and my aim was true."

I kissed his hand. "I'm sorry. Killing a man can be a hard thing. If you feel raw about it later, we can talk."

"I'm in fine spirits Captain. I killed men before they killed me. Not much more to say."

"Very well then. I'll excuse your earlier insubordination this one time, but if the Spanish resume their attack, you'll stick close to Mustafa's side as if you were his shadow. Understood?"

"Understood."

I turned my attention back to the field. Down on the beach the Spanish commander - not as stupid as I had first thought - was moving about restoring order. He sent one squad forward under a white flag to retrieve his wounded and reformed the rest of his battalion into a hollow square to defend against an attack. I was relieved when I spotted Testu and then I saw Zekowtah return with a handful of wounded.

"Mustafa, after I speak with Guillaume and Zekowtah, I'll see to our wounded. I suspect the Spanish have had enough and will retire to Nombre de Diós, but I don't think this Spanish commander is accustomed to losing, so I may be wrong. We must be ready for a second assault. Let's rotate the men to get water, ammunition and powder."

"The men will be ready Mary."

I found Testu and Zekowtah standing together at the stream washing blood off themselves and walked across the field to join them. Testu greeted me with a broad smile.

"What amuses you, good sir?" I asked.

"Why I am delighted, ecstatic, to see you unharmed of course."

"You look no worse for wear," I replied and nodded to Zekowtah.

"I have fought many battles and survived each one with hardly a scratch."

"You live a charmed life Guillaume."

"Ha, ha! I do, I do indeed. What are the Spanish up to?"

"They're collecting their wounded under a white flag."

"Your gunners were magnificent Mary. They carved the Spanish up. The Spanish commander will withdraw I think and wait for reinforcements."

"I suspect you're right."

"Let us hope good fortune was with Maurice and Jacob. Any word from Henri?"

"No. I fear the fighting aboard the *Pig* was fierce. I doubt Henri and his men can repel a second attack. What is your situation here?"

"We have counted over forty Spanish dead so far and we'll find more bodies in the woods and down by the shore. I lost seven men and have wounded. Zekowtah lost six I think?"

"Yes," Zekowtah answered, "though I still have men out running down Spaniards."

"And your losses Mary?" Testu asked.

"At least ten souls that I know of. I fear I'll find more once I make the rounds."

"Your men took the brunt of the fighting," Testu replied. "You had the worst of it. For the rest of my days I will bless you for bringing those glorious three-pounders ashore. Genius that was."

"More an act of desperation," I said honestly and then turned to Zekowtah. I noted the blood dripping from the axe tucked inside his belt. "Zekowtah, your boy?"

The Aztec nodded. "We fought side-by-side, father and son. When the other young bucks held back, Iztli rushed into the fight without fear. He brought down three Spaniards with his bow. I will make him *Cuachicqueh*."

"I'm glad he's unharmed and pray he'll live to see the day when the Cimarron can live in peace."

"Men have never lived in peace. There is no end to war."

"A harsh judgment of mankind Zekowtah, but I can find no fault in your words. Well gentlemen, shall we go see what the Spanish are up to?"

Testu and Zekowtah followed me back to the knoll where we found Efendi and my men repairing the berm. To my dismay, the Spanish hadn't left. The battalion commander had retrieved his wounded and had his men erecting a crude wall of sand and wood to protect themselves from our guns. He was waiting, as we were, to see whose ships returned first. Stalemate.

"What are our losses Mustafa?" I asked.

"Twelve dead. Fifteen wounded. Guillaume, Captain Henri sent a man with a message for you. He has lost half his men and the Spanish spiked his guns before they left. He asks for your permission to abandon the *Pig*."

Testu jerked his head back as if he had been slapped in the face. "With victory so close?"

"Victory?" I scoffed. "Your hatred of the Spanish has clouded your good judgement Guillaume. The price we've paid in blood for silver has cost us dearly and if that Spanish squadron returns before our ships do, we won't even have the silver."

"Look there, Mary!" Testu said, pointing at the ocean. "Sails! Our sails by God!"

Testu's eyes were better than mine. I could only see the faintest outline of a ship or two in the distance. But the Spanish commander must have seen what Testu saw, for his men began helping the wounded to their feet, or lifted them up on litters, and within minutes the Spanish were on the move, marching down the coast for Nombre de Diós. I silently walked away to tend to my wounded.

We had forty-four dead in all, nearly one third of our expedition, and as many wounded. We laid the dead out in neat rows along the shore, the brave Captain Henri among them. A grievous wound to his leg was beyond cautery. Testu was forced to amputate the leg above the knee to try and save Henri's life, but the brave Frenchman bled out and died peacefully an hour later.

Zekowtah permitted torches and cooking fires throughout the camp. Men sat quietly around the flames eating their suppers while I stood alone at the water's edge, waiting in the fading light for the longboats to drift in.

A deep sadness gnawed at my heart as I listened to the surf splashing against the sand. Death was nothing new to me, but this day had affected me beyond my understanding. Mercifully, my melancholy diminished when I saw Atwood and MacGyver's faces in the lead boats.

"Praise God you are alive Mary!" Atwood said and embraced me as he stepped off the first longboat.

MacGyver jumped off next and did the same. I hugged and kissed them both.

"Yes, I'm alive. I fear this day has made a good many widows and too many orphans."

"Mustafa?" Atwood asked with apprehension.

"God loves that man. He's well, as always."

Atwood considered the bodies lying side-by-side on the sand. "God's wounds."

"A bitter day," I said as I locked one arm around Atwood's waist and the other around MacGyver's and held them close. "Tell me about your day."

"A very good day all-in-all," MacGyver answered. "We have eleven lads to bury and a dozen wounded to care for. Maurice lost about as many."

"My heart aches for it. And the Spanish?"

Atwood grunted. "Their commander was not without skill. We traded many blows. But we had the faster ships and the bigger guns. We were lucky too. Without rhyme or reason, a rogue wave struck a Spanish nao as she made a sharp turn and she capsized. Most peculiar. The fighting stopped to fish her crew out of the water. After that misfortune, the Spanish wisely sailed off. I do not expect them to stay away for very long though. We should go."

"Aye..."

Then Atwood handed me a peculiar thin tube.

"What's this?"

Atwood pulled on the tube, extending its length. "A gift for you. We fished two Spaniards out of the water, one fellow had this eyepiece on him. Take a look, like so."

I looked through the tube and was shocked. Everything turned bigger and moved closer.

"What the devil?" I asked and pulled the tube away.

"The engraving along the side is Dutch," Atwood replied. "The Spanish use this glass to spy. This is how they saw us before we saw them."

"This is a fantastical device."

Then Maurice jumped down from his longboat. He took me by the hands and smiled.

"Mary, how wonderful to see you. Testu?"

"Guillaume is well Maurice, as is Zekowtah and his son. But we lost many men."

"Henri?"

"He died of his wounds."

Maurice saw the bodies and nodded. "He was a good man. The Spanish came at you hard."

"Aye. Three hundred Spaniards launched their assault from here and the rest came at us from the woods down by the swamp. The Spanish nearly broke through our lines. Thank God they didn't land men behind us. Thanks be to God you boys ran their ships off."

"How did they know you were here?" MacGyver asked.

"Ah, an excellent question Michael. I know not. We must ask Zekowtah. Perhaps the Spanish army stumbled upon us by mere chance. The Spanish often send out patrols or take to the field to practice their battle tactics, or so I've heard."

"This," Atwood said, "was a damn large patrol and is an odd place to practice."

I yawned. The day's ugly business had caught up to me. "Well," I said wearily, "the Spanish have plenty of ships and men to play with. Come, let's find Guillaume and Zekowtah."

We quietly walked back to camp and found the French digging graves to bury their dead. I would bury my own at sea as was our way.

After we ate our suppers, I took all my men back to the ships along with our dead. We offered up our prayers, gave the sea our fallen and then I shared a drink or two on deck with my crew. When I could drink no more, I went below and collapsed on my bunk, too weary to even strip-off my filthy clothes, and cried myself to sleep.

In the morning when I stirred, I awoke refreshed and in a better mood. I made my way in the dark to the galley where I found hot coffee and fresh biscuits set out for the night watch and helped myself to both. I made my way to the quarter deck to enjoy my early breakfast and was surprised to find Atwood and a dozen men, all wearing grim faces, waiting for me.

"What's this?" I asked, bracing myself for bad news.

Atwood and the men smiled, then stepped aside to reveal a large barrel filled with hot water underneath a makeshift tent behind them. "Your bath, madam," Atwood said with a silly grin. "Thompson, with the lady's permission, go below to her cabin and fetch soap, a fresh towel and some clean clothing."

I kissed Atwood on the cheek and shook the hand of each sailor. "Thank you for this kindness. I'm touched by your thoughtfulness. Promise me you'll do the same for your wives or sweethearts back home after we return and I promise you your reward will be rich indeed."

After a good bath and a hearty breakfast, I took thirty men with me in three longboats and went ashore. We rowed underneath a brilliant sky of cobalt blue with bands of soft turquoise and splashes of bold yellows and deep reds. I found Testu and his men on the beach, dragging the bodies of dead Spaniards up to the field and dropping them down into the pits we had dug. The air was thick with the stink of death and swarms of black flies.

Testu walked towards me, covered in filth, but wearing an easy smile. "Well, well, well, Poseidon's daughter has returned to us fresh and well-scrubbed and ready for a bright, new day!"

"You'll kindly keep your distance downwind sir."

"Ha! Nothing a little perfume can't cure."

"I don't see any of your longboats on the beach, Guillaume."

"No. We still have work to do."

I grabbed Testu by the forearm and pulled him aside. "Are you mad?"

"No? Why do you ask this silly question?"

"Guillaume - do not play the fool with me. We must depart these shores with haste. The Spanish will return with more ships and more men. Perhaps they're on the way already."

"Perhaps, perhaps not. The garrison at Nombre de Diós is small. The captain-general there will most likely send couriers to Ciudad de México and request reinforcements before he makes his move. It will be days before the Spanish return, if they return at all."

I could feel my cheeks burning. "Why? Why do you take this awful risk? How much more silver do you need? Haven't we lost enough men?"

"Just before the Spanish attacked, my men found another chest, only one, but there must be more."

"Aye. I heard the cheers and thought as much. Wait. You and your men have spent all night digging?"

Testu winced. "Well..."

"Auck! And you've found nothing more?"

"Thus far, no."

My tone turned testy. "The silver's luster has scrambled your brains. Don't become a greedy Midas!"

Seeing Testu and me exchanging heated words, Zekowtah and Maurice cut across the stream towards us. Atwood, MacGyver and Efendi did the same and soon we found ourselves holding a council of war amidst a pile of rotting flesh and dirty flies.

"Do we have a problem here?" Atwood asked gruffly with his hand on the hilt of his sword.

I gave the big Scot a reassuring smile. "All is well, Jacob. Our friends wish to stay. They intend to look for more treasure."

"Mary, I don't think we should -."

"Rest easy, Jacob," I said. "We aren't staying. Guillaume, we'll take our share now. Whatever else you find is yours. We can meet again in the Port of Spain if you like. I intend to return to Europe with New World goods and to see my men reunited with their families. Zekowtah, we'll happily take you and your men and your share of the silver back to Guna Yala if you like."

Zekowtah nodded. "I thank you, Mary. The Cimarron are not seafarers like your Carib friends. We dislike the water. We'll stay with our French brothers."

"Very well. I trust you and your people will think of me as your friend."

The Aztec warrior considered me for a moment before he spoke, then rested a hand on my shoulder. "I am proud to call you friend and ally. If providence favors us, we will stand together again..."

Chapter Ten

e said our farewells to our French and Cimarron brothers, took our share of the silver and returned to our ships before noon. I was impatient to reach the Port of Spain, though I knew not why, and was glad to put Panama behind us.

It is true I have a restless soul and often find myself in a hurry. But what drove me away from Panama was something oddly different, something peculiarly unsettling. I have a good nose for the weather and good instincts for approaching trouble. I scanned the horizon in all directions but saw only blue skies over calm seas and no hostile sails.

Atwood sensed my shifting mood. He brought one dram of whiskey for me and one for himself, though a dram measured out by a Scot is closer to two drams measured by others.

"'Tis only midday!" I said and laughed good-naturedly as I worked the ship's wheel, though I did not refuse the whiskey.

Atwood raised his glass. "As the captain of this ship, I decide the time of day. To wash away the brine, salute!"

I raised my glass and knocked the whiskey back. "You're a good man Jacob Atwood and you have a kind heart."

"God forbid."

We stood in silence together for a time as *Phantom* and *Diablo* glided across the gentle swells. The sky was without blemish. The sea glittered like a green jewel. I relished the crisp, clean air, a most welcome change from Panama's offensive heat and humidity.

After traipsing through the jungle, surviving on nuts and berries, I did not have much meat on my bones. The whiskey's magic spread across my body fast. My mind began to wander, churning out random thoughts. I thought of my mother, something I rarely did as she had died when I was very young. And yet the memories I had of her, fragments at best, now flooded into my head. Then, as real as life, Hunter stepped out of a mist before me. He wrapped his arms around me and kissed me. I could feel the warmth of his body against me. I could taste his lips on mine. And then my little Aliénor appeared, reaching up to grab my neck. But in a flash of light, she vanished into the mist holding Hunter's hand. I quickly offered up a prayer for her happiness and wellbeing.

A roar of laughter jolted me out of my reverie. Whatever malaise afflicted me was not shared by my men. I had a happy crew. And well I should. We had silver and profits to spend. I had rich men sailing for me. I took a deep breath to clear my head, grasped the wheel more firmly and focused on the way ahead.

Our voyage to the Port of Spain was blissfully short and uneventful. We dropped anchor in a crowded bay and I released half my men with five days' liberty, paying out token shares to each man. I kept the rest aboard the ships to work repairs and to guard our loot and took Atwood, MacGyver, Efendi, Kinkae and Fish with me to the tavern on the square. The tavern's proprietor, one of mine, greeted us warmly and seated us at a quiet table in a backroom. When he returned with glasses and pitchers of ale, he reached into his apron and handed me two letters, both from Cortés.

The Spaniard delivered as promised. He had found the cargo I wanted for our voyage home. I only needed to provide him a date, a place and the tonnage I wished to purchase and he would see to the rest. But I could not give Cortés an answer until I conferred with Testu.

We divided our time between the ships and the tavern, drinking, playing cards and games of chance. I never strayed far from either place and the days passed by slowly. The seaport, as always, depressed me.

Two tedious weeks after our arrival, a day or two before I intended to leave the Port of Spain without Testu, the Frenchman walked through the tavern's double doors with a look I had never seen on him before. Even in the shadows, I could see the sorrow in his eyes.

I waved him over to our table. I pulled a chair out for him and handed him my ale. "Guillaume, what vexes you?"

Testu wearily plopped down next to me and avoided my gaze. His lips were cracked. His skin was pale. His eyes were dull and lifeless.

He took a sip of ale to clear his throat. "Three days after you sailed, a plague swept through our camp. Spread to the ships. Nearly half my men perished! Half, Mary! Zekowtah lost Iztli. Maurice fell ill too. I am doubly cursed as alas we found no more silver."

I laid my hand on Testu's forearm. "Maurice is dead?"

"Zekowtah and his men carried Maurice back to Ronconcholan, as was his wish. I know not if he is alive or dead."

"The world is cursed my friend, not you."

"I should have listened to you, Mary."

"Each day we put our lives in jeopardy no matter what we choose to do."

Atwood poured Testu more ale and raised his tankard. "The fates are fickle, friend. To fallen brothers."

When I returned to the ships, I handed out chunks of coarse soap to my crew and plenty of it. I grabbed a bucket and a brush, got on my hands and knees and started scrubbing. My men grumbled a little but joined me as I knew they would. Once we finished scouring the ship, I made every man wash himself and his clothes with soap.

Testu agreed to cross the Atlantic with me and I agreed to remain in Trinidad for another week, to give his unhappy crew time to find their good morale in the pleasures the port had to offer. I sent one letter to Cortés at his home in Santo Domingo and another to his *hacienda* in Havana with my requirements and told him to expect us in Old Havana in three to four weeks' time.

Testu slid off me panting hard with sweat bubbling up from

every pore. I offered him a thin smile, an insincere smile, but it was the best I could do. No woman could ask more from her lover. No woman should need more. Testu was a dark and handsome man. His body was firm, pleasing to the eye and sensuous to the touch. He had an easygoing manner, a quick wit and he took pleasure in pleasing me. I had no right to want more. The emptiness I felt perplexed me.

I kissed the Frenchman on the cheek. I reached for my clothes and started dressing.

"What is your hurry, Mary?"

"The tide will be with us soon. I always inspect my ships and men before weighing anchor and setting out. You know this."

"*Très bien*. Most wise. All is well between us?"

I threw Testu a curious glance, then admonished myself. I had forgotten that men can be intuitive too, no matter how elaborate the mask a woman chooses to wear.

"What a silly question," I replied evasively.

"Yes? Good, good."

"What compels you to ask me such a thing?"

"Nothing, nothing in particular. Well, I suppose there is Panama. You were against our voyage to Panama. Of late you seem, well, aloof."

"Aloof? You think me a ship moving windward?"

"No, no. Aloof. *Ah, le mot en anglais*. Ah, distant."

"Distant is it?"

"*Oui.*"

"Hmmm. I accompanied you to Panama of my own accord and harbor no ill-will against you there. *Tous les Frencmen semblent penser qu'ils sont des experts sur les femmes.* But women are not easily understood. All is well *mon ami. Donne cette affaire sans penser à mon galant capitaine.*"

It pained me to be less than forthright with Testu. Like leaves carried off by the wind, we wretched souls must travel the path handed to us by fate. I offered Testu a reassuring smile and mercifully he did not press me. When I stood to slip my trousers on, he smacked me playfully on the rump.

"I am happy you are not cross with me, Mary. Your French is improving."

"I have a fine tutor."

"You are a good student."

"As are you," I said as I reached down to cup the Frenchman's manhood in my hand and squeezed.

The day was overcast. The air smelled of rain. I was thrilled to be out on the open water again, and far away from the Port of Spain. As *Phantom* skimmed across the water under full sail, I stood atop the forecastle watching the dolphins play.

We sailed in ballast in a diamond formation with *Cerberus* in the lead of course. We moved north-by-northwest tacking against a lively wind.

My thoughts turned to Ireland and my little Aliénor. Westport would have seen the year's first snow. I imagined her outside in her basket wrapped in a warm blanket, giggling with delight as snowflakes tickled her nose. I wondered if she would have any memory of me upon my return, or see only a stranger.

"Mary, Mary!" Atwood called out as he climbed the forecastle's ladder towards me. "We've got company," he said and pointed south.

I put my hands over my eyes and struggled to catch a glimpse of sails on the horizon. But I saw only whitecaps roiling across a bad-tempered sea with thick, low clouds swirling all around us.

"I see nothing but water, Jacob."

"Aye, but from the masthead O'Rourke has spotted a pack of ships two points off our port stern. The ships are closing with us."

"Warships?"

"Can't tell."

"Well, there is nothing to be done for it. We should hold this course. The weather is turning raw. I'll grab a pair of sea capes for us if you'll fetch some hot coffee."

"Something stronger would suit me better. I had a cask or two of

Mad Dog brought aboard before we put the Port of Spain behind us."

"I best keep to the coffee today, Jacob. Strong ale makes me sleepy and besides, that Mad Dog of yours tastes like oil. But if you were to add a thimble full of whisky to my coffee, you wouldn't hear me complain."

The ships shadowing us were small but fast. Their crews worked hard through the morning to close the distance between us. *Phantom* and *Cerberus* had more speed to give, but *Diablo* and *Vengeance* were sailing as fast as they could sail.

When the lead ship in the pack closed within fifteen hundred yards of us, I climbed the main mast up to the masthead to see things for myself and took the Spanish glass with me. I counted thirteen ships in all.

After I stepped back on deck, I took the wheel and nudged *Phantom* up alongside *Cerberus*. "Unless those are friends of yours Guillaume," I shouted across the water, "it would seem we're in for a brawl."

Always composed, always amused by the world around him, Testu smiled broadly as if he didn't have a care in the world. "So it would seem Mary. Today I am most fortunate to be sailing side-by-side with you. I suppose as a gentleman I should warn those rogues about your mercurial disposition. Only a knave charges blindly at a devious mind already planning his destruction!"

"I promise they'll find no joy this day," I said. "We must seize the weather gage for ourselves. Once those jackals are within a thousand yards or so, we can come about and go straight at them. You take *Cerberus* and *Vengeance* to the right and I'll take *Phantom* and *Diablo* to the left and we'll circle around these mystery ships. God willing they'll break and run to avoid our sting."

"And what if they do not? I am reluctant to split our ships against a larger force. They have us by three-to-one. We should stay together to support each other."

"If we were fighting on land, I might agree with you my friend. But what we lack in numbers, we can overcome with speed, agility and firepower. We are facing pirates, not the Spanish navy."

"Someone must have blabbered in port. Someone talked about the silver."

"Aye, some loggerhead with a loose tongue has put us all in jeopardy."

"Or perhaps we've been betrayed."

"It is of little consequence now Guillaume. We box those ships in-between us, we herd them in tight and then hit them hard on all sides. Those dogs will run. If I'm wrong, we can put in at Guadeloupe where we have friends. The island is no more than fifty leagues due east by my reckoning."

"Well I remember the day we first met Mary. You kept your ships close and traded speed for blunt power, to great effect as I recall. Won't you reconsider?"

I shook my head with a cocky smile.

"Mary..."

"Ready your ships for action *mon Capitaine* - hold on to your balls and follow me!"

Atwood moved next to me. "I've learned," he called out to Testu, "not to question our good lady on matters of tactics. She has a gift Guillaume. At the Battle of Cartagena, we faced a smaller force in calmer seas. Today we face a larger force in trickier winds. A different tactic is needed."

"Pardon? The Battle of Cartagena?"

Atwood laughed. "I thought you knew. We named the fight between us off the coast of Venezuela the Battle of Cartagena."

"Ah, *très bon*. Very well, we shall do things your way Mary. But if we survive the day, the honor of naming this battle is mine. That is my price."

"So be it," I said and waved Testu off. "Jacob, signal Michael to pull-up alongside us. We need to share the plan with him. Best have Mustafa ready the ship for action too."

"Aye, Mary."

"Any sage advice?"

"I like the plan, Mary. Those Trinidad tavern whores with their flimsy coasters are about to take on sturdy warships sailed by men of discipline and iron. Even so, Guillaume's ships are undermanned and he doesn't have your skill. I wish to God we had Maurice with us. This day looks to be bloody all around."

"We play the cards we've been dealt Jacob."

"True, true. If the action turns hot and there is fighting on the decks, you must not risk your life. If I tell you to go below, you go below without question. You have an infant child to care for now."

"Right."

"Promise me."

"Very well."

"Say it."

"Jacob!"

"Say it."

"Oh, bloody hell. I promise."

"Good. Ah, here comes our good Captain of the Guns now."

I turned on my heels to face Efendi. "Mustafa, Jacob is giving me orders. I may need your skills."

"I heard. You best heed Jacob's good advice Mary."

"Hmmm. Better to have the pair of you locked away below for mutiny."

Efendi looked over the stern rail at the vessels closing on us. "As you please. I might hold off on that order for a bit. You might yet need us."

I laid my hand on Efendi's shoulder. "If I were you, I'd see to my starboard guns."

After another half-hour passed, I had my men hoist a green streamer up the main mast, the signal for our four ships to turn about to the south as one and seize the tactical advantage. We sailed close-hauled, picked up terrific speed and sailed straight at our pursuers.

Our sails billowed full and strained against the lines. Water splashed over the rails. From head to toe I was drenched in sticky brine. But I didn't care. My blood was hot for battle.

Efendi returned to the quarter deck to stand with Atwood and me. "The deck has been cleared for action," he offered in a calm, confident tone. "The guns are primed and loaded."

"Very well, Mustafa. I see you have the swivels ready to mount as well."

"Quite so Mary. I'll send a squad of our best marksmen aloft when the time is right."

"Good. I'm surprised we haven't seen any rain yet. Even so, the lads best check their powder with all this sea spray and water spilling over the rails."

"I trust you'll straighten her keel out to give my gunners a level platform when it's time."

"I promise to give your gunners a wonderful array of targets to choose from Mustafa."

We were somewhere off the coast of Martinique, though visibility was too poor to see the island, sailing south in two parallel lines. Two thousand yards or so of water separated my ships from *Cerberus* and *Vengeance*.

And then I saw a puff of smoke and a tongue of flame spew out of the bow of the lead ship, followed by a mellow boom and a splash of water. The well-placed shot, a brilliant warning shot, landed between *Phantom* and *Diablo* and raised an eyebrow or two among my crew.

Atwood, standing at the wheel, didn't flinch. He didn't even look to see where the shot had landed. He kept us on a steady course and we forged ahead at breakneck speed. Nothing rattled that man.

"It would seem our new friends," I told him, "wish for us to heave to for a parley."

Atwood nodded and smiled as I fumbled with the plumb bob on my gunner's quadrant, trying to untangle a troublesome knot. Hunter had purchased Niccoló Tartaglia's newfangled device for me in Ireland a few years back. I was better than any man at using the quadrant to gauge distance.

"The intentions of those villains," he said, "seem plain enough. What's your pleasure, Mary?"

"We press ahead Jacob. I want to close the distance with those ships, but not so close that we find ourselves in the midst of their formation or we'll be fighting on all sides."

"Aye, Mary. I've kept my eye on Guillaume. He's slipped too far off to the west. This wind will carry him even farther."

"So I see. I fear he waited too long to make his move. He's lost position. Well, there is nothing to be done for it now. We must keep to the plan."

We continued on our line of attack. The men from Trinidad were brazen rascals. They made no attempt to flee or change course.

At a thousand yards my gunners would start hitting things. At five hundred yards my gunners could cause real damage and at two hundred yards or so my men would load the great guns with grapeshot and employ the swivels to inflict some truly horrific damage upon flesh, canvas and wood.

I walked across the quarter deck to the fore rail and took in the main deck below. Efendi's gunners, four men to a gun, twelve crews in all, looked ready. Each gun captain held a burning linstock in his hand, waiting for the order.

I steadied my gunner's quadrant on the rail to estimate the distance. At a thousand yards I waved my arm to catch Efendi's attention.

"Mr. Efendi, you may have your men run out their guns and fire as you deem best. Target the lead ship first, then move down the line as we pass each ship by."

Quiet, never boastful, Efendi simply doffed his English flat cap and nodded with the cold, grim eyes of a killer. I've seen the bravest man freeze at the sight of his war mask.

"Gunners," he shouted. "Run out your guns. Captains take aim, on the swell, steady, wait for it, when ready, fire..."

BOOM! BOOM! BA-BA-BOOM! BA-BA-BA-BA-BA-BA-BOOM!

The starboard broadside shook the ship from stem to stern. White smoke blew back into my face. The gunners hustled to swab the muzzles down as plumes of water splashed up all around the lead vessel from Trinidad. I couldn't believe my eyes, missed shots all! And then *Diablo's* guns thundered with a full broadside. I saw more splashes and more missed shots! And then: BOOOOOOOOOOM!

A tremendous explosion, the likes of Coruña, obliterated the lead ship in a ball of smoke and fire. The horrific blast bent the ship's deck upwards and snapped her masts in two like twigs. I stared, transfixed, as the ship's hull split in half. Her stern floated one way, her bow the other and then both halves slipped beneath the waves. In single moment, the ship and all her crew were gone.

"Merciful God in heaven!" Atwood cried out and crossed himself.

I gawked at the empty spot of water, too stunned to speak. I heard wild cheers from my crew.

I glanced over at Atwood. "We struck her powder magazine?"

"Possibly, Mary. More likely the damn fools brought their powder up on deck and stacked the barrels together in one neat pile. Either way, MacGyver's men landed a lucky shot."

We did not have long to gloat. Twelve ships, overcrowded with angry men wanting vengeance, started lobbing iron at us. Our foe had three and four-pounders at best, but they had a lot of them and shots rained down all around us. Most fell harmlessly into the sea, but several shots ripped through our sails and a few balls smacked against our hull.

"Stop your vents, swab your barrels down!" I heard Efendi bellow. "Jump to it! Prime and load, prime and load. Faster, faster, faster if you want to survive this day!"

Seconds later our guns barked back.

I looked over at *Diablo*, just as she fired another broadside too, and then looked for *Cerberus* and *Vengeance*. Testu had sailed too far off for me to see what was happening, even with my Spanish glass, but in my heart, I knew Testu was in trouble.

I turned again to Atwood. "Jacob, should we hold our course or sail towards Testu?"

Atwood answered me with a blank stare. I understood. Indecision had never been one of my flaws.

"Jacob?"

"Ahem. We stay our course Mary, we keep to the plan. If we turn and move towards Testu now, we'll be cutting straight through the middle of those heathens. Even with our heavier guns the risk is far too great. If just one well-placed shot disables either *Phantom* or *Diablo*, our goose is cooked. Are you well Mary?"

"Aye, I'm well enough Jacob. A peculiar mood vexes me today. You are right, I know. Still, we can afford to shave a half a league off our present course to gain some time. See those three ships at the tail end of the flotilla? Let's ease over to them and introduce ourselves."

Atwood handed the wheel over to a tall Swede named Larsson, a good man at the helm, and hurried to the quarter deck fore rail. With a voice like rolling thunder he barked out orders to turn our ship two points to starboard.

Fish and his Carib, wearing only trousers, raced up the rigging smartly. They spread out along the foot stirrups in their bare feet and let out more canvas while my Blackamoors worked the lines and braces under Kinkae's watchful eye.

No man could coax more speed out of a ship than Atwood.

Then the pirate flotilla surprised me and spilt itself in two. Nine ships turned away from us and sailed off to intercept Testu. The other three formed a skirmish line to keep us from following. I felt a knot in the pit of my stomach as I realized that I had underestimated our opponent. These rogues were not the usual, undisciplined pirate rabble we had engaged over the years. We were fighting a well-organized, determined foe led by a single commander and the man was showing skill.

I waved to Atwood and Efendi to join me at the helm.

"Guillaume is no doubt cursing your name about now Mary," Atwood quipped.

"No doubt, no doubt he is," I replied uneasily. "Perhaps he has good cause to do so."

"Nonsense Mary, your plan is sound," Efendi offered.

Atwood nodded in agreement. "Mary, Mustafa speaks the truth. We'd be in the midst of a bloody brawl at close quarters had we listened to Testu and sailed in a single formation. He has only himself to blame for being too far west. We need thirty minutes, no more, to close with those bastards standing in our way. With our faster ships and bigger guns, we can easily pick them apart. Then we can rescue our French friends."

"Aye," I replied half-heartedly, less certain. A part of me wanted hide away in my cabin and cry. Good men would die because I had misjudged the skill of our opponent. I needed a distraction and took the wheel from Larsson.

Atwood had an uncanny gift with time. Thirty minutes later, just as he had predicted, *Phantom* was close enough to engage the three ships trying to prevent us from sailing west. *Diablo* had fallen behind but I was in no mood to wait. We were facing two caravels, no heavier than two hundred tons apiece, and one handsome, two-masted schooner with decks and rigging crowded with an impressive array of well-armed men. We brought our guns to bear. We traded broadsides with all three ships to test the nerve of their crews. The pirates fought us off with short-barreled falconets, good for only close range, but run away they did not.

Efendi's gunners concentrated our fire on the last ship in the line as we closed the distance. We pummeled the caravel with our six and nine-pounders with good effect. The pirates were brave and fought back valiantly, matching us broadside for broadside with marksmanship that was better than fair. Against our overwhelming firepower and speed, any prudent captain would have turned tail and run. But the promise of treasure will rob most men of their senses.

At last the sun, if only briefly, broke through the clouds and I caught a glimpse of the fighting to the west. I was greatly relieved to find *Cerberus* and *Vengeance* still both in action. But I could see the pirates circling around Testu's ships in an ever-tightening noose. I excel most others at finesse in battle, but we had no time for tricks. If we were going to reach Testu in time, we needed to bludgeon our way through the pirate battle line in front of us.

I gave the wheel back to the Swede and called my officers over. Atwood, Efendi, Kinkae and Fish hurried to my side.

"Have we lost anyone, Mustafa?"

"No, Mary."

"Any damage to the ship?"

"Nothing that will impede our ability to maneuver and kill."

"Impede?"

Efendi grinned. "A new word I learned in Trinidad. The word means to *shackle the feet*."

Even with cannon booming all around us, Atwood slapped the rail and laughed. "Whoa, ho! Mustafa the Scholar."

"Gentlemen, we must cut right through those ships."

Atwood furled his brow and glanced at me askew. "We'll be vulnerable charging straight at them, we'll be close enough to spit at each other. A cracked mast or shattered rudder and *finis*."

"If we stay at this distance Mary," Efendi said, "we can make short work of those devils. Their three-pounders are no match against our guns."

"I understand the risks, but we're short on time."

Atwood rested a hand on my shoulder. "In men, they outnumber us by far. If they board us..."

I bit my lip and nodded. "I know Jacob. But without our help, I doubt Testu can survive much longer."

"Kinkae, Fish, see to your divisions," Atwood said tersely. "Prepare to fight at close-quarters."

I kissed Kinkae on the forehead and did the same to Fish. "God keep you both safe."

"Their ships are flimsy, poorly armed merchantmen built for speed, not battle," Efendi said as Kinkae and Fish rushed off. "Pain and sorrow will be their only reward this day."

Atwood grunted. "Ah, Mustafa the Boastful. We'll see soon enough. Best load half your batteries with ball, target rudders and masts, and load the rest with grapeshot to sweep their decks and rigging clean of vermin."

I placed one hand on Atwood's shoulder and the other on Efendi's. "I could not bear to lose either of you."

Atwood patted my hand. "No worries Mary. Mustafa is too ornery to be killed by some fuckin' pirate and I'm too ugly."

"Signal Michael to follow us," I said. "Let's give the schooner our close attention. Ignore the caravels. We finish this quickly."

"Remember your promise," Atwood said.

"I will do what needs to be done," I said and took the wheel.

When we turned into our foe the winds suddenly shifted without warning, robbing us of our precious speed. I was dumbfounded by our bad luck. We were no more than three hundred yards away from the schooner. She was a ninety-footer, a twelve gunner, with red sails. She raked us with one broadside and then another as we plodded straight at her. *Phantom* absorbed each blow and how we didn't lose a mast or spar is a mystery to me. At two hundred yards, I had the topmen take in sail and spun the wheel to port to bring our guns to bear. It was time to inflict our own pain.

"*FIRE!*" I heard Efendi bellow.

Our guns belched smoke and flame. Then Efendi gave the order to our men crouched behind the bulwarks to stand. They jumped to their feet, mounted the swivels to the rails, fifteen in all, and fired. We peppered the schooner with hundreds of mini-balls and pieces of shrapnel. Debris went flying off the schooner in all directions and bodies fell from her rigging.

The schooner's gunners answered us in kind as best they could with their paltry three-pounders. Six shots slammed hard into *Phantom*'s hull, doubled-planked with seasoned oak, and ricocheted into the sea.

Perched high up in the schooner's masts, skilled sharpshooters did more damage. Two of Efendi's gunners fell dead. I saw others go down with wounds. One ball drilled a hole through the brim of my hat.

I shouted new orders to the topmen. I slowed our ship down, turned to starboard, and tried to bring us around the schooner's stern. But her captain, no fool, turned his schooner as we turned, robbing our sails of precious wind.

With little more than one hundred yards between us, a lucky shot struck our main mast, splintering the wood. Though I knew Him not, I offered up a quick prayer and to my surprise the mast held.

And then one of the caravels peeled away to intercept *Diablo* while the other turned in to us. Suddenly we found ourselves wedged in-between two ships and taking a beating on both sides. The pirates were as good an opponent as I'd ever faced and had their ships been on par with ours, we might have been in real trouble. But their ships were not on par with ours and their commander was not my equal. He had sacrificed his line of battle, had allowed us to come in too close, no doubt intending to board us. I glanced at the schooner and then at the caravel. My men were inflicting horrendous carnage and yet the pirates would not quit.

"Jacob!" I shouted down to the main deck and shrugged my shoulders. His face was covered in black power and streaked in sweat. "Any thoughts on how we end this stalemate?"

But before he could answer, I saw MacGyver turn *Diablo* towards the schooner in a bold but risky move to cut across her bow and held my breath. *Diablo* wasn't *Phantom*. She didn't have her speed. The schooner turned to meet the new threat. Her gunners pummeled *Diablo* with canister shot. *Diablo's* bowsprit split in two, her jib sail went slack and her forecastle burst into flames. But with nerves of steel, MacGyver pushed on, buying me another chance to swing *Phantom* around the schooner's stern.

There was no time to realign our sails or to warn the crew. I took my sword and cut the braces to the mizzen sails and spun the wheel around. Men lost their footing as we turned. And as we circled around the schooner's stern, *Diablo* collided into the schooner head-on.

"Move, move, move!" Efendi yelled. "As your guns bear, *FIRE!*"

BOOM! BA-BA-BOOOOOOOOM! BOOM! BA-BOOM! BOOM! BOOM!

Nothing could survive our broadside at such close range, and yet I froze in horror when out of nowhere a large ball of fire smack into *Phantom's* side near the main mast. Tongues of flame shot-up along the starboard rail and began licking their way up the shrouds. I watched one of my men jump over the side with fire crawling up his trousers. Another man slipped from the rigging directly above my head and hit the deck headfirst in front of me. His skull cracked open, splattering my boots with bits of brain and blood.

Men scrambled to grab axes and buckets for the fire, but I knew it wouldn't be enough. I gave the wheel to Larsson and looked for Atwood.

"Jacob," I screamed as he lifted himself up off the deck. "Loosen the port gun tackles or cut them free. Now! Hurry! Then get the men over to the port rail and hold on!"

When Atwood stared at me bewildered and didn't move, Efendi rallied the men to his side. He understood. The men frantically started cutting away rope and tackle to set the guns free.

I took the wheel back from Larsson and sent the Swede forward to tell the topmen to trim our sails for a hard turn to starboard. I told him to hold on.

The flames spread rapidly across Phantom's starboard hull, devouring wood and hemp. We had only minutes before we lost the ship.

As I worked the wheel to catch the wind and current, *Phantom* picked up speed. I waited for as long as I dared and then spun the wheel hard over, forcing *Phantom* on her side. Guns, crates and barrels, anything not tied down, slid across the deck tipping the ship even more. Men went flying too. As the ship's starboard rail dipped below the waves, a wall of water surged across the deck. I struggled to spin the wheel around again before we capsized, but I was too weak and then I lost my footing. I would have gone over the side had Atwood not caught me by the arm. He pulled me up, we grabbed the wheel together and pushed and pulled with everything we had. With a great moan *Phantom* righted herself, then coasted to a stop in a cloud of smoke and steam.

Men rushed about to secure the guns. Others fished their mates out of the sea and then helped the wounded below.

"What the devil?" I asked. I turned to face Atwood when he didn't answer.

He was staring at me glassy-eyed. He doubled-over and heaved. I caught him as his legs buckled. I kicked away some bits of broken glass and eased him down against the bitticle. It was then I saw the ugly knot sprouting from his forehead.

"Here, take a sip of water Jacob," I told him and handed him a ladle from a water bucket. "Close your eyes and rest. You've hit your head but good. Don't move."

"Whew, aye, I think I'll heed your good advice for once. The world is spinning."

I looked over at the schooner. She was a heap of tangled wood and shredded sails drifting on the water and listing badly to port. The caravels moved in closer to save the schooner's crew.

Then I wrapped a line around my waist and lowered myself over the side to inspect the damages. A good portion of *Phantom's* hull was charred amidships. The chain plate securing the shrouds to the main mast was shattered. I saw snapped lines and rigging that had gone slack. *Phantom* was a mess, but all-in-all we had been extraordinarily lucky. The damages appeared superficial.

Efendi leaned over the rail to help me back on board. I hugged him tightly and embraced Kinkae and Fish too when they joined us.

"Get yourself below and have Stachel stitch you up," I told Fish when I saw the blood trickling down his face from a deep gash across his nose. "Kinkae, we have men in the water."

Kinkae pointed over the aft rail. MacGyver already had a boat in the water to rescue our men. I saw a plume of smoke rising off *Diablo's* forecastle, but no flames. She had drifted away from the schooner and her crew was busy cutting away her broken bowsprit with saws and axes.

Efendi knelt next to Atwood. "Now that's a bump worthy of a bear of a man like you," he said. "Fish, Mary sent you below, go. Kinkae, fetch some blankets for Jacob. We shouldn't move him until Stachel inspects his injury. Are you hurt Mary?"

"No, Mustafa. Did you see what hit us?"

"Aye, the schooner's men launched a fireball from a catapult mounted at the stern," Efendi replied. "I caught a brief glimpse of the war engine when they pulled a tarp off."

"A catapult?" I asked incredulously.

"Aye," Atwood said. "Who would be so stupid to light a ball of straw, tar, and God only knows what else, soaked in naphtha on a wooden deck and fling such an abomination through a maze of their own, combustible rigging?"

"Their stupidity," Efendi offered solemnly, "though desperate, nearly destroyed a far superior ship. That catapult nearly doomed us all."

"How many men have we lost?" I asked.

Efendi shook his head. "I know of a dozen dead for certain. We'll muster the crew and count heads after we restore the ship for action. We have men with bruises, bumps, broken bones and cuts, nothing that won't mend with time. A barrel rolled over one of our Carib lads though, crushing both his legs. Our surgeon says the poor fellow has a punctured lung as well and won't survive the day."

"I shall go to him," I said, "offer what comfort I can. How soon before we can sail?"

"Replacing the rigging is the worst of it. The rest can wait. An hour perhaps, maybe two."

"That long? Can we get the ship underway whilst we make repairs?"

Atwood glanced up at me. "Mary, we'll need every gun and every knot of speed for the battle yet to come. *Diablo* I think has a splintered bowsprit. I'm I right Mustafa?"

"You are."

"Well, there you have it Mary. You can't take on the other pirates without her. Please Mary, think with your head, not your heart."

No woman, no matter how meek or agreeable she might be, ever wants to be chastised by a man, any man, for considering her emotions - even if his words ring true. I stared at Atwood filled with indignation.

"It was woman with heart who gave you life Jacob Atwood. It is a woman with heart who bore you six fine children and manages your household for long stretches of time without any help from you. It is a woman with heart who has made you a modestly wealthy man."

Atwood looked away with a wounded look. I knelt down next to him and stroked his hair. I had no right to lash out at any man for offering me good advice, especially a man like Atwood.

"Forgive me, Jacob. You are right, of course. We'll need every gun and every knot of speed for the battle yet to come. We'll stay put until you decide *Phantom* is ready for action. Now rest."

Atwood smiled to let me know that all was well. "Without your quick wits Mary, well, you saved the ship."

I stood to look out over the water. The light of a gloomy day was beginning to fade. The hourglass was nearly empty. I could just make out *Cerberus* and *Vengeance* in the distance trading blows with nine pirate ships.

"A fucking Roman catapult," I mumbled to myself. "Well gentlemen tomorrow is not yet here, hence who can say how the day's final entry into the ship's journal will read. Jacob, don't you dare move. Mustafa, Kinkae, see to the repairs as best you can. I'm going below."

For reasons unknown to me, my Carib crewman took on Christian names. The injured Carib had taken the name Bobby. I found Bobby sprawled out across a table in the galley with his broken legs wrapped in bloody gauze. Fish was standing next to him, holding his hand as Bobby wheezed his life away. Stachel shook his head when he saw me.

"What's this now?" I asked and leaned over to stroke Bobby's cheek. He managed a brave smile for me, exposing his front teeth, teeth filed down into fangs. His body was heavily tattooed and he wore six gold rings in his left ear. Each ring represented an achievement in battle. "You are shirking your duties again I see? I always suspected you for a slacker."

"Gracious Lay, Lady Mary," he whispered. "Life, life is good."

"Shhh, rest now my brave warrior. We have more battles to fight together, we have more giants to slay."

"Please dear lady, if, if the thing is possible, bury me in Guadeloupe, not at sea."

I took his hand and kissed him. "I will honor your wish. Now rest my noble warrior. There is life in you yet."

Stachel pulled me aside. "My lady, I could repair his punctured lung if he were strong enough. I'm confident I can even save one leg, but not the other. If I amputate the bad leg, he will surely die. If I don't amputate the leg, marrow will seep into the blood or his wounds will fester and he will die. There is nothing I can do for him."

"We have laudanum?"

"Yes."

"Give it to him, as much as he needs to end his pain."

"By your will, madam."

I pulled Fish aside. "Fish, stay with him. Is there anything more we can do to comfort him?"

"No, Mary. This will go hard on Henry. Bobby is his favorite cousin."

I patted Fish on the shoulder and then checked his stitches. "After we finish this ugly business, we'll put in at Guadeloupe. I'll give Henry the sad tidings myself. Let me look in on the rest of the wounded. You rest now."

When I returned topside, Efendi was standing at the helm, barking out orders to the topmen to set the main sails. Night was closing in around us. A few yards away, the schooner was slowly sinking. The caravels were fleeing south for Trinidad with the remnants of the schooner's crew. To the northwest I could see only muzzle flashes dancing on the water, scattered shots here and there, no broadsides. Whether men were too weary to fight or powder was running low, I did not know.

I knelt down next to Atwood to apply a wet compress across his forehead. "The swelling is down a bit. How do you feel?"

"Like a mule kicked me in the head. Stachel says I have a nasty concussion, but I'll live. How's the Carib?"

"He's passing over, a blessing I suppose. What is our situation?"

"*Phantom's* main mast is cracked and that crack will rupture into a break if we put too much strain on the wood. Kinkae's men have blocked the fracture with thick splints and wrapped heavy cordage around the splints. God only knows how long the mast will hold.

We're taking on water too from an errant ball that split a seam. Kinkae's lads have braced the hull with timber, patched things up as best they can and he has men at the pumps. We won't sink, but a three-pound shot shouldn't have caused such damage. I suspect the ball struck a length of rotting wood or planking riddled with worms perhaps. Your sad attempt to capsize us certainly didn't help. We'll need to put the old girl in dry dock soon. Havana would be a good choice."

"Can we sail?"

"Aye, but don't push her hard. We can make the rest of the repairs on the move."

"And *Diablo?*"

"Michael's lads have fashioned a crude bowsprit and they've raised a new jib. I wouldn't trust either vessel in strong winds or heavy seas."

"Mustafa?"

"Michael lost six men and has eighteen wounded. We have twelve dead, four missing and twice as many wounded. The guns are ready and we have enough shot and powder. We can fight."

I suddenly felt overwhelmed and exhausted and plopped myself down next to Atwood. The day's ugly business and taken everything out of me.

"What's the plan, Mary?" Atwood asked.

"I was about to ask you the same question. I'm fresh out of ideas."

"We go straight in."

"This is not a happy day."

"Storms come and go Mary."

"We must honor Michael's gallantry later. His brazen maneuver straight at the schooner tipped the scales, broke the deadlock. After all we've survived over the years Jacob, to think a catapult from ancient times almost did us in."

"'Tis a perilous life we've chosen Mary. I have no regrets. Better this than standing knee deep in pig shit working some noble's farm."

"Quite so. I like your plan Jacob. This pirate commander is a tenacious *biche-sone*. I'd like to meet him. I'd like to meet him face-to-face."

Chapter Eleven

I didn't have much of a plan. *Phantom* was a crippled ship. *Diablo* was little better. I heeded Atwood's good advice and did not push either ship too hard. We had the bigger guns and by far the better gunners and I put my trust in that. Even wounded *Phantom* was a match for the whole pirate pack - or so I told myself.

Two long, excruciating hours passed before we reached Testu's ships in the dark. To my great relief, and to the relief of all my men, the pirates scattered when they saw our sails, except for one large frigate with a broken rudder sitting not far from *Cerberus*. The frigate's men quickly hoisted a white flag over the stern as we passed them by. Even in the dim lantern light, I could see the apprehension in their faces.

I looked over at *Diablo*, sailing in tandem with us, and cupped my hands over my mouth. "Michael, secure that frigate and take her in tow. Keep a wary eye out for any treachery. I would row over to *Cerberus* to see the damage done."

MacGyver nodded and waved me off.

It was well past midnight when Atwood, Efendi and I boarded *Cerberus*. Weary men, begrimed in filth, in soot and blood, were quietly repairing snapped lines and torn sails or chipping away at shattered wood with their hammers and chisels. I saw twenty bodies wrapped in sailcloth laid out in a neat row across the deck for burial.

"Welcome aboard Mary," I heard Testu call out behind me.

I spun around and saw Testu standing up on the quarter deck, looking down at me. He had a bottle in his hand and a bloody strip of linen wrapped around his neck.

"I'm delighted you decided to join the fight even at this late hour," he quipped.

I ignored his barb. "You are hurt?"

"A scratch. A splinter caught me in the neck. I have twenty-four dead and a shattered rudder. *Vengeance* lost nearly thirty men but Bertrand proved himself worthy of command.

"Bertrand?"

"With Maurice laid low in Panama, I handed *Vengeance* over to Maximilian Bertrand, a Pole who prefers to be called Piotr. For a navigator, he acquitted himself quite well during the action. We have close to fifty wounded. For some this will be their last night in this world."

"An evil day for all of us," I said evenly and walked towards the quarter deck. I carefully unwrapped the linen around Testu's neck and winced. The splinter was of good size. "Where's your ship's surgeon? We must attend to this wound at once."

"He is below with his blades and saws. Our good physician has been a most busy man this day."

"I brought our surgeon over with us. Stachel, to me! Captain Testu is in need of your skills."

Stachel slung a leather satchel over his shoulder and hurried up to the quarter deck. I held a lantern next to Testu's face as Stachel inspected the wound.

"*Monsieur*, this is not a clean wound. I will need to do a bit of cutting."

Testu took a long swig of wine. "So my own man told me. Proceed doctor, and I want a pretty scar."

We followed Testu to his great cabin and helped him to his bunk. I removed his boots and lit more lanterns and candles as Stachel laid out his tools on the captain's table.

"Captain Testu," Stachel said. "I have nothing for the pain. Drink. Lady Mary, perhaps you could hold the good captain down? I'll use this piece of cloth to tie his head securely to the bedframe. We must keep the captain still."

I did as Stachel asked and held Testu's shoulders down. Halfway through the cutting, Testu mercifully passed out.

After Stachel removed the splinter, cleaned the wound and stitched the torn skin together, I sent him down to the galley to help *Cerberus's* surgeon.

"How do you feel?" I asked when Testu stirred.

"I, ah, I think I'd prefer to be dead. Sweet Jesus what did your surgeon do to my head?"

I placed a wet compress on Testu's forehead and smiled. "I think you did that to yourself Guillaume with too much wine."

Testu glanced at the pile of bloody rags on the table. "Did he get all of it?"

"He thinks so, aye. Your own surgeon inspected the wound before Stachel closed it and approved his work."

"The pirates have fled?"

"All but one frigate with a broken rudder. Michael has taken her in tow."

"I suppose I was a bit gruff with you earlier Mary. I regret my callous words."

"I understand your anger. You had the worst of it. You lost men, but so did I. I do not regret my decision. I expected you to keep some distance between yourself and the enemy."

"An unfriendly wind turned on us."

"And you lost a rudder."

"True. Bad luck that was."

I leaned over and kissed Testu on the check. "Rest now. I'll return in the morning. Your wound is going to hurt like the devil's bite later and we have nothing for your pain. As soon as *Cerberus* can sail, we'll put in at Guadeloupe. The Carib are skilled at healing wounds and reducing pain with herbs and such."

I stayed with Testu until he fell asleep, then rowed back to *Phantom.* When I returned to *Cerberus* in the morning with a pot of hot chicken broth and fresh bread, I found the Frenchman sitting on the main deck in a chair with his back against the main mast.

"I'm glad to see you up and about," I said brightly. "How do you feel?"

Testu glanced over at the dead. "Better than those wretched souls."

I looked at the bodies and saw six more passengers waiting for the ferryman. "The dead are dead. Your color has returned at least Guillaume. I brought you breakfast."

"I am grateful."

I leaned over and felt Testu's forehead. The skin was hot.

"You have a fever," I said and handed him a handkerchief. "*Cinchona*. Chew it, then wash it down with water."

"As you wish, mother."

"Men have called me worse. If you are trying to goad me, you won't succeed. It is too fine a day for foul moods. I made a quick inspection of your rudder before I came aboard. *Cerberus* is seaworthy?"

"Yes."

"Good. Eat your breakfast, bury your dead and let's make haste for Guadeloupe before our friends from Trinidad return with more ships and men."

"Your gracious Majesty," I said with sincere respect as I knelt before the King of Guadeloupe. Carib by the hundreds had turned out of their huts to see us.

Henry received me in front of the great council lodge sitting on a common wooden stool. Wearing his magnificent feathered headdress, dripping with strings of pearls and seashells, and a red feathered cape draped around his shoulders, he looked upon me sternly as I bowed my head. Across his lap rested his uncle's spear. He stood, pointed his spear at me and motioned me to follow him into the lodge.

"What kind of a greeting is this?" Atwood whispered in my ear as we stood. "I think the sun has fried the little shit's brains."

I too began wondering how I might have offended the king. "We'll know the truth of it soon enough," I said.

"Well if the prick cuts off your head, rest assured we'll cast your body into the sea with many prayers and great fanfare followed by days and days of heavy drinking."

The lodge was dark and empty inside. Henry set his spear against the wall, and after he carefully removed his headdress and placed it on the ground, he broke out into a huge grin and wrapped his arms around me.

"Mary! My heart is glad to see you!"

"Your Majesty, it is my great honor."

"No, no Mary. I'm your Henry, not your chief!"

I kissed him on both cheeks. "You will always be my Henry. But you are now a great lord too."

"Yes, yes. I am King of Guadeloupe, of Dominica and of all the lesser islands from here to Trinidad."

"You've been busy."

"Yes. Not all my people agreed with Paka Wokili's choice to succeed him. I had to prove myself worthy of wielding the king's spear."

"So, you invaded the islands to the south. There was a war?"

Henry nodded. "More of a skirmish between kin. You and my Irish brothers have taught me well. I took the islands at night, one after the other, moving quick, quick, quick, catching the rebellious tribes by surprise. All have bowed to me. All have pledged their undying loyalty to me."

"Can you trust the leaders of the rebels to keep their pledges?"

"Oh yes, Mary. The pretend kings, greedy, little turds who sowed the seeds of discord among the tribes, with Spanish coaxing, are dead. Their own warriors cut off their heads and sent them to me in tribute."

I arched an eyebrow. The Henry I knew had a kind soul. The ruthless side of his nature caught me by surprise.

"You have consolidated your power and are the ruler of a great nation Henry. Congratulations. Even so, the tide from Europe will not recede. You must learn to live in peace with the Spanish, lest you and your people are swept away someday."

Henry looked away lost in thought for a moment and did not

answer.

"Henry, I bear sad tidings. Pirates from Trinidad attacked our ships two days ago. We lost many men, your cousin Bobby among them. Fish has told me that you were very fond of Bobby. I'm sorry."

"Ohhh... Did he die well?"

"He was a courageous warrior and suffered only a little. He was well-liked and respected by his shipmates as you know. His last wish was to be buried here. I've brought his body with me."

"It is the will of Tamosi and the *zemís*."

"The gods?"

"Yes. I will tell his mother and his father. I will call upon the *buyeis* to make prayers, to keep the evil spirit Maybouya away. Wakanili, this is Bobby's Carib name, has joined his ancestors at the great feasting table in the stars, I am sure."

"I pray it so."

"Why did the pirates attack your ships?"

"Treasure. We found buried silver in Panama, the very silver Drake took from the Silver Train in '73. After leaving Panama, we sailed on to the Port of Spain. We lingered there for some time. Someone with a careless tongue talked, or we were betrayed."

"Who?"

"I know not. One of my men, one of Testu's men. We may never know."

"My warriors did not see *Pig* sail into the bay, but they saw an unfamiliar ship in tow."

"We lost the *Pig* in Panama and took one pirate ship. There's a story to be told there."

Henry smiled again. "With you, Mary, there is always a tale to tell. Tonight, we'll feast and you shall tell me about your voyage west. I wish to see Fish."

"I brought Fish ashore with me. He's standing outside with the others."

"Most excellent. I have important matters to discuss with him."

"Of course."

"I saw a man being carried on a litter in the crowd."

"Aye. Guillaume was wounded during the fighting. The wound is festering and he has a high fever. Our physicians can do nothing more for him. I hoped one of your medicine men might help him."

"The best *pia* among my people is a woman, a very old woman who lives alone up in the hills. You know her."

"The woman who cared for me?"

"The same."

"How extraordinary. That was years ago and she was withered and ancient even then."

"You look weary Mary. I have a hut prepared for you. Rest. Tonight, we shall eat the fatted pig and drink Spanish wine. We will speak of many things."

That evening the King of Guadeloupe held a grand banquet in our honor. All were invited. I moved our ships in close to shore. I had the crews anchor them in a battle line and left enough men onboard each ship to man every gun. Too weak to attend the feast, I left Testu in the village with the medicine woman who had once brought me back to life.

We sat underneath a canopy of bright stars on grass mats around campfires set against the shore. We ate and drank and told our stories while children entertained us with the songs of their ancestors. And when we had stuffed our bellies full, Carib warriors fetched their drums, claves and calabashes and filled the night air with music while their women danced around the fires provocatively, arousing the passions of every man. The merriment was grand. And when men started drifting off to sleep, when the fires burned down to embers, Henry led Fish and me back to the great lodge.

"I did not see Maurice," Henry said as he filled three wooden bowls with *ouicou*. He handed one bowl to me and one to Fish.

"Guillaume," I replied, "left Maurice in Panama with the sweating sickness. I do not know if he is alive or dead."

Henry tipped his bowl of *ouicou*, spilling a few drops on the ground. "An offer to the gods. I pray Maurice is alive. He's a good man. Mary, Fish and I have reached an agreement. This is why you are here."

"Agreement? What agreement would that be?"

"We are of like mind on a matter of great importance to our people. I hope you'll find our decision to your liking."

"Henry, the wine has already dulled my senses and now you are plying me with *ouicou*. If you wish to befuddle me further with riddles, you are succeeding. You know my mind. I prefer plain speech."

Henry and Fish exchanged glances.

"Fish must stay in Guadeloupe, Mary. You must release him from his oath."

"Oh? Well if it is important to you, your Majesty, then it is equally important to me. The friendship between the Carib and Irish is precious and I will gladly honor your wish. Fish, I hereby release you from your obligations to the ship and to me. You've proven yourself a capable seaman, a fine warrior, and I'll miss your good company."

"Are you not curious to know why Mary?"

"I did not wish overstep, but certainly."

"Fish is the true son of Chief Paka Wokili."

"What? But I thought -."

"I am sorry for the deception Mary. Paka Wokili took many wives. My uncle's third wife gave birth to Fish. But when she accepted the Christ God and allowed a Jesuit monk to baptize her and her son, Paka Wokili banished her and rejected Fish as his flesh and blood."

I laid my hand on Fish's shoulder. "So, you are royalty!"

Fish smiled sheepishly. "Yes, Mary."

"And you are telling me this Henry for what purpose?"

"Mary, I wish to be chief no more. I have united the island tribes and my people are at peace. Life is good for all Carib. But I long to sail with you again. I will pass the chief's spear to Fish. The elders have given their consent. All is as it should be."

"Well, I, I hardly know what to say Henry," I replied, truly caught off-guard. I turned to Fish and bowed. "Your Majesty."

Uncertain of what to say or do, Fish simply stared at me and grinned.

"The men will miss you. I trust you'll think of me as your friend and ally."

Fish surprised me when he hugged me. "Henry called you sister. I will call you sister."

"I'm honored. What name will you be known by? King Fish doesn't seem quite fitting."

"I have chosen the name Joseph."

I bowed my head. "Joseph? A Christian name. King Joseph, my lord, I wish you a long and happy reign. Henry, when you've done what you must do here, report to Mustafa if you please and see to your division. Welcome home my brother..."

The coronation of Fish a few days later was little different from Henry's coronation, except of course no one needed to be buried. No Carib chief before, to anyone's memory, had ever willing walked away from the throne. After King Joseph was crowned outside the great council lodge, the people flocked to Henry with remarkable affection. Warriors embraced him, women took turns kissing him and children lavished flowers, trinkets and other simple gifts on him.

Henry was no less dear to me and I was overjoyed to have him back. The new king's reaffirmation of the alliance between the Carib and Irish before the elders filled my heart with joy and in return, Fish was pleased to accept my gifts of silver - along with the pirate ship and her crew to do with as he pleased.

With the sun melting into the sea, and lovely Venus on the rise, I made my way down to the shore where the Carib were gathering for the great coronation feast. Our ships sat peacefully in the bay not far off. I could see the night watch moving about, lighting the lanterns one-by-one. Then I heard a splash and saw *Cerberus's* crew lowering a skiff into the water, but thought nothing of it.

I plopped down on a blanket near a small campfire to warm myself. Even in the islands the air can feel cool at times.

"Ah, Mustafa, where have you been?" I asked as he sat down next to me.

"I've been on the ship overseeing the work."

"And the others?"

"Michael and Kinkae came ashore with me. Last I saw them, they were with Jacob sharing a keg."

"And how go the repairs?"

"The easy work is done. We need a new mast. Tully has reinforced the braces on the hull and fashioned a crude patch to plug the leak. The man has skill."

Tully, one of the newer men, had signed with us as the ship's carpenter back in Westport. He was a runt of a fellow from Wales with an ornery disposition but at carpentry, there was none better.

"I take it you and Jacob don't want me circumventing the globe quite yet?"

Efendi smiled. "That would be wise. A voyage around the world - what a vile notion."

"Agreed. How fares your young apprentice?"

"His strength and skills in the martial arts improve by the day. He has a keen mind. He is a capable seaman. He is fearless and loyal and proved his mettle in Panama and again in the fight with the pirates. I am considering taking Robert with me on a pilgrimage once we return to Europe."

I felt my heart skip a beat at the thought of losing Efendi. "A pilgrimage? A pilgrimage to where?"

"East."

"Istanbul?'

"Perhaps. More likely Krak des Chevaliers, a place north of Dimashq."

"That is near the Holy Lands?"

"Yes."

"What the devil do you hope to find in the lands to the north of Dimashq?"

"When you were very young, Lord O'Malley took you in when there was no one else. He clothed you. He gave you shelter and prepared you for the world. There is an ancient monastery near Krak des Chevaliers. When I was very young, when there was no one else, the monks there took me in. They clothed me. They gave me shelter and prepared me for the world."

"Christian monks?"

"No. These monks are not a religious order. They trained me in the art of combat, in all its forms. Nobility, like the Sultan, pay huge fortunes for men trained by Chevaliers monks."

"For what purpose?"

"Retainers, bodyguards and the like."

"The monks trained you to serve as a bodyguard for noblemen?"

Efendi grinned. "No, I despised the notion and I was rebellious in my youth. Mercifully, my master was a tolerant man. If he could see me now, he'd burst with laughter as I've become what I swore I would not."

"I see," I said, though I really didn't. "How long will this journey last?"

"More than a few months certainly, less than a lifetime. Do not be concerned, Mary. I will not abandon you. Never."

When the skiff from *Cerberus* slid up on the beach, a seaman holding a torch jumped out and hurried to me.

"Please, Lady Mary," the man said as he removed his cap. "Will you return with me to *Cerberus*? I fear *Capitaine* Testu is dying. He asks for you."

The man's words hit me like a blow to the stomach. "What? But Testu is on the island under the care of a Carib healer."

"Beg pardon my lady, but no. My *Capitaine* had us return him to the ship this morning."

"Why?"

"I cannot say. Please Lady Mary, I fear time is short."

The ship's surgeon and Bertrand, the new captain of the *Vengeance*, were standing next to Testu's bunk when I stepped into the cabin. My heart sank when I saw Testu. His skin had turned ashen-grey. His eyes had lost their sparkle. He was soaked in sweat and wheezing.

I took Testu's hand and looked at the surgeon. "Christopher, what is this?"

The surgeon shook his head. "I suspect the wound has poisoned his blood. His body was already weak from his illness in Panama.

There is nothing more to be done. He's in God's hands now."

He pulled Testu's shirt sleeve up to show me a thin, red line running along the inside of Testu's arm. "He slips in and out of consciousness. He asked to see you. He was most adamant about it."

I wiped a tear from my cheek. "How long?"

"Soon."

"Gentlemen, might I have a bit of privacy with Guillaume?"

"Of course, *ma dame*," Bertrand replied softly. With a jerk of his head the surgeon followed him up to the quarter deck.

I sat on the edge of the bunk. I caressed Testu's hair. I listened to him mumble gibberish for a bit and then he opened his eyes.

"Mary, how good of you to come."

"I'm sorry you're feeling poorly Guillaume. What can I do?"

"My time is near, I know."

"Nonsense."

"Mary, you should leave the lies to those with more skill."

"Hmmm."

Testu squeezed my hand. "I regret these past few months. We have drifted apart. I've been cross with you at times, unfairly so, and I am sorry."

"Stop. Save your strength."

"You are still in love with Hunter."

I hesitated. "No."

"*Oui*. But I hold no grudge."

Testu closed his eyes. I thought he had drifted off to sleep, but then he struggled to sit. I moved a pillow behind his back and helped him.

He looked at me and smiled. "I love you Mary, truly I love you. I have been jealous of a dead man."

I could feel my lower begin to quiver. I could feel my eyes welling up with tears.

"Please Mary, I want to hear you say it before I die, even if it is untrue. I leave this world with no wife to mourn me, with no children to carry on my name. I do not want to die alone. I do not want to die unloved."

"With an honest heart, Guillaume, I love you," I said and held him.

Testu closed his eyes again as if to savor my words. "The last wish of a dying man, fulfilled. Life is good. *Merci beaucoup, ma dame.*"

I kissed his cheek and smiled.

"Mary, Piotr is a good man. You can trust him. But look for Maurice. If he still lives, keep him close. You will not regret his friendship. My final will and testament is in a drawer underneath the desk. Take it."

"My dearest Guillaume, I'll keep you in my heart always. There is something I must tell you. But I am beset by shame and guilt. I beg your forgiveness."

"Whatever troubles you, it matters not. Keep such thoughts to yourself. I am content." He paused, managed a weak smile and winked at me. "Besides, I am no priest. I do not hear confessions."

"I must unburden my heart. I was waiting for the right moment to tell you. Do you remember that night in Davenport, with you and me and James, when we let our passions run wild?"

"No man could forget such a night of delicious debauchery."

"That night produced a child, a girl, your child."

For the briefest moment, Testu's strength seemed to return. I saw a flicker of light in his eyes.

I took his hand and held it against my breast. "I gave her a French name, Aliénor. She is in Westport in the care of a good family."

"Truly, I have a daughter?"

"Truly. And she is beautiful. She has my eyes and mouth, and my raven hair. She has your brow, your square chin and your strong, aquiline nose."

"Aliénor, a lovely name."

"Aye, Aliénor. Aliénor Muirgheal. She is half Irish after all."

"She is half French."

"Aye, she is your flesh and blood *mon amour*. Upon a day Guillaume, we shall all meet again out on the open sea with clear skies above our heads, with a fresh wind at our backs and with a promise of adventure in the air."

Testu nodded. He laid back on his pillows, closed his eyes and slept, never to wake again.

As was Testu's wish, we built a funeral pyre on the beach that evening and watched the flames consume his body. We offered prayers, I gave a eulogy and we scattered his ashes across the water with all the honors owed to a captain of the sea. There was not much to Testu's will. He bequeathed *Cerberus* to Maurice and *Vengeance* to Bertrand and gave me his share of the silver.

King Joseph agreed to send one of his great war canoes across the ocean on my behalf, to take a letter from me to Ronconcholan. The king's warriors would row south and hop from island to island until they reached Cumaná at the mouth of the Manzanares River. From there another Carib tribe living along the Spanish Main would carry my letter overland to Ronconcholan. I've heard Carib couriers move more swiftly than the Spanish post service. I addressed my letter to both Maurice, hoping he was still alive, and to Zekowtah, and informed them of Testu's death. I invited Maurice to Guadeloupe to take *Cerberus* and I expressed my sorrow to Zekowtah.

In the morning we broke camp. We took on water and fresh provisions, small livestock, dried fruits and vegetables mostly, and prepared our ships to sail. I was anxious to find a new mast for *Phantom*, secure our West Indies cargo and return to Ireland.

But before we could weigh anchor, Bertrand rowed over to *Phantom* in a longboat with only himself and three men. I greeted Bertrand with a friendly smile from the quarter deck as he worked his way up the rope ladder.

"Piotr, a good morning to you sir. To what do we owe this unexpected pleasure?"

Bertrand removed his distinctive copotain hat with its large brass buckle in the center, he was the only man on any of the ships who wore a copotain, and looked at me with a grim expression. "My Lady, forgive me, I have distressing news. A number of men aboard *Vengeance* have mutinied."

I let a tin of coffee slip from my hand. "What? When?"

"During the night sometime."

"The whole crew?"

"I do not how many are these mutineers, but they have taken prisoners."

"Why," Atwood asked, standing at my side, "didn't the damn fools sail off during the night?"

"Greed of course my good man, greed. They want the silver aboard *Cerberus*."

Atwood grunted. "All of it?"

"*Oui.*"

"Plainly they don't know the temperament of our good Lady Mary."

I glanced over at *Vengeance*. She was anchored off our port bow some two hundred yards away.

"Well, breakfast shall have to wait," I said. "Jacob, I'll have the anchor raised and the tops'ls let out if you please. Bring us up alongside *Vengeance*."

"Run out the guns and bring up the swivels?"

"Quite so."

I poured myself another coffee and poured one for Bertrand as my men eased us over to *Vengeance*. We were greeted by a mob of Frenchmen standing on the deck with muskets and swords, ready to repel boarders.

"What do you intend to do?" Bertrand asked me.

"You'll have your ship back before we finish our coffee," I said. "Or I'll have their heads."

I leaned over the rail and considered the faces of the mutineers. "Who speaks for you?" I demanded.

A large bear of a man, bigger than Atwood, climbed up on a barrel next to the main mast. "I do. We have no quarrel with you Lady Mary. This matter is between Frenchmen."

"Well, I have a quarrel with you. What do you want?"

"We have prisoners."

"So I've heard. What do you want?"

"We want the silver."

"Surrender your arms and I'll give you your share of the silver."

"We want all of the silver."

"What's your name?"

"Bayard."

"You intend to rob me of my silver, Bayard?"

"No, no, Lady Mary. We only want the silver aboard *Cerberus*. Bertrand hands the silver over to us and we'll hand our prisoners over to him."

"Some of that silver is mine. Testu bequeathed his share to me in his will."

Bayard didn't expect that and paused a moment to think the matter through. "He had no right. That silver belongs to us."

"I don't think Captain Testu would have agreed with you there my friend. No matter. If I hand the silver over to you, what is your plan after that? Do you think the longboats can accommodate all that silver, along with the provisions you'll need for you and your men?"

Bayard snickered. "*Vengeance* is our ship now. We'll put the prisoners ashore in Trinidad, or in Santo Domingo or Havana, after we are safely away. You have my word."

"The word of a pirate?"

"Those are our terms."

"Well, I like my terms better."

"We make the terms, not you."

"But you haven't heard my terms yet. You might like them."

The big man looked at me confused and hesitated, trying to think how best to respond.

I took a sip of coffee. "For Christ's sake man, I haven't got all day. That large head of yours might explode if you strain your tiny brain too hard. Here are my terms: take the boats, leave the prisoners and row away, to where I do not care. I'll let you keep your lives. If you don't like my terms, I'll splatter your guts across the deck, every last fucking one of you."

The ringleader drew his sword and pointed it at me. "No, I don't think you will. You would be killing the prisoners too."

"A price I'll unhappily pay. I'll not bargain with loathsome scoundrels. Your disloyalty turns my stomach. Captain Testu was a fair and good man and you have dishonored his memory. Shame on all of you! Decide quickly for my breakfast grows cold."

The mutineers exchanged nervous glances. They began whispering amongst themselves. Bayard was not altogether stupid. He could see he was losing control. He jumped off the barrel and climbed up on the rail to come closer to me.

"We have no quarrel with you, Lady Mary, we'll come back later for our silver," the big Frenchman said, then turned to his accomplices. "*Hommes, relevez l'ancre et déployez la voile. Nous pouvons revenir pour l'argent à un meilleur moment.*"

I looked down at the main deck and caught Efendi's attention. "My good Captain of the Guns," I called out in a loud voice for all to hear. "Are the guns primed and loaded? *Les armes sont-elles amorcées et chargées?*"

"They are madam."

"Grapeshot? *Mitraille?*"

"*Oui.*"

"On the count of three, I want that deck swept free of vermin. Prepare to fire. One... Two... *Sur le compte de trois, je veux que le pont balayé de cette vermine. Préparez-vous à tirer. Un... deux...*"

Before I could finish my count, we all heard the crack of a single musket shot. Bayard looked puzzled, then tottered for a bit before he plunged headfirst into the water. One of his own men had shot him.

"Jacob, let's tidy up this mess. Take Captain Bertrand and the men you need to secure that ship."

"Straight away, Mary. What do you want to do with the mutineers?"

"This voyage has seen enough bloodshed. Set them adrift in the longboats. I don't want to see their faces. Be quick about it too before I change my mind."

Bertrand narrowed his eyes at me. "I am curious my lady. Would you have fired your guns on those men? The innocent might have been slaughtered with the guilty."

I smiled. "I hadn't considered that possibility. Goodness, I'm famished. Off you go Piotr. Go and reclaim your ship, then we sail for Havana." After Bertrand walked off, I went below to my cabin, laid across my bunk and wept. I know not why.

BOOK II

Atonement

Chapter Twelve

Autumn, 1590

ove, the Great Lie. Truly, I say there is no love in this world. There are but fragile, fleeting moments between two souls reaching out for affection. A man, a woman, they declare their undying love before the world one day only to see their precious love dashed against the rocks the next. Love is no more enduring than the seafoam tumbling across the sand. Death, betrayal, jealously or greed - all lie in wait to bring love down. A husband looks for a fresh conquest, a wife needs something more and runs off, a child is cruelly taken. Love is an illusion of the mind, a sinister trick on a trusting heart.

We reached Havana with thirty fewer Frenchmen. I put *Phantom* in dry dock as she needed the most attention and we spent the next two weeks properly overhauling our ships. When we set sail again with new masts and spars and canvas, with sturdy vessels worthy of the sea, we sailed for Old Havana where we found Cortés, dressed in his familiar light beige suit and his ruffled cream shirt with white lace around the neck, waiting for us on the wharf surrounded by stockpiles of barrels, crates, boxes, chests and stacks of freshly cut lumber.

I sat with Cortés underneath a cluster of palm trees as we watched the men work. I shooed away a fly buzzing around my nose. I took a sip of wine. The day was hot and humid and I was glad to be sitting in the shade.

"I am saddened by the death of Captain Testu," Cortés said. "A tragic loss."

"Aye. I shall sorely miss him. Your daughter Elizabeth is well?"

"She is in excellent health and in fine spirits, but dear God she is a headstrong woman. She asked me to give you her warm regards."

"Please give her my warmest regards in return when you see her."

"I have heard you were in Panama recently," Cortés said cautiously and looked away.

"You are well informed."

"Men talk."

"Indeed they do."

"Your journey was successful?"

"Marginally so."

"Good. I have also heard that the Spanish army, a considerable force, engaged a large Cimarron war party along the coast of Panama at about the same time you were cruising near those waters."

"Oh? The Cimarron and Spanish are always trading blows, or so I've heard."

"True, true. According to the army's dispatches, the Cimarron were accompanied by several hundred French and English pirates. Quite a large raiding party."

"Hundreds of French and English you say? That is a substantial force."

"Indeed. These scoundrels were accompanied by an unusually powerful squadron of warships as well."

"Huh. I wasn't aware the Cimarron had ships."

"They do not."

"Do you think Drake has returned to the Americas?"

"Drake is in England."

"Pirates out of Trinidad then most likely, like the pirates poor Guillaume and I fought off Guadeloupe. Perhaps the very same men. Why does this trivial bit of news interest you?"

Cortés filled my glass with more wine. "There is more to the story. The fighting took place west of Nombre de Diós, in the vicinity where Drake buried the treasure he had taken from the Silver Train in '73. A fascinating coincidence, yes?"

"An odd coincidence to be sure Rodriguez. But as I recall, the Spanish recovered all of the treasure Drake left behind in Panama. Yes?"

Cortés shrugged his shoulders. "That is the official position of Madrid. Do you believe everything you hear?"

"I'd be dead if I did."

"I only speak of these matters to pass the time. I thought they might amuse you."

"Ah, ha. Well, I am amused. Thank you. I must say, this wine is delicious."

"I am fond of this particular vintage myself. I have a small vineyard in Spain, but I have never succeeded in producing anything of this quality. I brought cigars for Jacob and Michael."

"You shall join us for supper aboard my ship. Afterwards, you boys can smoke your awful tobacco up on deck and downwind from me."

"When will you depart for Europe?"

"As soon as we complete our business here."

Cortés made a broad sweep of his arm over the piles of cargo. "Forgive me, Mary, I have advanced a substantial sum to procure all of this. Do you have the balance due with you?"

"Have I have ever failed to pay?"

"No, never. You've always honored your word Mary."

"Quite so and I'm well aware of my obligations now. Those three wooden chests resting against that cracked piling yonder, the chests to the left, those are yours."

"*Maravilloso, gracias.*"

"Come now, let's go take a peek to make certain you are satisfied with the payment."

"No, no. This is not necessary."

"I insist."

I pulled Cortés up out of his chair and we walked over to the cracked piling. As I opened each chest for him, he stared wide-eyed at the silver bars stacked inside, silver bars bearing the royal seal of the King of Spain with the year 1573 stamped on each one.

"*¡Querido Diós!*" Cortés whispered and crossed himself. He quickly closed all three lids. "*El Tren de Plata.*"

"You'll want to remove those markings. I suggest we melt the bars down before you leave."

"*Sí, Sí. Gracias.*"

"*El gusto es mio.*"

"So it was you in Panama!"

"Aye, and a few of my friends. But the less you know the better I think."

"Yes, yes. I quite agree Mary. As you have honored your word to me, I shall honor my word to you."

"Oh? That sounds a tad ominous."

"The clan, Dowlin's son, he is asking questions."

My heart skipped a beat. Sailing through blustery winds howling like demons from hell with heavy, slashing rains and monstrous waves crashing over the bow trouble me not. But hearing the *Síol Faolcháin* was nearby sent a cold shiver down my spine.

"Dowlin, he's here in the Americas?"

"No. He sent three men to my home in Santo Domingo asking questions about you. The lead man was Irish, but the other two were peculiar fellows, foreigners from distant lands, lands to the east I think."

"The Americas are overrun with foreigners."

"These men were different. They wore black turbans with red-striped brown robes and their boots curled at the toe. They carried curved daggers with ivory handles tucked inside their belts with strange markings, like runes, engraved along the blades. Ottomans or Persians perhaps?"

I called Efendi to my side. "Rodriguez, tell Mustafa what you told me."

"Did they speak?" Efendi asked after Cortés repeated his story.

"No."

"Tattoos, earrings or marks of any kind?"

"No. But the day was unusually blustery. The robe of one fellow parted, revealing the chainmail he wore underneath his robe and around his neck hung a medallion with the image of a beast, like a tiger or a lion. I thought it odd."

"The dagger is called a *jambiya*. They are not uncommon. The medallion though... Describe the image of the animal you saw."

"The beast was on all fours. Its head faced its tail and in the beast's mouth it carried a swallow-tailed flag bearing a crescent moon. Etched around the rim of the medallion were many crossed spears and curved swords, *scimitars* I think they are called?"

Efendi removed a pencil and a scrap of paper from his pocket and quickly sketched an image of a beast on all fours holding a swallow-tailed flag in its mouth. "Something like this Rodrigues?"

"Exactly like that."

I saw something akin to fear in Efendi's eyes, something I'd never seen in him before.

"What is it Mustafa?" I asked. "What troubles you so?"

"There was once a powerful order of assassins led by the Old Man in the Mountain, Hasan-e Sabbāh. They called themselves the Hashshashin of the Nizari Ismailis. Stories abound about the mystical powers of these highly skilled killers. It is said they could scale any battlement and walk through walls unseen to reach their victims.

Noblemen were murdered inside their castles whist sleeping in their beds, even when surrounded by bodyguards. According to legend, when the Mongol hordes swept across kingdoms from China to Europe, a Mongol *tumen*, ten thousand men, was dispatched to the Nizari's stronghold in Persia to avenge some insult against their khan. The fortress sat atop a mountain, carved out of sheer rock, and had stood impregnable against the world for centuries. But the Mongols found a way inside and the fortress fell. The Mongols killed every living soul except for a clutch of the best Nazari warriors who escaped through a secret tunnel."

"I've heard such tales. I thought these Persian assassins were only myth."

Efendi handed me his drawing. "More than myth. This is the Ismail Lion carrying the flag of Islam, the seal of the Old Man in the Mountain. I've only seen this mark once before."

"But the Mongols destroyed the assassins hundreds of years ago you said."

"Those who escaped the slaughter fled west and rebuilt their order."

"These men are like you?"

"No, not like me. These men kill for gold. I kill to protect life."

"Huh, an interesting philosophical dilemma."

"If these men are Hashshashin of the Nizari, they are extremely dangerous. And they are relentless. They will not stop until they fulfill their mission, a sacred obligation in their faith, or die in the attempt."

"Dowlin," Cortés interjected, "I fear would not have sent these men to the West Indies without the blessing of the Spanish Court."

"What do you suggest we do Mustafa?" I asked.

"To kill a lion, you must track the animal back to its lair. I will remain behind with two of our men."

"No!"

"Mary, in this matter I do not ask for your permission. A monster is stalking you. Tell me my lady, do you prefer to be the prey or the hunter? I will answer for you. You are the hunter and I am your spear."

"But -."

"But I will find you once my work is finished. If I fail to return, run Mary. Run far away as fast as you can and never, never stop."

Encountering only modest gales and patches of rough seas here and there, we had enjoyed an unusually long stretch of good weather since leaving Westport. I don't recall ever seeing better. But once we entered the dark waters of the Atlantic for the Old World, our luck deserted us. That cold bitch can whip-up thrashing gales in winter as treacherous as any summertime *huracán* and she hit us and hit us hard with one vicious storm after another. For many days and nights howling winds slashed at our sails as towering waves crashed over the rails, violently smacking our ships to a fro. One ugly gale dumped freezing rains on us and wrapped our ships in ice. We lost twelve good men to the sea before we saw the friendly shores of Ireland. Never before had I lost so many men on one voyage.

Before we parted ways with our French friends off Lamb's Head, I reminded Bertrand that *Vengeance* was his free and clear, but that he was only holding *Cerberus* in trust for Maurice. He understood and agreed to rejoin us in Westport in the early spring for a new adventure to the west.

Spirits soared when we coasted into Clew Bay with our battered ships. We were all bone-weary, but we were home and I had purses fat with Spanish silver and New World gold to hand out to each man. I set aside one chest of silver for the queen, then paid the men their shares and gave them sixty days' liberty. Atwood caught a packet ship for Dublin and from there he would catch a ship to Ayr. MacGyver travelled as far as Dublin with him and then hurried on to Rush. Henry and Kinkae stayed on the ships with their men and I went ashore with young Robert.

The day turned blustery and cold with Westport's grey skies threatening snow. I found myself missing the warm, sensuous breezes of the Caribbean.

"So, Rob," I asked as we walked along the pier, "once Mustafa returns, I understand you intend to desert me for piles of sand in the Syrian Desert?"

Robert smiled. "Mustafa has warned me that the journey will be arduous, but aye, I will travel the road with him."

I stopped at the crossroads near the center of town to embrace Robert. "My, my, Master Robert. Holding you is like embracing a pillar of stone! You didn't have these muscles when we left Westport."

"No, Lady Mary. Much has changed."

"Where a boy once stood, I now see a man. Such a handsome lad you've become too! Well off you go, give my warm regards to your father and to your brothers. I'll see them soon enough at the tavern and I'll expect you to buy the first round."

I saw the boy in Robert return when he giggled, and then he hurried off while I took the road to the Fitzgerald house. My heart began to sing as I pictured little Aliénor in my arms. I quickened my pace, fool, fool, fool that I am.

I froze in horror in the middle of the road when I saw the charred carcass of a home. The stone chimney and a few burnt walls were all that remained standing of the Fitzgerald house.

"They an't here," a rickety, old voice called out behind me. I spun around and came face-to-face with a shriveled, old woman staring up at me, clutching a threadbare shawl against her bent shoulders. She offered me a toothless grin.

"The family who lived in that house grandmother, do you know where they went?"

"He, he, he. No, no. I do not. I suspect far, far away from here tho'."

"Did they take a baby with them?"

"God have mercy, this cold bites deep into the bone. Could you spare a coin your ladyship?"

I dug into my pocket and handed the woman a handful of shillings.

"Oh, this will do nicely," she said and started walking off.

"Thank'ee kindly darlin'."

"Wait, please. The baby, tell me about the baby."

The old woman spun around and laughed. "My, my, an't you the arrogant one, demanding this and that from a poor, sickly, old woman. Why seek ye the dead among the living?"

I stared at her aghast as she turned her back on me and started walking away again, mumbling nonsense to herself. "Old crone," I shouted after at her.

I walked through the ruins, looking for some clue of where the Fitzgeralds may have gone but found nothing. I sat on the burnt remains of three-legged stool to gather my thoughts. Snowflakes began falling all around me. And then an elderly gentleman with a walking stick doffed his hat and waved to me from the road.

"You be Lady Mary?"

"Aye."

He pointed towards the center of town. "I live down that way. Name's Griffin, ma'am. Friar Thomas asked me to keep an eye out for you. I heard you were back in town."

"You know Friar Thomas?"

"Not terribly well, but when he comes into Westport, we sometimes share a pint or two."

"Please sir, can you tell me what happened here?"

"I don't truly know. But the Fitzgeralds and the children left before the fire. Friar Thomas said he'd wait for you at the old priory on the road east of Castlebar. Do you know it?"

"Aye," I answered. "I do. Thank you, Mr. Griffin."

The man touched his stick to his forehead and walked off. And then I saw Robert racing down the road, sobbing. I hurried to his side.

"Rob?"

He took one look at the Fitzgerald house, grabbed me by the shoulders and looked at me with wild eyes. "Where's Aliénor?" he asked me frantically.

"I do not know. What's wrong? Why do you weep?"

Robert buried his head in my shoulder, shaking. "Men gutted

the *Fúmsa an Díoltas* with fire. Folks say my fath, father, and my bro, brothers are, are, are dead. They say their, their, bodies were hack, hacked to piece, pieces and left in a, a cart out in the woods. Hacked to pieces Mary!"

I fought down the bile rising in my throat. I tried to shake-off the ugly thoughts racing through my head. I took Robert by the hand and we ran to his father's tavern. When I saw the burnt-out shell, I fell to my knees in the middle of the road and wept.

A few curious town folk gathered around us. None had much to say. No one knew who had set fire to Shaw's tavern or to the Fitzgerald home. No one knew the whereabouts of the Fitzgeralds. I found reason to hope.

Robert leaned over and vomited. I could see him shivering and wrapped my arms around him.

"Mary, they, they killed my, my father and kil, killed my brothers. What do I do? Tell me, I beg you. Wh, wh, what must I do?"

I kissed his eyes, I kissed him on the forehead and led him to a nearby tavern. I had the barkeep bring us hot tea with honey, cinnamon and a little whiskey and mixed them altogether.

"Drink, Rob," I said as I reached across the table to hold his hand.

We sat quietly together for some time drinking our strong tea. The day turned dark as the flurries changed to snow. A fresh wind from the north railed against the tavern's windows.

The barkeep, a bald, round, short little fellow with a friendly smile stoked the fire in the tavern's small hearth and then brought us a loaf of warm bread and hot soup to fight the chill. He laid a hand on Robert's shoulder.

"A great evil has befallen Westport," he said. "I'm sorry for your loss young Robert. Your father was a good man and well-liked. Your brothers were fine lads."

"What happened here?" I asked.

"Word is *Phantom* is back in port. You be Capt'n Mary?"

"Aye."

"Name's Tom Flynn, madam. I only know what you've probably

already been told. Strangers came to town one night and torched the *Fúmsa an Díoltas* and the Fitzgerald home. The next day Shaw and his boys were found dead out in the woods. No one has seen the Fitzgeralds. That's all I know."

"Should you hear of anything more Tom Flynn, I trust you'll seek me out. My generosity is well-known."

"If you're after justice my lady, I need no reward to punish the loathsome scoundrels who murdered good, Godfearing men in cold blood."

I nodded my thanks and turned to Robert as Flynn walked off. "Rob, I must ride to Castlebar. There is a man, a friar, at an abbey there who may know something. He's a good friend. Rob, do you have any family in Westport or somewhere nearby, or should I take you back to the ship?"

Robert looked at me with bloodshot eyes and a runny nose. "I'll be coming with you, Lady Mary."

I could not say no. With Flynn's help, we borrowed two good horses and rode fast and hard through biting winds and driving snow. We rode through Castlebar and reached the priory just before dark.

The priory, a modest stone building in disrepair, stood in the middle of nowhere surrounded by woods. A sad, little stable sat off to one side with a few scrawny chickens strolling around the yard and one thin pig.

A slim man with greasy, disheveled hair and grey stubble on his chin answered the front door with a candle in his hand when I knocked. I took the fellow to be the priory's caretaker. He let us inside after I gave him my name.

Robert and I followed the man into a poorly lit room with a dirt floor and a roughhewn table surrounded by a dozen chairs. Off in one corner I saw a crude bookcase with no books and along the walls I saw sconces without candles. The room's fireplace, being small, gave-off little heat.

"I'm Doyle," the man turned and said, bearing a set of badly stained teeth. "Are ye family?"

"I've known the friar since I was a little girl," I replied.

"Friar Thomas said to expect you. When the priory moved to Galway awhile back, I agreed to stay on with Friar Thomas and tend to this place. Lord, I know not why. Friar Thomas keeps to his room these days. The small allowance Galway sends us each month is barely enough to buy food. The friar is too frail to leave his bed, but his mind is as sharp as it ever was. We don't get many visitors. You'll brighten the friar's day for sure."

I sent Robert outside to fetch more firewood, in an effort to distract his mind, while Doyle led me down a musty hallway to a small room where the old friar was resting on a cot. The bedroom was dingy and unkept and barely large enough for the friar's cot, one cheap nightstand, a narrow dresser and a small coal brazier. The only decoration in the room was a simple cross of wood hanging over the bed-board.

I lifted a candle off the nightstand, held it close to the friar's face and was taken aback. The robust, portly man I knew had withered away to bone and skin oozing puss from scabs and open sores. I noted the twitch in his left arm and the drool trickling down his chin. I saw clumps of hair around his pillow and on the floor.

"Friar Thomas," I said, gently nudging him on the shoulder to wake him.

"Mary, you've come home," he said.

"I'm sad to see you like this. What ails you father?"

He grabbed me by the arm and choked back tears.

I could feel my body tense as a terrible dread spread through me. "Friar Thomas, do you know where Aliénor is? There was a fire at the Fitzgerald's house."

"She's, she's gone."

"Gone? Gone where?"

"Mary, Mary, Mary, Aliénor is with our Lord."

"NOOOOOOOO!" I heard myself scream.

My heart stopped beating. I fell to my knees. I couldn't breathe as I felt the walls of the room closing in on me. Different thoughts raced through my mind as I struggled to catch my breath. I had misunderstood the friar of course. Yes, yes. He is a feeble, old man I told myself. His mind had turned to pudding.

Then, behind me, I felt strong arms lift me to my feet. Robert.

I looked down on the friar filled with rage. I had an urge to shake him.

"Have you lost your wits you stupid, old man? Aliénor is not *DEAD*! She's with your brother and his wife. Tell me now, where is your brother? Think! Where can I find your brother?"

I could see the horror in the friar's eyes. He could no longer hold back his tears.

"Mary, your loss has filled me with unbearable grief. The *Síol Faolcháin* sent men to Westport. The *Síol Faolcháin* have killed them all."

The room started spinning. My knees buckled and I fell. I vaguely remember Robert catching me and carrying me to the front room. He sat me in a chair next to the fireplace, wrapped a blanket around me and tossed more logs on the fire.

I stared absently at the flames. I felt numb and couldn't focus. I knew only that Friar Thomas had to be mistaken. The clan had no knowledge of Aliénor. I remember I wept for some time before I drifted off to sleep that day.

When a shaft of sunlight brushed my cheek in the morning, I awoke curled-up on the floor wrapped inside a blanket with the fragments of an ugly dream lingering in my head. Faceless demons clawing at my legs had tried to pull me off a ship to drag me to the bottom. I took in the unfamiliar room and found Robert sleeping next to me. And then I remembered. The priory. Friar Thomas. Aliénor and an endless stream of pain.

Robert stirred, sat up and took my hand.

"Rob, I'm sorry," I said and kissed his hand. "You are hurting too. This is all a terrible, terrible mistake. We'll find your father and your brothers. We'll find my little Aliénor."

But as he looked at me and as I looked at him, we both saw the truth in the other's eyes. We wrapped our arms around each other, held each other close, and cried for a good, long time.

"Mary, I'll brew us some tea," Robert finally said. "Can you eat?"

"No. I have no appetite. Tea, yes tea."

Then Doyle walked through the front door carrying a basket of eggs. He removed his cap and bowed his head when he saw me.

"Lady Mary, I'm sorry for your troubles."

And then we heard the friar coughing. Doyle set his basket down and I followed him into the friar's room.

The friar's eyes were closed. He held a rosary in his hand and was mumbling something to himself.

"Father, I, I am sorry," I said in a hoarse voice as I placed my hand over his. "I pray you can find it in your heart to forgive me. I shouldn't have lost my temper with you."

He opened his eyes and squeezed my hand. "Oh child, there is nothing to forgive. You're most precious to me."

I leaned over to embrace him. I found it difficult but forced myself. "I should never have left Aliénor here, or anywhere in Ireland. I should have taken her to France or to the United Provinces, somewhere across the sea and far away."

"Mary, do not punish yourself. I beg you."

"Are you certain about what you said? Is it possible you are wrong?"

"No."

I felt my lower lip begin to quiver. I had the urge to heave and I would have too but for my empty stomach. "How? How did she die?"

"Who is the boy standing in the hallway behind you?"

"This is Robert Shaw. His father was the proprietor of the *Fúmsa an Díoltas*. Folks in Westport say his father and brothers are dead."

The friar winced. "I'm sorry lad. I'll pray for their souls. I did not know your father or your brothers well but I knew them. I see the likeness now. Mary, perhaps we should speak alone?"

"Whatever you have to say to me Father, you may say to Rob as well. He and I are family now."

I turned to look at Robert, guilty that I had neglected his grief. "Rob the choice is yours to stay or to wait in the other room."

"I would stay and hear the Father's words."

I walked over to Robert, rubbed his arm and kissed him on the cheek. "Very well then. Friar Thomas?"

"Please, help me sit up."

Robert and I each grabbed an arm and raised the friar up on his pillows. When I lifted his blanket up to pull it over his chest, I saw his filthy nightshirt and was hit with the overpowering stink of old urine.

"Mr. Doyle, might the priory have a tub?" I asked.

"No, we'd need to bundle Father up and take him into town for a bath, but I fear he's too weak."

"I see. Perhaps you could fix us all some breakfast?"

Doyle nodded and left the room.

Friar Thomas cleared his throat. "Doyle is a bit slow, but he's been a faithful steward of this priory for many years."

My opinion of Doyle was less charitable, but I held my tongue. "Father, you have a story to tell," I said with impatience.

"Aye. Three months ago, the *Sons of the Síol Faolcháin* came to Westport asking questions about you Mary. Shaw warned my brother John and John, being no fool, left Westport in haste and brought his family here."

"Aliénor was here?"

"Aye, briefly. With the money you left me, I helped John secret Aliénor and his family out of Ireland. John and Katerina travelled on to Dublin with the children, sailed to Liverpool and then travelled on to Edinburgh. From Edinburgh they sailed across the Channel to Ostend. I know these things because John sent me a letter after they reached Ostend safely. The letter is in the top drawer over there."

"The clan found them in Ostend?"

"No. The road was long and hard though. The weather was dismal. Aliénor caught a cold and later died with a high fever."

I looked away. "In Ostend?"

"Aye, Mary, in Ostend."

"What happened to your brother and his family?"

"After they lost Aliénor - I tell you John and Katerina loved her like their own - they returned to Westport thinking they'd be safe. But the *Síol Faolcháin* had men waiting for them and murdered them all."

I should have, I knew, shown the friar some compassion, but I had none to give. I pressed on with my interrogation.

"How did the clan learn of Aliénor?"

A coughing fit seized the friar before he could answer. I sent Robert to the kitchen for a cup of wine. After Robert returned, the friar greedily drained the cup.

"Ah, better," he said. "Thank you. I know not, Mary. I can only suppose."

"Then suppose."

The friar glanced up at Robert. "Lad, what I have to say will be hard to bear."

"Say what you have to say Father," Robert replied.

Friar Thomas glanced at me and I nodded.

"Very well then. Tho' I've had plenty of time to think on these terrible matters these past few months, truly I do not know the answer to your question Mary. I believe the *Síol Faolcháin* came to Westport after they learned you were still alive. It was no secret you frequented Shaw's tavern. I suspect they took Shaw and his sons to some quiet place to talk, then killed them in the woods after heard what they wanted to know."

I rested my hand on the friar's shoulder when he started sobbing.

"I, I don't think the clan knew anything about Aliénor before then. That, that is all I know."

"Rest now," I said.

After the friar closed eyes and fell asleep, I wrapped an arm around Robert's waist and led him back to the front room. But he stopped me in the hallway.

"This," he said, showing me a small vile in the palm of his hand, "was on the priest's dresser Mary."

"Aye, medicine no doubt. What of it?"

Robert shook his head while he removed the cork from the bottle. He poured a drop of liquid onto his little finger and put his finger to his nose. Then he touched the drop with the tip of his tongue and spit.

"The liquid has no odor and is tasteless."

"And?"

"I only saw the friar once from a distance, not too long ago. He had thick hair, pink cheeks and a round belly. He walked with a strong step."

I nodded. "Aye, now he's old and dying."

"Aye, he's dying, but not from sickness or old age I think. This liquid is laced with poison."

"What? How can you know this?"

"Mustafa has been teaching me many things. He has been instructing me on how to make and how to identify the use of different poisons. The friar's sudden loss of weight and hair, his drooling and his trembling hands, are all signs of slow poisoning. The friar smells of garlic and his fingernails are discolored with white stripes. These are the symptoms of one particular poison: arsenic. Depending on the dose, arsenic can kill slowly or quickly."

"Doyle."

"By your leave Mary, I should like to have a chat with our good steward of the priory."

"Rob, the horses need to be brushed, watered and fed. I'll see to the other."

"We both hold equal claim."

I placed my hand on Robert's cheek. "A fair point young man. Still, I would have you keep your hands clean in this ugly matter."

"Lady Mary, you are my mistress. I swore my fealty to you. But if I must choose between obeying you in this matter, or obeying Mustafa, I must obey Mustafa. Before we parted ways, I swore to him that I would protect you with my life, even if it meant disobeying you."

"Doyle is no threat to me."

"Please Lady Mary, leave Doyle to me."

Too distraught to argue, I nodded and quietly took a seat close to the fire. An hour passed before Robert returned from the stable. His shirt was splattered with blood. I pointed to the table where I had set out two bowls, wine and a basket of black bread. I had breakfast simmering in a pot hanging inside the fireplace.

Robert took a seat and drained his cup of wine as I filled our bowls with pottage. "When the *Síol Faolcháin* learned that John Fitzgerald and the friar were brothers," he said in a low voice, "they came here to the priory, eight men in all, looking for Aliénor. When Friar Thomas denied knowing Aliénor, they beat him. They beat him harder and still he denied knowing Aliénor. But when they started on Doyle, he talked. He told the clansmen what they wanted to know. He told them that the Fitzgeralds had left the priory with an infant girl, but that John Fitzgerald had not said where they were headed. The clansmen paid Doyle to kill Friar Thomas and didn't much care how he did it. Doyle chose slow poison so he could continue collecting the stipend Galway sends each month. When the friar received his brother's letter, Doyle read it and sent word to the clan that Aliénor had died and that the Fitzgeralds were returning to Westport."

"Could Doyle describe any of these men?"

"Aye, he gave me a good description of two of the bastards."

"Rob, I've brought this evil upon you. I will understand if you blame me for the death of your father and your brothers. I'll give you all the money you need to start your life anew. If in your heart you hate me, I pray you can forgive me with time."

Robert looked at me dumbfounded. "Hate you? Mustafa warned me about this."

"Pardon?"

"Mustafa said there are times when you say the silliest things and that I must learn to ignore you when you say them. You told the friar we are family. Is this not so?"

I reached across the table for Robert's hand. "For my part, it is so. We are blood."

"We are blood," he said and took my hand.

"Very well. Tomorrow we'll ride into Castlebar and find someone to properly care for Friar Thomas."

"And then?"

And then I had no answer. Without warning the grief swept over me. As I broke down in tears, Robert wept with me. We moved over to the fire and held each other until we could weep no more.

Later, before the sun settled on the land, we dragged Doyle back into the woods and tossed his body into a deep hole. In the morning we rode to Castlebar where I found a kindly woman to care for Friar Thomas. I sent a letter off to Galway, informing the friars there that Doyle had run off, and then Robert and I returned to the old priory with the woman and a cartload of supplies. After we bid the friar farewell, Rob and I rode back to Westport.

For weeks I kept to my great cabin, wallowing in my great grief. Pain and I are no strangers. First Gretchen, then Gilley, Hunter and all the others, and now my sweet, little Aliénor, a blameless infant child, the people I had loved most in this world, all murdered by the wretched *Síol Faolcháin*. Those I choose to love pay a terrible price for my affections. The *Síol Faolcháin* - my hated foe - I could think of little else.

The days passed by slowly as I frittered away the hours knocking back the whiskey. The nights were cold and lonely. My only comfort was sleep and sleep was often hard to find. At the darkest hour, I caught myself staring at the loaded pistol I kept near my bed.

When the days turned warmer, I packed a sack with food, blankets and warm clothing and left my great cabin to go ashore. Henry and Kinkae tried to come with me, but I would not let them and luckily Robert was in town purchasing fresh victuals for the crew.

I walked for miles until I reached *Cruach Phádraig* and made my way up a rocky, narrow path until I reached the mountain's snowcapped peak. If the legends be true, Saint Patrick had fasted on that peak for forty days and forty nights. A silly notion had rattled around in my brain while I was languishing in my cabin. Perhaps, I thought, God might hear my prayers from the place where Saint Patrick had once spoken with Him. But after three days and two nights up on that damn, windswept mountain, when God refused to even give me a nod, I retraced my steps back to the ships chilled to the bone and disheartened.

A day later I caught a fever. I drifted in and out of sleep with visions bizarre in nature and devoid of any good purpose. At times I felt so cold, and my body shook so hard, I prayed for death to take me.

When awoke one morning feeling better, I found Efendi sitting in a chair next to me, dozing.

"Mustafa," I whispered, you've returned. When he didn't stir, I leaned over to try and wrap my arms around him and nearly fell out of my bunk.

Efendi caught me, lifted me back on the bed and put a hand to my forehead. "Good, good. Your fever has broken," he said and took my hand. "Mary, Rob has told me all. I have no words."

"No, there are no words," I said. Had I any tears, I would have started crying.

"You have no meat on your bones. Let me bring you something to eat. A piece of toast or warm broth?"

"Later perhaps. You are well?"

"I am."

"Allah be praised my friend. Tell me then Mustafa, tell me a story about a pair of mad jackals running loose in the New World."

Efendi reached into his pocket and handed me a medallion, like the one Cortés had described with the figure of a lion holding a swallow-tailed flag in its mouth. "The beast's two cubs are dead."

"Will the Nizari send others?"

Efendi shook his head and squeezed my hand. "I know not. But never forget who we are. You and I are the hunters, fearsome hunters, not the prey, never the prey."

Two months to the day after we had dropped anchor in Westport, I received a letter from Bertrand informing me that he was on his way, and then my own men started drifting in. Atwood and MacGyver were among the first to return.

"Enter," I said when I heard a light rap on the door to my cabin.

Atwood stepped inside and removed a new, stylish, capitano hat. "Mary."

I stood to embrace the big Scot. "You've spoken to Mustafa."

Atwood held me and kissed my hair. "Aye, aye."

"All is well with your family?"

"All is well. Mary, I'm here to tell you that I'll be heading out soon. I'm taking Mustafa and some of the lads with me, about thirty or so in all. You rest and wait for us here."

"Heading out? Heading out to where Jacob?"

But I knew the answer already. Atwood bit his lip, said nothing.

"Jacob, I'll not let you ride to Youghal, not into the stronghold of the *Síol Faolcháin*, not even with a hundred men."

Efendi then stepped into my cabin. "The men are ready Jacob."

"Have them stand down Mustafa," I said sternly. "Summon the others. Now if you please."

When Atwood and Efendi returned with MacGyver, Henry and Kinkae in tow, I pointed to the table and each man solemnly took his seat. "My brothers," I said with a quiver in my voice. "I'm deeply touched by your willingness to take on the *Síol Faolcháin*. But what has changed that we might win such a war? Nothing. The clan has more ships and more men than we do, men who have fought the English, men hardened by battle."

Atwood grunted. "The *Síol Faolcháin* has murdered innocent folk on O'Malley land. Where's their outrage? Where's their thirst for blood? I'll wager the O'Malleys have more men and more ships than the *Síol Faolcháin*."

"The *Síol Faolcháin* attacked me, not the O'Malleys," I said. "This is not their fight."

"Jesus Christ, Mary. Lord Eoghan Dubhdara O'Malley was your father. You are the daughter of a king. If the O'Malley clan had any honor, they'd march side-by-side with us against the *Síol Faolcháin* and rid Ireland of this pestilence instead of hiding behind in their castle walls whimpering like whipped dogs."

"I'm nothing to the O'Malleys, Jacob, except a source of profit.

Besides, the clans cannot afford to slaughter each other with English armies camped on Irish soil. The O'Malleys are looking out for themselves. We would do the same."

"Shaw was our friend," MacGyver blurted out. "Your daughter, Mary. We must set matters right..."

I stood to look out the stern windows. I could see the summit of *Cruach Phádraig* in the distance, rising above a mist that had settled over Westport. The last flicker of daylight had bathed the mountaintop in a hallo of golden light against a steel-blue sky. I found comfort in the mountain's stark beauty.

MacGyver rose from the table to stand by my side, then kissed my hand. "Forgive me, Mary. I apologize for my callous words. You and Rob have suffered terribly. I'm sorry."

I gave MacGyver a reassuring smile and returned to my seat. I filled each man's glass with wine.

"Does any man here think me weak or feeble-minded?"

Silence.

I clenched my teeth and pounded the table with my fist. "Good," I said in a firm voice. "By God, I swear there'll be a reckoning one day. But we must bide our time. We must take our revenge at a place and time that favors us. We wait. Perhaps we wait for months or even years - but we wait. Let the *Síol Faolcháin* feel secure for now. I'm learning patience as the years go by - but my memory is long." I turned to Efendi. "We are the hunters, not the prey."

Bertrand sailed into Westport in the early days of March with *Cerberus* and *Vengeance* as promised. His ships were loaded down with a wonderful assortment of Old World goods and finished products. As I had neglected selling-off our own cargo, we had to delay our departure for a week or two.

But I had no interest in selling or buying cargo and left the matter in Atwood's hands. I went ashore, borrowed a good horse and drifted here and there, losing all sense of time. I took the road south and moved from town to town for several days until I reached Galway. I know not why I chose Galway. I told myself that I had heard the mountains of Connemara, the *Na Beanna Beola*, the Twelve Bens, beckoning me.

I found an inn with wholesome food and a talented lute player with a wonderful voice and was halfway through a delicious rabbit pot-pie when Efendi stepped through the tavern door. He saw me, walked to my table and plopped down into a chair across from me.

"Mary."

"Mustafa. How did you find me? Never mind my silly question. What's wrong?"

He helped himself to my ale. "Nothing is wrong. What are you doing?"

"Plainly, I'm eating my supper."

"Mary..."

For no particular reason, I began to cry. "Damn my foolishness," I said, wiping away my tears with my sleeve. "I'm sorry."

"You have no reason to be sorry."

Then a deep and menacing voice behind me interrupted us. "Is this foreigner troublin' you miss?" the voice asked.

"The lady is fine," Efendi said. "Move along."

"I'm not speakin' to you. You've upset the lady. 'Tis time for you to leave."

Efendi calmly placed his hands on the table. I've seen Efendi break a man's leg while seated.

I turned to face the intruder. He was a big man, more fat than brawn, but even a fat man can be dangerous and no doubt he was with friends.

I offered the Irishman a disarming smile. "You're most kind, sir, to be concerned about my wellbeing. All is well. This man is my friend."

"We don't fancy foreigners around here. If you're with him, you best leave too."

On any given day, the big Irishman would have been helped out of the tavern with a broken bone or two and I would have finished my meal in peace. But I was not myself.

I pushed away from the table to stand. "Mustafa, I've lost my appetite. Let's take a walk outside."

"Mustafa?" the Irishman asked. "What kind of name is Mustafa? Why you're one of those filthy, shit-eating Arabs, a heathen who spits on our Lord and Savior!"

I pulled a knife from my boot, jumped to my feet and I held the blade against the Irishman's throat. I hissed at him like a snake. His eyes bulged in terror as I leaned on the blade and drew a trickle of blood. The tavern fell silent.

"My friend is not Arab, he's a Turk," I said calmly. "Not that it matters. I'm doing you a favor by shutting your hole before you make me angry. Consider this your lucky day. Any further rudeness from you and your friends will be carrying you out of this fine establishment a bloodied, broken fool."

I turned to look at the faces around the room. "All is well, or do we have a problem?"

Folks looked away and returned to their own matters.

"You can pay for my meal," I told the fat Irishman as Efendi and I slowly started retreating for the door and stepped outside.

"Jacob is beset with worry, Mary," Efendi said as we ambled down a deserted street.

The night air was chilly, raw and smelled of snow.

I buttoned up my coat.

"Oh?" I said.

"He has men scouring County Mayo looking for you. You should not have left as you did."

"I do believe you are scolding me."

"Praise Allah you are well. That is all I have to say. Please, let us return to the ships."

"Are we ready to sail?"

"Yes. Jacob has sold all of our cargo from the Americas and has purchased new cargo for the voyage. The ships are in prime condition. The men are eager to sail."

"Excellent. How is Rob?"

"The boy is angry at the world. He is angry at you in particular for deserting us without a word. He'll mend. I am more worried about you."

"No need. Let's return to Westport. But I'll not be sailing on this voyage."

"Beg pardon?"

"And neither will you or Rob."

"What the devil do you propose we do in Ireland?"

"Not Ireland my friend. I have a chest full of silver for the queen. I will sail to London. You and Rob may accompany me to London if you like and there we shall part ways."

"Part ways?"

"Aye. I cannot see the world clearly. I do not trust myself to lead. I need more time Mustafa. You will take Rob and travel east on your pilgrimage."

"No, Mary. I will not leave you alone."

"You will. The time is right for your journey. Rob will mend, I agree, but I think he'll heal faster if he takes this pilgrimage of yours."

Efendi nodded thoughtfully. "I will do as you ask, but on one condition."

"On one condition says you? If I recall, Gilley tried that once."

Efendi cracked one of his rare smiles. "So he did. I remember you threatened to toss him over the side."

"So I did."

Efendi dropped his smile and looked hard into my eyes. "Swear to me, Mary. Swear to me that you will take no action against the *Síol Faolcháin*. You must keep far away from the clan."

"I have no wish to kill myself, Mustafa. You have my solemn word."

Upon our return, I gave my officers their orders. None were too keen to sail without me, but they obeyed. Efendi and Robert traveled with me as far as London. I kissed them both and shed a tear - as any mother might when bidding her sons farewell - and watched them from the dock as they boarded a ship for Italy. Then I hired two dockmen to help me carry my chest of silver and made my way into the city.

I walked directly to the Council of Marine to find the presiding officer, whoever that might be. I decided against trying to deliver the silver to the queen in person as I had no desire to answer a lot of questions.

A minor clerk sitting behind a half-wall at the Admiralty took in my rough clothing and refused me entry. The fool then compounded his error by ignoring my request to see someone of rank. After I had the dockmen place the chest on the floor and sent them on their way, I showed the clerk the silver. He bolted from his chair and ran down a long hallway. When he returned a few minutes later with a man plainly full of himself at his side, I smiled. The man, dressed in expensive silk apparel, looked me up and down with a haughty manner. I took him for a younger son of some wealthy nobleman, one rank above a ne'er-do-well.

"I wish to see someone of authority," I said evenly. "I'm on the queen's business. Who might you be, sir?"

The man put a handkerchief to his mouth to stifle a chuckle. "On the queen's business you say? Oh my. I am Captain Holbrook, George Holbrook."

"I'm pleased to make your acquaintance, my lord. I am Lady Mary."

"And I am delighted to make your acquaintance dear lady, though I am no lord. I'm a captain in Her Majesty's Royal Navy. At present I am serving Charles Howard, the First Earl of Nottingham, the Second Baron of Effingham. Lord Howard is the presiding officer of the Council of Marine and I am his humble secretary. In his absence, I can speak for him."

"You have a position of great prestige, sir, for one of your youth."

He looked at the chest sitting on the floor. "May I?"

"Of course."

He opened the lid and removed one of the silver bars. "Dear me. This bar has been stamped with the Spanish Royal Seal."

"Oh? How odd. I hadn't noticed. Do you wish me to return the chest to the Spanish ambassador my dear Captain?"

Holbrook smiled politely. "No need to be rash. James, fetch two men and - with the lady's permission - have the chest brought to my offices on the double." The captain offered me his arm and escorted me down the hallway. "Tea, Lady Mary?"

The captain's office was small and cramped but he was a gracious host. He poured one cup of tea for me and another for himself.

"Still hot," he said and motioned me to sit. He handed me my tea and took a seat behind his desk, then picked up a small, silver box and offered me a pinch of snuff. I shook my head and declined.

"Are you sure?" Holbrook asked. "Many of the ladies in London partake. A pinch of snuff is all the fashion."

"Not for me Captain Holbrook, but thank you." I reached into my cape to retrieve my *Letter of Marque and Reprisal* and handed the document to him. "Signed and sealed by Her Royal Majesty. I'm not quite the bumpkin your clerk imagined me to be."

He unrolled the document and laughed. "Ah, a royal license to play pirate. And I thought this treasure was for me!"

"Alas, no."

Two men dressed in buff trousers with matching red jackets trimmed in blue piping briefly interrupted us when they carried the chest into the captain's office. Holbrook had them set the chest on his desk and then dismissed both men.

"Bless me, we have a woman on the throne and now we have female captains! The world's been turned upside down."

"A monarch or a commander hardly needs a pair of stones to be wise or skilled in battle."

"I dare say I agree my lady! I have a capable, headstrong niece, an extraordinary girl, who desires nothing more than to be a doctor, though such a thing is of course impossible. I pity the man who attempts to tame her."

"Send her to me and I'll help see her desires fulfilled if she has the talent."

"Hmm. I believe you would. Captain Mary, yes I've heard the name."

"I pray you judge me not by what you've heard."

"I must confess, your attire threw me off. Do you dress in common seaman's clothing as a disguise?"

"Did you think me some trull from the waterfront when you first laid eyes upon me? I much prefer these clothes to silk dresses and fancy lace when driving ships hard across an angry sea."

Holbrook smiled. Then there was a rap on the door and a young man carrying a tray with a fresh pot of tea walked in. I could feel his eyes on me.

"Thank you, Moses," Holbrook said. "Be a good fellow and add a log or two to the fire and then you may close the door behind you."

Holbrook stood to pour two more cups of tea after the young man left. "You must have a fascinating story to tell Lady Mary, or do you prefer Captain Mary?"

"Mary, just plain Mary will do."

"Excellent," he said as he exchanged my old cup for a new one. "By all means, please call me George."

That was when I knew the captain was flirting with me.

"May I?" he asked after he returned to his desk.

"Of course."

Holbrook carefully removed the silver bars from the chest and stacked them on his desk in two neat rows, counting them with something approaching reverence. "A handsome sum, Mary. Did you acquire this silver at sea or in the West Indies?"

"I do have a tale to tell George, but that story is for the queen. I trust you'll see this silver delivered to her majesty, along with my compliments."

"I understand. I assume this silver is the queen's rightful share under the terms of your commission?"

"Just so," I replied, though this of course was not quite true. I owed the Crown one-third of whatever I took in plunder under the terms of my commission. But in my mind, I hadn't plundered the silver from the Spanish or under my commission. I had recovered treasure lost by Drake and didn't owe the Crown a thing. Even so, the queen might not agree if she ever learned the truth. This one chest was my compromise.

Holbrook flipped one bar over. "Ha, I see that these bars were minted in 1573."

"Aye. But if I were you, I'd keep that fact to myself, Captain. The queen places a high price on discretion."

"I dare say she does. You were with Sir Francis and Robert Devereux in Spain last year I think?"

"That is true."

"Sir Robert is a very dear friend of mine."

"Though I'm but a lowly commoner, I too consider Sir Robert a friend."

"A commoner? Some say you are of royal blood, that you are the bastard daughter of one Irish king or another."

"How sailors love to gossip!"

"Will you stay in London long?"

"No, not long."

"Perhaps you would consider joining me for supper before you depart. I know several wonderful establishments."

"Perhaps."

"Excellent! Where are you lodging?"

"I have yet to secure accommodations."

"How will I find you?"

I smiled demurely at Holbrook. "I have other business in London. If those matters do not detain me too long, I'll find you."

Holbrook was a handsome fellow with a fine physique and not without his charms. But I had no interest in lingering in London to play. I had accomplished what I needed to do. In the morning I slung a canvas bag over my shoulder and caught the first packet ship I could find for Ostend.

The Opal Coast was blanketed in thick fog with a cold drizzle that cut straight into the bone. I couldn't stop my teeth from clattering after I stepped off the ship. I couldn't feel my toes. I spent a nearly a week in dreary Ostend, suffering the gloom of that city just long enough to find my little Aliénor's grave, and to drink away my pain.

When I had had my fill of sorrow, I collected my things and walked down to the waterfront in a driving rain to purchase passage back to Ireland. When the ferryboat was late, I slipped into the nearest tavern to warm myself, but I did not tarry there long. The tavern was packed with vulgar, smelly men and the very thought of liquor turned my stomach, so I returned to the dock and waited in the rain. I passed the time wondering how I would keep myself busy over the next few months. I needed a distraction. And then a marvelous inspiration tickled my pickled brain. I decided I'd rebuild Shaw's splendid tavern and gift the new tavern over to Robert.

When the ship for London finally pulled in, I stepped into a line with the other passengers while a boy walked down the line passing out tins of hot coffee, compliments of the ferry company. I took two. As I pressed a coin into the boy's hand, I felt someone tap me on the shoulder.

"Mary, Mary, Mary," I heard a familiar voice behind me call out.

I spun around to find Martin grinning at me.

"Bless me, John Martin. You're looking fit, much better than when I saw you last in Portugal. You are well?"

"Thanks to you, I'm very well indeed. You however are blue in the face woman."

"Aye, I'm cold! What an odd coincidence our paths have crossed again here in Ostend."

Martin answered me with a furled brow and a playful smirk.

"Ah, not a coincidence."

"No. How the devil did you become marooned in this dreadful place? Dear God, you haven't lost your ships *again*!"

Despite my melancholy, Martin, the least humorous man I knew, made me smile. "I simply came to Ostend to see a friend."

"Ah."

"And you, what business brings you to Ostend?"

"I'm here for you of course. I have a newbuilt frigate parked a few blocks away with better accommodations than this old barge can offer."

"How did you find me? Oh, never mind. Well I know you are a man of many secrets."

Martin leaned close to my ear. "The queen wishes to see you."

"Oh? Why?"

"I suspect it has something to do with Spanish silver."

"I see. I take it you're back in the queen's good graces?"

"I am most pleased to report that I apparently never fell from her majesty's good graces."

"I'm glad. Did you ever find our mutual friend?"

"I did."

"Is he dead?"

"No, not yet. For now, his life has some value to us, but his time is very near. What is my lady's pleasure? You are free to choose. The queen wishes to see you, but she does not command your presence. My orders are to see you safely to your destination, wherever that may be."

I shook my head and sighed. "Let's go see this frigate of yours."

"The queen will be most pleased. She was concerned when she learned about your travels to Ostend alone."

"Do you keep spies in every port?"

Martin laughed, locked his arm in mine and walked me to his ship.

Martin accompanied me all the way to Windsor Castle and this time I had no difficulty gaining entry inside. The palace guard promptly escorted us to a parlor where the queen and two of her ladies-in-waiting were reading poetry. Martin and I stood at the doorway and bowed.

The queen excused her ladies and gave Martin a kindly smile. "John, we thank you for your good service. You look famished. Why don't you visit the kitchen and have the cook prepare you a hot meal?"

"Your Majesty," Martin replied, bowed again and walked backwards until he was out of sight.

The queen stood to embrace me. "Oh, Mary. When we heard the wicked news, news of these nefandous crimes, it was like a dagger to the heart."

I thought I had exhausted all my tears. But no. My body trembled and I broke down again in the queen's arms.

"There, there, child," the queen whispered and rubbed my back. "Shhh, shhh. What can we do?"

"Nothing, Madam. There is nothing you can do."

She took my hand. She led me to a chair and poured me a cup of tea.

I took a sip to help compose myself. "Aliénor, Aliénor Muirgheal was her name."

The queen placed a hand over mine. "Lovely."

"She was a lovely child."

"We need not speak of these evil matters if the speaking of them brings you pain. I cannot begin to fathom the depth of your suffering. I'm glad you accepted Captain Martin's invitation. I wanted to express my sorrow and my deep and abiding affection for you."

I forced a brave smile. And when the queen asked me to stay, I did and we talked of many things over several hours. The queen was exceedingly kind and patient and I was surprised by how open and frank she was with me. We talked about God, the Reformation, politics and war. We even discussed what the Irish were calling the War of Decimation. England's methodical eradication of everything Irish - Plantation - had killed and displaced tens of thousands of Irish men, women and children and the Irish warlords were striking back.

When a servant appeared with Martin at his side, I knew it was time to leave. "Your Highness, rest assured I will never disclose the things we have discussed this day. I know you have shared some of your private thoughts with me and I am humbled by your trust."

"I have no doubt you will show discretion for I know your mettle. You are an intelligent and fair-minded woman with wonderful good sense. The fact that you are also Irish has made our discussions, particularly on the Irish matter, all the richer and I respect your point of view. No burden is heavier to carry than the suffering of my people. The great kingdoms of Europe outmatch us in wealth and power. England, Scotland, Wales and Ireland must stand united as one, lest we find ourselves groveling at the feet of some foreign prince with gluttony in his heart who would carve us up to satisfy his appetite."

I nodded. "I do not envy you, your Majesty. You are a great queen to your people. I find the burden of command over a paltry one hundred men a taxing enough challenge each day."

"The silver was a most welcomed gift. I've instructed my Secretary of the Council of Marine to melt the silver down and destroy any record of it. He and his subordinates are forbidden to speak of the matter to anyone. I think it is best if Drake does not learn about your gift. He can be pugnacious and not always of fair mind. The silver belongs to the finder in this instance, not to the one who lost it, but I have no wish to quarrel with Drake over such matters."

"I fully understand, Madam."

The queen placed her hand against my cheek. "Fair thee well, Mary. God keep you safe in His Divine Constancy. And do not think again you can deliver gifts at my doorstep and ignore me - lest you enjoy being kidnapped by my navy."

After we left Windsor, Martin insisted on returning me to Westport. The queen was sending Martin back to the Americas and Ireland was only a little out of his way. He was to quietly explore the lands north of Florida up to Virginia, named after her majesty, and then the lands to the west while gathering information on Spanish settlements in those territories.

I spent my days in Westport giving life to my inspiration. I spared no coin in rebuilding Shaw's tavern. And when the work was well-in-hand, I spent my days riding. I found peace roaming about the countryside or hiking up into the mountains. I savored those carefree days. In the spring I rode out to Castlebar to see Friar Thomas, but my visit was brief as he passed away several days after my arrival. His death saddened me, but I did not weep.

Beyond the tavern, I had no plan. I had no dreams or desires. Worst of all, I could find no purpose to my life. I breathed. I ate. I slept. I was simply killing time before time killed me. An awful thing to do. Before he died, Friar Thomas had assured me that I had a part to play in God's plan. I had strong doubts.

On the first day of May, the beginning of *Lá Bealtaine*, the foreman overseeing the work on the new tavern handed me a hammer to drive in the last nail. The tavern had a modicum of elegance and was larger than before and I was well pleased.

The next morning, a day of striking beauty, I heard *Cruach Phádraig* whispering my name. I quickly dressed, ate a breakfast of oatmeal porridge and saddled my horse, a spirited mare with a flaxen mane and tail, white socks and a rich, chestnut coat that I had purchased a week before. Like me, she was a wild beast with stamina and we raced the wind together on our way to Louisburg.

I stopped at a market along the way to purchase a basket of fruits, cheeses and a loaf of bread. I replaced the wine in my waterskin with water.

I walked to the highest point of the mountain, laid a blanket across the ground and enjoyed my midday meal underneath a pretty sky with white, puffy clouds. I could see the fishing boats below trolling the waters between Clare Island and Inisturk. I could see for miles all around. I laid my head down, closed my eyes and slipped into a deep and peaceful sleep. Aliénor came to me in a pleasant dream. She was sitting atop Hunter's shoulders, laughing and waving at me to follow them into a field of golden wheat.

I awoke to a wonderful warmth spreading across my body. My heart felt lighter. My mind seemed sharper too. Gone were the muddled thoughts that had plagued me through the winter. I began to believe that the magic of *Cruach Phádraig* had touched me.

I stood, I stretched, I looked out over the horizon. Though a part of me I knew was forever broken, the world seemed good to me again. And then I spied four full-rigged ships sailing in a line under a rising full moon towards shore. They were too far off to recognize, but in my heart I knew they were mine and I hurried back to Westport.

Standing on the dock, I spotted Atwood at the tiller in the first longboat, holding a lantern in his hand and sporting a full beard. He stepped off the boat and wrapped his huge arms around me.

"Mary, thanks be to God! Are you in good health?"

I kissed his cheek, I touched his beard and smiled. "I'm well enough. I like this new look. A good journey?"

"A good journey. What sorcery brought you out this night to look for us?"

"I rode up into the mountains to pass the time. By mere chance I spotted our ships sailing into the bay."

MacGyver, Henry and Kinkae stepped onto the dock and took turns hugging and kissing me. The longboat crew surrounded me and each man shook my hand.

"You lads," Atwood said, "are released. Travel safe. Sixty days' liberty Mary?"

"Sixty days seems right, Captain Atwood. Have you lads been paid your shares?"

The men nodded.

"Good. Off you go to your wives and sweethearts then. You can share your stories with me later upon your return."

"Mary, 'tis good to see you smile," MacGyver said cautiously.

I could see the hesitation in Henry's and Kinkae's faces as they waited to see how I would answer MacGyver.

"Lads, all is well," I said. "I'll not lie, the past few months have been difficult. We bury our dead, we grieve and then we move on. Put your minds at ease. My heart is filled with gladness this night! Welcome home."

"Mustafa and Rob," MacGyver asked, "travelled to the east?"

"They did indeed. I received a letter from them not long ago. They were somewhere in Syria and in good health. Efendi expects to be back in Ireland in a month or two. Any trouble?"

Atwood shook his head. "No. We were most fortunate on this voyage. Cortés continues to honor his word and we found a friend."

"Oh?"

Atwood pointed to one of the longboats drifting in. "Speak of the devil."

I turned, looked at the water and saw Bertrand at the tiller of one boat with Maurice sitting at the bow, waving at me with a broad smile. My heart filled joy.

"I've rebuilt Shaw's splendid tavern," I said, "and the place is open for business. Let's release the rest of the men and set the night watch. I'm eager to hear your stories!"

I embraced Maurice warmly when he stepped off the boat and kissed his cheeks. "Maurice, my dear, dear friend. This is a happy, happy day! You are a wonderful surprise!"

"It is good to be alive, Mary. Thank you for what you have done."

"I did no more than you would have done for me," I said and turned to shake Bertrand's hand. "Piotr, welcome to Ireland. Come gentlemen and join us. We must celebrate our reunion!"

Chapter Thirteen

or the next two months, while the crews enjoyed their liberty, I turned my attention to readying my ships for our next voyage. At times the darkness still tried to snare me, but the magic of *Cruach Phádraig* had blessed me and with each new day I grew a little stronger. I had lost a child, but I still had my sword, my pistols and knives. These were my children now, and how I spoiled them. Each day without fail I sharpened my blades to a keen edge. I cleaned and oiled my pistols with meticulous care.

I spent a fortune on *Phantom*. I had the shipwrights strip her down to her keel and then had her rebuilt with the finest woods I could find and with the best designs I could buy. For years *Phantom* had been the queen of the sea. Few ships could match her speed or agility. But shipyards across Europe and the Americas were launching sleeker, faster ships like *Cerberus* down the ways and I would not sail with a ship of lesser quality.

Irish shipwrights are gifted craftsman. They construct fine ships. But the Irish know how to build fishing trawlers and small freighters, not warships. So, at great expense, I brought two marine architects renowned for their bold ideas over from Europe to help me. One fellow was from Amsterdam, the other from Boulogne. The Dutchman's specialty was building merchant ships with grace and speed using novel and intricate rigging plans. The Frenchman's specialty was building warships with strength and balance. He laid out the gun deck first and then built his ships around the guns, maximizing the ship's stability on a rolling sea. The two men bickered constantly at first and listening to them savage each other tested the limits of my patience. But after many fits and starts - and my extraordinary generosity - the two men strolled into Shaw's tavern one evening bursting with enthusiasm and placed a set of drawings in front of me. And as they took turns explaining their new design to me, they praised each other's genius and traded triumphant smiles.

With my two architects, now fast friends, in agreement and eager to begin construction, I hired the best shipwrights I could find. I tripled their wages to work night and day and placed my Carib and Blackamoors at their disposal.

My perseverance was richly rewarded when we launched *Phantom* in record time. She was a marvel to behold in every way. The Dutchman had removed her cumbersome bonaventure and lateen sails and replaced her fore, main and mizzen with sturdier, taller masts pickled in nearby saltmarshes for strength to carry longer, heavier spars for her larger sails. The Frenchman had eliminated *Phantom's* fore and aftercastle, lengthened her gun deck and double-planked her hull and bulwarks with *quebracho*, the Spanish word for axe breaker, one of the hardest woods in the world found in the forests of the Provincia de Tierra Firme. The Dutchman and the Frenchman had transformed *Phantom* into a three-masted frigate with sleeker lines, a tougher hide and a razor-sharp bow.

Waiting for the workers to finish the odds and ends exhausted me. But when she was finally ready, I took the architects with me into the Atlantic for her trial run. *Phantom* was astonishingly fast and nimble. I marveled at how well she handled in both strong and light winds. She was by far a better ship.

After two days of hard sailing, we coasted into Clew Bay and as we neared the docks, a small sloop with a single sailor came out to greet us. Atwood had returned.

"What ship is this?" he called up to me as the crew took his sloop in tow. "She's missing a mast."

"She's a wonder that fires the imagination and tantalizes the senses," I replied, giddy with excitement. "You won't miss that mast, I promise. Welcome back. All is well in Ayr?"

"Aye. Martha asked me to give you this," Atwood said as he stepped aboard and handed me a small box.

Inside the box I found a short letter and a book of prayers. Martha's letter and her gift touched my heart.

I leaned against Atwood's chest and shed a tear or two. "Martha's words are lovely," I said after I reclaimed my composure. "I have no skills at letter writing, but I must write something to thank her."

Atwood kissed my head, then took in the ship. "I hardly recognize the old girl. She's a good sailor?"

"I surrender the helm to you, my good Captain. You be the judge."

"Looks like about half of the lads are back. I didn't see *Cerberus* or *Vengeance*."

"Maurice and Piotr should be on their way."

"Any word from Mustafa?"

"Aye. I received a recent letter from him. They were close to Calais and not far from home. Now Captain, take the wheel and let me see what you can do with this newfangled war machine. I'll introduce you to the two gentlemen standing on the quarter deck. They are the men responsible for breathing life into this marvel."

A week later Maurice, a prince of the Cimarron, sailed into port with *Cerberus* but without the *Vengeance*. Bertrand had decided to pursue less risky endeavors closer to home. A few days after Maurice's arrival, a pair of weary pilgrims covered in the dust and the grim of the road rode into town on two mules. I hardly recognized either man. Efendi and Robert were dressed in robes and turbans and had grown full beards.

I ran to them. "Oh, how I've missed you both!" I said excitedly. I hugged and kissed them as they dismounted.

"It is good to be back, Mary," Efendi said plainly.

"Lady Mary..." Robert said and embraced me again.

"Rob, my dear Rob. Let me have a look at you. How you've sprouted! Tall, handsome and strong, Westport best lock away her daughters. How are your spirts?"

"I'm well Lady Mary, and you?"

"I'm better. Well, don't tease me. Did you rascals find Krak des

Chevaliers?"

"We did Mary," Efendi replied with a broad smile.

"Did you find the fountain of youth or fabulous riches there?"

"Not that I recall."

"Did you at least find God?"

"No, Mary. But we did find this," Efendi said and turned to Robert. "Rob."

Robert removed a leather pouch from his belt and dropped a heavy object wrapped in a soiled cloth into my hand. I carefully undid the cloth and found a stunning crucifix of solid gold studded with rubies, sapphires and emeralds. The craftsmanship was exquisite.

"Oh my," I said. "Did you scoundrels rob the Vatican?"

"We found this cross by accident buried in the sands of the Syrian Desert outside the ruins of a castle," Robert explained. "Mustafa believes a knight, or perhaps even a prince, lost this in battle during the Crusades hundreds of years ago."

"This is magnificent Rob."

"This is my gift to you."

"No, no, this gift is much too rich for me. This is a rare treasure and you must hold on to it. Perhaps it is even a talisman."

But the boy, now a man and as headstrong as his teacher, shook his head no. He folded his hands behind his back and stepped aside when I tried to slip the crucifix inside his robe.

Efendi shrugged his shoulders when I turned to him for help.

"I see your holiday to the east has done nothing to cure your insubordinate ways," I said. "I shall keep this treasure safe for now, but upon a day, I shall return it to you Rob. Thank you. Well, is it not our custom that one gift deserves another?"

I pointed to the new tavern down the street. "Come, let us quench our thirst and fill our bellies."

"This is splendid," Robert said as we stepped inside.

"I'm glad you're pleased," I said. "'Tis my gift to you. You are now the proud owner of the finest establishment in all of County Mayo. But do not think to charge me for my meals when I take my supper here."

"But Lady Mary -."

"There'll be no discussion about it."

"This is more than I deserve, Lady Mary. You are most generous."

"We are bound by blood you and I. Henceforth, you may address me as simply Mary."

"Aye, Mary."

"Our Aztec friends have taught me the importance of names. Give the matter some thought and choose wisely."

"Why not *Mary's Tavern?*"

"You," Efendi interrupted, "I see still have more to learn. We keep to the shadows. Something less conspicuous would suit me better."

Robert acknowledged his error with a boyish grin.

"Gentlemen, I'm famished," I said. "Let's eat. I'm told the fare here is quite good, though after looking at the two of you, I worry about the riff-raff this place will attract."

Efendi raised his hand. "First, I too have a gift Mary."

"This is like Christmas Day."

"Before Rob and I set out on our journey, you asked me a question. You asked me if the Nizari will send others. I can answer your question now. The Nizari will not."

"How can you be certain?"

"After Rob and I left Krak des Chevaliers, we travelled farther east. We purchased peace with the Nizari."

"This is wonderful news," I said with some suspicion. "And the price?"

"The life of the Grand Master of the Order."

"You killed the grand master?"

"No. We kidnapped the man. The price for peace was his life. He readily agreed to our terms and we released him."

"God's wounds, how did you reach him? Didn't you tell me that the Nizari's stronghold is a fortress?"

"I did."

"You can walk through walls like the Nizari?"

Efendi smiled. "No. Rob and I tracked the man down to his favorite brothel where we caught him, ahem, at an indelicate moment."

I couldn't help but laugh. "How can you be so certain this man will honor his word?"

"The only reason the grand master agreed to send two of his assassins to Spain was because he owed King Phillip a favor. He holds no grudge against us. He did not know his men would be sent to the West Indies to settle some insignificant grudge between Christians of no importance. His debt with Phillip has been settled in full."

I looked at Efendi in disbelief. "The King of Spain wants me dead?"

"No. I very much doubt the king has ever heard of you. But the *Síol Faolcháin* has friends in the Spanish Court. It is not difficult to imagine the king owed money or a favor to one of his nobles who in turn owed money or a favor to the clan."

"An interesting possibility. The grand master I must say seems to have taken all of this rather well. Does he know his men will not be returning?"

"I handed him the other medallion, he knows. And he understands full well that I can find him again. The grand master is a practical fellow. He will honor his word."

After supper, I sent Robert back to the ship to fetch Atwood and the others and told him to bring Maurice too. Efendi remained behind with me.

"Mustafa, you and Rob shared many interesting stories about your journey and yet you have not told me why you travelled to Krak des Chevaliers," I said as I poured him more ale. "I know it was not to find the Nizari as you intended to travel east before we knew anything about the Nizari."

Efendi shook his head. "I cannot say."

"Why?"

"I am sworn to secrecy."

I threw Efendi a dirty look. "Auck! I'll ask Rob then. He'll tell me."

"No, he won't. He proved himself worthy and the brothers have accepted him."

"Who?" I asked, annoyed that I even had to ask.

"The brothers of the order."

"What order?"

"An order whose name I cannot say. Had you been born a man Mary, I would have taken you with us. I will only say this: my loyalty to the brotherhood does not, and never shall, conflict with my loyalty to you."

"Forgive me, Mustafa. Your loyalty is beyond reproach. I don't much care for mystery and secrets though."

Efendi broke the tension in the air between us with a rare and hardy laugh. "You love mystery and secrets as much as anyone!"

"Hmmm," I mumbled under my breath as Atwood and the others filed through the tavern doors to join us. "So, but for a missing pair of balls dangling between my legs I could be a knight or a priest or whatever it is you are in this secret fraternity of yours?"

"Mary, in truth you have the largest balls of any man I know."

I told Maurice and Robert to wait outside and led the others to a private room in the back of the tavern, a room I had designed and furnished myself. And when all was ready, I sent a boy out into the street to fetch the two men. Atwood, MacGyver, Efendi, Henry and Kinkae sat quietly around a long table when Maurice and Robert walked in. I stood off to one side, holding a dead fish in my hand.

"Gentlemen, our rules require a unanimous vote by this assemblage for what I am about to propose," I said and slapped the fish on the table. "Are you willing to swear an oath of loyalty, a blood oath, to me and to the men around this table if they accept you as a brother?"

Maurice and Robert exchanged glances and replied "aye" together.

"Excellent. It warms my heart to hear you say so. Rob, will you honor the Ten Rules?"

"Aye, I will."

"And you, Maurice?"

"Yes, my lady."

"Very well. Rob, you first. Robert Shaw, you stand before us now to give your binding oath before God. Do you swear, on your life, to faithfully honor the Ten Rules with the Almighty Father as your witness?"

"Aye."

I smiled. "You must say the words my young friend."

"Oh, sorry. I swear to each of you, on my life, to faithfully honor the Ten Rules. I swear this before Almighty God as my witness."

I nodded and pulled a dagger from my boot. I stabbed the fish through the heart and left my dagger quivering in the table.

"Understand this Robert Shaw: I will, by Christ, hold you to your sacred oath."

"I understand full-well Mary."

"Very good. What say the rest of you? Are we all agreed to accept Rob as our true brother, or does any man here desire to express his objection?"

Atwood was the first to cast his vote. "Rob has proven his mettle to my satisfaction time and time again. I say aye."

"You have my blessing too, Rob," MacGyver said.

Henry and Kinkae both nodded their consent while Mustafa remained suspiciously quiet.

"Mustafa, why do you withhold your vote?" I asked.

The Turk kept his eyes fixed on Robert. "Rob, you and I are compelled to obey another oath, an oath no less sacred than the one you just now swore. Before I vote, I would know the answer to a simple question: if you were forced to choose between your loyalty to Mary and to these men, or your loyalty to the order, how would you choose?"

Robert took a moment to find his words. He looked at me and then looked back at Efendi.

"You've asked a hard question Mustafa. But I do not think one oath is in conflict with the other. You must agree with me brother for you are here and bound by the same two oaths. To be clear though: Mary and I are bound in blood and no earthly power can sever this bond between us."

Efendi stood, clasped Robert by the shoulders and shook him. "Rob has my vote Mary. Keep your eyes fixed on your North Star my friend and you'll never go far astray."

I was well pleased all my brothers thought as much of Robert as I did.

As was our custom, I had Shaw kneel before me. I anointed his hair with seawater - our lifeblood - and kissed him on the head. When I raised my glass of whiskey, everyone stood with me and raised their glasses too.

"Welcome to the fold Rob," I said. "The meaning of the skewered fish is plain enough. The seawater is our *aqua vitae*. To good fortune, long life and fellowship."

After we drained our glasses, I had Maurice to step forward.

For the next few years we smuggled our tax-free goods back and forth between the New World and Ireland with near impunity. Oh, one brazen rascal or another tried to test our resolve on occasion, but they all fled like dogs when they felt the sting of our six and nine-pounders. *Phantom* and *Cerberus* proved themselves more than a match for all challengers and *Diablo* was no toy. Maurice's crew, a mix of Blackamoors, French, Carib and Cimarron, more or less became mine. Our alliances with the Carib and Cimarron nations grew stronger and with Cortés as our trusted agent, we made a tidy sum. We lost men to the sea, to disease and in battle of course, but for the rest of us life was good.

And yet we all saw the warning signs. We knew our days of leisure sailing and easy profits could not last. The King of Spain was consolidating his power in the New World, spending enormous sums improving key fortresses and building bigger, deadlier ships. Spanish warships infested the Caribbean. Spanish garrisons doubled in size. Pirates, smugglers and gentlemen adventurers fought amongst themselves for the scraps. With our faster, better-armed ships, our

Caribbean allies and my ring of spies, my men and I fared better than most. But with each new voyage we saw our risks increase and our profits dwindle.

As for my great matter, my desire for vengeance against the *Síol Faolcháin*, I was forced to bury my hatred. As Spain's fortunes soared, the clan's power rose too. I had to consider the repugnant possibility that the *Síol Faolcháin* might forever remain beyond my reach.

When we returned to Ireland in the early spring of 1595 with our West Indies cargo, we found ourselves returning to an unfamiliar land mired in turmoil. Once again, we had to find ways to adapt to a new and changing world.

I spent my days in Westport helping my Blackamoors, Carib and Cimarron with routine repairs on the ships while the Irish and the French travelled, some traveling only a little ways and some far, to their homes and families. When I ventured into town or saddled my horse and rode out into the country, the word I heard on every tongue was war. In Ireland there is always talk of war, but the talk in the towns and villages I passed through was far different from the usual noise. Irishmen by the thousands were taking up arms. Counties to the east and to the north and south were in full rebellion. But the most shocking news I heard was of the great Irish victory over the English at a place called Clonibret in County Monaghan. With field cannon and powder supplied by the Spanish a man named Hugh O'Neil, the Lord of Tyrone and a powerful Gaelic chieftain, had routed an English army in pitched battle. Folks claimed after the victory that O'Neil had even offered the Irish crown to King Phillip! The thought of swearing allegiance to Spain turned my stomach.

I imagined the queen sitting on her throne, full of rage. But I did not think Elizabeth would despair or panic, not that prideful woman of iron will. She would take the defeat in stride and press on.

I also learned that my notorious half-sister, Grace O'Malley, known by many as the Pirate Queen, a woman I had never met, had boldly sailed to London to meet Queen Elizabeth to secure the release of her two sons. The English Governor of Connacht, Sir Richard Bingham, a man known for a heavy hand in parceling out English justice in Ireland, had taken the boys prisoner. In exchange for peace with the O'Malley clan, Queen Elizabeth agreed to set the O'Malley boys free.

"John Martin, you old rogue!" I called out to the Englishman as he strolled into Shaw's tavern, renamed *Banshee's Lament* by its young owner. "Come and join us."

Martin eased himself into a chair next to me at the tavern's bar. "My Lady, gentlemen."

"You are looking fit. Tell me, what brings you to Westport?"

"Just passing through madam, just passing through."

"Ha, aren't we all!" I said. I had never met anyone more evasive than Martin - and well I knew he never appeared by chance.

I poured him a full tankard of ale. "Permit me to introduce my officers. You've met Jacob Atwood and Michael MacGyver and Mustafa Efendi of course." Martin reached across the bar to shake each man's hand. "And these other fine fellows are Kinkae, Henry, Maurice and Robert Shaw."

"'Tis a genuine pleasure to meet all of you."

"We were just about to retire to a private room in the back for supper, will you join us John Martin?" I asked.

"Ah, most kind, most kind. I will indeed for I am famished. Could we speak alone for a moment first Mary? I have a personal matter to discuss."

I nodded and led Martin outside to an alley behind the tavern. "Are you coming from or going to the Americas?" I asked.

"To."

"Ah, we're making ready to sail to the west ourselves. And how is our queen?"

"At sixty-one years of age, she is a spritely woman who enjoys remarkably good health."

"Spritely?"

"Ah, one of those newfangled words, from France I think. It means lively. She asks about you."

"Please tell her majesty, when you write your report, that she has my love and affection."

"I will do so. I assume you've heard what happened at Clonibret?"

"Aye."

"The news has caused quite an uproar in London. Are you aware of the meeting between Grace O'Malley and the queen?"

"I've heard of this."

"Clan O'Malley is at peace with England."

"Good."

"The war between Spain and England drags on though Mary. Neither side has found a way to checkmate the other. But Spain can afford a protracted war. England cannot. Between the war with Spain and putting down the rebellions here in Ireland, England is bankrupt. The royal coffers are empty. Parliament has been forced to impose new taxes on the people and to make matters worse, England has experienced one poor harvest after another. Englishmen are suffering. Dissatisfaction is rampant. There have even been reports of riots in York, Durham and Northumberland."

"England will survive. I'm less confident about Ireland."

"Yes, the Irish dilemma. But any monarch must bring rebellious subjects to heel or lose his throne. If the clans unite and form an alliance with Spain, Ireland will be a dagger pointed at Elizabeth's throat."

"Well, Ireland is not my concern. I'm a woman of the world."

Martin came as close to a smile as he was able. "Indeed, you are. There is nothing provincial about you and your pragmatic view of the world is one of the many qualities I admire about you."

"Out with it, John. Our supper is turning cold. You are here to ask me for one favor or another. Speak your mind."

Martin bowed his head. "Power in London has shifted. Robert Dudley, the First Earl of Leicester, Sir Francis Walsingham and Sir Christopher Hatton, once the queen's most capable administrators, and all devoutly loyal to her majesty, are gone. New men rule the Privy Council now, ambitious men driven by politics and greed. Not even the esteemed Lord Burghley, William Cecil, can control these ribald scoundrels."

"What is this to me?"

"Her majesty will not live forever. Her greatest desire is to leave her people strong and secure after she is gone. Her majesty believes England's destiny lies to the west. She is determined to colonize the northern regions of the Americas."

"King Phillip might have a word or two to say about that."

"No doubt. What I've said so far is common knowledge, what I am about to say must not be repeated, not even to your officers, leastwise not yet."

"I understand. I'd never betray the queen."

"I know. The queen has given her blessing to send a powerful invasion fleet to the Caribbean. There will be plenty of opportunity for plunder."

"When?"

"Soon."

"Godspeed to you Martin. I trust England will succeed in her bold endeavor and I wish the queen all good things."

"England needs you, Mary. No one is more familiar with the Caribbean than you. Your strong friendship with the Carib and Cimarron has great value. Your network of spies is better than my own."

"You exaggerate John. England will win or lose the battle with or without my participation. But tell me, Drake will be in command again?"

I could hear the disdain in my own voice as I uttered Drake's name.

"As you say, Mary, our supper is turning cold. Shall we eat? This discussion should not be had on an empty stomach."

I was against sailing into war with the English again. I did not trust Drake and I did not trust the English to share any plunder, not fairly. But most of all I didn't think the English could win. The days of cheap and easy victories against the Spanish in the New World had long passed.

Martin again intended to assemble his own squadron of privateers to augment Drake's fleet and he promised my men and I would sail with him. And he gave me his solemn word: if Drake and I crossed swords again, he would, with the queen's blessing, stand by my side. While Martin failed to win me over, I agreed to put the matter to my men.

As more of my men started drifting into Westport, some returned with their wives and children pulling carts behind them with everything they owned. Families were desperate to escape the death and famine ravaging north Ireland. I purchased the old priory in Castlebar and secured other lodgings nearby for them. I lost thirty men or so to the rebellion too and had to hire new hands. When I finally put Martin's proposal to a vote to my men, the majority, dissatisfied with our shrinking profits and intoxicated by the prospect of easy plunder, urged me to ignore the risks and accept Martin's offer.

Bloody, brutal war, the maker of widows and orphans, the pestilence of the world, ugly but exhilarating just the same, was rising over the horizon. I could see it, hear it, taste it. A part of me loves the thrill of battle. It is not the killing I enjoy, though I have no qualms about killing when killing must be done. I relish the intellectual challenge of war, the challenge of devising a stratagem and the tactics needed to outwit one's opponent. The joy of leading men into battle is undeniable too. If this be a sin, I am prepared to pay the price. I did not choose this life. This warrior's life chose me and I'll not apologize for who I am.

We did not set out in the spring of '95 as planned of course. Politics at Court, divisiveness among his own officers and a lack of finances - and no one had forgotten the debacle of '89 - kept Drake tethered to Plymouth for long, tedious months.

Martin meanwhile used the gift of time to quietly assemble his squadron of privateers. He positioned ships in Westport, Galway and Limerick, far away from prying Spanish spies lurking in English ports.

In early August, Martin and I were summoned to Buckland Abbey in Yelverton, the grand and princely estate Drake had purchased for himself after circumnavigating the globe. I left my ships in Westport and sailed with Martin to Plymouth aboard his fine raider, *Queen's Grace*. A valet, an abrupt, pasty-skinned fellow, greeted us at the door and promptly let us inside. We followed him past the laughter of men somewhere on the first floor and up a stunning, winding staircase to a small study where we found Drake sitting at a desk writing letters. Drake was surprisingly cordial towards me. He smiled, as if our petty quarrel in Cascais had never happened.

"Captain Martin, Lady Mary, how good to see you both," Drake said with sincerity. He rose from his chair to shake Martin's hand. Then he kissed my hand and motioned us to sit.

"You are well, Mary?"

"I am, thank you."

"Good, good."

"How goes your preparations, Sir Francis?" Martin asked.

"I think well enough John. A few members on the Privy Council object to an enterprise to the West Indies. Ho-hum I say. Those knaves, these timid, little men worry Spain might use my absence to invade England. God forbid any of them had to pick up a sword and fight."

"Are their concerns so farfetched Admiral?"

"I'm hardly stripping England of her defenses Martin. In any case, her majesty has summoned me to Court. She wishes to hear more about my prior voyages to Nombre de Diós and the details of my plan."

"Perhaps the queen is having second thoughts about the expedition?"

"I'm confident the queen will give me her blessing."

"May I ask how many ships you've secured so far?"

"Excluding the vessels in this secret squadron of yours John, twenty-five by my last count."

"All this waiting," I interjected, trying to be amiable, "must be frustrating for your grace."

"Quite so, Mary. One of the many burdens of command. I've kept myself busy though. I am overseeing the construction of improved fortifications around Plymouth and I've built several flourmills."

"Flourmills?" I asked.

"Aye, to make fresh biscuits and bread for my men. I even have pure water delivered to the mills daily. Whilst we sit in port twiddling our thumbs day-after-day, my men can at least fill their bellies."

"I pray you keep these flourmills a secret Sir Francis lest my own men hang me from the yardarm for not doing the same."

Drake chuckled. "It shall be our secret, Mary. Well, permit me to introduce you to the gentlemen downstairs."

"Sir Francis," I said and took a step towards Drake. "I do not wish to be too bold, but your last voyage to the Caribbean was nearly ten years ago I think?"

"That's about right. I took Santo Domingo, Cartagena and St. Augustine and the Spanish paid one hundred and fifty thousand gold ducats in ransom for me to spare the torch."

"A glorious feat-of-arms your grace, but things have changed in the West Indies. The Spanish have much improved their defenses on land and at sea."

"As has England, Mary, as has England. John has informed me of the same. But the Spanish have never seen the likes of the might I shall bring to bear on the Americas."

When Drake turned his back on me, I said no more. He led Martin and me downstairs into the Abbey's formal dining hall. The great room was large and elegant with handsome paneled walls, marble floors and a beautiful, coffered ceiling. The room smelled of fresh paint and cigars. I counted about two dozen men in the room, mostly officers, but I saw a handful of fashionably dressed gentry, a few moneymen and a politician or two.

"Gentlemen," Drake said. "Your attention please. Allow me to present Captain John Martin and Lady Mary to you. Captain Martin is assembling an auxiliary squadron of privateers for our expedition. He enjoys the queen's favor so don't be rude. For those of you who may not know Martin, he is, shall we say, a man of intrigue. Lady Mary has three privateers under her command and is well-acquainted with the Indies. Some of you may recall Mary sailed with me against the Armada and then again in '89."

An awkward silence fell across the room as men gawked at me, then the whispering started. I was just a silly woman, a lowly commoner, a laborer dressed in men's clothing. But I was also a woman with a pretty face and a fetching figure and I had warships to contribute to the cause.

I broke the unpleasant moment with my best, flirtatious smile. "Gentlemen, it is a great honor to stand here amongst England's greatest champions," I said and curtseyed with a bit of flourish.

Then, starting with the oldest fellow in the room, I worked my way around a very long table to shake each man's hand. The elderly gentleman introduced himself to me as John Hawkins and Drake's second-command. He was known as "old leaden foot" by his men because he moved so slowly. I knew that Hawkins and Drake were cousins and had sailed against the Spanish together many times.

Next, I met a man named Brutus Browne, to my surprise an Irishman and the first officer of Drake's flagship, the five-hundred-and-fifty-ton race-built galleon *Defiance*, and Michael Meryall, the first officer of the six-hundred-and-sixty-ton race-built galleon *Garland*, Hawkins's flagship. I met Captain Gilbert Yorke and his first officer, Master Edward Tyllesley, from the six-hundred-ton race-built galleon

Hope and Captain John Troughton, who commanded the six-hundred-ton race-built galleon *Elizabeth Bonaventure*. Then there was Captain William Wynter from the three-hundred-ton man o' war *Foresight* and Drake's younger brother, Thomas Drake, who had command of the two-hundred-and-fifty-ton frigate *Adventure*. All six Royal Navy ships were on loan to Drake from the queen.

Then Sir Thomas Baskerville, a colonel in the English Army who had distinguished himself in France and Holland against the Spanish, introduced himself to me. Baskerville would lead the army.

Drake was a gracious host. He plied us with good wine while his cooks prepared a handsome feast. As we waited for our supper, Martin and I sat quietly in a corner of the room watching Drake and his officers discussing plans and strategies as they stood hunched over a stack of sea charts. I was surprised when the discussion turned testy. Drake wanted to attack the Canarias before sailing on to the Caribbean and Hawkins was adamantly opposed. For all to hear Hawkins called Drake's plan folly, a diversion and a waste of precious time. I half expected Drake to draw his dagger and was relieved when servants marched into the room carrying covered trays. With good food and good wine, men relaxed and the mood around the table turned cordial again as we talked of menial things.

Halfway through dinner, a nervous, young lieutenant carrying dispatches from London, and plainly in a hurry, stepped into the room. The lieutenant apologized for the intrusion and handed Drake an oilskin pouch. Drake removed two letters from the pouch, read them to himself, and then held his hand up for silence.

"Gentlemen. One of these letters is from the Privy Council and the other is from the Admiralty. A large Spanish force has landed at Mount's Bay. They've taken Mousehole, Newlyn and Penzance!"

"Damn!" Drake's younger brother blurted out and pounded his fist against the table.

"How large a force?" Hawkins asked.

"Four galleys, the *Nuestra Señora de Begoña*, the *Salvador*, the *Peregrina*, and the *Bazana*. Don Carlos de Amesquita supposedly is leading the attack with about four hundred men."

Hawkins grunted. "Amesquita is under the command of Admiral Pedro de Zubiaur. We must assume a larger Spanish force is lurking somewhere nearby. Amesquita may only be leading the first wave of a larger assault or perhaps, God forbid, a full-scale invasion!"

Martin stood to stretch his legs. "Your grace, dare I ask what happened to the English militia at Cornwall?"

"You may ask," Drake replied. "But the answer will give you no comfort. It would appear the militia tossed away their weapons and ran. Cowards all. But I know the Deputy Lord Lieutenant of Cornwall, Francis Godolphin. Godolphin is a competent soldier with grit. He'd never betray our queen. He's either dead or a prisoner. The Spanish have taken hostages. They are putting hundreds of homes to the torch."

Hawkins drained the last of his wine and with the help of Meryall, slowly rose to his feet. "We must ready the fleet for action. We must counterattack at once!"

Drake tossed his napkin on the table and jumped to his feet. "You are right of course, John. We can be in Penzance before morning if we move with haste. Gentlemen, to your ships!"

Men bolted from the table and rushed outside to their carriages and horses. Drake's younger brother paused before Martin and me.

"Captain Martin, I understand your ship is laid-up in drydock," he said. "The *Adventure* is a small vessel. I cannot offer either of you luxurious accommodations, but if you wish to accompany the fleet, you may sail with me."

"If the lady is game, so am I," Martin replied.

I tossed my head back and laughed. "I love a good adventure, sir. Lead the way Thomas and I shall gladly follow."

We rode with the younger Drake in his carriage to the River Tamar in the fading light of a setting sun. We found his ninety-footer resting peacefully against the quays. *Adventure* was a full-rigged, three-masted frigate with one bank of oars, sixteen to a side. She carried twenty great guns, a mix of small falconets and fowlers, with a ship's complement of one hundred and twenty men.

Drake assembled his crew on deck and after he quickly explained matters, his men moved out smartly to prepare their ship to sail. Martin and I stood with Drake on the quarterdeck as men cast-off the mooring lines and unfurled sail. Once we were underway, he graciously offered me his cabin, but I declined. I was no stranger to sleeping on a deck surrounded by snoring men.

With *Defiance* in the lead, we sailed through the night, six warships in a line. When we reached Mount's Bay in the morning, we saw plumes of smoke rising above Penzance, and a harbor filled with boats gutted by fire.

Fearing the worst for the town folk, Martin and I went ashore with Thomas Drake and fifty men. Amesquita had sacked and burned the town but, in an act of old-fashioned chivalry, he had taken no hostages or English lives. With nothing more to be done at Penzance, and the Spanish nowhere in sight, Admiral Drake led us back to Plymouth and then he hurried off to London to see the queen, taking Martin with him.

Stranded in Plymouth on my own, I passed the time sampling different taverns while reading *A Short Account of the Destruction of the West Indies*, by a Dominican friar named Bartolomé de las Casas who told of the many atrocities against the Indian peoples in the New World, and a delightful comedy, a play, titled *The Taming of the Shrew* by a young upstart named William Shakespeare.

One morning as I was walking about, I stopped to listen to a Puritan, a man I had seen strolling up and down the streets each day whipping up large crowds with his fiery preaching. I thought him entertaining. He promised to bring any who would follow him to a land of milk and honey, to a place far away from the corruptions of Rome. He promised the crowds paradise in the New World. Plainly the poor fellow had never been to the Americas.

When I was summoned back to Buckland Abbey, I was greeted by the same gruff valet as before who escorted me to the great hall where Drake and his senior officers were already gathered. Drake's appearance took me aback. He looked nearly as old and as frail as his cousin Hawkins. I saw Martin's friendly face and was glad when he waved me over to an empty chair between himself and Hawkins.

"We've only just begun Mary," Drake said. "Gentlemen, we are all agreed then that the ships in Plymouth and Portsmouth can be ready to sail before month's end. John, what say you? Will your privateers be ready too?"

Martin turned to me and I nodded. "The privateers shall be ready your grace," he replied.

Hawkins started to speak but stopped when a violent coughing fit seized him. He spit phlegm into a handkerchief as he struggled to stand.

I mixed some wine and water in my glass and handed it to him.

"Thank you, madam, thank you," he said and took a long sip. "How many, ahem, how many ships have you, Lady Mary?"

"Three," I replied. "Two vessels are nearly the equal of your race-built galleons. The third ship is smaller and not as fast, but she's a match and then some for either *Adventure* or *Foresight*."

Hawkins glanced at me suspiciously. "If I'm not mistaken dear lady, you're a merchant by trade, some say a smuggler. I've never heard of a smuggler sailing across the oceans in war galleons."

"Lady Mary," Drake interrupted, "is not exaggerating, John. If memory serves Lady Mary, one of your ships is the *Phantom*, yes?"

"Your memory is sound, Sir Francis," I replied in a respectful tone. "And she's been completely overhauled and refitted. She's faster and better armed than when you last saw her."

"Excellent. John, I can vouch for Mary's ships. *Phantom* is a very fine battlecruiser."

Hawkins suffered another coughing fit and paused to drink more wine. The room waited silently for him to recover.

"Are you ill, John?" Drake asked.

Hawkins waved the question off. "No, no. God have mercy though, this detestable damp climate will be the death of me! Three good ships it is then, though I wish you had thrice that number. Captain Martin, how many ships have you in your squadron?"

"With my raider and Lady Mary's three, only four ships your grace, though I have commitments from the owners of seven more vessels. Whether these men honor their pledges or not I cannot say."

"Good, good. That old rogue Serrocold is bringing ten of his ships to the party with him and there is another squadron of privateers being assembled in Liverpool I hear."

Drake stood. "Well, shall we to business then? The queen and her Privy Council were most distressed by the attack on Cornwall. Some of the queen's advisors worry that this latest Spanish insult against our shores was more than a random raid. They fear the attack was a reconnaissance-in-force to probe and test our defenses, a prelude to a second invasion, and they are urging her majesty most strenuously to nullify our plans to invade the West Indies. These men would keep us bottled-up in Plymouth indefinitely for an invasion that may never come."

Drake paused and waved a sheet of paper in his hand around. "But the game has changed. I received this letter from Lord Burghley earlier today. The *Begona*, the flag galleon of the Spanish treasure fleet, was severely damaged in heavy seas off Puerto Rico. The fleet left her behind with a shattered mast and a damaged rudder. She managed to limp into the Bahía de San Juan on the thirtieth day of March and is sitting in the harbor like a fat pig with a broken leg. Now here's the part that will interest all of you: *Begona* is carrying two million and a half in gold ducats..."

"Good God," Hawkins said. "Did you say two million, five hundred thousand ducats, Francis?"

"I did and our good and gracious queen is now most keen to see us embark upon our journey. We are free to sail with the first good wind - but the Privy Council insists we return to England within six months. To quote Lord Burghley, "and not one day later." We have six months, more than enough time to do what must be done."

All agreed their ships would be ready to sail before the end of August, though Drake could not be dissuaded from advancing on the Canarias first. As a compromise with Hawkins, Drake agreed to send Martin's squadron directly on to Guadeloupe in advance of the fleet to secure good water, fresh provisions and any intelligence on the Spanish we could find. Martin and I gladly hurried back to Westport to make ready.

The day before we were to set out for the Americas, Martin found me at the *Banshee's Lament* and invited me to ride with him. There was something he wanted to show me he said and had two horses already saddled and tied to a hitching post outside. We rode quietly side-by-side for a bit until he turned down the road to the old mill. I pulled up on the reins of my horse and stared uneasily at Martin.

"John?"

Martin brought his horse around. "Fear not, Mary. We can turn back if you like."

"What is there to see this way?"

"Down that bitter road Mary, you will see how I settle my debts."

"Very, well, lead the way," I said sharply, as I discretely touched the pistols tucked inside my belt and made sure my sword would slide freely from the scabbard. I liked Martin. I even trusted the Englishman. But I would kill him before he killed me if he had murder in his heart.

When we reached the scorched stones and charred timbers of what was once the old mill, Martin pointed to the riverbank where I saw a man dangling from a cross out in the open for all to see. "Dear God!" I blurted out. "That poor fellow was crucified."

"That poor fellow was a man named Cox. He's the traitor who shot me down. He's the scoundrel who lured you here from the tavern. He's the vile snake who betrayed us both to the *Síol Faolcháin*."

I nudged my horse closer. "So it is," I said. Even with the buzzards picking at the dead man's flesh and a swollen face, a bloody mess, I recognized the man. A placard with the word "traitor" scratched into the wood hung around his neck. I stared hard at the corpse.

Martin had taken two burnt timbers from the mill to make his cross. He reached over and gently placed his hand on mine.

"He eluded me for some time. 'Tis a gruesome sight to behold I know, but I thought you would want to see. I pray I've not upset you."

"No, no. You were right to bring me here. Why crucify him?"

"I pride myself on my calm dispassion. Shooting this miserable prick would have been easier. But when Cox dropped to his knees and began whimpering and groveling like a dog, when he begged me to spare his life and swore to me that he was a Godfearing Christian, when he told me that he deserved my mercy and compassion as a fellow Christian, well, I allowed my emotions to get the best of me."

I drew my sword, I ran the sharp steel through the dead's man heart. "I too have debts to settle..."

Chapter Fourteen

n the 28th day of August 1595, Drake slipped out Plymouth in the dark, without fireworks or fanfare of any kind. England's legend was sailing off to war with only twenty-seven warships and a gaggle of penances and flatboats. He had only fifteen hundred sailors and twelve hundred soldiers clad in morion helmets, half-mail and brigandine. Drake sent the English privateers - mostly small frigates, barks and galiots, led by a London merchant named David Serrocold and the captain of the three-hundred-and-fifty-ton *Concord* - out as a vanguard to scout the waters ahead. After clearing Plymouth Sound, the fleet sailed south-by-southwest for Las Palmas off the Moroccan coast.

After we received word of Drake's departure a few days later, Martin led our secret squadron of four, sailing in close formation, out of Clew Bay into hefty, rolling seas and fluky winds for the West Indies. Despite the Atlantic's foul mood, we made fair time and glided into Guadeloupe's fine harbor without losing any men. It seemed an auspicious beginning.

The King of Guadeloupe and his royal entourage were standing on the beach waiting for us as we rowed ashore in our longboats. Dressed in his magnificent headdress and his war cape draped across his shoulders, and carrying the king's spear, King Joseph greeted us with open arms and a broad smile. And then I saw a fearsome *Cuachicqueh* warrior, an angry bumblebee, standing next the king and my heart began to sing. Zekowtah was alive. Some inexplicable attraction of the spirit had drawn me to the Aztec from the very first.

I knelt before my former lieutenant. He laid his hand upon my head and greeted me with words of friendship and when I stood to embrace the king, dozens of children, unencumbered by their nakedness, pushed through the ranks of Carib warriors to grab my hands and hug me by my legs, eager to see what gifts I had brought them.

"Thank you for welcoming us to your island your Majesty," I said as the children continued tugging at me.

"It pleases me to have you back Lady Mary. Captain Martin, I remember you. If Spain is still your enemy, you are welcome to my island."

"England and Spain are very much at war," Martin answered.

"Good. Ah, my brother Henry!" the king said and stepped forward to clasp Henry by the arms.

I turned to embrace Zekowtah, he looked fit and strong. "Zekowtah, what ill-wind has brought you here, so far away from your people?"

Zekowtah saw Maurice working the tiller of *Cerberus*'s longboat some fifty yards from shore and waved before answering. "The end of days has at last found my people. I have seen blood and tears enough to fill the ocean. The Spanish have crushed the Cimarron in Panama."

I gasped. "Nooo."

"One Spanish army came down from México. Another marched up from Gran Columbia. Trapped between two great armies, we had no chance. The Spanish butchered thousands. Nothing is left of Ronconcholan but ash and bone."

"The children?"

Zekowtah shook his head. "Those who survived will work the mines until they die. The Spanish show no mercy to rebellious slaves, no matter their age."

"How many Cimarron escaped with you?"

"We are a nation of about three hundred."

"Guillaume told me about your son. Iztli was a fine young man. The news of your loss was like a dagger to my heart."

Zekowtah looked away. "With Iztli's death the line of my ancestors is forever broken.

"I cannot begin to fathom your pain," I said, seeing no need to burden Zekowtah with my own loss. "Have you come to Guadeloupe seeking refuge?"

"I knew you or Maurice would return someday. I have warriors. Have you returned to the Caribbean to trade with the Spanish or to kill them?"

"We've come to fight. Drake is on his way with a powerful fleet."

"Then you have fifty more warriors, brave, strong men and good fighters."

I sent the children, still pawing at me, over to the longboats to claim their presents from the sea chests my men had brought ashore and then looked for the king. Fish was mingling with Henry and some of his former Carib shipmates a few yards away, laughing at one story or another. I took Zekowtah by the hand and pulled the king aside and waved Martin over.

"Your Majesty, we must talk. Drake will be here soon with many English ships. He'll need provisions before sailing out to engage the Spanish."

"My warriors, King Joseph," Zekowtah said, "will fight with Mary."

I laid my hand on Zekowtah's bare shoulder. "You and your people have suffered enough. There's Maurice coming ashore now. Go to your brother. We shall speak of these matters later."

Fish enjoyed merrymaking as much as his father, Chief Paka Woliki, and had his people prepare a great feast to honor the friendship between the Carib and Irish. The entire village turned out. Women lit the cooking fires up and down the shore while the men slaughtered pigs and chickens to be roasted on the spit. The children carried baskets of fresh fruit and vegetables, cooking pots and jugs of beer and wine. The king also put his army on alert. He doubled the number of lookouts up in the mountains and sent out additional war canoes to patrol the waters around his island.

Fish and Zekowtah sat with my officers, Martin and me. All around us there was lively music, singing and dancing. But the gaiety could not hide the sorrow moving through the camp like an early autumn chill. As we ate and drank our fill, we mourned the Cimarron dead and wept for those wretched souls wasting away in the mines. The demise of the Cimarron nation was a terrible reminder to all Carib that their days were numbered too. One morning they'd awake to find Spanish warships anchored in their bay.

I spent the days waiting for Drake in one of my darker moods. Though I owed the Spanish a pain or two, England's war was not my war and I had no wish to sail with Drake. The temptation to abandon the expedition was nearly too much for me. But I stayed, the reluctant warrior, with another purpose in mind.

A commander strives to have three advantages over his opponent before he commits to battle: speed, surprise and firepower. Luck is always welcome too. Drake left England with firepower, but the delays in launching the expedition and his decision to sail for the Canarias first had cost him surprise and speed. I counted twenty-four warships in all when the fleet glided into the bay in early November. *Defiance* was not among them.

"Thomas!" I cried out to Drake's younger brother as his longboat plowed into the beach. "Welcome to Guadeloupe."

"Lady Mary, I am delighted to see you made it safely across the ocean."

I took his arm in mine and led him to my tent, set underneath the shade of two palm trees. "Have you ever had *ouicou?*"

"No, what is it?"

"It's a Carib concoction. It'll make your toes curl, but you must try some."

"Ah, my brother warned me to be on my guard around you."

"You should heed his good advice, Captain. Pray tell me, where is your brother? I don't see *Defiance*. And I see John Troughton's boat coming into shore over there, but I don't see Admiral Hawkins with him."

"I suspect old Hawkins is still pouting and will keep to his cabin. He and Francis nearly came to blows at Las Palmas."

Earlier that morning I had rolled up the sides of my tent to let in a pleasant ocean breeze. I kept a small camp table and two chairs in my tent and motioned Drake to sit as I poured us each a drink.

Drake took a sip and winced. "Woah!" he exclaimed. "A potent concoction indeed, Mary."

"I'm glad you like it Thomas."

"Thank you. In answer to your question Mary, the privateer *Francis* is missing. Five enemy frigates swooped down on the tail end of the line using the wind to good advantage and engaged several of our ships. *Francis* is small and slow and fell behind. We eventually lost sight of her. My brother took *Defiance* and *Delight* to make a sweep around the island, hoping to find her."

"I fear the Spanish almost certainly have the *Francis*."

"Yes."

"What happened in the Canarias?"

Drake drained his tin and helped himself to another. "We arrived off Gran Canaria on the sixth day of October. Sir Francis led half the fleet into Las Palmas in plain sight of Santa Catalina Castle whilst Baskerville took several ships and landed several companies of musketeers at Arguineguín. Baskerville was confident he could take the small fort of Santa Ana there and then flank Santa Catalina. But his men couldn't even advance beyond the beaches. Spanish mountaineers dug-in along the high ground, with plenty of men and heavy artillery, forced Baskerville to withdraw under heavy fire."

"Casualties?"

"Several dozen dead and wounded. The Spanish ambushed one of Baskerville's patrols and took ten men prisoner. The guns at Santa Catalina wreaked havoc on the fleet. Four ships suffered significant damage and we lost several days repairing them. My brother is the greatest Englishman to ever put to sea and I love him, but Hawkins was right. Attacking the Canarias was a mistake. As you said at the Abbey, we are fighting a different enemy. My brother convinced himself the Spanish would shit their pants and run at the sight of our mighty force. They didn't. The world has changed and I have my doubts whether the admiral can change with it."

"Aye. Well, drink up and rest your bones. I shall introduce you to the King of Guadeloupe later. I'm on excellent terms with the king."

"Oh?"

"Not long ago he was one of my lieutenants," I said with a wink.

Defiance and *Delight* coasted into the bay two days later without the *Francis* and if the Spanish had the *Francis*, they'd torture her crew for information. To my disgust, Drake seemed in no hurry to set out. We spent long days in Guadeloupe doing very little. I was bored and jealous when Drake sent Martin off to God knows where and forbid me to sail with him.

I saw very little of Drake and when I did it was only from a distance. Hawkins came ashore briefly but could barely walk and did not tarry on land for very long. I saw the younger Drake quite often. We enjoyed each other's company. He was plainly smitten with me, though I did not encourage him.

When Martin returned, Drake summoned his senior officers, along with Serrocold and me, to his tent for a council of war. Hawkins was carried into Drake's tent on a litter.

"All is ready," Drake said. "We keep to our plan to attack San Juan. We sail with the morning tide."

I suddenly felt ill. I couldn't believe my ears. I must have misunderstood.

"Beg pardon, your grace," I blurted out. "But the plan has been compromised, we've lost surprise. Surely the Spanish will be waiting for us in San Juan. Surely the Spanish will strengthen their defenses there and move *Begona's* treasure ashore as a precaution."

"Ah, we have a seer with divine powers in our midst," Drake said mockingly. "How is it you and you alone can foresee the future Mary?"

"I have my wits, your grace, no more."

"Wits alone are not enough to win a battle. Steel your courage woman. I didn't win fame and fortune by running away from a fight. Attack the enemy head-on when you find him and never hesitate. I suppose you're against sailing to Panama as well?"

"Panama, Admiral? Without your Cimarron allies, aye I'd avoid Panama and look for easier pickings."

Hawkins struggled to sit-up on his litter. "The lady's words have merit Francis," he said in a weak voice and started coughing.

Drake dismissed us both with a flick of his hand. "I promised the queen rich plunder and rich plunder is what I shall have. The treasure sitting in San Juan is ours for the taking. Gentlemen, lady, I expect each of you to do your duty! Let's break camp tonight and return to our ships for on the morrow we depart these pleasant shores to win new glory!"

All around me Englishmen raised a rousing cheer. And when the cheers subsided, when men wandered off to attend to their own matters, a gentle hand pulled me back as I took a step towards Drake.

"Mary," Drake's brother whispered in my ear, "no need to cause a raucous and stir up trouble. I know when my brother's mind is fixed and cannot be turned. Nothing good will come from provoking him."

"You're right, of course, Thomas," I said. "I can be too pigheaded for my own good at times. This expedition though is beginning to feel more and more like Coruña and Lisbon."

"Perhaps. And yet the disappointment of Spain and Portugal is but a distant memory. Besides, my brother and Hawkins have always enjoyed extraordinarily good luck in the Caribbean. Luck can carry a man a long way."

"Let us see what Martin knows. Oh John, will you accompany Captain Drake and myself for a stroll along the beach? Perhaps I can even entice you both into sharing a late-night libation with me, if you're game."

Martin walked alongside the younger Drake and me and gladly shared everything he knew from his reconnaissance mission to, as I had suspected, San Juan. He had taken a dozen men ashore at night to probe San Juan's defenses. They found the poor *Francis* in the inner harbor, tied to one of five heavily-armed Spanish frigates in the harbor, and captured a handful of prisoners.

The prisoners told Martin what we already knew: the Spanish were expecting Drake, that soldiers and civilians alike were working side-by-side day and night improving the city's defenses. But the prisoners also disclosed that *Begona's* crew, after moving the galleon's guns and the treasure into Castillo San Felipe del Morro, a fortress on the eastside of the Bay of San Juan, had scuttled their ship at the entrance of the bay to block the English fleet from entering.

Morro Castle is a massive fortress on a three-tiered platform built from large quarried-stone pieces reinforced with concrete and iron and is blessed with many *garitas*, or turret boxes. On the Isla de Caras, or Goats Island, on the westside of the bay, stood a smaller fort the Spanish called El Cañuelo. The prisoners claimed both forts were well-supplied with victuals and with enough ball and powder to withstand a long siege. The Spanish had five hundred soldiers, a mix of professionals and militia, three hundred sailors and thirty-six massive harbor guns at Morro Castle alone, the superior bronze pieces, to protect San Juan.

The Governor of Puerto Rico, Colonel Pedro Suárez de Coronel, appointed General Sancho Pardo y Osorio, a soldier known for his tenacity in battle, as his supreme commander. Osorio in turn entrusted the city's shore defenses to Admiral Gonzalo Mendez de Cauzo and handed command of the frigates over to Don Pedro Tello de Gúzman, a gifted seaman by reputation.

None of this intelligence had alarmed Drake any.

At first light the following morning, Drake sent boats around the fleet to deliver his orders. Mine were predictable. My ships were to guard the fleet's north flank and lend support to the army as it landed on the beaches, not unlike the mission Drake had handed me six years earlier at Coruña. As soon as crews secured their boats, the fleet weighed anchor, dropped sail and we headed west. One Aztec prince and fifty of his warriors sailed with me.

We moved through tranquil waters until Virgin Gorda appeared off our starboard bow, an island I had never been to. Drake led us into a bay well-protected by a ring of sheer-faced mountains of striking beauty.

After we dropped anchor, Drake invited me to join his fleet officers, along with Martin and Serrocold, for supper aboard *Defiance*. The crew had removed a partition from Drake's great cabin to accommodate the large group. Hawkins did not attend. After a hearty meal of lamb stew, fresh biscuits and a good Tuscan wine, Drake spread a map of San Juan across the table and we spent the evening polishing the details of his plan. I must confess, I was impressed.

The key to Drake's plan was to find the sunken *Begona* and a way around her. If Drake could get his fleet inside the bay, he could reach the inner harbor, destroy Tello's frigates and then attack Morro Castle by land and sea from the south where to fortress was most vulnerable. The mood in the room was confident, even jovial, and for once I held my tongue.

At dawn bad fortune found us though. The morning watch and I looked on as *Garland's* crew hoisted an enormous black streamer up the mizzen gaff with the Hawkins coat-of-arms attached. The old knight was dead. Hawkins's death hit Drake hard. The admiral kept to his cabin through the day and the fleet didn't move. Drake boarded the *Garland* that evening and buried his cousin at sea with full honors.

Among my newer men there were murmurs. The loss of the *Francis* and the death of Hawkins were evil portents of things to come they said. Even among some of my veterans there was talk of fresh misfortunes to follow. I dismissed such prattle as superstitious nonsense.

On the twenty-second day of November, nearly three months into the campaign, the fleet at long last arrived off the serene waters of San Juan. Drake brought us in close to the bay and we dropped anchor. But someone had badly miscalculated the effective range of the Spanish harbor guns. The batteries at both Morrow Castle and El Cañuelo boomed in anger at us. The Spanish lobbed heavy iron into the middle of the fleet, giving the English race-built galleons, especially Drake's flagship, the choicest target, their close attention. We watched plumes of white water sprout up all around the English dreadnoughts. We saw several ships take hits. One ball nicked

Defiance's main mast and sent debris flying everywhere. Another smashed into her stern. Around the fleet, crews scrambled to weigh anchor.

We sailed beyond the range of Spanish guns and dropped anchor and lost another day as the English repaired their ships. From ship-to-ship word spread like wildfire that the ball that had smashed into *Defiance's* steerage had struck the very stool Drake had been sitting on while he was drinking beer with four of his officers. Drake escaped unscathed men said, but all four of his officers suffered injuries. A captain named Clifford died instantly and the Irishman Browne died a few days later of his wounds. Men saw Drake's close brush with death as one more bad omen, a warning Drake failed to heed.

In the morning Drake sent sixty brave men in three longboats into the bay to find *Begona*. We watched from afar as the English methodically rowed back and forth across the water, ignoring the shots falling down around them from the shore batteries at El Cañuelo as they took soundings. The work was slow and dangerous. When the English found the galleon, they quickly marked her grave with red buoys, then put their backs into their oars and returned to the ships without loss.

Drake set the next part of his plan into motion as night closed in around us. He sent my three ships out to sea a little ways where we formed a skirmish line to protect his north flank. Any Spanish ships trying to relieve San Juan would need to fight their way through mine. And then at ten of the clock, the English galleons opened fire on Goats Island, peppering the El Cañuelo with everything the English had while Baskerville slipped into the bay with twenty-five flatboats and twelve hundred men. My crew lined the rails to watch the action with me. Muzzle flashes streaked across the water. Fuse bombs bursting over the fort lit up the night sky. I'd never seen anything like it.

Baskerville split his forces into two. He sent half his men to the right to land on Goats Island to take El Cañuelo and led the rest to the left into San Juan's harbor to destroy the Spanish frigates.

The plan was bold and fraught with risk. Drake was sending half his army against a fortified position without siege equipment and the other half against well-armed frigates. In the old days, when Spain's defenses in the New World were crude and flimsy and she kept the best of her soldiers in Europe, Drake's use of sheer, brute force might have won the day.

Atwood, Efendi and I watched the battle from the quarter deck sipping whiskey. We watched in awe as the fighting raged back and forth.

When the English stormed the craggy beaches of Goats Island, the navy's bombardment stopped and the Spanish garrison opened fire. The fort, though small, was built of stone and surrounded by flat, open ground with clear fields of fire in every direction. Wave after wave of English infantry charged across the open ground with ladders, desperately trying to reach the stronghold. The English were very brave and held nothing back. But Spanish gunners forced the English back each time under a withering barrage of round shot and lead. The Spanish fought like demons and matched English valor man-for-man.

Baskerville appeared to be having better luck in the harbor. He brought his flatboats in close, within spitting distance of the Spanish, close enough for his men to lob their firebombs, grenades and torches and shoot their flaming arrows at the frigates. Tello's sailors and marines held fast. They stood along the rails and up in the rigging, pouring volley after volley of musket fire into the English flatboats. English oarsmen - with glorious resolve - ignored the bullets raining down on them and kept their boats in position.

And then triumph! We saw the forecastle of one frigate burst into flames. The fire quickly worked its way along the rigging, spread to the bowsprit and up the fore mast. Then a second frigate caught fire followed by a third and my men erupted into a thunderous cheer. The English seemed poised to win a great victory.

But then, with losses mounting, and unable to reach the last two frigates, Baskerville suddenly pulled his flatboats back. He stopped at Goats Island to help the others off the beach with cannon balls falling down all around them. We saw one flatboat explode and break in two. Another caught fire, collided into a third and both flatboats capsized. The evacuation turned into bloody mayhem. The Spanish continued pounding Baskerville's flotilla until the flatboats reached the ocean. Then the Spanish secured their guns and the world, except for the Spanish frigates still burning, turned dark and quiet.

What had looked like an English victory at night, turned into a horrible, costly disaster in the morning. El Cañuelo stood unscathed and we saw only one Spanish frigate still burning. Tello's men had saved the other two. The attack had cost Drake eight hundred dead and wounded, half his army, and ten flatboats.

As I reflect on these matters now, I don't think Drake understood, and therefore could not accept, defeat. The very notion was utterly foreign to him. He saw only victory, or the occasional setback before victory. On that third day off San Juan, I was certain *El Draque*, for thirty years the scourge of the Spanish Main and the great champion over the Spanish Armada, would see what the rest of us saw and set a course for home. But not that prideful man. Though the bay, barely a thousand feet wide at the entrance, was partially blocked and defended by Morro Castle on one side and by El Cañuelo on the other, and with four frigates lying in wait in the harbor, Drake sent the word out to every ship: prepare for a full attack! My officers and I looked at each other too stunned to speak.

When Drake's men shot a green signal flare into the sky before breakfast, the fleet weighed anchor and one-by-one warships slipped in behind *Defiance* to form a single line of battle. And I had a decision to make.

"What's your pleasure, Mary?" Atwood asked me with a grin. "Follow Drake into the lion's den or stay put outside the bay to guard Drake's flank? One could interpret his orders for us either way."

Before I could answer Atwood, El Cañuelo's heavy guns shattered the morning's quiet as *Defiance* approached the entrance of the bay. Drake's gunners didn't answer, saving their precious shot and powder for the greater battle yet to come.

"Damn, Jacob," I replied, shaking my head. "We shouldn't be

here. The thought of losing even one man in this foolishness turns my stomach."

Atwood absently scratched his beard. "You'll hear no contrary word from me."

"The lookout has scanned the horizon for other sails?"

"Aye, and he has nothing to report."

"Let's fall in behind the last English ship. When we reach the bay, we'll see how Drake's plan prospers before we decide."

"Wise, most wise," Atwood said, then slipped below to fetch us breakfast.

When he saw Drake sailing towards the bay with the entire English fleet behind him, Tello, no fool, knew what he had to do. The quick-witted Spaniard had his men cut the anchor cables and set the sails and within minutes Tello had his four frigates charging across the bay, racing straight for *Defiance*.

I rushed to the bow with Atwood and Efendi to get a better look as we moved in behind Serrocold's ships. We were at the tail end of the English line some two thousand yards or so north of the entrance of the bay. The guns at El Cañuelo on our starboard, and at Morro Castle on our port, targeted the English galleons and ignored the rest. Geysers of white water shot up all around the dreadnoughts with Tello's squadron closing fast. Fearless, indefatigable, Drake pressed on. I watched in awe as two possible futures collided.

At first, I thought Tello intended to take Drake head-on in a desperate act of honor. But no, the plucky Spaniard led his squadron over to the English red buoys where the doomed *Begona* lay and we watched - aghast - as his men turned their guns on their own ships and blew gaping holes into the hulls below the waterline. Many a brave Spaniard drowned as their ships went down. Tello had sacrificed of four of his frigates in a brilliant move to seal-off the narrow gap Drake was hoping to slip through.

With the no way into the bay, Drake had no choice but to turn his ships around. With fine seamanship, the entire English fleet came about in good order and we headed out to sea. The battle for San Juan was over.

Drake led us west for a time, keeping close to shore, and then gave the order to drop anchor when the English spotted cattle grazing in a field. He sent a large landing party ashore to slaughter the cattle and to secure fresh water and used the time to summon his highest-ranking officers to his cabin for another meeting of the council.

Sitting rigidly behind his desk, Drake stared grimly at our faces in the dim light of a single lantern swaying back and forth above his head. He did not stand to greet us. He cracked no jokes. He offered no beer or wine. He seemed to me a broken man.

I took in the damage to his cabin. I saw the large hole where the ball had punched through the stern. I saw the shattered wood where the ball had smacked the floor and then ricocheted through the forward bulkhead. The planking beneath my boots was stained in dark blood.

I caught Drake grimace when he shifted uncomfortably in his chair. I saw the dry blood splattered across the sleeve of his jacket. He took a sip of water. He used a napkin to dab the beads of sweat off his brow.

"Gentlemen, my lady, I propose we leave San Juan behind us for now," Drake said wearily. "The treasure sitting inside Morro isn't going anywhere. I will bring you to twenty places far wealthier than San Juan with riches easier to be gotten. Let us try our luck in Panama next and after we've plundered Panama, perhaps we'll visit Veracruz or Havana - I've already dispatched Martin to Veracruz to have a look - and before we return to England, we can return to San Juan to collect our gold. We'll land the army at night a few miles east of Morro and take the castle in the morning by land."

No one uttered a word, not a sound, not even Thomas Drake, the one man who might have been able to talk Drake away from stepping off a cliff. The somber mood around the cabin turned sour.

I rowed back to *Phantom* disillusioned and depressed. I summoned my all officers to me and invited Zekowtah too.

"I assume Drake is returning to England, Mary?" MacGyver asked as I poured the wine.

"No."

"No?"

"No, at sunrise we sail for Panama."

Atwood grunted, as he was want to do when something offended him. "Folly, sheer folly. What riches does Drake hope to find in Panama? This expedition is sailing against the wind and under an unlucky star. If Drake doesn't have the good sense to return to England, we should quit the fleet and look to our own matters. He's gone mad."

"Drake cannot return yet," I said softly. "I see it now. A man like Drake doesn't know defeat. He can't go back to England and face the queen or his peers like this. He'll be disgraced and never sail again. I fear if we cut away and run now, Drake will charge us with cowardice and desertion upon his return to England. How does that help our cause? I propose we sail on to Panama with Drake as I have my own plan. But I put the matter to a vote."

"Might we know your thoughts first, Mary?" MacGyver asked. "What in Panama interests you? New tales of buried treasure?"

I reached across the table and took Zekowtah's hand in mine and did the same with Maurice with the other. "No, not for buried treasure. Zekowtah and Maurice believe some Cimarron may be hiding up in the mountains. I'd like to give them the chance to find their people and bring them back to our ships. Cimarron lives would be treasure enough for me on this voyage."

First Atwood, then MacGyver, followed by Maurice, Efendi, Kinkae, Henry and Shaw one-by-one voted aye.

"Very well," I said. "Zekowtah, do we have your blessing?"

Zekowtah nodded. "I will never forget this kindness."

"It is settled then," I said. "Let's drink."

We lost two more days as the English sat bobbing up and down on the ocean's swells replenishing their stores and repairing their ships. When the fleet was finally ready to sail, Drake led us to Rio de la Hacha at the mouth of the Rancheria River on the Columbian Pearl Coast before sailing on to Nombre de Diós. This is where, according to the stories, Drake's unrelenting hatred of the Spanish had been born years ago from one grievous wrong or another.

Drake sent Baskerville with three hundred men ashore and I accompanied the English with fifty of my own out of curiosity. A small Spanish garrison fled with the flamingo birds into the jungle when they saw us coming. We wandered into town without a shot fired. The village elders came out to greet us and after a bit of haggling, Baskerville agreed not to burn their village in exchange for ransom. Within the hour six stout Wayúu tribesmen met us on the beach carrying three small chests filled with pearls and silver coins. The total was barely enough to cover the expedition's expenses for a week and I heard grumbling amongst the English. Drake had promised them much more.

I was surprised by my new orders waiting for me in my cabin when I returned to my ship. With Martin gone, Drake instructed me to take *Phantom*, the swiftest ship in the fleet, and scout ahead for any trouble. I wasted no time. I promptly had the crew weigh anchor, I had them let out all our sail and before long we were skimming across the waves at exhilarating speed racing against fast-moving clouds under a pale blue sky.

We arrived off Nombre de Diós in fog and rain the following morning, well ahead of the fleet. The town's modest harbor was empty of any warships and the wooden fort on the hill overlooking the bay was quiet. We dropped anchor a few hundred yards from shore and waited.

Atwood made his way up to the quarter deck carrying two tins of hot coffee with a chicken on the loose nipping at his heels. "Miserable weather," he said and handed me a tin.

"Thank you for the coffee," I said. I took a sip and winced.

Atwood smiled. "Strong, eh?"

"I can feel my toes curling. Has our cook risen from his hammock yet? I'm famished."

"I found Antonio dozing. A swift kick in the arse did the trick, tho' breakfast will be late. I had to brew the coffee myself."

Atwood and I stood together in silence for a time, watching the men stumble on deck. Then more and more men appeared and soon I realized the entire crew was assembling.

I gave Atwood a puzzled look. "What's this?"

"Ship's company!" Atwood bellowed as Efendi, Henry, Kinkae and Shaw joined us up on the quarter deck. "Form ranks, doff hats!"

My men, as disciplined a crew as any crew on any ship in any navy, smartly fell into formation, well as best they could on a cluttered deck. They removed their hats and caps in unison.

Atwood handed me a leather pouch. "My lady."

"Oh my," I said as I undid the cord and took a peek inside. I removed a necklace made from colorful seashells with alternating silver and gold beads from the pouch and held the necklace up for all to see. Dangling from the center of the necklace were three pink conch pearls.

"Every man had a hand in making this," Atwood said proudly as he fastened the necklace around my neck. "One pearl for each ship, Mary. Happy Christmas Day!"

"God bless you Lady Mary," a voice cried out on deck and then the whole crew erupted into a hearty cheer. One man began playing *The Coventry Carol* on his lute and men began to sing with him.

I could count the number of gifts I'd received in my life on one hand. I leaned over the rail and smiled. We were a mix of Christians, Muslims and Jews, with a good number of pagans mixed in, from many different kingdoms. It mattered not to me.

"This gift is very fine," I said, teary eyed. "Whether you believe in Christ or some other deity, I wish each of you a Happy Christmas, a day of peace and gladness. Captain Atwood, I suspect we won't see the fleet today. Certainly, we'll see no action. What say you men, should we celebrate the day with music and games and libations all around?"

A great roar rolled across the ship.

I turned to my officers. "My brothers, it is my good fortune to share my life with you. You've touched my heart. Thank you."

Drake was quick to action when the fleet arrived the next day.

He sent Baskerville and what was left of the army ashore in a light drizzle, bolstered by two hundred privateers. Drake took fifty men from Serrocold and the rest from me, more from me because Serrocold had lost men on the beaches of Goats Island. I was not happy, but I could not refuse Drake if I wanted to keep to my plan.

I stood at the rail and looked over the side at the two flatboats the English had sent over to transport my men ashore. We loaded fifty men into each, dressed in marions, breastplates and half-mail the English had stripped from their dead. I wore the armor too.

"As you asked Mary, one hundred and fifty men," Atwood said softly.

"Thank you, Jacob."

"I picked our very best fighters. Please, won't you reconsider?"

"No," I replied and turned to Efendi. "Are you and your men ready Mustafa?"

"Yes, Mary."

"Good. And if the ships are gone when you return, everyone knows what to do?"

By that I meant our rallying point. This time we picked Bahía Sapzurro, Port Pheasant, a secluded, well-protected bay to the south discovered and named by Drake himself years ago.

Efendi nodded.

Atwood gently grabbed my arm. "Mary, I should be the one to lead our men ashore this time and you should be the one to stay with the ships."

"No. I want Michael with the ships and I want you at my side. I'll not send men into danger watching them from a ship's rail."

Atwood sighed. "Very well. Mustafa, do you see that thin column of smoke to the south towards Guna Yala? That will be Maurice, Zekowtah and Zekowtah's fifty warriors."

Efendi squinted, searching the shoreline. "I see the smoke."

I kissed Efendi on the cheek. "Go as far as Ronconcholan, but no farther. I want to help our Cimarron friends if we can, but I don't want to lose you, or any of our men. You are on a mission of mercy, no more. Godspeed."

Efendi squeezed my hand, then disappeared over the starboard rail. As Efendi and fifty men rowed towards Guna Yala in two longboats to rendezvous with Maurice and Zekowtah, I climbed over the port rail and down a rope ladder into the first flatboat which, as the name implies, is nothing more than a leaky, wooden box with oars and a half roof. I recalled the landing at Peniche when one flatboat capsized in heavy surf with all hands lost, the English drowned in their own armor, and I can't deny the queasiness I felt in the pit of my stomach as I stepped into that boat. Atwood followed me in the second flatboat and we landed on the beach with two-thirds of our men.

After the English brought the rest of my men ashore, Atwood formed them up in a column and we marched into Nombre de Diós in a heavy downpour. Most of the Spanish had abandoned their town. Even the garrison had fled.

I saw Baskerville standing inside a doorway hiding from the rain with a map in his hands. "Sir Thomas," I called out to him as I stepped away from the column.

"Ah, Lady Mary, I'm delighted you are here. I thought you might have gotten lost."

I glanced down at his map. "Ha! It appears to me you may be the one who is lost Colonel."

The old soldier cracked an easy smile. "*Touché.*"

"Where do you want my men?"

"Allow me," Baskerville said and reached over to adjust a strap on my helmet to keep the brim from slipping over my eyes. "There, better?"

"Yes, better, thank you."

Baskerville then called a sergeant over to us. "I hear your men are good fighters. I'm placing you and your lads in the middle of the column. This man will show you were to go. I'll join you directly."

"Where to, Sir Thomas?"

"Viejo."

"What is in Viejo?"

"I wish to God I knew."

With no Cimarron allies to guide us, with no intelligence about what lay ahead, we slogged our way through puddles and muck up to our ankles down the only good road out of town. Baskerville had five companies, about five hundred men, supported by Serrocold's gentlemen adventurers of unknown quality and my men, seven hundred souls in all. The English brought ten pack animals with them to carry supplies and five three-pounders too but soon abandoned the guns along the side of the road. Each English soldier carried rations for nine days, mostly hard biscuits, salted beef and dried fruits, and forty rounds of ammunition.

I do not think Drake had given Baskerville much of plan. We were to march on Viejo, sack the city and then scour the Panamanian countryside for more plunder. Drake's plan seemed desperate to me, though I understood his interest in Viejo. Viejo is a small town on the Pacific coast used by the Spanish to store the silver brought up from Columbia every few months. Once or twice a year the Spanish move the silver by caravan from Viejo, along with the gold from México, to Nombre de Diós where it is then loaded aboard the treasure ships bound for Spain. But as we marched in the rain, no one knew what, if anything, was in Viejo. Unperturbed, Baskerville, the good soldier, forged ahead without complaint, determined to win new glory for his queen and country.

Not long into our journey we left the road for the Capirilla Pass, an impressive name for a footpath barely wide enough for one man. We traveled over rugged mountains and down steep gorges in single file, losing half our mules along the way. In one spot the pass had been flooded by the unusual rains for Panama's dry season and we were forced to trudge through chest-high water for several miles.

Once we climbed out of the river the trail widened and we were able to march four men abreast. We moved through woodlands and thick foliage, stopping every few hours for a few minutes rest. The battle for Viejo was fought in the woods, in the rain and the fog.

BOOM! A single cannon shot startled all of us.

I could hear the officers at the front of the column barking out orders, but could not see them in the thick fog that had settled over the land. The English company in front of us disappeared as they rushed forward. I had no orders, so I did not move.

Atwood grabbed me by the arm and pulled me down to the ground. "Good place for an ambush," he said calmly.

"What do you think, Jacob?"

"I think the Spanish don't want us here."

I pushed my helmet back and gave Atwood a dirty look.

He sighed. "We should spread out in a line, two men deep, and watch our flanks."

And that is what we did. We stood and formed a skirmish line and advanced through the trees over flat ground. Then we heard the crackle of musket fire in front of us, random shots at first followed by whole volleys. The English company behind us moved forward with us but kept to the trail.

When we reached the action, I saw Baskerville had deployed one company of arquebusiers in a line, straddling the trail as we had, with one company of pikemen standing behind them formed up in a square. Beyond the English, through swirling smoke and mist, I caught a brief glimpse of a wood and earth parapet. The Spanish had built themselves a three-sided stronghold across the trail with ten-foot high walls. I saw many muskets and the nose of at least one cannon protruding over the top of the wall.

I led my men into a gully cutting across the trail about fifty yards behind the English pikemen. We dropped to our knees in the ditch for cover. A cannon boomed, belching smoke and flame, and tore a hole in the English line. I heard men scream.

Baskerville shouted orders in a calm, strong voice. He called out to the companies by name, Wolf, Tiger, Eagle and the like, and called out to the platoons by number. If he was nervous, he showed no sign of it.

Then the arquebusiers picked up their fork rests and fell back in good order. They redeployed to the left of the trail behind the trees while the pikemen shifted over to the right and suddenly I found myself holding the center of the English line. And then two companies of musketeers rushed past us. One company turned left to join the arquebusiers and the other moved right towards the pikemen, leaving one English company and Serrocold's men behind us in reserve.

From nowhere an arrow whistled over my head. I turned to Atwood.

"*Indios auxiliares?*" I asked. I had heard stories about Indian tribes fighting for the Spanish.

Before Atwood could answer the earth exploded around us, burying both of us in mud and dirt.

"Are you all right Mary?" Atwood asked.

I brushed the dirt off Atwood's face and shoulders. "Fine, fine, you? I see no blood."

"Fine. That arrow came from the woods to our left. Aye, Indians, a small war party I pray. I'll find Serrocold. We don't want to find ourselves surrounded out here."

A quiet settled over woods. The English had moved off the road and out of sight and Spanish had no reason to attack. I used the time to eat my noonday meal with the rest of my men. Our biscuits were soggy but our cornmeal flat cakes, prepared and wrapped in leaves by our Carib friends, were good and we had plenty of *ch'arki*.

Baskerville plopped down next to me as I ate. I handed him a piece of *ch'arki*.

"Many thanks, Lady Mary," he whispered. "Across the road ahead of us is a small wall made of dirt and logs, hastily thrown-up I think, but effective nonetheless. The Spanish have two, maybe three cannon with satisfactory fields of fire. My men have reconnoitered the area to the east and west and we cannot turn either Spanish flank. The terrain is much too difficult. To the right is a sheer cliff, to the left is thick jungle and swampland. The Spanish chose this ground well."

"Aye, I saw the wall and heard the cannon. Do you intend to attack?"

"Yes. My scouts returned with one prisoner. The enemy force is smaller than our own. Perhaps two hundred men, no more."

"Who is their commander?"

"The Viceroy of Peru has entrusted the defense of Panama to Don Alonso de Sotomayor."

"You know this man?"

"I do, he's an exceptional officer."

Baskerville struck me as a capable soldier with reasonable, good sense. Still I treaded lightly.

"Colonel, is it wise to attack a fortified position head-on? We have no artillery and the ground in front of the wall is narrow. Your men will be packed in tight, advancing into well-protected muskets and cannon."

Atwood then came up behind us and rested a hand on Baskerville's shoulder. "My lady is no fool, Colonel."

Baskerville smiled. "No, Lady Mary is no fool. But we must try to dislodge the Spanish. If we succeed, the road to Viejo will be open to us."

"Are you aware the Spanish have an Indian war party with them?" Atwood asked. "They're in the woods to our right and maybe to our left."

"Yes, even so we must attack."

I bit my tongue. I knew Baskerville's answer was the only one he could give. The expedition was running out of time and he could hardly return to Drake to report that he had run away from a fight.

"Lady Mary, will you advance, say one hundred paces, and hold the right and left flanks whilst my lads move up the middle and take that redoubt? If we breakthrough that barrier, the Spanish will break and run. I know you and your men are here for plunder, not to fight a pitched battle, but we English are in a bad fix here. Fifteen volleys, fifteen shots per man is all I ask and then you and your lads can retire back to this position."

"You need us to keep the Spanish occupied for fifteen minutes or so?"

"Fifteen minutes would be most welcome."

"And what if you succeed? The Spanish will fight to the death to keep Viejo."

"I am a simple soldier following his orders. To try and fail brings no dishonor. But not to try at all..."

"Very well. I do not do this for Drake or England or honor. I do this for brothers in difficulty."

Baskerville nodded and glanced at his pocket watch. "I am most humbly grateful to you, madam. I'll not forget the bravery of you and your Irishmen. By my watch it is half past two of the clock. Do you carry a watch?"

"Jacob does."

"We shall attack at three. What happens after that is in God's hands."

Baskerville jumped to his feet, patted Atwood on the back and walked off into the mist.

I gathered as many of my men around as I could. "Lad's, in thirty minutes the English will attack. Half of us will move out to the left and form a line running north and south to protect the English flank and the other half will do the same on the right whilst the English advance up the center and storm the Spanish barricade. I promised Colonel Baskerville we'd hold the line with fifteen shots. The Spanish will retreat, or they won't. That's it. That's the plan. Spread the word down the line to the others."

At quarter to the hour, we checked our powder boxes and replaced any wet powder cartridges with dry ones. We dropped our backpacks and our bandoleers. Some men discarded their armor too. The steel was hot and heavy and I wanted to do the same but Atwood wouldn't let me.

We waited for the English companies to move into their attack positions, then climbed out of the gully and formed a skirmish line running perpendicular to the English line on both flanks. I took the left and Atwood took the right and the English rear guard with Serrocold's men moved up to the gully to protect our line of retreat.

At exactly three of the clock, three English companies, three hundred men, moved forward in a fine drizzle with one company in reserve. The Englishmen walked shoulder-to-shoulder without music or flags, not even a battle cry. A queer tranquility settled all around us as the English advanced. Even the birds stopped chirping. With the mist turning thicker, we could see no more than fifty paces or so in front us. I moved forward slowly, gingerly stepping over fallen logs, boulders and a few dead bodies.

And then, as if the devil himself had risen out of the bowels of hell, the earth exploded in front of me. A severed arm struck me in the face. I thought the arm was mine. One of my men rushed to me, grabbed me by the shoulders, shook me and asked me something. But my ears were ringing and I couldn't hear him. I looked down, saw my arms and hands still attached and nodded.

On our left, the woods crackled with musket fire. A line of Spanish musketeers emerged from the trees and moved towards us. I took a knee, found an easy target and fired. *Click-boom*! My men did the same.

I couldn't tell what was happening to Atwood and his men on the right. But I could see the English companies rushing towards the Spanish redoubt and I could see the Spanish pouring cannon and musket fire into their ranks. I fell to the ground and reloaded.

"Take cover!" I heard Atwood bellow and then I saw a muzzle flash. The Spanish had wheeled a cannon into the woods on the right. Mini balls and bits of sharp metal pierced the air above my head.

As we reloaded, a mix of Spanish musketeers and Indian warriors with spears and axes charged straight at us.

"Keep on your bellies, lads!" I shouted. "On my command, fire one volley, then fall back ten paces. Stand and *FIRE*!"

We rose as one, fired our muskets and retreated a few yards back into a cloud of smoke.

"Reload!" I screamed and waited for the smoke to clear. "Steady. Hold. Stand and *FIRE*!"

We fired a second volley, again fell back and reloaded. I saw one of my men fall on his back with an arrow in his shoulder. Another spun around with a hole in his chest. The poor fellow twisted in agony and fell dead at my feet.

I turned to look for Atwood. His men had taken the cannon, but I saw Atwood sitting on the ground with his face buried in his hands. I grabbed the nearest man, a man named Todd, one of the ship's gun captains, and told him to take command while I ran over to Atwood.

"Damn, damn, damn!" Atwood repeated over and over again, rocking back and forth.

"Let me see Jacob," I said and gently pried his hands away. Blood flowed down his cheek from a nasty wound to his left eye. I reached into a small leather pouch attached to my belt for a strip of linen and carefully wrapped the cloth around his head.

"There now," I said. "Let's get you away from here."

"I've lost my eye, haven't I?"

"Hush now my brave captain. I don't know."

"Damn, damn, damn," he said again. As I helped Atwood to his feet he raised his pistol and fired at the woods.

"Come now, I'll help you back to the rear," I said.

"No, we need every musket Mary."

When Atwood wouldn't budge, I took a moment to survey the fighting raging back and forth all around us. We were mired in shit and piss and gore and I couldn't tell which side was winning. I could see Baskerville sending in his reserves, to make the final breakthrough or to plug the gaps in a crumbling line, I did not know. Todd and his men were holding fast on the left, as were Atwood's men on the right, and that raised my spirits some.

Then the mist lifted just long enough for me to see the English climbing over their own dead, struggling to reach the top of the wooden wall. Spaniards were wildly swinging their muskets around like clubs trying to beat them back. And then the mist returned, closing in all around us.

"Lads!" I shouted. "We hold the line. No falling back. Pick your targets carefully. Fire as you please!"

My men and I fired one shot after another until we had nearly exhausted all of our dry powder. Then the Spanish and their Indian allies on our flanks melted back into the woods just as Baskerville's men emerged from the mist stumbling towards us. The English attack had failed.

I pulled Atwood's watch from his pocket to check the time. The battle had lasted for over an hour.

The English collected their dead and helped the wounded and we retraced our steps back down the trail until we found a stream with good water a safe distance away where we made camp. As men lit the cooking fires, I tended to my wounded. One of my men, knowledgeable about injuries to the eye, deftly plucked Atwood's damaged eyeball out with a quick twist of his knife and then stitched the gash together. Mercifully, there was no need to cauterize the socket. I had twenty-eight wounded and fifteen dead. Nearly one-third of my men had paid a heavy price for nothing.

I looked for Baskerville as weary, bloodied Englishmen trickled into camp but did not see him. The number of maimed and wounded I saw broke my heart. I quietly helped the English surgeon where I could. Neither of us had much to say.

When I could do no more for the English, I sat down next to Atwood. He was fast asleep and snoring.

Then Baskerville plopped down next to me and handed me a skin of wine.

"*Merci*," I said and took a sip.

"A hard day."

"A hard day, Colonel. Back to Nombre de Diós?"

"Aye. With our victuals altogether spoiled, the powder in our pockets wholly lost and our match greatly decayed, we cannot press forward. I had hoped to find some weak spot in the Spanish defenses but alas, we found none. The Spanish built themselves a sturdy wall and used the terrain to good advantage."

"Even if we regroup and somehow succeed in taking all of Panama, what then?"

"His grace is supremely confident we'll find much treasure in Panama."

"His grace is a desperate man, flirting with disaster and disgrace," I replied harshly. "I see only blood and death awaiting us here, no treasure."

Baskerville made a heavy sigh. "Aye. How many men?"

"Twenty-eight wounded, fifteen dead. You?"

"I don't yet have a final tally of the causalities. Our losses were severe. I lost three company captains, brave lads all."

"A hard day," I repeated softly and looked away to stare into a nearby fire. I could feel the fatigue and sadness spreading through my body.

"A day that would have been harder still had you not kept your word and your composure under fire Mary," Baskerville said and looked over at Atwood. "How bad?"

"He lost an eye."

"Perhaps our surgeon should have a look."

"He did already."

"Well, I'll let you rest then. I wanted to thank you. I must see to the night watch. We'll strike camp at first light."

In the morning Atwood awoke with a mild fever and I gave him *cinchona*, but I had nothing for his pain.

"Jacob, can you walk?" I asked.

"Of course, I can walk," he answered crossly and stood.

"Good. We're returning to the coast."

"Good. I see fifteen crosses on the other side of the stream. Ours?"

"Aye, ours. We have twenty-eight wounded to move. Three will need litters. The English suffered far worse."

"No surprise there. I have yet to see a man beat his head against a wall and win. How are the lads?"

"Spirits are low. I wish to God we'd never come to this awful place. I'm sorry, Jacob, truly very sorry."

"Sorry? Why?"

"I've been careless with our lives."

"Nonsense. Each man followed you of his own free will. I lost an eye. Better an eye than an arm or a leg. Better eye than to be planted in the ground over there across the stream."

"Even so, my heart aches for you and all the others. I'm sorry, terribly, terribly sorry."

Atwood grunted and looked away. "Fair warning," he said in a loud voice for all to hear. "The first son-of-a-whore who calls me Capt'n Cyclops will feel the sting of my boot up his arse - and I have a very big boot."

His threat raised a chuckle or two around the camp.

I placed my hand around Atwood's waist to help him sit. "Let me change your dressing and then you must eat. I'll heat some cornbread for you and make you tea. I see our English friends are already busy breaking camp."

"The lads shouldn't see you doting on me! It's -."

"It's what Jacob Atwood? I'll dote on whom I please. Now sit still."

Atwood sighed. "Ah, very well. "To hell with tea. I'll take a little whisky if we have any."

With so many wounded to care for the journey back to Nombre de Diós was slow and difficult. We had to use rope and tackle to move the men on litters over the gorges and across the streams where the water was deep. We had enough to eat but the fair weather didn't last. The heavy rains returned, adding more misery to our journey.

When we finally reached Nombre de Diós four days later, some men cheered and some dropped to their knees and wept when they saw the fleet still anchored in the bay. Drake had setup camp along the shore and we saw scores of men sitting around the campfires or casually moving about. The admiral's command post was easy to spot. His men had raised the Tudor colors, the red cross of St. George over a field of horizontal green and white stripes, to the top of a church steeple and had planted two spears in the ground outside the church doors with pennants bearing Drake's coat-of-arms, an argent fess wavy between the pole-stars Arctic and Antarctic over a field of sable.

I saw MacGyver and Kinkae rushing towards us from the beach with a dozen men. I exchanged a nod with Baskerville and we parted ways. He walked on to the church and I hurried over to MacGyver and Kinkae.

"What a joy to see you," I said and hugged them both. "We have wounded."

"The town has a good hospital with a fine doctor," MacGyver

said. "He's a Spaniard but has shown us no ill-will."

"I'll see to our wounded, Mary," Kinkae said. "Lads, with me."

"Where's Satchel?" I asked.

"He was down with dysentery," MacGyver answered, "but is on the mend."

Atwood then joined us with the blood-stained linen covering his left eye.

MacGyver gently laid his hand on Atwood's shoulder, took his musket and helped him remove his backpack. "Let me take you to the hospital, Jacob."

"No need Michael," Atwood replied.

"He lost an eye, Michael," I said. "Still, the dressing must be changed Jacob and the wound cleaned. I'll drag you to the hospital myself kicking and screaming before all of our men if I must."

"An English messenger," MacGyver said, "returned to camp two days ago with dispatches from Colonel Baskerville. We heard about a battle fought on the Capirilla Pass. What happened?"

Atwood grunted. "We got our fuckin' arses kicked."

I turned to look at my men. We were a ragged, filthy lot. Kinkae and the others were helping the wounded to the hospital while the rest stood on the road waiting to be told what to do.

"Lads, this was the most miserable of marches," I called out to them, but stopped in midsentence when Atwood grabbed me by the arm.

"Mary," he whispered. "Don't you dare apologize to these men. You'll insult them. You have their respect, even their adoration. Ahem, right then, I'll go to your hospital, but only after I find some whiskey first."

I nodded. "Lads, I just want to say how proud I am to serve with you. No captain could ask for better. Let's wash-up, rest and later we'll crack open a few kegs of beer and ale, or whatever you have a taste for."

The men quietly shuffled towards the tents pitched along the shore.

"How many did we lose?" MacGyver asked.

"Seventeen, we lost seventeen good men," I replied solemnly. "Fifteen in battle, one died from his wounds on the march back and another slipped off a cliff and fell to his death. What news Michael of Mustafa and the others?"

"Nothing yet."

In the evening Drake summoned the usual crowd to the church for a council of war, but this time he also invited every ship captain. I was happy to bring Atwood and MacGyver with me. Between the whiskey and the laudanum, Atwood felt no pain.

Drake's men had gutted the church. Every crucifix and statute, every symbol of the Catholic faith had been removed. I saw broken pieces of the Virgin Mary on the floor next to a back door. Crates of shot and barrels of powder had been stacked against the walls. The air reeked of urine.

Drake was sitting in a chair where the priest's ambo had once stood. He looked more sickly than before and when he tried to speak, he mumbled. Thomas Drake moved to his brother's side and started speaking for him.

Despite suffering heavy losses, dwindling supplies and men falling to disease, despite having no good intelligence on the strength or whereabouts of the Spanish Army, Drake was determined to win victory in Panama. We would, the younger Drake said for his brother, spend a few days resting, healing and cleaning weapons and then move the fleet to Portobello, a new Spanish settlement a few miles away to the west. We'd take whatever plunder we could find in Portobello and then march on Viejo again.

Drake's new plan to take Viejo was to sail the fleet into the Rio Charges as far as the river would allow and then send the army downriver in the flatboats. Once Baskerville reached the Pacific coast he could march on Viejo from the west, a move the Spanish would never expect, or so Drake imagined.

The admiral struggled to his feet with the help of his brother. "Within our grasp," he said in a low, raspy voice, "is a fabulous amount of treasure. Sitting inside Viejo's walls is gold and silver worth four million *pesos*. True, the Spanish fought ferociously at the

Capirilla Pass and yet Sotomayor has revealed his weakness. He has but two or three hundred men at most to defend his precious town."

I heard grumbling amongst the congregation. Men were losing faith.

"We are doomed," a faceless voice in the crowd cried out.

The admiral suddenly sprang to life. He drew his sword and struck the hilt against his chair's armrest three times. "Enough!" he roared. "It matters not, man. God hath many things in store for us. And I know many means to do her majesty good service and to make us rich, for we must have gold before we see England!"

The church fell silent.

"Before first light," Drake said sternly, "we'll put Nombre de Diós to the torch. We'll put every town and village in Panama we pass through to the torch. The fleet sails in the morning. Make ready. You are all dismissed."

In the morning I stood on the beach watching Nombre de Diós burn. I saw no victory in the flames. I saw no honor.

We hastily broke camp and rowed to our ships as the village smoldered, but as the English fleet began to stir, I did not follow. Efendi and the others had failed to return. I could not bear losing Efendi or Maurice or Henry or Shaw and I had grown very fond of Zekowtah.

I had sent Atwood over to *Cerberus* earlier and waved him off. He wasn't the first buccaneer to wear a patch over an eye - but he looked far more menacing than any I had ever seen before. Atwood and MacGyver would sail west with the English fleet while I took *Phantom* east to Guna Yala to look for our men.

When we found nothing at Guna Yala, we sailed on to Port Pheasant and I began pacing back and forth on the quarter deck, fearing the worst. We reached the port just before a vicious gale descended upon us, tormenting us with heavy rains and thumping winds. Terrifying lightning bolts and bloodcurdling thunder ripped the heavens asunder as we hurried into the bay for shelter. We furled all sail, dropped three anchors and rode out the storm below. The winds howled through the night, snapping rigging lines and battering our poor ship to and fro. *Phantom* creaked and groaned against the huge rollers smashing into her side. Many, me among them, had a touch of *mal de mer*. When we started taking on water more than one man thought we were doomed and at the darkest hour I thought so too and offered up a prayer. They say *huracáns* do not strike during the winter. I'm not so sure that's true.

In the morning the world made peace with an angry sea. The sun peeked through the clouds. The winds abated and the waters calmed themselves. I dressed, washed my face and went to the galley for coffee but stopped when I heard the lookout cry out. I rushed up the companionway to the quarter deck.

Kinkae pointed to a plume of smoke rising from the beach when he saw me. I went to the stern rail to have a better look, then grabbed my sword and my muskets and rowed ashore with twenty men.

When I saw Efendi emerge from the jungle waving at me, I wept. Then Maurice and Zekowtah, leading a long line of Cimarron men, women and children, followed Efendi down to the beach. Henry and Shaw raced ahead of them to pull the longboat in. I jumped into the surf to embrace and kiss them both.

Efendi shook his head in disgust when he reached us. "Robert, Henry, do not spoil our good Lady Mary. It's undignified. She knows how to drive a boat into the sand."

Then Zekowtah and Maurice joined us and offered to shake my hand. I laughed and hugged and kissed them too.

"I see you've brought new friends," I said with a light heart.

"We did indeed, Mary," Maurice replied. "There are more in the woods yonder."

"How many?"

"Over four hundred souls," Efendi said as he rested his hands on my shoulders. "We have Spanish regulars not far behind us, a company at least, maybe two. They set an ambush for us at Guna Yala and have been pursing us for days. No doubt they think they have us trapped here against the sea as they seem in no hurry to move in for the kill."

I laid the palm of my hand against Efendi's cheek. "Did we lose anyone?"

"No, you?"

"Aye, we fought a bloody battle near Viejo. The Spanish fought us from behind a fortified position in the woods and had cannon. We retreated with heavy losses."

Zekowtah gently took my hand and pointed to the line of Cimarron walking towards us. "I am saddened by the loss of your men Mary. Yet here is good. Your men purchased the lives you see with their blood."

"All is as it should be," I said. "I'd be a poor friend indeed if I ignored the plight of your people. I think I must address you as King Zekowtah now."

The Aztec shook his head. "We have no land. We are too few to need a king."

I placed my hand on Zekowtah's shoulder. "The Cimarron must have someone to lead them, if not you, who? Well gentlemen, shall we? The ship will be exceedingly cramped, but we'll make do. Why is that woman over there, the one sitting in the sand, weeping?"

"She lost her infant son during the night," Maurice answered. "A branch broke free in the storm and killed the child."

"Ohhh... Let's get her aboard the ship and to my cabin."

I had my crew bring *Phantom* in close - with her guns run out, primed and loaded. We took the Cimarron off the beach first and then ourselves. The evacuation took us the better part of the morning. Mercifully, we never saw any Spanish.

"We have a one-eyed pirate amongst us now," I said to my officers as we rowed back to the ship in the last longboat. "But if you value your lives, I'd pretend not to notice if I were you."

"Who?" Shaw asked.

"Jacob."

Efendi chuckled. "Allah is known to humble the strong and the proud."

We crammed as many Cimarron onboard as we could and took two longboats in tow packed with men. We sailed slowly for Portobello, stopping along the way when we could to let the

Cimarron stretch their legs on shore and used privy buckets when we couldn't. The ship reeked of foul orders from stem to stern and I fretted over our lack of cleanliness.

When we reached Portobello, we saw *Cerberus* and *Diablo* riding anchor a good distance away from the rest of the fleet. We eased *Phantom* in-between both ships and dropped anchor.

"Mary," Atwood called over to me from *Cerberus*. "You've hired a larger crew I see."

"I did indeed. Why are you anchored way out here?"

"A storm hit us and hit us hard, blew the fleet westward. Strong winds and heavy seas carried us from Portobello to the Isla Escudo de Veragua in the Golfo de los Mosquitos. The English went ashore after the storm blew by, we did not. Sickness and death followed the English back to their ships. Drake pulled away from the island as soon as he had the wind and we returned to Portobello."

"Malaria, the plague, the bloody flux?"

"Hard to say. Take your pick."

"Did Drake send Baskerville and the army down river?"

"No, the English are too weak to fight."

"Can the ships sail?"

"Aye. You need but give the order."

"Then let's leave this Godforsaken place."

"Where away Mary?"

"Guadeloupe."

"You don't intend to ask Drake for permission?"

"I suppose I should. How can he refuse me when the queen herself commanded him to return to England at the end of six months? It's nearly February. I wonder though. Perhaps Drake has come to Panama as much for revenge as treasure. Drake has never concealed his fondness for his Cimarron allies. When I row over to his ship and tell him what we've done, he might be pleased and even well-disposed towards us."

Later, I decided on the cowardly approach and wrote Drake a letter, explaining my need to quit the expedition. If I went in person to see Drake and things went badly, Martin could not protect me as the *Queen's Grace* had not yet returned.

I never did deliver my letter. The following morning, on the 28th day of January 1596, we watched *Defiance's* men hoist the black flag with Drake's coat-of-arms attached. Drake had passed away during the night from the bloody flux men said. But I did not think some base affliction killed Drake, not that titan among men. I think Drake died from his wounds received in battle at San Juan and was too proud to give the Spanish, his hated foe for thirty years, the satisfaction of knowing that a lucky Spanish ball had brought the great Dragon down.

Whatever the truth, Drake's officers and crew, to the sound of subdued trumpets and muted drums, assembled on deck later that afternoon with great solemnity to honor England's legendary admiral and to and bid a great man farewell. The skies turned threatening and the winds turned cold as Thomas Drake offered a fine eulogy, recounting his brother's many heroic deeds in rich detail. Then men gently lowered a lead coffin over the side. It was Drake's final wish to be buried at sea in the New World, dressed in his full body armor.

After the funeral, Colonel Baskerville assumed command of the fleet. He scuttled any ship that could not be trusted to make the hard journey back home and set a course for Plymouth. The wretched expedition was at last over. As the English sailed off, I took my ships, laden with treasure far more valuable than any gold, and pointed us towards Guadeloupe.

Chapter Fifteen

was pleased when the King of Guadeloupe welcomed our Cimarron friends to his island with open arms. Zekowtah and his people, for a time at least, were safe and in return the ranks of the Carib army swelled with many fine, new warriors.

For days we rested and feasted. Our hosts treated us like royalty.

Once our ships were in fighting trim, after we had loaded fresh provisions onboard and said our farewells, we dropped our sails and headed west for Santo Domingo. The expedition had cost me plenty and I had men who needed money for their families. I had no intention of returning to the Old World empty-handed.

Luck was with me. I found my favorite Spaniard at his fine home just outside the city. But we learned from Cortés that the Spanish Royal Navy was scouring the Caribbean, looking for Drake or for any ships that might have sailed with him. Cortés procured what he could in haste and we left Santo Domingo in a hurry with only half our usual load.

The sky was clear, the breeze was delightfully fresh as I strolled up and down the deck, pretending to inspect the guns. I turned to face the bow when an odd voice, a soft voice, cried out to me.

"Lady Mary..." I heard the voice say in a pleading tone.

I glanced over to the fore mast and saw two men dragging a smaller man towards me. The man's face was hidden underneath the brim of his straw hat.

"Mr. Chance, Mr. Castellanos, what's this?" I asked.

"We've found ourselves a stowaway," Chance answered.

"A stowaway?"

"Hiding below in the ship's rope locker Mum," Castellanos added.

Efendi walked over to me when he overheard the word stowaway.

"Who are you?" I asked the man in the straw hat.

When the man refused to answer, I removed his hat to see his face. "Good God!"

"I'm sorry, Mary. Please, I beg you, do not be angry with me."

"Elizabeth! How the devil did you get aboard my ship? Oh, never mind that now. What were you thinking? We're on our way to Ireland, not to one of the Caribbean islands."

Elizabeth looked down at her shoes and didn't answer.

I looked at her wide-eyed. "Nooo! Great God, please tell me you haven't run off with one of my men! Your father will hang me from the gallows!"

Elizabeth started sobbing. "No, madam."

I scolded myself for being too harsh. I gently lifted her chin to see her face. "What then?"

"My father was about to marry me off to one of his friends at King Phillip's Court, a nobleman from Toledo named Don Ruy de Estrelle."

"Ah, and you disapprove of this match?"

"He is a vile, wrinkled, old man. He is fat and he is bald and he stinks of tobacco! His teeth are black and he suffers from gout!"

"He must be the most hideous man in all of Christendom," I said.

"I will not marry him!"

"I'm sympathetic Elizabeth, truly I am but -."

I paused when I saw the sudden gleam in her eye, when I saw her triumphant smile. She had one more card to play.

"He is a slaver, Mary. The man has made his fortune in slavery!"

"You think you can win me over because I dislike the business of slavery? Clever girl. What am I to do with you? We are hundred leagues from Santo Domingo."

"I will earn my keep, I swear I will. And once we reach Ireland, I shall make my way back to Spain. I have money."

I took her hands in mine to soften the blow. "Elizabeth, I fear my question was rhetorical. I know what I must do. I cannot be an accomplice to this scheme of yours. God forbid you fell victim to some evil. Your father, and my friend, would never forgive me. Mustafa, let Jacob know we must come about and return to Santo Domingo."

With surprising quickness and agility, Elizabeth pulled away from me. She scurried up the main mast shrouds with the dexterity of a cat before I could pull her back.

"Elizabeth, have you lost your senses? Come down from there at once before you fall and we lose you to the sea!"

She ignored me, reached for the crosstrees and continued working her way up the main top mast.

"Where the devil are you going Elizabeth?" I called out sharply, more frightened than angry.

She paused to look down at me. "I will stay in the masthead."

"For how long?"

"Until we reach Ireland," she said defiantly.

Efendi chuckled.

"What amuses you, Master Efendi?" I asked, annoyed. The entire crew had come up on deck to watch the entertainment.

"It would seem Spanish ladies are as stubborn as their Irish sisters. Turkish women are far more obedient."

I arched an eyebrow at that and turned to Elizabeth. "Please, Elizabeth, I could not bear to lose you. Come down from there now and let us talk. I promise I'll listen to all you have to say."

But Cortés's strong-willed daughter ignored my offer and moved higher up to the top gallant mast. "I do not need you to listen Mary. I thought you would have compassion. I will not wed a man I do not love, a man whom I despise. I will not. I will not let my father condemn me to a life of wretched loneliness. I would rather die!"

Even from a distance I could hear the quiver in her voice. Not from fear, but from sadness. I could see her shoulders shaking as she forced herself up higher. She earned my admiration.

At that very moment a rogue wave smacked the ship off-balance, if only for an instant. Any experienced sailor at the masthead would have shrugged the moment off and laughed. But Elizabeth lost her footing. I gasped when she fell backwards. She would have fallen to her death had the rigging not snagged her by the leg. She dangled precariously upside down. But she didn't scream, she didn't panic, and that too earned my admiration.

Shaw pulled me back as I started for the shrouds. He bolted up the rigging and when he reached Elizabeth, he tied a safety line around her waist, cut the line around her leg and then slowly walked her down. The ship burst into applause and cheers when Shaw stepped back on deck with Elizabeth in his arms.

I embraced her and held her close as she buried her face into my shoulder and wept. "Shh, shh, all will be well," I said as I stroked her hair. "I swear it. Rob, well done. Please escort the good Lady Elizabeth to my quarters and keep her company. There'll be no more theatrics today. I'll be down directly."

As Shaw led Elizabeth below, I turned to Efendi. Atwood had left the ship's wheel during the commotion and was standing next to him.

"Now what do we do?" I asked both men.

Efendi chuckled for the second time in one day. Unheard of.

"*You*, Mary," he replied. "What do you do now, not *we*."

Atwood removed a small flask from his vest pocket and offered me a sip. "To cure whatever ails you."

"Auck, you're both about as useful as a pair of rusty, old nails," I said and stormed off.

I was wrong - and weak - and knew it. I did not turn the ship around. After we reached Ireland, I'd write Cortés a letter. I'd explain to him that we had been too far out to double-back to Santo Domingo, even if untrue. I'd tell him that I'd put Elizabeth on the first good ship I could find sailing for the West Indies. But that too was untrue. Elizabeth had won me over.

I could feel the spirit seize me.

"Hold the line!" I shouted to my men with all I had to give.

A surging tide of angry men, armed with muskets, swords and axes, roaring like wild beasts, charged wildly at us. They climbed over the rails and swung over on ropes to board us. I stumbled backwards when a musket ball grazed my temple, searing my flesh like a hot iron.

"Courage lads!" I cried out. "Courage! If you falter, if just one of you bolts and runs - we all die. Hold I say, hold!"

My men and I tried desperately to hold the pirates back, but there were far too many. We were overwhelmed. The decks ran red with streams of blood.

I jumped off the quarter deck and landed squarely on the gun deck, bent on slaughtering as many wicked souls as I could before they slaughtered me. An ugly brute of a man, a mountain of quivering flesh, stepped in front of me. He grinned before he fired his pistol at my heart. I stared in disbelief as I saw a red stain spread across my shirt. So, this is my wretched end. Killed by animal for nothing. And then my world turned black.

"Mary, Mary!" I heard a familiar voice cry out.

"What?" I asked, struggling to get my bearings.

A strong hand shook me by the shoulder. "Arise and shine my lady, for thy light has come and the glory of the Lord is risen upon thee."

I rubbed the sleep from my eyes and found Atwood standing over me sporting a new, red eyepatch. "Are you reciting scripture to me?"

Atwood handed me a tin of hot coffee and laughed. "The rocky shores of Ireland looming on the horizon before us. We're home."

I sat upright in my bunk, glanced down at my chest and felt a chill race down my spine as I recalled my disturbingly vivid nightmare.

I was greeted by biting winds lashing at my flesh as I stepped on deck. Flurries danced all around me. I tightened my wool scarf around my neck and stomped my feet. And then I caught Maurice waving goodbye from *Cerberus's* gun deck. After I waved back, he swung his ship south for France while we veered north for Clew Bay, plowing through the hefty swells of an ornery sea.

We found Westport dusted in snow when we landed. As was our custom, I paid the men their shares, a disappointing amount to all, and gave everyone their liberty. To the families of our fallen, I sent fifty pounds sterling to each, a handsome sum by any measure.

Elizabeth stayed with me in Westport, as did Efendi and Shaw. Atwood returned to Ayr of course and MacGyver travelled on to Rush. Over the past few years I had often allowed my Carib and Blackamoors to stay behind in Guadeloupe with their families when I returned to Ireland. But I needed them in Westport with me now and kept them on the ships.

Elizabeth was a joy and I loved her more each day. She had blossomed at sea. She had applied herself day and night with vigor, learning every shipboard skill she could. She was bright and eager and full of energy. The crew had shamelessly indulged her. And when she begged me to teach her navigation and gunnery, I happily agreed. Efendi and Shaw introduced her to the martial arts and it did not take her long to trade her delicate figure in for a sturdy physique wrapped in hard muscle. I marveled at her transformation. She absorbed everything around her. She was becoming one of us. She was becoming me.

I am a proud and stubborn woman. I am full of rage. Oh, what a toxic brew to choke on.

The image of Martin's traitor hanging from a cross had never been very far from my thoughts. Martin had exacted his revenge and I longed to do the same.

Efendi found me strolling around the quarter deck in circles lost in thought. The afternoon was warm and bright. Men were busy replacing fatigued wood and sanding *Phantom* down before repainting her. The ship from stem to stern smelled of fresh-cut wood. I could hear the men aboard *Diablo* and *Cerberus*, anchored only yards away, doing the same. With spring in full bloom, Westport's harbor was bustling with ships of every sort and kind.

"All but a few of our men have returned Mary," Efendi reported.

"Excellent."

"You've been distant of late, Mary."

"Have I?"

"Yes."

"Hmmm. I suppose it's time."

"Time?"

"Please Mustafa, come with me."

Efendi followed me to my cabin where his gaze quickly fell upon a map of Ireland spread-out across the table.

"What is this?" he asked.

"Though I've been patient, though I've shown enormous restraint, I've hardly been idle these past few years. It has taken me time, and no small amount of money, to gather the information I needed to bring my great matter to a close."

Efendi leaned over the table and took in the names written by my own hand in the margins of the map. He read the notations I had scribbled next to various towns and villages and took a deep breath.

"Oh my."

"Oh my indeed Mustafa."

"How?"

"I've quietly, carefully and with the utmost deliberation, hired eyes and ears across Ireland. I had help too. With the queen's blessing, John Martin lent me certain resources in Ireland."

"Impressive."

I handed Efendi a letter, one of seven letters I had written. He read the letter to himself and nodded approvingly.

"Extraordinary, Mary. Legends are born from such bold deeds."

"No, Mustafa. No one will ever know. No one but us must ever know. This vicious whirlpool of killing and retribution we've been trapped in ends now."

Efendi leaned across the table to kiss my forehead. "Your will, my lady."

"Please round-up the lads for me. 'Tis time for the final act."

I handed each man a letter as Efendi led Atwood, MacGyver, Maurice, Henry, Kinkae and Shaw into my cabin. "My brothers, please read the instructions I have handed to you. You are free to follow these instructions or not."

Each man looked at me in stunned silence after reading his letter.

"There it is then," I said.

"How long?" MacGyver asked. "How long has it taken you to put this plan together?"

"It is fitting that you be the one to ask, Michael. Since that day seven years ago in Rush when you put a ship and crew into my hands, my mind has been quite busy."

I turned to Maurice. "This is not your fight Maurice. But you are one of us. This is why you stand here now. I don't expect you or your men to join me in this matter. You may sail on to the West Indies and wait for us there if you like."

Maurice shook his head. "I will be ready. The men I choose to bring with me will be ready."

"Thank you, Maurice. What say the rest of you? Stand with me or walk away. Each of you has my love regardless of your decision. Once I've settled my great matter, we'll set our sails and journey back to the New World."

"Each of us," Atwood asked solemnly, "is to pick forty men?"

"Aye. My plan requires two hundred men in all."

Atwood whistled. "*Ambitious* is the word that comes to mind."

"Ambitious, aye. If you're with me, we'll discuss the plan in more detail tonight at supper at Rob's tavern. Rob has closed his place to outsiders for the evening. We'll not be disturbed."

Every man stood with me of course. Though we were an odd assortment of riff-raft, I loved them and they loved me. Around the table stood an Indian, a Cimarron, an African, a Turk, a Scot, two Irishmen from different counties and one flawed, deeply scarred woman with debts to settle. The sufferings we had endured together between two worlds had forged an unbreakable bond between us. I took a moment to consider the faces staring at me and smiled back with pride.

"Very well then. Set mind, body and heart to purpose, lay hands on sharpened steel, on unblemished ball and deadly powder. There is yet much work to be done. But first, let's fill our bellies with wholesome food and strong drink. Let us be merry and celebrate the fellowship that binds us."

That evening we tweaked the details of my plan here and there and agreed to set-out on the road before week's end. The plan had risks of course, but every man was with me.

After supper I returned to the ship. I stood alone on the poop deck next to the ship's wheel, taking comfort in the calm surrounding me. All the stars in heaven shone brightly against a pitch-black sky. The bay was as smooth as polished stone. All was quiet in Westport as she slept.

Men though were about to die. Husbands, fathers, brothers, and sons. All were on my list. I had time to change my mind. We could sail off to the West Indies or beyond and leave the evils of the Old World behind us with no one the wiser. God knows I considered the possibility. But no.

I am like a mountain I told myself, immovable, implacable, impervious to the ill-begotten, wretched winds forever seeking to level me. I am like a volcano, spewing ash and fire with rising fury, incinerating everything in my path. I *am* the monster lurking in the dark. A witch's black cat, a harbinger of grave misfortune some say, has better sense than to step in front of me.

In the morning I gathered my things and went ashore into town. I hired three horses and took the low road to Youghal with Efendi and Shaw riding at my side. I am like the mountain. I am like the volcano. I am the monster lurking in the dark, bearing gifts for old acquaintances, gifts I prayed that would be well received.

Chapter Sixteen

he room was dark and cold. Sleet beat against the windowpanes as ferocious winds whipped the trees around outside. Winter's last, dying gasp.

I laid my pistol gently down on the desk, took a seat and waited. I lit the two candles standing at opposite ends of the desk and watched the flames flicker in a draft, casting eerie shadows against the far wall. A clump of dying embers in the room's small fireplace offered little heat, so I buttoned up my sea cape and rubbed my hands together for warmth. The New World had thinned my blood, though I did not complain. My poor Shaw, hiding outside behind the trees to keep a sharp eye out for any trouble, had it worse.

I took a moment to admire the twin candlestick holders on the desk. The matching nudes, cast from dark bronze, were rising from the ocean depths with outstretched arms to embrace the light above. I would have pilfered the exquisitely crafted sea nymphs for myself but for the vile creature who had touched them.

And then my prayers were answered. The door creaked open and the figure of a tall, sinewy fellow stepped into the room. I smiled and reached for my pistol. The man stared at me with an even mix of shock and panic.

Our paths had crossed only twice before. On the first occasion I was but a child when I watched this same man slice my stepfather's throat open with a knife inside our home. And then years later I saw him again in Westport at the old mill on the Carrowbeg when he killed my poor Hunter and all my men. Wherever this pig travelled, murder followed in his wake.

"YOU!" he said.

"Master Kayne Dowlin," I replied with no charity in my tone. I paused to savor the moment. "How very good it is to formally meet you at last."

He considered the pistol in my hand. He balled his hands into fists and clenched his jaw. His nostrils flared as he snarled at me like an animal about to pounce.

I cocked the hammer back on my pistol. "Don't," I said. "You're not fast enough and I'm an exceptional shot."

He considered my words, then quickly switched tactics. He relaxed his jaw, opened his fists and smiled at me with an air of superiority.

"Why so quiet?" I asked when he didn't speak. "Cat got your tongue? Here now, lest you think me rude, you sit whilst I stand. This is after all your home and your desk."

With my pistol levelled at his heart, I stood and slowly moved around one side of the desk over to the door while he moved around the opposite side and plopped down in his chair.

"How?" he asked. "How did you escape the fire?"

I laughed at him. "That's your first question? You wish to know how I escaped from the old mill? Hmmm. A far better question I should think would be: *where is my son?*"

I saw the hate seep into his eyes. He started to rise from his chair.

"Still yourself, Dowlin. Unless you want a bullet in the gut, sit back down. No harm has come to your son. I sent the maid home and merely tucked your boy in whilst you were out and about the town. He's a beautiful child. And those blonde curls! All the pretty girls will throw themselves at him one day. About two years old or so I think? Well, never mind. I should think your next question would be: *how do I survive this night?* Bless me though, your first question was about my welfare. I'm touched."

Dowlin eased himself back into his chair, leaned over and spit. "I should have done what my Uncle Romulus intended to do. I should have brought you back to Youghal and cut you up into little pieces. I would have kept you alive in some filthy, rat-infested cellar for weeks in unimaginable pain for my own amusement."

"Are you this charming with all the ladies? Let me answer your question about that night at the old mill, that night you ambushed me and my men. We have a little time yet. After you set the mill on fire with me inside, I escaped through a crawlspace underneath the floorboards once used by the mylnweard to access the mill's great wheel."

Dowlin shook his head in disgust. "How fortunate for you. And then you slipped into the river and slithered off like a snake whilst my men and I watched the old mill burn."

"My, my, aren't you the clever one? Just like your father, I see."

"You bitch."

"Ah, we can agree on that. I am a bitch. *I'm the bitch men dread.*"

He laughed. "I have no fear of you, none at all. We both know you can't touch me. Sail across the world, it matters not. The clan will hunt you down. And as you well know Mary, my men will not stop after they kill you. Your death, and a gruesome death it will be, will only whet their appetite for more. They'll snuff out every life of everyone who was ever dear to you. Run now little rabbit whilst you still can."

"Spare me your empty threats. You sound like a silly child, not a man. I'm not running from anyone. Certainly not from the likes of you. But, as to the reason why I am here, I did not come to kill you as you might suppose - though it would give me great joy to end your miserable life I must confess."

I could see the confusion in Dowlin's eyes.

"What then?" he asked. "You intend to rob me? I keep no gold or silver in this house. You've wasted your time if that's your purpose here."

"I think if I came to rob you, I'd need to kill you too. No, I'm here to reach an understanding with you."

Dowlin leaned back in his chair. "Oh? What kind of understanding?"

I sensed the subtle change in Dowlin's tone, the smugness in his demeanor. He thought he had gained the upper hand. I was happy to let him think so.

"I came to make peace with you. I'm here to end the bloodletting between us. Too many have suffered on both sides for our hatred."

"Why would the *Síol Faolcháin* make peace with you? Why would I make peace with you? You murdered my father - you beheaded him they say. You butchered my uncles in front of me. You took *Medusa's Head* and stole our gold. You're a filthy pirate, a murderer and a thief."

I casually laid my pistol down on an armoire standing against the wall next to me and folded my arms. "You speak of murder? Hypocrite. You slaughtered an innocent, unarmed man in Dublin nearly thirty years ago. You brutally murdered him in front of his daughter and then let your apes violate the child. You were young, little more than a boy back then. I was younger still, but the memory of that night is burned deep into my soul."

The animal showed no remorse. But I could see, even in the room's ghoulish candlelight, that he remembered.

"Oh, how delicious!" Dowlin exclaimed with a crooked grin. "You were the girl in the butcher shop! My, my, my, small world. How things turn."

I couldn't believe the pig was smirking at me. I took a deep breath to steady myself.

"Whose tongue has the cat grabbed now?" he asked with a chuckle. "The butcher owed the clan money and the fat toad couldn't pay. He got what he deserved. He was my first kill by the way. As for you, my men made you a woman. Without the skills they taught you, an orphan girl would never have survived the streets of Dublin. You should thank me."

"Your brutes raped a child!" I blurted out.

Dowlin shrugged his shoulders with indifference.

I forced a smile. "Well, let us move on to consider your treachery in Westport. After I showed you and your men my mercy and set you free, you turned around and ambushed my men at the old mill and then killed them all. I could hear you and your boys chanting over and over again: *blood for blood, blood for blood* as the old mill crackled and burned. That was day I first recognized your face. That was when I realized you were the young fellow with the knife at the butcher shop. And ever since that day, I've been thinking about this day. As for your father and your uncles, they were rabid dogs who killed for pleasure and I put them down. I did the world a favor."

Dowlin stared at me, seething with contempt. "And you think this settles the accounts between us?"

"No. But there's more. After you discovered I was still alive, you sent your lackeys up to Westport. They killed innocent men, women and children trying to find me. By your hand, Friar Thomas, the Shaws and the Fitzgeralds are dead. There was also a baby, my daughter."

I looked away to hide my tears.

"I know nothing about a baby."

"She died on the road when the Fitzgeralds were on the run. Your men killed her just the same. But the dead are dead. You and I still live and we both have friends and family who are dear to us. We make peace between us. We end the killing this night for the sake of those we love."

Dowlin - as I knew he would - made his move.

"Let bygones be bygones, eh?" he asked. "I have a better idea," he said as he reached into a drawer beneath his desk. He pulled a pair of matching pistols from the drawer and pointed them at my head.

"Mary, Mary, Mary, you stupid, arrogant cunt. There can be no peace between a wolf like me and a snake like you. After I shoot you in the face, I'll cut off that pretty head of yours and toss your body into the bay to rot next to your poor, sweet Gretchen. You remember her? Oh, yes, you can add her name to your list of my accomplishments. Once my father was finished with her, he handed her over to me. She did not die well. But you will, lucky girl. Farewell you bastard of a whore..."

Gretchen too. I should have known.

I heard the click-boom of one pistol followed by the other. I saw the flash of gunpowder and smoke. I relished the moment and smiled when Dowlin's expression turned to horror. Then I pulled two musket balls from my pocket. I held them up for him to see. I tossed the balls across his desk and watched them roll into his lap.

"You think yourself my equal?" I asked. "Fool. You've just killed yourself."

That was Efendi's cue. My brave and loyal Turk stepped out of a water closet behind the desk where he had been patiently waiting. He silently came up behind Dowlin and gently placed a knife against Dowlin's throat.

Dowlin slowly craned his neck around to look up at Efendi. "You're a dead man if you harm me," he said.

I walked over to the desk and came nose-to-nose with Dowlin. I stared hard into his eyes.

"Thank you, Mustafa," I said softly. "I think we have Dowlin's full attention now. Mustafa's blades are sharp. But I have something more interesting in mind for you Dowlin. The time, Mustafa?"

Efendi pulled a watch from his pocket. "'Tis a few minutes before midnight, Mary."

I carefully removed a needle from the lapel of my vest. I pricked Dowlin's hand with it. I stood back and smiled.

Dowlin howled with laughter. "This is meant to intimidate me? You stab me with a fucking pin? You've had your fun, now *RUN*! I'll give you and your Saracen dog a day's head start before I send my men."

Dowlin tried to rise from his chair but couldn't. He struggled to catch his breath.

"You're as predictable as was your father," I said. "Don't die on me yet. This is not the worst of it. I need your heart to pump a little longer."

"Bit, bitch," he mumbled, struggling to say the word. "What, what did, did you do to me?"

I caressed his cheek with the back of my hand. "I forgot. I've heard you dislike the sea and avoid the water whenever you can. You've never been to the New World, have you? Well, in the jungles of the Spanish Main there is this colorful, tiny creature, no bigger than your thumbnail, known as the dart frog. Oh, but of all the animals in the jungle this smallest of creatures is the most deadly. When the dart frog is threatened it secretes a poison through its skin. A great Cimarron warrior taught me how to extract the poison from the frog. There is no cure."

"I will -."

I shut his jaw with my hand. "You'll do nothing because you can do nothing. Your legs are already paralyzed, yes? Your arms are starting to feel heavy. You can't even make a fist. Soon the poison will spread to your lungs and then seep into your heart and brain."

"The clan will avenge myyyy, my murd, murder."

I used the tip of the scarf around Dowlin's neck to dab the drool running down his chin. "No, no one will think you were murdered you silly goose. You are about to die unexpectedly at your desk from a bad heart whilst reading a book. I brought one with me you can borrow, *The Prince* by Niccolò Machiavelli. You might find Chapter Eight on criminal virtue particularly enlightening. Here, I'll turn to the proper page for you."

Dowlin placed his hands on his desk and tried to stand again. He raised himself up and inch or two before I forced him back down.

"You shouldn't exert yourself, my friend. The poison works more quickly if you fight it. But death I fear is not your punishment."

"Wh, wha, what?"

"As we've been having this pleasant chat, all across Ireland, here in Youghal and in Cork, Mallow, Limerick, Dublin, Wexford, Waterford and in other villages in-between, I have sent squads of men, two hundred strong in all, to the homes, taverns, gambling dens and whorehouses of your lieutenants. Every man who has insulted me is being dragged out into the streets and hanged, stabbed or shot. By morning, there will be no more *Síol Faolcháin.*"

"Im, imposs, possible."

"Impossible you say? No, not at all. After my daughter's death, her name was Aliénor Muirgheal if you care to know, I laid low and bided my time, not an easy thing for me to do as I'm not by nature a patient soul. But I needed that time you see to place men inside the

Síol Faolcháin, to infiltrate your ranks. I needed time to put my elaborate scheme in place."

"Liar."

"I have no reason to lie. You'll see your men soon enough. Ask them when you do. There's more. Stay with me. I've not yet told you the worst of it. This is why I did not let Mustafa open your carotid artery. I wanted you to linger for a bit so you may know the full and terrible extent of my fury. He is a Turk by the way, not a Saracen."

"Wha, what?"

"Your son. No, no - I see the alarm in your eyes - I'll not harm him. Who but a wretched pig would harm a child? They say you beat your wife to death and it pains me to think of the boy as an orphan. I'll take him and raise him as my own. I'll name him James after, well, you know. I'll teach him to despise the clan. His children and his children's children - your bloodline - will all learn to hate the Dowlin name. How like you my plan now my Lord Kayne Dowlin, prince of the disemboweled *Síol Faolcháin*? Speak quickly now, you haven't much time."

My words had the desired effect. Dowlin's skin turned purple, his eyes bulged from their sockets. His cheeks and lips swelled grotesquely. His face contorted into something inhuman.

"Fu, fu, fuck you," Dowlin mumbled with his final breath.

I walked behind him as his throat closed on him, as he began to suffocate. I placed my hands on his shoulders, on the shoulders of the man who had killed so many I had loved.

I leaned close to his ear. "When we spit in the face of the gods, beware," I whispered. "The gods spit back - and they spit venom. Tell your father and your uncles and all your friends in hell when you see them tonight, tell them that you are the architect of this wreckage. I offered life. You chose death. I suppose we both knew it had to end this way. One of us had to die. Well, I have miles to go with a young child in my arms and your time is at an end - and the *Síol Faolcháin* ends with you. I leave you with these final words to take to your grave: *blood for blood* my friend, *blood for blood...*"

I left Youghal with my arch enemy slumped over his desk holding *The Prince* by Machiavelli in his hand. And my men carried out their part to near perfection. Oh, a handful of *Síol Faolcháin* captains and lieutenants here and there had by chance survived the night of bloody slaughter. I had expected that. I'd hunt them down later and the lives I took would not be missed. All across Ireland families were disappearing in the middle of the night as the English rounded up the Irish. When folks heard talk about the *Síol Faolcháin*, a clan with strong allegiances to Spain and active in the rebellion, they would see English hands at work in their disappearance. No one would come looking for me or mine. I had used England's policy of Plantation to my own advantage. With one swift, devastating blow, I had gutted the brutal *Síol Faolcháin*. I had shattered the unrelenting circle of vengeance and reprisal that had cost me so dearly.

I returned to Westport with little James Hunter Ryan fast asleep in my arms. He was a quiet, shy little boy with alert and happy eyes. I found a good and loving family to care for him while I journeyed across the sea. The boy would grow into a man never knowing the sins of his father.

One final loose end was settled a few months later in Spain. My men caught up to Cortés's former colleague, Don Villanueva, a man who had betrayed me to the Twins for gold. They say Don Villanueva died in Seville at his desk from a bad heart while reading *The Prince* by Machiavelli.

Alone atop *Cruach Phádraig*, I stabbed the earth with my sword. I plopped myself down on the ground and closed my eyes to let the magic of the mountain wash over me.

My mind began to drift as I reflected on my own journey. I've been luckier than most. I've known great love, sublime and sweet. I've made my way through life sailing across the broad oceans and exploring new worlds with a swift ship under my feet and a loyal crew at my side. I've secured great riches for myself and for others and I've vanquished all my enemies. I've been blessed with keen wits, good health and great beauty. I should have felt content.

But the years of pain and sorrow had taken a heavy toll on me. Alone, and with youth beginning to fade, I longed to feel joy again. I yearned to find some bit of happiness before old age took away my wits, my health and beauty away. Perhaps I should have heeded the queen's good advice years ago and settled down with Hunter somewhere safe and far away from trouble. But then again, no. We must be true to who we are.

In the end, when the hour glass is empty, there is but one question that matters: with all of our flaws and all of our misdeeds, can any of us find redemption? Can my soul find redemption? I know not the answer.

I fell into a deep and blissful sleep underneath the warmth of a summer sun and didn't stir until a stray raindrop struck me on the nose. When I propped myself up on my elbows, I saw the sun darting in and out of fast-moving clouds above with an empty sea below churning with whitecaps. Towering thunderheads had gathered to the west and I could see faint flashes of lightening streaking through the clouds. What had started off as a delightfully warm day had turned stark and cold. A storm was barreling down on fair Ireland.

I packed my things and grabbed my sword. I buttoned up my jacket and raised the collar around my neck. If I hurried, I had a chance to beat the rain.

I took one last look at the beauty surrounding me. My nap had reinvigorated me. My head was clear and buzzing with many thoughts. I decided the time had come to gather my men, though I still had no plan. Something would come to me.

And then I saw two riders, a man and a woman, racing up the mountainside. The man leaned over and tried to kiss the woman, but she laughed at him and spurred her stead on. She was an accomplished rider and easily took the lead. The man dug the heels of his boots into his horse's flanks and tried to catch her, but she was too fast for him. She turned in her saddle and blew him a flirtatious kiss as he spurred his horse on. Robert and Elizabeth were coming to save me from the storm. I loved them both dearly and had high hopes for their happiness.

Then out of the blue I remembered something Testu had once told me in Ronconcholan. He had said to me that the Cimarron hid their gold and silver and pearls taken from the Spanish in the muddy waters of the Chepo. I had thought nothing of it at the time as this treasure belonged to my friends and allies. But Ronconcholan was no more and the Cimarron had scattered. God only knew if any of it still lay buried in the riverbed. And even if there was still treasure there, finding it would take a miracle. The challenge intrigued me though and I smiled.

I threw my bedroll over my shoulder. I picked up my backpack and started down the mountain. For the first time in years the world seemed fresh and full of promise.

I was born a child of the gutter. I am the daughter of a whore. I am the youngest child, the bastard child of the last of the kings of Umaill though a butcher, a commoner, raised me. I am an adventurer, a soldier, a schemer, a buccaneer, a smuggler and a thief. I am who I was meant to be. I have regrets, only a fool would not, but I have no regrets about the life I've lived.

This is who I am. I was born in blood and I will die in blood, or so the story goes...

Afterword

Jealousy, greed, fear - even love - these are the seeds of war. Men thrive on wealth and power and in their arrogance will kill to acquire both. Small wonder the world is doomed to perpetual conflict.

Two seminal events, with breathtaking cultural, religious, intellectual and political consequences, ignited global war in the 16th Century. The first occurred in 1492 when Christopher Columbus discovered the New World for Spain (followed by the discovery of gold in 1519 by Hernán Cortés de Monroy y Pizarro Altamirano as he methodically annihilated the Aztec Empire). The second happened in 1517 when a lowly German monk named Martin Luther posted his revolutionary pamphlet *The Ninety-Five Theses* to the door of the All Saints' Church in Wittenberg, Germany, sparking the Protestant Reformation.

New World riches allowed King Phillip II of Spain to strengthen his military and to expand his empire. The Protestant Reformation allowed King Henry VIII of England to annul his marriage to Spain's Catherine of Aragon and marry his mistress, Anne Boleyn. While Catholic Spain embraced the world as an emerging superpower, England embraced the Protestant faith causing an irreparable schism with Rome.

Envious of Spain's great wealth, and fearful of her growing military might, England and France turned a blind eye to piracy in the Caribbean during the mid-16th Century. For decades, English sea dogs and French buccaneers flocked to the Spanish Main by the thousands, raiding Spanish towns and plundering Spanish treasure ships at will.

Full scale war broke out in 1585 when England sent ships and men to the United Provinces to help the Dutch Protests in their fight for independence against Spain. This war, known as The Anglo-Spanish War, would last for twenty years with fighting stretching from the farm fields of Europe to the jungles of the Americas and across the oceans of the world.

When Spain's attempt to invade England with the most powerful fleet every assembled ended in a spectacular disaster in 1588, an English victory seemed assured. But England's counter invasion of Spain the following year, led by England's living legend, Sir Francis Drake, was an even greater fiasco.

The two military blunders though did not equal a stalemate. Hapsburg Spain, with her fabulous wealth pouring in from the Americas, and a population of nearly nine million (including Portugal), could easily replace her losses while England, a poorer kingdom with a population of only four million (including Scotland and Wales), could not. Spain emerged as the world's first global superpower with an empire stretching across Europe to India, the Philippines and the Americas.

Drake's last voyage in 1595 to the West Indies, a place where he had beaten the Spanish time and time again over the years with daring and cunning, was the act of a desperate, unwell man. As Mary explains in our story, the West Indies had changed. Over the years Spain had spent enormous sums fortifying her possessions in the Americas to protect them from men like Drake. Inexplicably, Drake had learned nothing from his mistakes in 1589 when he squandered the lives of his men attacking heavily fortified walls.

When England failed to humble Spain, she cast a jealous eye towards Catholic Ireland. The English redoubled their efforts to pacify the island with great cruelty, sparking a massive rebellion known as the Nine Years' War.

Two Irish chieftains, Hugh O'Neill, the Earl of Tyrone, and Red Hugh O'Donnell, the Lord of Tyrconnell, united the clans and took to the field with Spanish support. The Gaelic chieftains proved themselves able commanders and defeated the English in several battles in and around Ulster and Munster. Ultimately the English prevailed with superior numbers and the Gaelic nobles fled, many to Spain, in what was known as the "Flight of the Earls."

The rebellion cost both sides dearly. An estimated 100,000 Irish men, women and children died from disease, starvation or were killed in battle (ten percent of the population) while England suffered roughly 30,000 dead and incurred between £2 and £3 million in debt, nearly bankrupting the kingdom.

As pertains to 16th Century women, which is the heart of our story, women were considered chattel under the law. Women could not own property or inherit estates or enter into professions. They could not become clergy, politicians, lawyers or doctors. And yet a number of women overcame the prejudices and barriers of the age. Smart, powerful women, remarkable women, such as Queen Elizabeth I, Grace O'Malley (the Irish "Pirate Queen"), and the Islamic "Pirate Queen of Tétouan," Sayyida al Hurra of Morocco (her name means: 'noble lady who is free and independent; the woman sovereign who bows to no superior authority') commanded whole fleets and armies of men. There were also women from the lower classes, commoners, who also achieved success. Some became ships' captains and even explorers.

Through Mary's eyes, though she is a fictional character, we are provided some glimpse of the world these extraordinary women survived and even thrived in. I sincerely hope you enjoyed our story.

Odds & Ends

Queen Elizabeth I   Sir Francis Drake

An anonymous seaman's account of Drake's death:

"At 28 and 4 of the clocke in the morning our Generall sir Francis Drake departed this life, having bene extremely sicke of a fluxe... The same day we ankered at Puerto Bello, being the best harbour we found along the maine both for great ships and small... After our comming hither to anker, and the solemne buriall of our Generall sir Francis in the sea: Sir Thomas Baskervill being aboord the *Defiance*... M. Bride made a sermon, having to his audience all the captaines in the fleete."

Drake's Burial at Sea
Bronze plaque by Joseph Boehm, 1883

From 1589 to 1591 English privateers seized about 300 prizes worth approximately £400,000.

English race-built galleon *Ark Royal*

Double chart, in pen and water colors drawn on vellum, depicting the harbors of A *Coruña* and *El Ferrol* (probably prepared for the Drake-Norreys expedition of 1589)

Santander in 1590 by Joris Hoefnagle

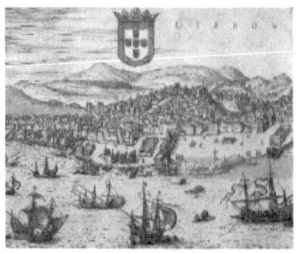

Lisbon in 1572 By Franz Hogenberg & Georg Braun - cropped lower and higher parts from Civitates Orbis Terrarum

Letter from Queen Elizabeth I to Drake and Norreys during the siege

of Lisbon demanding Robert Deveureux return to England

Stature of María Pita in A Coruña

When María Pita's husband, a captain in the Spanish army, was killed defending A Coruña by a bolt from an English crossbow on the 4th day of May 1589, María picked up a spear to take his place. And when an English flagbearer reached the highest part of the wall and all seemed lost, María killed the man with her spear and shouted: "*Quen teña honra, que me siga!*" ("Whoever has honor, follow me!"). King Phillip II honored María's heroism by giving her the pension of a military officer for life.

A Dutch eyeglass maker named Hans Lippershey applied for a patent in 1608 for the first known telescope. His patent was denied.

A quick note on style. As with *The Butcher's Daughter*, I've written in a contemporary voice because we live in contemporary times. Even so, I've tried using words that the men and women of the 1500's would have understood and used and to this end the Online Etymology Dictionary was a wonderful resource.

God bless us all.